"This is the part where you tell me your name," he said, dropping his hand to his side. He stared into my eyes and his expression turned serious. "That's so strange. I know we couldn't have, but have we met before? I know it's impossible, because I'd never forget those eyes…but it feels like I know you. Like I've always known you."

D1211092

PRAISE FOR THE
WORKS OF EM SHOTWELL

"BLACKBIRD SUMMER harkens to a time of mysticism and magic, painting old world beliefs and mindsets onto a contemporary palette. The depth of emotion and atmosphere created in the story is nothing short of amazing."
- *Award-Winning Author, Tina Moss*

"THE CHANS leaves you wanting more! I can't wait until BLACKBIRD SUMMER comes out so I can read Logan and Tallulah's whole story and figure out just what is up with this town and its inhabitants!"
- *GoodReads Reviewer, Amanda*

"Loved, THE CHANS, this sneak peek behind a new series by a fabulous debut author that is going to rock the socks off fans of Beautiful Creatures!"
- *Award-Winning Fantasy Author, Heather McCorkle*

"I'm so excited to read Blackbird Summer! And THE CHANS is a great way to jump in."
- *Paranormal Romance Author, B. Hughes-Millman*

"Fans of Sookie Stackhouse and Beautiful Creatures who are looking for their next fix from the sticks should look no further than BLACKBIRD SUMMER. I can't wait for the next book in the series."
- *GoodReads Reviewer, KChase*

Blackbird
Summer

Em Shotwell

CITY OWL
PRESS

BLACKBIRD SUMMER
Blackbird Series: Book One

CITY OWL PRESS
www.cityowlpress.com

Cover Design by Tina Moss. All stock photos licensed appropriately. Edited by Heather McCorkle

For information on subsidiary rights, please contact the publisher at info@cityowlpress.com.

Print Edition ISBN: 978-0-9862516-7-2
Digital Edition ISBN: 978-1-5199376-9-8

Printed in the United States of America

For the many story-tellers in my family.

I learned from the best.

- Em

Chapter One

The old green truck lurched forward as I down shifted.

Please don't die! I begged the ornery vehicle, pressing harder on the pedal.

Three cars in front of us, a tractor crept along, stopping every so often. The snail's pace made driving a stick a real pain in the ass.

The afternoon sun winked off tin roofs as we lumbered past. Across the street, the magnolia trees that lined the sidewalk stretched their branches skyward in full bloom, showing off like pageant contestants vying for a crown. The sweet, lemony scent of their flowers mingled with the ammonia-like odor from a chicken house located out near the highway. The putrid union of the two smells forced me to breathe through my mouth, and then burned my throat.

At least it's pretty out. I sighed. We'd gotten stuck behind the tractor shortly after turning onto the main road in town. It had been twenty-five minutes. Twenty-five minutes for the standard eight minute trip.

I tried to peel my sweating thighs from the ripped vinyl seat without popping the clutch. On the bench seat next to me, my younger sister Delia yanked a brush through her tangled tresses.

"Pawpaw really should get the A/C fixed. I can't go anywhere without ending up looking like a wild woman," she grumbled. "It's either roll down the windows or sweat to death." A knot of hair stuck in the brush. "Or in today's case both." Her words were weighed down by the same slow accent carried by everyone in southern Mississippi.

I shook my head, used to Delia complaining about the truck.

Truth was, while most twenty-one-year-old women would have been embarrassed to drive such a machine, I loved my Pawpaw's old Ford. For years, it had been his work truck. Now, instead of being used to haul crops or gardening equipment, he kept it as an extra vehicle for his grandkids to borrow. One that was bumpy, and needed a little coaxing to start, but hadn't let me down yet. In fact, the truck gave me the only bit of real freedom that I owned.

Whenever I was behind the wheel, I was free to daydream of driving across country, and escaping to a place where I wasn't confined by family expectations and lists of rules. I dreamed of a place where I could blend in and get a job, get married, or even go to a *decent* college, instead of our puny satellite campus that only offered courses in things like dental assisting and pet grooming. *Not that it had stopped me from applying.*

The old Ford was my sanctuary where I could pretend that Brooklyn, Mississippi didn't exist. Or at least that I hadn't been raised in a family that was treated as modern day lepers, living outside of a town that prided itself on being the shiny, self-righteous buckle of the Bible Belt.

Only, unlike lepers, we weren't hated because we were diseased. We weren't. Neither was my family guilty of being Yankee, gay, or Muslim: the three cardinal sins of the Deep South. The folks in our town viewed us as worse, much worse.

But on days when I sped through the Mississippi back roads with the windows down and my long hair flying, none of that mattered. In those moments, I wasn't Tallulah Caibre, the girl from the "evil" family your Mama told you stories about. In those moments, I was free.

I sighed again and snapped back to reality as a gray haired lady decked out in pearls and a crimson pant suit dinged her bell and zipped by on her bicycle. The yorkie nestled in the bike's basket yipped at me as they rode past.

"Oh this is ridiculous!" Delia said, tossing up her hands. "Can't you go around them?"

I turned my head and looked at my sister, eyebrows raised. "Yeah. Okay. Why didn't I think of that?"

Delia smirked, and then dunked her hand into the plastic cup of melted ice. Without saying another word, she flicked droplets of water at me from her fingertips. I was surprised they didn't sizzle as they landed against my skin.

"Joke's on you," I said, "that feels great." I stuck my tongue out at Delia, the same way I'd been doing since we were kids. She giggled.

Outside, antebellum homes inched by, a hundred years past their prime, with peeling paint and sagging, wrap-around porches. They mixed with the few small businesses that dotted the main road. The result was an odd mesh of old and new. An ancient bank, long closed, sat next door to the strip mall that was erected in the nineties. A Burger Boys Drive In sat across the street from a boarded-up historic home, whose neglected yard boasted a majestic live oak, dripping with Spanish moss.

The combination of rundown grandeur and flowering trees next to pitted parking lots and cheaply crafted buildings gave the impression of an old lady clinging to her youth. No matter how much she fought it, her beauty was determined to fade. Maybe I was being cynical because a part of me longed to see other places; maybe it was the heat.

I stared with childlike longing as a potbellied man set up a snow cone machine under the shade of the biggest magnolia as he did most summer and spring afternoons. In the fall, he sold boiled peanuts, in the winter, pralines and hot chocolate.

I raised my hand to wave. The goody-man, as he was known to most people, smiled and waved back. I guess not everyone in our small town hated my family.

The tractor pulled off the main road, and I hit the gas, accelerating to speed limit.

"Finally," Delia said, shoving her comb back in her bright gold purse. She pulled out a compact and frowned as she assessed the damage done to her by the humidity and summer temperatures.

We turned into the parking lot of Sugar's and I tried not to cringe. The sign was hot pink, and the faceless mannequins in the window were dressed in bright colors of whatever pattern and fit that happened to be trending. Each one was gaudier than the one before it. The purses that dangled from their permanently crooked arms practically shouted, *Look at me! Look what I can afford!*

I had gone inside one time, and then only stayed long enough to gasp at a price tag while the snotty girl behind the counter gave me the bitch face.

"Lord that purse is so tacky," Delia said, pointing to a royal blue, rhinestone number showcased front and center.

"Don't you have that bag?" I asked.

Delia looked at me like I didn't have two brain cells to rub together. "Well duh. But that was before I saw that Maureen Purdue carried the same one. Can you imagine? Me and dried-up old Maureen with the same purse? I walked into the truck stop, and she was standing there behind the counter with the bag flung up in front of her like it was some kind of trophy. Of course, I had to turn right around and go put mine in the car."

"Good grief, Delia. That's kind of mean, don't you think?"

"Like you wouldn't have done the same thing."

"I wouldn't have spent a month's pay on one purse." I pulled a face at her. "Your money would go a lot further if you shopped somewhere else. I swear you keep Sugar's in business."

"Come on, Tully. You know you're jealous of my sense of style." Delia grinned at me.

"Yeah. You're right. That's it." I laughed.

For Delia, every payday meant a new purse or outfit, but I was fine with my cutoffs and t-shirts, thank you very much.

My sister took one last look in her mirror before sighing and snapping the compact closed.

I managed the hulking truck into a parking spot near the back of the lot and shifted to neutral. Delia shoved open her door and hopped out, landing on the three inch heels of her strappy sandals as easily as if she were wearing running shoes. Not that she would ever be caught dead in running shoes. Or running, for that matter. At five foot eight and naturally slender, my sister didn't break a sweat if she could absolutely help it. That's saying something in the wet heat that is southern Mississippi summertime. Water springs from your pores like so many tiny geysers if you so much as step out your front door.

"I'll be back in an hour," I reminded her. "Try to be waiting out front or else...you know..." I moved my hand up and down, pretending to honk the truck's horn.

"Yeah. I know. Beep, beep," Delia said, rolling her eyes. "I swear. You *like* embarrassing me!"

She wasn't wrong.

"I don't know what you're talking about, sister dear." I grinned. "But I can tell you, I'm not setting foot back in that store, and I'm not going to wait around in the parking lot for an hour either. Honking the horn can't be helped."

"Yeah, well. You don't have to enjoy it so much. If we had cell phones—"

"Not that again," I interrupted.

She knew there was no point in us having cell phones. Daddy wouldn't pay for the service because the only place to get a signal was in town, and as far as he was concerned, the less time we spent here, the better. I sure wasn't going to pay for one just so I could call Delia to tell her to hurry up.

My sister rolled her eyes. "I'm just saying." She grabbed the door handle and reared back to slam it shut. I couldn't blame her for that; it was the single way to get the door to stay closed.

"Forgetting something?" I called, before she had the chance.

"Oops. Sorry," she said. She let go of the door and dug some money from her bright, ugly bag.

"Uh-huh," I said. It wasn't the first time Delia had tried to get away without paying.

She slapped a ten into my palm a little harder than necessary. The deal was, I would give her a ride, but she had to buy me lunch. Ever since her incident, Daddy didn't turn her loose on her own. And I couldn't blame him, even if it did mean I had to play chauffeur.

"Thank you, ma'am! And remember, one hour. And don't use your discount!" I said, wiggling my fingers.

Delia smiled back at me, fanning herself in a last ditch attempt to save the make-up that had taken her at least an hour to apply.

"Go to hell, sister dear," she said, her words slow and so saccharine they made my teeth hurt.

Despite her sometimes foul mouth, with creamy skin and huge green eyes made bigger by a small puggish nose and cupids-bow mouth,

Delia resembled a Disney princess cartoon. One that wore a little too much eyeliner and whose jet-black hair was blown-out and sprayed into perfect beauty queen submission. She looked so sweet and innocent, but if you mentioned it, that was when she told you to go to hell. For a minute you took it as a compliment, as if she were suggesting some kind of exotic vacation. People, at least the very few that didn't have some kind of preconceived notion about us, wanted to like her.

She smiled, cat-like, and slammed the truck closed again. Before she turned to walk away, I caught the telltale flash of green in her eyes.

I knew it was silly to worry. It had been years since Delia had gotten into trouble and exiled from the local shops. Everything had been made right by phone calls from Mama and promises from Daddy, but I couldn't help it. That sudden spark in her eyes made me feel uneasy. My sister was fearless, daring, and carefree. And when she got an idea in her head, you'd have better luck stopping a train than changing her mind.

I waited in the parking space while Delia strode across the lot, her hips moving from side to side, purposefully drawing the attention of anything with a Y chromosome. Two teenage boys stared as she moseyed by, their shared cigarette held between them, forgotten. Delia looked at them over her shoulder, lapping up the attention like a stray puppy.

She was almost to the shop entrance when the door opened and petite, redheaded Shanon Johnston sashayed out. Shanon's older cousin owned Sugar's, and the spoiled seventeen-year-old hung out at the boutique during the summer months. One more reason for me to avoid the store. I clasped the stick shift in a white-knuckled death-grip, watching as Shanon stood with her hands on her hips blocking the shop door. As Delia approached, the smart mouthed girl cocked her head to the side and pointed to the two boys in the parking lot. Delia started to laugh, but then Shanon said something that made Delia pause.

For half a second, my sister went rigid, before relaxing back into her practiced, 'I don't give two shits what you think, but hey look at me,' stance. *Shoulders back. Hips forward. Careless expression.* She could have been working the runway on America's Next Top Model.

Anyone else would have missed the momentary chink in Delia's armor, but not me. Shanon's words—whatever they had been—

penetrated my sister's steel façade.

Delia stepped closer to Shanon, and placing her hand on the shorter girl's shoulder, she leaned down and looked the redhead in the eye. I shifted from neutral to park, ready to hop from the truck if need be. I held my breath and waited. Not for a fight, but something worse.

Come on, Delia. Don't be stupid.

No words passed between them, only a look, *the* look. Dammit, so much for not being stupid. A sort of glazed expression came over Shanon and I could practically see her will turn to mush, leaving her as pliable as clay, ready and wanting nothing more than to please my sister. The happy current of her particular Gift emanated so strongly, I could feel it from where I sat in the truck. I counted it as a not so small blessing that her Charm only worked on those unGifted.

A second later, Shanon pushed the door open and held it for my sister, giggling like a schoolgirl sharing a secret with her favorite playmate. She reached into the pocket of her skirt, pulled out a few dollars, and offered the money to my sister. Delia looked back to where I sat in the truck before shaking her head. Shanon stuck the bills back into her pocket. The hate that had colored her face a moment before evaporated, replaced by a look of peaceful complacency.

Delia again turned toward the truck smirking, and as she waved me away, her eyes danced and flashed with the telltale sign of magic.

Oh, Delia. At least she hadn't taken the money. That was all we needed, for Delia to be called a thief...again.

My sister had been forgiven last time, but the people of Brooklyn weren't too keen on second chances, at least where my family was concerned. I glanced across the parking lot, but Delia and Shanon were the sole ones around. The smoking boys had disappeared around the corner of the shopping center. No one had seen the exchange, and Shanon wouldn't be talking.

As I eased the truck from the parking lot and onto the road that functioned as Brooklyn's main street, a navy and silver police cruiser rolled past me, turning into the lot next door.

I watched in my mirror as the cruiser pulled into a blue lined parking spot reserved for the handicapped, and Chief Rucker stepped out. His belly strained against the buttons of his uniform while he adjusted his belt.

I swallowed back the vinegary taste of dislike that filled my mouth.

Of course, he'd park in a handicapped space. The rules that he lives to enforce don't apply to him. My teeth ground together.

Pious bastard. He loved nothing more than giving my family a hard time. I thought of my strong willed sister shopping, and considered going in to get her. But I knew better. Delia would make a scene or give me hell the whole ride home.

I sighed uneasily as I drove away. *Delia, for once, behave.*

Chapter Two

Myrtle's Diner was the only place to eat in Brooklyn that didn't have a drive thru. Housed on the edge of town in a squat building with a flat roof, the bricks were painted the color of peanut butter. A white rectangle on the side denoted the previous tenants, the old men of the Brooklyn Masonic Lodge, who had painted over the only window in an attempt to keep prying eyes at bay. On the whole, the building resembled the world's ugliest Lego block. It was a testament to Myrtle's food that business thrived, despite such a hideous external appearance and busybody owner.

The bell jingled overhead when I walked in.

"Hey there, Tallulah," Myrtle drawled from behind the counter. Her hot pink lips stretched painfully across her face.

"It's me, Myrtle."

Her smile eased with the realization that Delia wasn't going to totter in behind me.

"Good. You know I don't judge your family like some do, but I'm not comfortable around that sister of yours. It's not right what she did to me," Myrtle said, making sure that her voice carried throughout the empty diner.

Myrtle would never actually say anything to my sister directly. She may not admit it, but the woman was terrified of Delia. I, on the other hand, was the safe Caibre sister. The one less Gifted.

My family wasn't supposed to use our magic. Especially not around outsiders. It had always been the golden rule, the most important one on a long list of things we weren't allowed to do. With my Gift, it was an easy rule to keep. The Gift of Suggestion isn't that great anyway, but the task had proved harder for my little sister. She started breaking it before she was even out of a stroller.

When Delia's magic was running high, it coated the air in a feeling of good cheer that can only be described as Christmas-like, lulling those around her with a sense of peaceful happiness. If you breathed in the leftover dredges of her magic, you found yourself longing for evergreen trees and family and eggnog. Anyone within hearing distance could feel the happy current.

She had always used her Gift to get her way with little things, nothing big, free candy or a cut in line at the goody-man's booth, but she was sixteen when she messed up. If you ask Delia why she did it, she'll tell you Myrtle had it coming.

After hearing a particularly harsh rumor the woman was peddling about one of our cousins, Delia waltzed into Myrtles, leaned across the counter, and Charmed Myrtle into cooking her whatever she wanted, free of charge. She ordered things that weren't on the menu, exotic dishes like cheese soufflé and duck comfit, and then laughed when the older woman went out of her way to try and prepare the elaborate meals before eventually failing. The two were alone in the restaurant, and Delia didn't let up until she was bored with her game. My sister said it was the most fun she'd ever had, but when it was all said and done, Myrtle wasn't laughing.

Delia had left the restaurant with a doggy bag of Myrtle's deep fried consolation food in tow. She hadn't even made it back home before the fog cleared from Myrtle's head and she personally started calling every store in town to tell them what that "dangerous Caibre girl" had done to her. Anywhere else, she would have sounded like a crazy-woman, but our Gifts were the worst kept secret in a town that hated us for them.

Thankfully, there was juicier gossip a couple of months later when it was discovered that the third grade teacher at the primary school was running a web-cam peep show from her bedroom. Delia's drama had been hearsay from a less-than-credible source, but poor Veronica Washington had been "caught" on camera by the head of the P.T.O.

Delia became old news, left alone as long as she tiptoed on the sidelines and didn't draw any more attention to herself. Which my parents made sure she didn't.

If you asked Delia whether the free food was worth the trouble, you'd likely get something thrown at you.

Myrtle stared at me, smugly waiting for a reaction to her jab.

I ignored her and instead, ordered a hot fudge sundae.

"Fine," the older woman said, clearly annoyed I hadn't taken her bait.

She pushed off the counter and sashayed through the swinging door that led to the kitchen. The ridiculous uniform she had chosen for her wait staff crinkled with her every step. I think the outfit was supposed to resemble a fifties style soda shop girl. Instead, the gaudy hot pink skirt and top combo, complete with poufy crinoline petite coat, resembled something from a 1950s theme night at a strip club. At least, I thought it did. I hadn't ever been to a strip club, but you get what I mean. The outfit was especially wrong on Myrtle, who would own up to being thirty-five, but who my Mama said was forty-seven. Although years of tanning booths and a two pack a day habit left her with leather skin and looking like a hard sixtyish.

I'd heard someone call her "rode hard and put up wet," but that sounded disgusting.

From his place hanging on the wall in the corner, the Elvis clock rocked his mechanical hips and sang a shortened verse of "Love me Tender," signaling it was 3:00. The lunch crowd had long cleared out, and it would be a few hours before the supper crowd started trickling in.

I had thought I was alone in the dining room, but from the corner of my eye, I caught a flash of movement from a booth near the back of the restaurant. A man was sitting with his back to me, bobbing his head in time to whatever music was playing through his ear buds. With no book, and nothing else to do, I leaned forward to try and see what he looked like. His wavy, dark hair was glossy as lacquer, and long enough to be tucked behind his ears. The skin on the back of his neck and arms was a good four shades darker than my own not exactly pale, but not exactly tan complexion. His was that perfect shade that sunbathers strive for, the color of coffee that had a little too much milk added to it. Delia, whose favorite past time was lying on a beach towel in our backyard in her bikini, would have been jealous.

Now, I know there's a fine line between curious and creepy, but for some reason the need to see the man's face pulled me forward. He was so free with his movements, enjoying his music like he was home alone or didn't care what anyone thought or said. It was the kind of freedom that made me prickle with envy.

I stood on the bottom rung of the barstool and stretched further across the counter, knowing there was no way to explain myself if he turned around. But for some unknown reason, I didn't care. It was as if the energy of his freedom was contagious, and it was washing over me, making me brave.

The swinging door to the back burst open, snapping me back to reality. Heat spread over my neck and ears when Lorretta stepped through the door three seconds before I could recover. The tiny blonde rolled her eyes at me, and stalked across the room to where the man was sitting, her every step designed for attention. The uniform that was pathetic on Myrtle somehow worked on Lorretta's athletic frame. She extended her toned arm, placing her palm onto the booth table, and leaned in low.

"You need a refill, Hun?" The words poured out of her mouth, slow as ketchup out of an old glass bottle.

"Nah. I'm good."

His voice was deep. Not the booming baritone of a middle aged man, but smooth and young, and accented in a way that said he wasn't from Mississippi. It added to his mystery and damn if it wasn't sexy.

Lorretta looked over her shoulder and caught me still staring.

"Freak." She mouthed the word before returning her gaze to the customer, leaning close enough for him to smell her brand of shampoo.

Finally, she rose and pushed away from the booth. Taking her time, she swayed back across the restaurant, only pausing long enough to shoot me with one more dagger before shoving open the kitchen door and stomping through. My face burned even hotter as I stared down at my hands. I could never in a million years so obviously flirt with someone. But Lorretta had a reputation for being obvious, among other things.

The door was still swinging on its hinges when Myrtle came back into the dining room.

"I'm sorry if I upset you about your sister, hun." Myrtle set a glass ice cream dish in front of me with a thunk.

Everything about Myrtle, from her bleached hair, to her habit of always talking a little too loud, begged for someone to notice her. The incident with Delia may have freaked her out, but I was willing to bet that in her mind, the attention the story bought her was more than worth it. It was two years later and she still milked it every chance she got.

"You didn't." I managed to get along at Myrtle's by keeping my words sparse, and letting her do the talking.

"So. Anything new?" she asked.

"Nope. Same old, same old." I gave her my usual response.

"You still working the fruit stand?"

The question made me wince, as it was no doubt meant to. Everyone else my age was off at college pledging their Mamas' sororities, or long married, barefoot and pregnant. Myrtle liked to remind me of that.

"Mm. Hmm," I said around a mouthful of vanilla bean ice cream.

I had been peddling produce from the glorified shed that stood at the end of our long driveway since I had been old enough to make correct change. Grandma's Gift allowed us to keep it open year round. The people who lived around Brooklyn had plenty to say about us, but they had no qualms with buying our produce, sometimes passing up one or two other fruit stands on their way to ours. Maybe it was wrong to take pride in that, but in a place where we were hated for being a branch on the wrong family tree, I'd take what I could get.

"Now how are you ever going to meet anyone if you stay out in that shack all day? Don't you wanna go off to college? Or at least have a little fun?" Myrtle asked, continuing down her usual list of questions.

Part of me wanted to blurt out that I was going to school at the community college next semester, and then pull the acceptance letter from where I kept it folded in my back pocket and stick it in her face. But I didn't dare. I hadn't told Mama or Daddy yet. I was waiting for the perfect moment, and telling Myrtle was as good as putting it in neon. I wasn't ready to deal with my parents, and I wasn't going to rush to rub this woman's face in something she had no business knowing.

Myrtle picked at the cuticle of her thumb, pulling off a tiny piece of dead skin and flicking it onto the diner floor. The only reason she was paying me any attention at all was because there was no one else to talk to. It wasn't like she was going to talk to Lorretta.

Myrtle had told Maureen Purdue, who worked out at the truck stop on the other side of town, that Lorretta, who was rounding up on thirty, was sleeping with Maureen's eighteen-year-old son. Maureen had stormed into Myrtle's and made a big stink, calling Lorretta a whore loud enough for everyone to hear. Myrtle had sat back and enjoyed the show.

But there weren't that many women around town who were looking for full time waitressing jobs, and even less who would wear Myrtle's ugly uniform. So Myrtle hadn't fired Lorretta. And unless you wanted to drive thirty-five minutes into Peachton, there wasn't anywhere else to wait tables, so Lorretta hadn't quit. The two women kept working as if the ordeal hadn't happened, only shooting each other dirty looks across the dining room floor from time to time.

And the sole other person in the diner today was the man listening to his earbuds. If he hadn't been someone from out of town, Myrtle probably would've tapped him on the shoulder and started pestering him. I was the bottom of the barrel when it came to finding out gossip. Unfortunately, for me, the barrel was empty.

"I don't want to go to college," I lied. "And I'm not worried about meeting anyone right now." At least that part was true.

"Well did you hear about Chief Rucker's son?" Myrtle changed the subject. She smiled, her top lip curling a little too much.

I guess my well-rehearsed answers weren't juicy enough. *Good.*

"No. I haven't. His son Jason?" Normally I didn't let myself get drawn into Myrtle's drama, but the Brooklyn Police Chief was a callous man who didn't even attempt to hide his dislike for my family.

"Yeah. Jason. He's about your age." Myrtle rubbed her hands together like she was about to tuck into something delicious. "Last weekend, someone was making a lot of noise in that motel out on

Liberty road. You know? The Palm Tree Inn?" She paused, waiting for me to nod. I did know the place she was talking about. Mainly because I had always thought it was a stupid name. There weren't any palm trees anywhere around. My family didn't even grow them, and we could grow anything. The Pine Tree Inn would have made a lot more sense.

"They were really going at it! Grunts, moans, the whole nine yards. The other 'guests' were none too happy, but I guess Joe Smithy, the guy who owns the motel, couldn't be bothered about it," Myrtle said, wagging her eyebrows, and raising an imaginary bottle to her lips.

Everyone knew that Mr. Smithy was a drunk, but the Palm Tree Inn didn't have a reputation for attracting the kind of people who minded.

"Someone called the Police instead. Chief Rucker was down in that direction anyway, so he answered the call himself...and guess what?"

"What?" I asked, reluctantly. I knew good and well once Myrtle started, she wouldn't leave me alone until she had finished her story.

"The Chief knocked on the door, and who should answer, but Jason butt-ass-naked!" She clapped her hands, smiling.

"So what's the big deal with that?" I took another bite of ice cream, taking my time before continuing. "Even I know that lots of men who go out drinking at the Bug-Lite end up sleeping it off at the Palm Tree Inn." I was proud of this little tid bit of information I had gleaned from a conversation overheard while pumping gas.

The truth was my Daddy would have buried me under the house if I ever so much as pulled into the parking lot of either the bar or the hotel. The fact that I was old enough to actually buy a beer wouldn't have even factored into his decision. And it wasn't just my crazy, overprotective Daddy, either. Any self-respecting father around would do the same. Both places were sketchy.

Myrtle rolled her eyes. "That's not all! Are you kidding? The Chief was surprised to see his son in the dumpy hotel, and even more surprised he came to the door naked, but probably figured he had himself a hooker, or something. So then he told Jason to keep it down and was about to leave when what do you think he heard?"

"What?" I asked.

"Another man's voice! Well, Chief Rucker pushed into the room and, lord have mercy, there he was! Another man sprawled out on the bed." Myrtle wrinkled her nose.

"Yikes." I took another bite of ice cream and swallowed. "That sucks for Jason. To be caught in the act by your Dad, and then to be outted to the whole town."

Myrtle put a hand on her hip and narrowed her eyes. "Don't you even feel sorry for the Chief? For a decent man like that to end up having a *gay* son…how terrible! Makes me wonder what happened to him as a boy to turn out like *that*."

Poor Jason. I didn't know enough about his personal life to know if him being gay would be surprising or not, but I could tell you Brooklyn, MS was not the most forward thinking place to live. I imagined Myrtle's view would be the typical one.

Lord only knows where Chief Rucker's views stood. He probably considered being gay along the same lines as robbing a bank or shooting a puppy. The man loved playing the part of the good ole boy. The small town police Chief who looked after everyone's best interest and moral integrity. He judged the Magnolia Festival beauty pageant every year, sat on the board of trustees for the small private kindergarten at the Presbyterian Church, and any conversation with him that lasted more than five minutes made it clear he thought that he was the ultimate say of all that was good and right in our town. Did I mention he hated my family?

I wondered how Chief Rucker was going to flip this to his advantage. Men like him pulled no punches when it came to keeping up appearances.

"And honey, that's not all," Myrtle continued. "Apparently the man had real green eyes." She paused and looked at me, expecting a reaction.

"And?" I asked, when she didn't continue.

Myrtle raised her penciled-on eyebrows. "The kind of eyes like your kind have?"

My spoon stopped half way to my lips as what Myrtle was getting at clicked.

Everyone knew we were Gifted. My family even profited from it. But we were very careful to keep the specifics of our magic a secret. Of course, there were always rumors, usually stories dreamt up by old women, told to entertain each other at the beauty shop. Sometimes though, every so often, someone would get it right.

Could they have figured out how to spot magic in a Gifted person's eyes?

Our irises acted like emerald screens, behind them magic danced and crackled, biding its time until it could escape. It wasn't obvious, but it was there if you knew what to look for. It had been a well-kept secret, hidden in plain sight.

But Myrtle knowing how to spot magic wasn't what bothered me.

I took a deep breath, and silently counted to three, determined not to say something I would regret.

"In fact," she continued, "it's going around town that the man with whom Jason was, I can't help it, caught with his pants down, was like you and yours. Some are saying he was like your sister. That poor Jason was a victim. That he was," she paused and looked around the restaurant, "*Charmed.*"

I swallowed my tongue.

Myrtle stood up straighter and practically belted, "And I certainly know that you can't help what you do when you're Charmed."

I glanced at the man in the booth. His head never missed a beat. He was for sure going to have hearing damage if his iPod was up loud enough to miss Myrtle's performance.

The last thing I needed was for Myrtle to see she had upset me. I didn't want to give her that satisfaction. But despite the fact that I had grown up near a town that considered us second-class citizens, my parents had managed to instill in me a good dose of self-worth. I had to say something. I physically could not sit there and not say anything.

"That's bullshit, Myrtle. So Jason happens to be gay. Yeah it sucks that his Dad walked in on him. Hell, it sucks that his dad is Chief Rucker. But nothing you have said could suggest he was doing anything against his will!" I shook my head. "Why? Because his, um, boyfriend had green eyes? Tons of people have green eyes and they have no Gifts. Besides, my 'type of people,' as you call us, we don't do that. We don't even date, so you can bet we don't go hook up in seedy motels. Not to mention I don't know of anyone outside of my family with Gifts who would be in this part of the country. Also, if you want to know what I really think, it's that Chief Rucker saying his son was taken advantage of saves face for him, and gives him a reason to give us more hell than he already does. Which is more than a little. So you need to keep your lies to yourself!" I quietly spat the last words from my mouth, intentionally keeping my voice low.

I risked looking at the man in the booth, who was still listening to his earbuds, oblivious to the drama unfolding behind him. *Thank God.*

Nausea squeezed my stomach, and I dropped my spoon into the half-full bowl of ice cream. Telling Myrtle off did not bring the relief I'd imagined.

Myrtle's eye's narrowed into thin creases, and her lips spread across her face in two vicious lines. Neither of us said anything for a minute.

And then.

"Oh?"

She had heard something she liked. I should have known better.

Crap.

"I gotta go. I don't have time for this." I stood up, and tossed Delia's ten onto the counter.

"Calm down now, Tallulah. Of course I don't think that! That's what is going around the old rumor mill. You know I'm never one to talk bad about people. I figured I should let you know. Just in case you knew the fella." She paused. "I tell you what," Myrtle picked up the ten and pressed it back into my hand, "This sundae is on the house. You know you can talk to me about anything, right?" Her transition from troll to wise barkeep was seamless perfection as she walked around the counter to stand close to me.

She cannot seriously think that I'm going to spill my guts to her? If you wanted everyone to know something, you told Myrtle. If you wanted them to know pronto, you told Myrtle but added, *Now don't tell anyone.* I bit down on my tongue. I had said more than enough for the day.

"Why don't you tell me what this is about you all not dating? That seems odd for a pretty girl like you. I would imagine that you, and especially your sister with that voodoo of hers, would have boys lined up to take ya'll out." She scrunched her brows in fake concern. "It's not your daddy, is it? He isn't doing anything…inappropriate?" She gave my shoulder a squeeze, making it clear she expected me to talk.

Anger crept through me, starting in the pit of my stomach, replacing the nausea with a tight knot. I swatted Myrtle's hand off my shoulder. Loretta was still in the back and the man in the booth was still swaying to music only he could hear.

Good. Swallowing back my words, I tried to force coherent thoughts into the jumbled, shocked mess that was my mind. The fact that Myrtle, who had seen me at least monthly since I was old enough to drive, would suggest something so vile just to get information she wanted, stripped away any idea that me and my kin were viewed as anything but rotten fruit. I knew she was self-serving, but this? This was beyond disgusting. I had never heard her even suggest something so terrible about anyone before. When she had turned people against Delia, there had been truth in what she said. This was an out and out lie.

My family had lived on the same 200 acres of land for over a hundred years, and maybe it hadn't always been perfect, but generations of our people had made it work. In one hour, I had single handedly managed to put it all in jeopardy. If I didn't play Myrtle's game, she would pretend to suspect my father had done things I couldn't even think about. Nasty things. Horrible things that even a hint at could ruin a well-liked man's life.

Daddy would be crucified.

I had to fix this, but I had to be careful. There were things we kept secret, and for good reason. It had always worked in our favor that the townspeople hadn't known exactly what we were capable of, not really.

Many people from Brooklyn, the same ones who preached us into hell, were happy to pay for services only we could provide. They always came at night, ashamed of needing us, and the next day never acknowledging the transaction. Never mind how many times Daddy assured pretty weather for the wedding of some dumb bride who didn't have the foresight not to plan her outdoor nuptials during hurricane season. Or how many times my Uncle Drew called the wind to blow a downed tree off someone's driveway. Or even when my cousin Rebecca delivered the greatest kindness of all by visiting the elderly at the end of their life, and helping them to feel peace and slip into a calm rest. But no matter how good the deed, our mercies were viewed as deals with the devil, and their dependence on us only deepened the hate many people from Brooklyn felt.

This delicate balance of need versus fear was what kept us safe in a world where magic was supposed to exist only in children's games and fairytales. Without even realizing it, the townspeople had woven our safety net, one string at a time, whenever they called on us for help, and every time they whispered a story that made us out to be grander than we were. But that net would snap like cheap thread if Myrtle started spreading such ferocious lies. We might have powers, but they had numbers.

"Myrtle, I appreciate your concern. I really, really do. But that's not the case. My Daddy is one of the most Godly, upright men you could ever hope to meet. He would never do something so vile."

"Oh hunny! I am sure he is! But I know it has to be stressful running a family business and all. And you and your sister are so pretty. If something was going on, you know that it wouldn't be your fault. Victims get brainwashed, you know. It would be hard, but you'd need to tell someone." The words rolled out of her mouth, poisonous but coated with a good dusting of sugar to try and sweeten their ugliness.

I clenched my trembling fists at my sides. It took every ounce of reserve I had in me not to let one fly up and punch Myrtle Delacroix in her ugly, lying face.

"Myrtle, dammit, Daddy isn't like that. I'm not like that. No one in our family is like that. That's disgusting!"

So much for calm and collected.

Myrtle jerked her hands to her hips, and pursed her lips. "Well, what kind of woman don't date? That ain't natural!" She stood on her tiptoes and leaned closer to my ear. "You know, sugar," she whispered, "folks love to believe bad things, especially about the people they don't like."

I squeezed my eyes shut. Anything that came out of my mouth was sure to hit the ears of everyone who walked into the restaurant that week. Using my Gift was too risky, and anyway, I wasn't sure if it would even work.

The Gift of Suggestion wasn't that helpful as far as magic goes. Never mind I'd never really tried it out.

When I was younger I'd played around and attempted to use it on Delia, but she'd tattled, and I'd gotten a tongue-lashing. After that, I'd ignored the fact that I even had a Gift. Easy thing to do with something so...slow acting. If I could lock eyes with someone, I should be able to plant an idea in their subconscious. Like a seed, the idea should stretch out and grow, twining and snaking through their mind, covering it like a weed. In the end, sometimes days later, the person shouldn't even realize the idea wasn't their own.

I'd always been a little jealous of my sister's ability. Which was stupid and useless, I know, because a person's Gift was as much a part of them as their hair color or skin tone. And like some people had hair thicker than kudzu, or a baby doll complexion, others, in my family, had more powerful Gifts. It was the luck of the genetic lottery, or as my Grandma had always told me when I complained about my puny ability, "You get what you get."

Now I wished I had been more of a rule-breaker, like my sister, and honed my magic. But I was the good sister. The rule-follower. And now my Gift was as useless as a muscle that atrophied after years of neglect. Sure, it was there and maybe had potential, but it would take time. I didn't have time. I had to figure this out now.

Sweat broke out across my forehead, despite the cooled air was blowing in from the vents overhead.

"Myrtle, try to imagine how hard it would be for me to date someone without Gifts. You see how we're looked at right here in town, where our family has lived as long as anyone else? People think we're evil, or else they want to see what they can use us for. It would be the same if any of us tried to have a romantic relationship with someone not Gifted. They would either be repelled or in it to see what they could get." I repeated the facts that had been drilled into my head since Mama had deemed me old enough to wonder about boys.

"So what do you do, then?" she asked. Her eyes widened with a sudden thought. "You don't *really* in-breed, do you?"

"No!" I snapped. That's disgusting!"

"Oh. Well what?"

I took another deep breath. I had to tiptoe through this part. It concerned not only my family's business, but that of other Gifted families as well. We were already outsiders, but we weren't truly alone. If I broke the trust we had with others like us, well...that would be bad.

"My Great Aunt Trudy makes arrangements for us when we turn

twenty or twenty-one. We aren't forced to marry or anything like that, and if we need a little more time then that's fine, but for the most part, when we turn twenty-one, we start seeing suitors." I kept the words as emotionless as I could. Anger was threatening to rip me clean in two.

"So ya'll have arranged marriages?" Myrtle had the nerve to sound let down. Arranged marriages might be juicy, but not as juicy as inbreeding. "Where does Auntie find these matches?"

"I don't know, Myrtle. I haven't ever thought about it."

"But these suitors…they all have powers, too? Earlier, you said that no one outside of your family that has Gifts would be in this part of the country. There are other families like yours?"

"Yes. Of course. I mean, think about it. We all have powers, and we aren't inbred." It was my turn to get snappy. She had what she wanted and I was done with the conversation. "Now. If you don't mind, I have got to pick up my sister." I turned to leave.

"Just one more, teeny thing, sugar." She said, grabbing my arm.

"What?"

"Is it true what they say about your Grandma?"

"I gotta go, Myrtle. If you want to know anything else about anyone in my family, you should ask them. I can bring Delia with me next time and you can pick her brain all you want. Then maybe she can pick yours."

Myrtle paled.

I pulled my arm from her grip, ran out the door, and jumped in my truck. "Shit! Shit! Shit!" I pounded on the steering wheel. Tears stung my eyes. "Why didn't I leave? I could have walked right out of there without saying anything."

I wiped my eyes on my t-shirt, and then pulled the truck onto the street, squealing the worn tires on the pavement. How was I going to tell my Daddy? Or my Pawpaw? Just the thought of repeating the allegations to either one of them was too much. Bile rose, threatening the back of my throat. I rolled the window down, needing air.

I loved Pawpaw Rex so much, and the thought of disappointing him sent an icy shiver through me, even though it was hot enough in the truck to fry an egg on the dashboard. Of everyone's Gifts, his was the most obscure. He had the Gift of Yesterday. He could remember.

Everything. He always said he remembers being born, and he probably does.

The disappointment he would feel when he finds out that his granddaughter had broken the family trust would not lessen with time, and even though I knew that his love was unconditional, the thought of my sweet Pawpaw carrying that memory around with him...it killed me.

It was a memory I could not give him. I wouldn't. Me, the responsible sister, the grandchild who did what was expected, would not be the one accountable for turning the tides against us. I didn't know what Myrtle could do with the information she had dragged out of me. Maybe nothing. But now that I was away from the diner, I knew I couldn't leave things like they were.

My hands shook as an idea formed. I held hard onto the steering wheel of the old truck and focused on not driving into the ditch.

The thought of using my Gift to fix things felt sour, fermenting my insides. It was against everything I had been taught, and I wasn't Delia, who had no problem tossing aside the lessons that were drilled into us since girlhood.

But then there was my Pawpaw...I couldn't be the disappointment.

At the next turn around, I cut the wheel sharp and headed back towards the diner.

Chapter Three

I parked in the same space I had just left and slid from my seat onto wobbly legs. Saying that the plan was simple was being generous. I would go into the store and tell Myrtle I wanted to apologize. Then I'd act like I was going to hug her. Instead, once I leaned in, I would lock eye contact and hope for the best.

The problem was I didn't know exactly what I was going to try to persuade Myrtle to do. I knew I didn't want her to repeat her lies. But I also didn't want her to tell anyone our family business. I could try to get her to think it was bad to speak ill of my family altogether, but that would be a long shot. Not that the whole thing wasn't a long shot.

No matter what, though, I could not let her figure out I was using magic, or she'd likely spread her rumors out of pure spite.

Before I could talk myself from the whole thing, I shoved open the door and marched in.

"Myrtle I need to…" I started, my eyes trained on my sneakers. My heartbeat filled my ears and I dried my palms on my jean shorts. "I want to apologize." I said to the floor, scared if I looked up I would lose my nerve.

"She's in the back," said the deep voice from earlier.

I jerked my gaze upward. *Crap.* I had been in such a hurry, I hadn't thought about the other customer. Or even Loretta, who I knew would love to see me squirm.

The man from the booth was standing by the counter in the front of the diner.

I clenched my mouth shut, embarrassed at the thought of what this man might have heard, and scared that if I talked I would only make it worse.

The holes in my plan now stood out in my mind, gaping wide and taunting me with how dumb the entire idea had been. *Things could not get any worse.*

"Are you okay?" The stranger asked.

I was wrong.

The back of my neck prickled, the way it always did whenever my face decided it was a good time to turn scarlet. Something too strong to be called butterflies stirred in my stomach. It was how I imagined stage fright must feel. Both exciting and terrifying.

I breathed deep.

He was tall. As a girl of five foot nine, I always noticed height. He had to be at least six foot two. And slim, but not skinny, built with the long muscles of an athlete. The dark hair that had been tucked behind his ears, now hung loose around a wide face decorated with high cheekbones, and the kind of full lips that made women jealous.

All of these things made him gorgeous, but his eyes made him breathtaking. They were large, almond shaped, and the color of moss. Green, but not magic green, and they stood out against his tan skin. I had seen good-looking men, but this man was startling. And he definitely had to be from out of town. In a place the size of Brooklyn, you learned most everyone's faces, even if you didn't personally know them. I was certain I had never seen this man before. I would remember a face like that.

And he had just said something, while I was staring at him. *Dangit.*

"Excuse me?" I asked.

"I said that you shouldn't apologize to her. She was rude to you. You have nothing to be sorry for." His lips parted, showing white, straight teeth that wouldn't have been out of place in a toothpaste ad.

Of course his smile would be as beautiful as he is. I touched my tangled ponytail, and for the first time in my life, I wished I had listened to Delia and actually fixed my hair and changed clothes before coming into town.

But he had spoken to me. That meant I had to answer. I tried to think, but every word in my vocabulary decided to vanish, leaving me mute. *Mute and homely, a winning combination,* I thought.

I shook my head. *Good. At least I could move.*

"I didn't mean to eavesdrop, but that whole bit about the dude with green eyes? I mean come on. I have green eyes and I'm not gay. I mean, there isn't anything wrong with being gay, but I'm not. And I'm not related to you either. At least, I hope I'm not. What I'm saying is that, I'm sure your family is lovely, it's only that, I can't be related to you," he paused, and nervously rubbed the back of his neck. "I mean. I know I'm not because I'm not even from here. What was all that about anyway? Green eyes and your people?"

I was stupid in my silence, but his rambling was somehow adorable.

"You heard that?" I croaked.

My family's freakiness had been on full display. And then, there were those disgusting threats. Myrtle's accusations churned in my stomach, curdling and sour like old milk. The feeling clashed against the butterflies and their eager fear, and suddenly I felt ill. I clamped my mouth shut and took a deep breath through my nose as a cold sweat prickled across my upper lip. Throwing up would have been bad, but throwing up in front of this man, who was a million times better looking than me, and had just heard from the most horrible source on the planet about how weird I was, would be a whole new kind of terrible.

I couldn't be the story about that time that he met this nut-case girl in po-dunk Mississippi and she threw up all over his shoes.

Oh God. Calm down, Tallulah.

"You were explaining about your family to her. She was being a real asshole. This place is crazy. That one lady yells at you, and that other girl acts offended because I didn't want to, I don't know, take her in the back room. I guess here you get dinner and a show."

He stuck out his hand, and smiled. "I'm Logan, by the way."

I stared open-mouthed at the hand in front of me. Every part of me wanted to grab that hand, twine my fingers through his, and keep them there forever.

Instead, I stood stock-still.

Something about him pulled at me. I wondered if he felt it, too. This beautiful trance wouldn't let me turn and leave, but terrified me too much to simply reach out and shake his hand.

My heart pounded the seconds as they lumbered by.

"This is the part where you tell me your name," he said, dropping his hand to his side. He stared into my eyes and his expression turned serious. "That's so strange. I know we couldn't have, but have we met before? I know it's impossible, because I'd never forget those eyes...but it feels like I know you. Like I've always known you."

"Um. I. I don't—"

"You ain't nothing but a hound dog..." Elvis' voice sang out from the ugly clock on the wall, snapping me from my stupor. It was 4:00. I had to get Delia.

"I. I gotta go," I mumbled, turning on my heel and bolting out the door.

I jumped into the green truck, and for the second time, wheeled from the parking lot. When I was far enough away from the restaurant to be sure that the man, Logan, couldn't see me, I whipped the truck onto the side of the road.

Simply thinking his name sent a rush of dangerous bliss through me, making me feel things that I had never allowed myself to imagine possible. Romance. Lust. Those were words on the pages of the paperbacks I read to fill my days working at the produce stand. The married couples in my family loved each other, sure. But their love grew to be. There was no locking eyes and intense feelings. It was all very proper. Planned. Analytical, even. Inquiries sent from one family to another. *That's how it has always been. That's how it has to be*, the familiar lecture ran through my mind.

My emotions tore at each other, at war inside me. Fear that I'd somehow made things harder for my family. Hatred and anger at Myrtle. Unexplainable desire and excitement over Logan. Sadness because nothing could ever come from those feelings. And if I was honest, maybe the tiniest bit of relief that it was out of my hands.

Most of all the unfairness of everything settled over me.

It was too much.

I threw open the door, barely making it out of the truck and to the roadside before throwing up all over the shrubby tangle of wildflowers.

***

"Well. You can't tell Daddy," Delia said, matter of fact like.

"What are you talking about, I can't tell Daddy? I HAVE to tell him, Del! The other families could get pissed…" My voice trailed off.

"Why? What good is it going to do you? Besides, the bitch didn't give you much of a choice, and I think that the tiny bit of info you gave her was worth the trade-off. I mean really, who cares about who we marry anyway? If they use their brains then most of them have figured that out by now."

"Maybe. But it feels wrong not to tell." I was an adult, but I'd broken an important rule. The responsible thing to do was tell my father, so he and the other elders could sort it out.

"Think about it. If you tell him, what possible difference could it make? He isn't going to let anyone go 'fix' it. All it's going to do is upset him and make you feel bad." Delia frowned.

"But it feels like I'm lying. And I'm not a kid. I can't just make a mistake and lie to cover it up. Not when it affects other people."

I had been a mess when I picked up my sister. Delia had been waiting for me in front of the store, chatting with the boys who were smoking earlier, with no sign of Shanon in sight. She had listened as I recounted what happened, her eyes growing greener whenever I said Myrtle's name. Like always, though, the aura of good that seemed to roll out of her pores calmed me down.

"It isn't lying. Not at all! And like I said, all it would do is upset him. And nothing bad will happen. You didn't tell her anything important. So who cares?" Delia said again. She reached over the giant shopping bag that sat between us on the seat and squeezed my knee. "We can go back and I can try to Charm her…"

"No. That's okay. I guess you're right." I sighed. "Maybe it would be worse to upset everyone over nothing."

"Of course I'm right! Plus, we don't want Daddy angry when I ask him if I can go to the fair tonight." She grinned.

"Seriously, Delia? Is that why you don't want me to tell? The damn fair?" I should have known. "If Daddy won't let you even go into town to shop, why in the world do you think he's going to let you go to the fair?"

"I didn't ask you what you thought about me going. Only that you not upset Daddy until after I talk to him. But if you must know, Jack said he would go with me if Daddy says yes." Her devilish grin widened. "Which I think he might."

"Yeah, because that won't mean trouble," I grumbled.

Jack was our cousin. With his dark hair and clear skin, he and Delia were boy and girl bookends, both with the Gift of Charm. When they were little, people had always asked if they were twins. That's not that strange considering our Mama and Uncle Gavin, Jack's daddy, really are twins.

"Come on. You know what he's going to say," I groaned. "There will be people there who hate us, Del. And with all that crap you pulled a few years ago, there's no way you can blend in. And Jack taking you isn't going to help, either. You've been bossing him around since diapers."

"Geez, Tully, it's a fair, not a bar! I'm eighteen and all I want to do is walk around, eat something on a stick, and maybe ride the Ferris wheel. There will be little kids there with their families, not a lynch mob!" Delia's eyes flashed green as her magic rose with her voice, ironically blanketing us with cheer.

I couldn't lie to myself, the fair sounded amazing, and even I wanted to go. The food, the lights, the games…all of it seemed almost magical. The carnival would draw people from Peachton, and maybe even as far away as Brookhaven.

Maybe Logan will be there… The thought made me smile, despite that I was trying to talk sense into my sister. I couldn't help it. But unlike Delia, I lived in reality. And in reality, going to a place filled with town people who didn't like us was a monumentally bad idea.

"Whatever, Del. Do what you want. You always do, anyway," I stated.

We sat in silence as the truck bumped down the familiar back road. I knew the ruts and potholes by heart, and could have steered around them in my sleep, but after being attacked by Myrtle, and then embarrassing myself in front of Logan, I was too drained to make the effort. Arguing with Delia was icing on the cake.

A few minutes passed, and Delia rolled her eyes. "I'm sorry all of that happened, Tully. I really am. But seriously, I wouldn't say anything if I were you. It's not going to help anything." She paused for a moment, "And if you do, wait until after I leave for the fair."

"You are so shallow!" I yelled at my sister, who burst into giggles.

"Chill, Tully! You are too easy! Now, why don't you tell me more about this Logan?"

I knew I would regret telling my sister about the handsome stranger, but everything had spilled out of me as soon as she'd gotten into the truck: from the beginning, to why I ended up crying in the truck in Sugar's parking lot, smelling like barf.

"There's nothing to tell." I shrugged. "He was gorgeous. I was a hot mess. He asked me my name, and I ran out like an idiot. That's it." My teeth gnawed at my bottom lip. "Besides. I'm twenty-one, so there's no point."

Delia frowned. "I guess not," she whispered, surprising me.

I had assumed my sister would be looking forward to the year of dates I was about to embark on, even if the idea left me squeamish. I hadn't liked the idea of arranged dates even before seeing the handsome stranger at Myrtle's. Now the whole thing really drove home how little control I had over my own life.

Neither of us said a word on the rest of the ride home.

Chapter Four

Delia had purchased a tiny yellow sundress from Sugar's. It was the type of dress that hung loose from the shoulders with an open back and a hemline so far above the knee, it was about a finger's length from being a shirt. And it would look amazing on my sister.

Too bad she had a better chance of growing a third leg than being allowed out of the house wearing it.

"I can honestly say, even if Daddy did let you go tonight, there's no way you would be going in that!" I pointed to the item in question. "Really, Del, if you try and get on the Ferris wheel in that thing you'll get arrested for indecency."

We stood in Delia's room on opposite sides of her full-sized bed, with the new sundress carefully spread over her down comforter.

"Well, sister dear, I guess I had better wear some pretty panties, then."

"Delia!" I snapped. "No way would you show your unde…"

Delia burst into giggles.

"What?" I asked, and then realized she was laughing at me. The thing is, nothing surprised me with my little sister, and it really wasn't hard for me to believe she would have a "to hell with it" attitude about flashing her drawers around for all the town to see. She wasn't a bad person. Nor was she some kind of closeted floozy. She never saw what the big deal was…about anything.

Well, anything other than clothes.

Or purses.

Or make-up.

"Would you relax a little, Tallulah?" she said, catching her breath. "Geez! No! I would not flash my. My—" Delia erupted into another fit of laughter. "My *lady business!*" She thrust her hips back and forth, stabbing the air with her crotch.

When the words "lady business" left her mouth, I couldn't hold back my own giggles, knowing she said the ridiculous word to tease me. According to my sister, I had the propriety of a seventy-year-old lady.

"Really Del? Lady business? Who even says that?" I gasped between laughter.

When we finally started to catch our breath, Delia snorted, setting us off in another fit. "I-I'm going to pee my pants!"

"Yeah," Delia said, "Pee your pants with your lady business."

"AAH!" I screeched, tossing a throw pillow at her.

Each chuckle seemed to purge some of the grimy feeling that had clung to me since Myrtle's threats at the diner. Delia could cheer me up in that way only best friends could, by bringing on bouts of hysteria from seemingly nowhere, and then keeping the giggles going until we were both all laughed out. One of her many non-magical talents.

"Ok. Ok," I said when we finally managed to stay sane for a good minute. I chanced a look at Delia, who was hugging the Sugar's bag to her chest.

"But to answer your earlier concern, I got this to wear over it." She pulled dress number two out of the shopping bag. It was long and navy, with a peter pan collar, and left absolutely everything to the imagination.

"That's from Sugar's?" I asked. The shapeless blanket of a dress was beyond terrible. I sniffed the air. "Del, that thing smells like a wet dog!"

"Actually, I pulled this out of the donation bin on the side of the building. The one for the 'crazy church'," she said, ignoring the wet dog comment.

The "crazy church" was our name for Embers of the Righteous Fire, a "church" whose preacher, Reverend Joshua Armstrong, had a long list of things he demanded his followers hate.

The one and only good thing that came from that nut job's cultish congregation was that they gave to the poor. Of course, the poor were subjected to hours of Reverend Armstrong's version of fire and brimstone preaching, followed by them "choosing" to get baptized into the church, and only then were they allowed to dig through the stuff that everyone in town had deemed not worth keeping or giving to a family member.

It was hard to imagine Delia, in her heels and dress, standing in the heat and pulling clothes out of the bright red donation bin. Then again, there had been those two boys eyeballing her in the parking lot. They would have been no match for Delia, all tarted up and feeling like Christmas. I decided not to ask.

"Ew. You are going to get the mange!" I pulled a face. "Besides, Daddy will know that you are up to something the minute you walk downstairs in that...thing."

"I'm not going to catch the mange from a dress! But you might!" She shrieked, and tossed the dress at me.

I jumped out of the way, letting it fall to the floor. Dust motes scattered above where it landed in a heap on the carpet. "You'd better wash that thing before you wear it."

Delia shook her head, like I was hopeless. "Daddy doesn't notice clothes. Trust me, he won't suspect a thing. Mama might, but I'll avoid her until Jack picks me up. You should come. We stand a better chance of being able to go, if we go together." Delia paused and then added, grinning, "Besides, that hottie might be there!" She wiggled her eyebrows.

I couldn't help but smile. I knew it was silly, but I wanted to see him again in the worst possible way. Bad enough maybe even to help Delia try and convince Daddy us going to the fair wasn't the craziest idea in the world.

Chapter Five

Three hours later, Delia had locked herself in her room, crying, and angry at the unfairness of life. Daddy was stomping around, fuming about how his daughters had no sense whatsoever, and Mama was trying to be the peacekeeper. I hung in the background, not surprised one bit. Delia and Daddy were always butting heads, and the routine was as familiar as it was unpleasant.

The argument between the two had lasted maybe fifteen minutes, but the aftershocks would last until the next morning. Delia would stay locked away in her room and Daddy would grumble until he fell asleep in front of the weather channel. Tension would hang over the whole house, heavy as a miserable cloud until they made up. While telling an eighteen-year-old—let alone someone three years older—that they couldn't go out may seem completely overbearing, in our family, it was more about self-preservation than control. If Delia went, even with me as a chaperone, she was bound to get into trouble, possibly of the magical variety. And we lived under Daddy's roof, so we really couldn't argue.

I cleaned the kitchen alone, sweeping the floor and washing the few dishes we had dirtied. I wiped the last of the spilled spaghetti sauce off the stovetop, and decided it would do me some good to get out of the house. I had enough tension for one day.

I pulled on my sneakers and yelled to Mama that I was going to Grandma's. Neither she nor Daddy complained. They trusted I would go where I said. Mostly because Mama had her own way of checking up on me, but also because they knew I'd never given them a reason not to trust me. *Me. The straight-laced responsible sister.* It was one of Delia's favorite digs when we were arguing.

I winced as the screen door slammed behind me. I was always forgetting to ease it shut, and half-expected Mama to stick her head out the door and give me a lecture.

She didn't.

Our driveway looped and turned many times, connecting everyone's houses and the many gardens on our property. So when I explained to people that my Grandparents lived at the other end of our drive, it meant their house was actually a good piece away…if you follow that path. I had been cutting through the back woods and apple orchard since I was a little girl. Delia and I had made the trek so many times growing up, there was a dirt footpath where grass struggled to grow, despite Grandma's Gift.

Overhead, a crow called to me with its throaty "caw." At night, the birds were usually off doing whatever it was crows did after the sun went down. The tension in the house must have gotten to Mama for her to send one after me for the short trip to Grandma's.

Mama could understand birds. All birds. But crows love to gossip, and they loved Mama for listening. Growing up, Mama had always sent a crow or two tagging along with me and Delia, ready to report on whatever dastardly deeds a couple of little girls were sure to commit. As you can imagine, it was more than a little difficult to get up to any mischief. We'd still managed, though.

"I'm old enough to walk to Grandma's at night without a babysitter," I called out.

"Caw," the bird replied.

Rolling my eyes, I shined my light through the trees to try and locate my flying nanny. I squinted into the darkness, and finally found him perched in one of the apple trees. The crow stared at me, no doubt waiting for me to keep going so he could follow and report to Mama that I had made it in one piece. After Delia's scene, I could hardly blame her for wanting to keep an eye on me. Still, it grated on my nerves. I was twenty-one for Pete's sake. It needed to stop.

I clicked off the flashlight and continued through the woods. The smell of the apple trees, spicy from their fruit baking in the sun, hung heavy in the air, taking me back to my childhood. I had grown up climbing in the branches and knew every tree in the grove. Some of my best memories were of games played on the path. The walks to Grandma's would often last all day with the orchard becoming an enchanted forest from where me and Delia, the princesses, would have to find our way to the queen's castle. Other times we were gladiators caught in a maze with no way out, or even witches zooming through our secret woods on broomsticks.

There was something calming about being in these trees alone, while familiarity enveloped my senses. From the many years of running wild and barefoot, I even knew exactly what the grass would feel like: dewy and soft, with the occasional squish of decomposing fruit between my toes.

Our life is separate from the world, but it is good. Blessed in its own way, I thought.

Sure, I had been homeschooled, and maybe the only church I had ever been too was in the barn. True, I wouldn't get to meet my husband the same way as most women. But I had a lot. I had a Daddy who lit up the sky with rainbows on my birthday, and a Mama who could tell you what the bluebirds were singing about. My Grandma radiated life itself, keeping us from getting sick, and my Pawpaw could tell you anything from the history of his lifetime because he remembered every detail. I had aunts and uncles who could do things most of the world thought was impossible. I had a family that loved me. Wasn't that enough?

Then why doesn't it feel like it?

The feeling of butterflies, dark hair, and a perfect smile flashed through my memory.

Because a life is made of choices, and my choices are made for me. The thought popped into my mind fully formed and with such intensity I almost had to sit down in the grass and catch my breath. Was it true? If I didn't make these decisions on my own was my life really mine?

After a while I rose and continued down the path, the happiness from the childhood memories all but gone, replaced by a feeling of despair. *Stop being so dramatic, Tallulah! You know why it has to be that way!*

The trees, like everything else alive, thrived in Grandma's presence, and crowded closer together in gnarly twists near the edge of the woods. They leaned toward Grandma's home, like a sunflower leans toward the sun. I squeezed through the opening Daddy had cut and re-cut for Delia and me. The underbrush was already starting to grow dense again, scratching my legs as I stomped through.

Grandma was on her back porch, sitting across from a couple who looked as if they'd rather have been anywhere else. The porch was where she saw her clients who insisted on coming after dark, which happened to be most people.

"If they are too good to come in the light of day, they aren't good enough to set foot in my house. They want to come and see the evil old woman? Well then, let the mosquitos feast while they wait," she often said. Of course, Grandma was never bitten by mosquitos. Or maybe she was and the bites healed before they had a chance to itch.

The woman sitting across from Grandma had her legs crossed at the knee, bouncing her foot up and down in a hard, jerky motion; no doubt counting down the seconds until she could get up and leave. The man sitting next to her wiped his palms on the front of his slacks before reaching over and giving the woman's hand a squeeze, but his tightlipped smile was not up to the challenge of masking the wild fear that shone in his eyes.

Grandma made a show of laying both palms on the not yet protruding stomach of the woman's green and white checkered dress. She leaned down slowly, placed her forehead even with the woman's abdomen, and closed her eyes. Grandma stayed like this, mumbling what I knew were nonsense words—probably her grocery list or something—before springing back to her feet.

It was all for show. She had known what was developing in the woman's womb before the pregnant lady had even sat down, but people paid more for theatrics.

Smiling, the man drew the woman into a deep kiss, before remembering where he was, and pulling away mid-embrace. He stood and tugged his wife to her feet, and like that, they disappeared around the corner of the house. A second later, a car engine roared to life and the couple was gone. When people would ask them how they knew what color to paint their nursery so early on in the pregnancy, they would no doubt attribute it to a strong hunch, and their friends who already had children would shake their heads, knowingly. They would never admit to visiting Grandma. That's how it was in Brooklyn.

"Ya'll drive safe now," Grandma called after them, in her slow, southern speak. She never spoke rudely to anyone, especially if they deserved it.

I walked from my hiding spot in the trees, careful not to step on any of the toys that littered the yard, left behind by younger cousins who spent their Saturdays playing at our grandparents' house. I picked my way around the many blackberry bushes and muscadine vines that seemed to multiply every year and eventually made my way to the porch.

"Lord, I ain't ever seen such a nervous couple," she cackled.

"They were from the crazy church?" I asked.

Joshua Armstrong might condemn us all to hellfire to anyone who cared to listen, but I guess curiosity won over religion. Because when the ladies of his congregation were expecting, they came at night like everyone else, with their best smiles pasted on, and eager for Grandma to touch their bellies and satisfy the questions they couldn't stand to wait a few weeks to have answered at their doctor appointments.

"No doubt about it. Wanted my help, though. The woman was real sweet. The man kept eyeing me like he wanted to spit," she said, shaking her head. "Before I even had a chance to find out what they were having, he asked me if I could make sure it would be a boy. Can you believe that? Those people are really confused about what it is I do here." She rolled her bright green eyes and twisted her pointed finger in a circle around the side of her head.

"Too bad for the mother. If her husband hadn't been such a sourpuss, I wouldn't have had to charge them the asshole tax." Grandma laughed, and patted her pocket.

"So what are they having?" I asked, plopping myself into the porch swing.

"A boy, thank God. I wanted to tell him a girl so bad, but I thought it would be mean to put his poor wife through that. Men like that…Well, they just ain't good." She moved from her seat and joined me in the swing.

"What do you think Rev. Armstrong says to get them so riled up?" I sat back, getting comfy. "What did we ever do to make him hate us so much?"

"No telling." Grandma sighed. "And Joshua Armstrong ain't ever needed a reason to hate anybody. He's always been evil, but I reckon it got worse after his wife passed. It's been, oh, going on fifteen years. I reckon he still blames me."

"Why would he blame you?"

"Oh, men like that have to blame somebody. He ain't going to blame God. Then he'd be out of a job. And for all his hootin' and hollerin', he ain't no more than a medium sized fish in this tiny pond. There's nothing he can do to the doctors over at the Medical Center in Jackson. So, at the end of the day, that leaves me."

"No, I mean, why would he have a reason to blame you?"

"I suppose because I can't do the miracles people say I can." She shrugged. "I actually helped his wife, Helen, with two of her pregnancies, and the whole time she was scared to death her husband would find out. She sat on my couch, shaking like a leaf, as meek and kind as Joshua is horrible."

She shook her head. "Years later, when she came down with breast cancer, rumor has it that he wouldn't let her see a doctor. That he said that there was no way God would dare take his wife from him. He had everyone in his church all riled up. His congregation was a lot bigger back then, you know. Before he went completely off the deep end."

Grandma rubbed her eyes with the back of her hands, before tears had a chance to collect and fall. Happy people had a hard time hiding their grief.

I put an arm around her shoulders and gave her a squeeze.

"Well, Helen got a lot worse before he finally relented and took her to the hospital. By then, they sent her home and suggested hospice. Joshua couldn't admit he might lose his wife. He stayed locked up in the house with her for a full month. Didn't preach. Didn't leave to go to the store. Nothing. No one saw him or talked to him. We'd started to wonder if they were still alive. People talked of getting the law involved, but no one did."

"Then one night, after me and your Pawpaw had been in bed for a while, someone started beating on our door. I was shocked when I opened the latch and Joshua was standing there, doing his best to hold up his poor wife. We let them in and he laid her on the couch and demanded I fix her. He was eat up with resentment and hate, but he was desperate. It took a lot for him to come and ask for my help, so I do believe that in some demented way he loved her. But it was too late. Helen's poor breasts were twisted and hard. I could tell from touching her that the cancer had settled in and taken root in other parts of her body. Poor thing wasn't so much alive as not yet dead."

Grandma paused and drew in a deep breath. I gave her another squeeze and she finished the story. "Tully, I wanted to help her. I did. If there'd been anything I could have done, you rest assured, I would've done it. I can't watch a person suffer. But she was too gone. Joshua had been bouncing from foot to foot, like he was scared for any part of his body to be in contact with anything we owned, even our floor. When I told him there was nothing I could do, he became still. So still. It chilled me to the bone. I didn't want to kick them out for Helen's sake. She was a good person, but Joshua stood there staring at me, and your Pawpaw finally had to ask him to leave. They laid Helen to rest not even a week later."

"I'm so sorry," I whispered. "Just because he blames you, doesn't mean you should blame yourself."

"Oh, sweetie, I don't. I don't. It's only a heavy thing for another person really and truly to believe you are responsible for a death. Even if the person that believes it is as crazy as a loon."

"You said you helped with his wife's pregnancies. I didn't know Reverend Armstrong had kids?"

Grandma's eyes flashed green. "They beat a fast path out of town after their mama died. Shows you right there what kind of person Joshua must be behind closed doors. Not a single one of his four boys wanted to stick around."

We continued to rock in comfortable silence, letting the tension ease. A smile crept onto Grandma's unlined face, and she poked me in the ribs.

"What?" I asked.

We were interrupted as the screen door creaked opened and one of my younger cousins stuck her head outside.

"Hey Tully!" a gangly girl with more legs than much else said.

"Hey Dory," I answered.

"Grandma, can I watch TV in your room? I'm trying to watch Jeopardy, but Pawpaw is snoring on the couch and I can't hear the answers real good."

Grandma chuckled. "That's fine, Dory. We can have a girls' night and you can sleep in there with me if you want. We'll kick old loud Paw out. Go ahead and get comfy."

Dory beamed. "Yes ma'am!" The screen door slammed behind her as she hurried back inside.

"Now where were we?" Grandma asked.

"Oh, I have a feeling you were about to tell me a secret?"

"Oh yes. Well. Don't tell her I told you, but I know that Trudy has been working on finding you a suitor. I expect she'll be wanting to talk to you before long."

"Ugh," I said, my shoulders tensing.

"It ain't so bad as that. Look at your Mama and Daddy. They're happy and in love. My aunt matched me and your Pawpaw." She patted me on the leg. "I couldn't have found a better man myself."

Grandma was nine months older than Pawpaw, but her Gift kept her skin tight and glowing. She could easily have passed for his daughter. That didn't matter, because the way Grandma looked at him said it all. My Pawpaw, with his combed back gray hair and a paunch of a belly that rounded out his overalls, was her other half.

"I know. But it's so weird to think in a year I could be married to someone I don't even know. I try NOT to think about, if you want to know the truth."

"Tallulah, baby, that could be the case for anyone. If you were to go off to college—and it's not too late, you still can—and start dating like the majority of girls, then you still might end up married in a year."

I snorted. "Yeah. College. Like Mama and Daddy are going to go for that. They want me married off, living down the road and popping out babies." The words came out sharper than I meant.

Grandma shook her head. "You need to give your parents a little more credit. Besides, Delia told me you applied."

I turned to face Grandma. "She did? I should have known she couldn't keep her mouth shut."

"Oh, don't be mad at her. She was hoping I would talk to your Mama for you. She thinks that you will 'chicken out' if someone don't intervene."

"What did you say?"

"I said that if you wanted it bad enough, you'd do it. Really, Tallulah, I don't know what you're so upset about. Your Mama went to LSU and got a degree in education."

"Yeah, but that was a long time ago. The rules are different now. More rigid." I bit the inside of my cheek. "Fat lot of good it did her, anyway. She's never had a real job in her life. Besides, it's not that I'm scared of talking to them. It's that I know they have this plan for me. I don't want to disappoint them, I guess."

"You don't think teaching you girls, plus all of your cousins, to read and write and do math was a real job? Because I can tell you, I couldn't have done it!" It was Grandma's turn to sound sharp.

"I didn't mean that."

Grandma smiled and pulled my hand into her lap, giving it a squeeze. "I know you didn't. And believe it or not, I do understand about not wanting to upset your family." She stared into the wood line, and I knew that she was looking beyond the trees, to a memory tucked away inside her. "Tell you what," she said, finally, "I won't tell your secret for you, but when you do get ready to talk to your Mama and Daddy, I'll be there too, for support."

"Thanks Grandma." I scrunched low in the swing, so that I could lay my head on her shoulder.

"Now. Back to Trudy."

"Ugh."

Grandma ignored me. "You know better than to think anyone would make you marry someone you don't like. And if you have babies or not is your decision."

"I know. It's just that, I feel like my parents barely know me. Aunt Trudy doesn't know me. And they'll be picking my dates. Deciding my future. I can't understand it." Grandma opened her mouth to speak, but

I cut her off. "I know that's how it's done…but that doesn't mean I'm excited about it."

Grandma said nothing, only pulled me closer to her in the swing. She hugged me tight, like she had when I was little. I pressed my ear against her shoulder, and listened to the comforting, quiet, hum that came from her soul. It was the sound of prosperity coursing through her, her magic strong, capable, and wonderful. Like the scent of outside things mingled with cinnamon, for me, it meant, "Grandma."

I sat snuggled next to her, rocking gently, and listening to the constant night song of the crickets. Within minutes, she had dozed off. I pulled away, careful not to wake her, and walked back into the orchard.

Grandma's Gift, the Gift of Vigour, was the most important power someone could possess, and in Grandma, the Gift was stronger than usual. Everything alive, from trees to babies, couldn't help but respond to her, soaking in her magic and becoming the best versions of themselves. One of my favorite memories was of sitting on a picnic table with Grandma in her backyard, eating slices of watermelon and spitting the seeds as far as we could. The next morning, watermelon vines formed a tangled circle around where we had sat. A week later, fat, green and pink melons, sweeter than anything I had ever tasted, grew.

Because of her Gift, our trees and gardens never disappointed, offering crops year round, regardless of temperature or season. It allowed us to keep the produce stand open and thriving all year long. There were rumors about how our fruit could improve mood, or heal minor ailments. Customers at the produce stand often whispered about these claims in hushed tones, their eyes darting from me and then to each other as they thumped melons or checked bananas for bruises. Every once in a while, someone would find the courage to ask directly. I'd shrug and smile. The fruit was beautiful, but it was simply the product. The magic was in Grandma.

Her Vigour was also a large part of why we lived together on our property. Her Gift protected us, keeping us healthy and safe. I never had a fever. My Mama and the other mothers in my family all had their babies at home without pain or complications. The only time I remembered anyone needing the hospital was when Jack fell out of the top of an apple tree and broke his arm. I was pretty sure if given enough time, the Vigour could have healed the break, but the bone needed to be set, and Uncle Gavin wasn't willing to take the chance on his son's arm.

I picked my way back into the orchard, the nostalgia from earlier long gone, thanks to the marriage conversation.

The thought of being married off to someone I didn't know knocked the wind out of me. It was like, for my entire life, I had something to distract me. Early it was playing games with my sister, and later it was doing schoolwork and manning the fruit stand, but now the distractions were over and I was stuck in limbo, waiting on a life to start that I couldn't get excited about. I didn't especially dread my future, but there was nothing in it for me to look forward to. I moved onward, sleepwalking and letting things happen because, for me and my family, there was no choice. It was the only way to ensure our safety and to keep our secrets.

Being magic in a world that only has room for science or religion could be a dangerous thing, with neither side wanting to admit our existences. The fact that we did, despite their theories or sermons, offended them. So we had to be careful in every area.

Including marriage.

Knowing that Aunt Trudy had started the process of finding me a mate meant that sleeping was out of the question, maybe forever, but definitely for tonight. I needed to burn some energy.

Chapter Six

I cleared the orchard on my parents' side of the property. My head spinning with too many thoughts, I walked around our house to the gravel driveway. Booger-lights sitting on the tops of tall poles and spaced about six yards apart lined the drive, offering the intermittent glow of eerie yellow light. I started at full sprint down the drive, going from one circle of light, through a long stretch of shadows, and into the next circle of light, forcing myself to focus only on the sound of the rocks crunching under my feet and the air I could not inhale fast enough.

I am not a runner. Not really. I don't know any tricks or techniques. I put one foot in front of the other, and don't stop until my lungs are on fire and my knees work about as well as Jell-O. I'd started running when I was thirteen, when going on drives to "escape" hadn't been a possibility. I would run and run until the only thing I could focus on was sucking in enough air to keep from passing out. It was a habit that had stuck.

Night runs had added perks. Not only could I focus on exhausting the anxiety from my body, I could even pretend I had some semblance of privacy. I had not seen another crow after the one that trailed me to Grandma's house was satisfied and left to report to Mama. And it was almost guaranteed that unless directly ordered otherwise, the black birds were gone for the night.

Not thinking, however, was hard. The very act of trying to force away a thought could bring it to the forefront. Screaming lungs and aching calves helped though, and by the time I reached the fruit stand and turned to run back to my starting point, all thoughts of Aunt Trudy, and even Logan, had been pushed aside. My mind was focused solely on the weight and movement of my legs.

On my second lap to the fruit stand, my pace slowed. I passed through the final circle of light as I neared the end of the drive close to the main road, when I heard it.

The chugging, whirring sound of a car idling.

It was late. No one except family should have been on the property this time of night. *Grandma stopped taking customers at 9:00, and besides, why would someone visiting leave their car idling on this end of the driveway?* The thoughts sat in a jumbled lump in my head, but while my mind was failing me, my gut screamed for me to hide.

I jumped into the shadows.

Crouching down, I forced my brain to cooperate. I didn't know the car. No one in my family drove a hatchback. I didn't recognize the model or year, only that with its round back and faded red paint it made me think of an Easter egg. It was the type of car that if seen at a red light, would make you think of children and family, but stalled on the side of the road, in the middle of the night, gave me the creeps.

The driver's side door opened, and it took every ounce of will I possessed to fight the urge to run. A man stepped out. I dug the toes of my shoes into the dirt, forcing my feet still, and held my breath as he walked to the back of the car and popped open the trunk. A red bandana was tied bandit style over his nose and mouth, and a dark baseball cap was pulled low on his forehead. Chills worked their way across my skin, despite the muggy night air. The light from the trunk sliced through the dark night, giving me a better look.

I couldn't pull in another breath.

Deep red stains splattered across his white t-shirt.

Blood stains.

My legs trembled, and I slapped a hand over my mouth, hoping to hold in the scream on the other side of my lips. It wasn't hunting season. Even if it were, it didn't make sense to go hunting in a hatchback.

In a white shirt.

At night.

On our property.

There was nothing good that could explain away what was happening right in front of me. My heart pounded far harder than it had during my run. Moving was impossible. I was too close. If he didn't see me, he would definitely hear me. I was stuck until he drove away.

I prayed silently and hard. *Please let him leave. Just let him leave.*

I looked around the treetops, up at the dark sky, desperate and wishing for a crow. I squinted into the darkness, hoping to see the faint outline of one of the birds perching on a fencepost, or circling around overhead, lazily following me like a good winged jailer. But there was nothing.

I was alone.

The man reached into the hatchback and hoisted something over his shoulder. Something with thick, dark hair. Something naked, with arms tied behind its back and blood running down long legs.

I started shaking and reached out to steady myself. The bushes I knelt behind rustled as my arm brushed against them.

The man paused and stared into the shadows. Towards me. I braced my hands on my knees, unable to move, knowing at any moment my limbs might give out.

Something fluttered from underneath the fruit stand a few yards in front of me.

Thank you, God, I thought. *I'm saved.* I gave in to my fatigued legs and sank to my knees. Tears poured from my eyes. *A crow. A crow could get help. Family would come.*

The man stilled at the sound of the wings, looking as I was, to the fruit stand. A bat flew from the overhang and into the night.

No!

I froze.

Every fiber of my body wanted this person to go away. Needed him to leave. *There was so much blood.*

The sourness of bile was heavy in the back of my mouth. I swallowed the pungent taste as dots blinked before my eyes. Anxiety made me lightheaded, and I stumbled to the ground, falling against the bush with a grunt.

The man jerked his gaze toward the noise. He took three steps in my direction, stopping at the edge of the shallow ditch that snaked along next to the main road. He tossed the girl from his shoulder and into the ditch, his eyes never leaving my direction.

A chill laced its way around my spine, and in that moment, I knew I was going to die. This man was going to find me, sitting and helpless, and do to me what he had done to the girl he had tossed away like roadside litter. He stared, and I knew he could see me. I trembled as the tears continued down my cheeks. *I should run.* But I couldn't make my legs work. My arms were rubber.

Somewhere down the driveway, a door slammed. The man looked away from me and walked to his car.

I couldn't breathe. Fear wrapped its decaying arms around my waist and squeezed the air from my lungs.

The man got into the hatchback, but instead of speeding away, he rolled forward a few feet, bringing the car directly in line with where I sat, crying. He stuck his arm out the open car window and pointed at me. He didn't move, but kept his arm raised, trigger finger pointing directly at me.

I peered hard, trying to see his features, but he was covered as much by the shadows as his disguise.

Finally, the car eased away.

Remembering the girl in the ditch, I tried to push myself up, but my arms and legs still would not cooperate. I closed my eyes, and breathed, forcing air deep into my lungs. Slowly, much more slowly than I wanted, I was able to get on my knees, and from there, onto my feet. I took a step toward the ditch, again wishing I could run. The man might return. I needed to get help, but I couldn't leave the girl lying, exposed on the side of the road.

Dried, crusted blood covered her from the waist down. Ugly purple and green bruises already had started forming up and down her thighs. She lay face down, and her hair fell matted across her back, caked with more blood and dirt. I could see now her hands were bound with grey duct tape, and her left foot was twisted and swelling. She was still. So still. Her naked back didn't rise and fall with the steady motion of a person sleeping.

Even beneath all the blood and bruises, I recognized the body.

"Oh God no! Please no," I whispered.

I stumbled into the ditch and sank to my knees next to her. With every ounce of strength left in me, I managed to roll my sister onto her back.

Delia's eyes were black, and new, slick blood leaked from her nose. I laced my arms under her armpits and pulled hard, hoisting her into my lap as best I could.

"Come on Delia. Come on," I breathed into her ear, hugging her close, covering her nakedness as much as possible.

"Help! Someone help me!" The words tore from my throat, primal, raw, and cutting.

Pain bit me from behind my eyes, and a dull ache started at the base of my head.

Still I screamed and screamed. "Help us! Someone help us!"

The coppery taste of pennies filled my mouth as blood poured from my nose, dripping down my chin and onto my lips. Pressure grew in my temples and I thought my head might burst. But my only thoughts were for my sister. The need to help Delia overwhelmed me. Consumed me. My little sister, my best friend on this Earth, could not die in my arms.

Help! Please! Somebody. EVERYBODY! Help us!

Breathing became a laboring chore as my lungs grew tighter and tighter with the agony of worry, and blaring white dots again danced around the edges of my vision.

I held Delia tight, wrapping my arms around her, and pulling her up. My screaming had become an unconscious act, the sound exploding from inside me with the power of my fear and rage.

The rustle of a thousand tree limbs shook in the wind.

But there was no wind. The night was sticky and humid. There had not been a breeze all day.

I looked up to see a sky filled with hundreds of little black feathered bodies, working as hard as they could, pumping their wings to get to where I lay.

I stopped screaming. The ink colored creatures spread above me, blocking out the moon.

"Mama," I rasped.

Then, with a final skull cracking pulse of pressure, everything went black.

Chapter Seven

I inhaled the familiar scents of cinnamon and wild honeysuckle, and rubbed the scratchy yarn of the afghan against my cheek, keeping my eyes closed. These things, the smells and the afghan, meant love. They meant safety, and the happy place of my childhood.

They meant Grandma.

I stretched, enjoying the sweet spot of seconds between dream and reality. The place before waking. The place before remembering.

Next to me, the springs of one of the vinyl chairs that made up my Grandma's furniture groaned in release as someone stood.

I opened my eyes and the night crashed into me.

"Delia!" I said, sitting up. The afghan fell to the floor.

"Shhh. Tallulah. It's okay, now."

Daddy stood next to the couch. The avocado colored chair across from me was still dented from where he'd been sitting, waiting for me to wake. I rubbed my eyes and looked around. Old cups of coffee sat cold and abandoned by their owners on end tables and windowsills, and my ancient Uncle Louis lay dozing in Pawpaw's brown recliner in the corner. Some kind of commotion sounded from the large wrap-around porch outside, where I heard the muffled swears of one of my uncles or cousins. I couldn't tell which.

I shivered through the thin material of the undershirt someone had dressed me in while I was unconscious. It was a white V-neck and hung to the tops of my thighs. I had also been changed into a pair of boys jogging shorts, probably a pair left at my Grandparent's house by Jack. My hair was pulled back and my face cleaned. A look down showed my arms were scrubbed free of any trace of the blood that had been pouring out of my nose in fat drops, dotting my arms, chest, and chin.

"Where's Del?" I asked Daddy, tears already beginning to sting my eyes. "Is she…" I couldn't say the word. It wasn't possible. My sister, who was always so full of life that it congregated around her in a hazy cloud, could not be dead.

"Is she…okay?"

Daddy's eyes were heavy, and his jaw was held tight in an unnatural way, like he was trying hard to look fine, but wasn't. At all. I had never seen such a look on him. My rock and safety net, bigger-than-anything Daddy.

It was the look of a deep-seeded pain. One that reminded me of the blood and bruises that had covered my baby sister's thighs and legs. My stomach lurched. I closed my eyes, swallowing hard to resist the urge to vomit.

"Daddy, is she okay?" I repeated, the words coming out as cracked and broken as I felt.

"She's alive," he said. "She's in the other room with your Mama and Grandma. Your Grandma is helping her."

"Oh thank God!" I sobbed. Hot tears blurred my vision. Something deep inside me twisted apart. I knew that once the tears began, they would have to continue until they ran dry. I wouldn't be able to stop them.

Daddy sat beside me on the sofa and wrapped me in his big, working man arms. This was the place that all of my childhood problems had been solved. But this wasn't a childhood problem, and it wasn't something a hug could fix.

Tears continued down my cheeks, making wet circles where they landed on my borrowed t-shirt. Gut wrenching tears, the kind that contorted the face, and made snot pour out of your nose. The kind that purged the soul with their heat.

"Tallulah, what happened?" he asked.

I opened my mouth, but instead of words, a groan escaped, and again, tears trailed down my face.

"It's fine. Take your time."

I scooted over, putting some space between us, and tried again, starting with my run, and how I saw the parked car. Ending with passing out in the ditch. The story was peppered with sobs, and when I finished, Daddy's eyes flashed green with angry magic. Outside, a deep thunder rolled across the sky that had nothing to do with the weather.

"We all felt you, Tallulah. We all knew you needed us to come to you," he gave me a meaningful look, "All of us."

"What do you mean?" There was no way I screamed loud enough for everyone to hear me.

"We felt it. We felt your fear and panic. We could feel you calling us to you. Everybody. Your aunts, grandparents, cousins. Everyone, Tallulah." He looked down at his hands. He was trying very hard to hold it together. I had never seen my Daddy cry. Ever. "But we didn't know where you were."

"You heard me?" I asked. "You mean, in your head?"

He nodded.

"That's impossible." I blinked in disbelief. "That's not my Gift." My forehead scrunched toward my nose. I was no telepath. As far as I knew, our family had never even had a telepath. My Gift, my tiny Gift, was Suggestion.

The corners of Daddy's mouth raised in a sort of sad smile. "Have you ever heard of Reflection?"

I shook my head.

"It's not a Gift, exactly. It never shows up on its own. It's more like an add-on that breaks free in people with certain abilities. And it's a rare one. In fact, I've never known anyone that's had it. That's what me and Uncle Louis were talking about." He nodded toward the snoring man in the corner.

A lump of chewing tobacco created a bump in old Uncle Louis's cheek and black spit bubbled out the corner of his mouth with each loud exhale. A red solo spit-cup sat on the floor next to the recliner. The flannelled old redneck looked like anyone's uncle. But as our Familiar, he knew more about Gifts than anyone. If Uncle Louis said it existed, no one, not even Daddy, could argue.

As infants, Uncle Louis coaxed our Gift to the surface, reading us and making it known. He named me Suggestion, and no one had ever doubted it. Now, if he said I had an add-on, it must be true. Still...

"I don't understand," I said.

"Reflection lets you take an aura, either yours or someone else's, and reflect it onto another person. It's similar to Suggestion in a way. With Suggestion, you can plant an idea. With Reflection, it's a feeling."

"Well why do you think that I have it?" I asked. "There wasn't even any eye contact involved. And why now? I wasn't trying to use my Gift, much less one that I didn't even know I had!" I didn't understand why we were even talking about this. My sister was lying broken in the other room. That was what was important. Not Gifts, mine or anyone else's.

Daddy shrugged. "The big difference, and the reason that Reflection isn't a true Gift, is that while Suggestion is named from birth, Reflection shows up much later. Usually there's some sort of trauma involved that brings it out in those who possess it."

He ran a hand over his stubble. "Honestly, though, there are a lot of unknowns about it. Maybe you don't need eye contact with family? Or maybe not with others who are Gifted? All I know is we felt your need for us so strongly. We felt your pain and panic. Your terror. I knew we had to get to where you were. I didn't know why, only that you needed me." Daddy took a deep breath. "We looked upstairs and realized that Delia was gone too. We panicked. We called your Grandma, and she said that she and your Pawpaw were about to get on the four-wheeler and ride to look for you. That's when I felt you really reaching out to us. Your poor Mama lost it."

My eyes widened. "The crows."

Daddy rubbed his lids, taking another deep breath. Even as an adult, I still very much thought of him as bigger and grander than me. Wiser. It was unsettling to see him this way, unguarded, and raw.

"I have known and loved your Mama for twenty-five years, and not once have I ever seen her like that. She feels responsible. When I was on the phone with your Pawpaw, your Mama went into the yard, and by the time I came outside, there were so many crows the ground looked like a black pool, rippling and moving."

He stared toward the window, his voice distant, like he was talking to himself. "It was unlike anything I've ever witnessed. All these birds, sitting there, silent and watching your Mama. Waiting on her. When she sent them out, they all took off in one fluid movement, and we followed them."

He looked at me, his face ashen, and his voice tight. "When we found you and Delia in the ditch, laying there, bloody and not moving..." His voice cracked. "We thought we had lost our girls."

Outside, the thunder stopped, at the same moment Daddy let out a shuddering breath. Sharp raindrops began to beat against the windows, sounding like a snare drum as they pounded the single paned glass. As much as it rained here, these weren't in the forecast. They were something else entirely. Daddy hugged me close so I wouldn't see the actual tears that fell from his eyes. But I felt them echoed in my heart.

Daddy never cried. He had always been even tempered and quick to smile. Delia could get him worked up, but it was always the same. They fought, she stomped off, and then in a huff, Daddy read or watched television, grumbling to Mama. The next morning everyone was always fine. He never held a grudge. He prospered in a town that didn't like us; he could call the weather down and command tornadoes.

He just didn't cry.

I sat still for a few seconds, before Daddy awkwardly turned me loose, and again fixed his face into that wrong, frozen expression. "When we saw that you and Delia were alive, me and Gavin tried to pick ya'll up, but as soon as he touched you, you started screaming. You wouldn't stop. It was like you couldn't see us. Rebecca met us here, and she was able to calm you and give you sleep. Do you remember any of that?"

"No," I said.

I thought back to my dreamless night, and waking up to thoughts of Grandma's house.

"No," I said again. "I don't remember, but I'm glad you called Rebecca. I don't think I could have calmed down otherwise. Much less slept. I don't think I'll ever be able to sleep on my own again." I shuddered, recalling the man pointing at me, slowly, like a hunter lining up prey between the crosshairs of his weapon. Without thinking, I scooted closer to my father.

His eyes flashed and again thunder cracked outside. He glanced at the window, surprised. Inhaling deeply, he closed his eyes, and within seconds, the rain and thunder stopped.

"Your Mama was torn. She hated leaving you out here, but your Grandma checked you over and said you were strong, so she and your aunts changed your clothes, and cleaned you up. Once she knew you were going to be fine, she went into the room with your Grandma and sister. I sent everyone else home to get some sleep."

Another round of muffled swearing came from the porch.

"I sent *almost* everyone home, I should say." He glanced at the door. "Your cousins Darren and Baron, and Baron's wife Tina insisted on 'standing watch'. They're posted at the door like those queen's guards, the ones on television that wear those funny hats." Daddy rolled his eyes. "They even got their shotguns. No doubt loaded, too."

"Lord," I mumbled. Two men that could shoot ice from their fingers like daggers, and a woman who could wipe your short-term memory as easy as buttering bread, were more dangerous than the metal and powder from a round of buckshot could ever hope to be. They didn't need those shotguns. And with Daddy inside watching over his girls, we didn't need a guard posted either. But that was Darren and Baron, high strung but with good intentions.

"You'll want to give everyone a call tomorrow to let them know that you and Delia are okay. I know they'll want to hear your voice."

I flashed back to my sister, naked and bloody in the ditch. She wasn't okay. She might never be. Hell, I wasn't okay and I had only seen the aftermath of what happened to her.

"I need to see Delia."

"Sure, baby," Daddy said, rubbing a hand over his graying hair. "But first I need to tell you something. Your sister..." His jaw tightened impossibly more as he said through gritted teeth, "She was raped."

Another crack of lightening lit the yard, and the thunder that followed shook the old house right to its cinderblock foundation. I understood his need to say it so directly. Daddy was not the kind of parent that talked to his girls about things such as sex. Much less something as horrible as rape.

I couldn't respond. Some part of me had known when I saw the blood trailing down Delia's naked thighs.

"Your Grandma is in there with her now, so she'll heal, but it's still important she go to the emergency room. Delia didn't like the idea when your Mama brought it up earlier. She's been through so much, and we don't want to force her. But she really needs to go, Tallulah. There could still be evidence, and..." he trailed off.

I knew what he meant. I had watched enough Law and Order to know there needed to be a rape kit. "I'll talk to her."

"I hate to ask you to, honey, but she'll listen to you. I hate that it has to be done. I hate it. And if I ever catch the sonofabitch who did this," more thunder crackled, "he'll pay for it."

I didn't have to see the lightning storm outside to know he meant it.

***

I walked down the short hallway to the bedroom that Delia, my Mama, and Grandma were in. Mama dozed in the rocking chair in the corner of the room, while Delia was propped up against the cherry headboard, looking tiny under a mountain of quilts. Grandma was next to her, lying on top of the covers and clasping her hand.

"Hey you," I said, because what else was there to say? What could be said to my little sister after something so horrible?

"Hey yourself," she replied. I walked to the side of the bed and crawled in next to her.

Grandma smiled, showing the two rows of perfectly straight teeth that, unlike most women her age, were all hers.

"I'm glad you're up, Tully. I'm going to fix you girls some hot tea." Grandma leaned over and kissed first Delia, and then me, on the cheek. She climbed out of the bed and shook Mama awake. The two left together, shutting the door behind them.

"Well," Delia fixed her gaze on me, "that was obvious. They want you to tell me I need to go to the E.R.?"

I nodded. It *was* obvious. I leaned over and wrapped my arms around her. Relief seized me. My sister was alive.

She sat for half a moment, awkward in my hug, before putting her arms around me and hugging me back. Something felt different. There was no Christmas in this embrace. None of the "Charm" that usually rolled off her, as natural to Delia as her dark hair or creamy skin. The trauma had stripped away a part of her. The part that made her upbeat.

The happy part.

Inside, I burned with anger. This was my little sister and someone hurt her, and I could do nothing to reverse it. I swore to myself that I would never argue with her again. I would work all of her Saturdays if she wanted. I would stop dreaming of a life beyond Brooklyn, of going to college, of everything forbidden. None of that mattered without her. I squeezed her tighter, praying for her sake for her Charm, and the happy feeling that came with it, to return.

"Oh, Tully. I know. You don't even have to tell me. I know that I have to go. I just…I can't imagine. I feel so dirty. And I hurt. I hurt Tully, even after Grandma has been sitting with me. The thought of someone else looking at me, touching me right now, it makes me sick. It makes me nauseated. The thought of…Oh god, I have never not wanted to do something more in my life." Delia paused and pulled away from me.

"And besides. It won't matter. I know what everyone will say. Everyone knows about my Gift. Even if I go to the hospital and they do a rape kit. Even if we skip the Brooklyn hospital and drive over to the bigger one in Peachton, and the nurses and doctors don't know me and they treat me nice, even if there's a match made instantly at the police headquarters or wherever they send the kit, IT WON'T MATTER." Her voice broke, before she continued, "As soon as they realize who I am, they'll say it was my fault. They'll say there's no way that it can't be my fault. God. I am so stupid."

I looked at my sister. My beautiful, younger sister. Her face was shaded with the greens and blues of healing bruises, with the in between parts splotchy and red from crying. Jagged, red lines crisscrossed through the whites of her puffy eyes. All of her tears were used up, and I knew she was right. Even though no one in the their right mind could ever believe that consensual sex could leave a person looking like that, once they knew who Delia was, that would be it.

But we still had to go. It was the only chance we had at finding the person who had hurt her so badly. Next to Delia getting better, finding the bastard who'd hurt her was the most important thing. He could not get away with this. *He won't.*

"I want to shower. I want to pretend today never…" Delia

stopped. She forced her swollen eyes open big. "Oh God. Everyone knows. How can I look at Pawpaw again? Or Daddy? Oh Tully! What did I do?"

I was pissed that this had happened to my sister. I was pissed at Delia for sneaking out. I was pissed at myself for being mad at Delia, because no one deserved this, and it was not her fault.

The monster who hurt her will pay.

"Delia, look at me!" I grabbed her arm, making her face me. It took everything I had to hang onto my anger when she flinched. But I refused to back down. "Look at me and listen. You can blame a lot of people, but don't you dare blame yourself. You did NOT deserve this!" I did my best to sound like the strong, older sister. I believed the words I was saying, but the shock of the night still clung to me, and my head still ached.

Delia looked down. "But Tully, if I would have stayed at home like you...If I would have listened to Daddy, this wouldn't have happened."

"Shhh. Yeah. You could have stayed home. But that doesn't matter. All you wanted was to dress up and go to a stupid fair. What happened...that isn't because of anything you did." I felt my resolve harden inside me. "It doesn't matter what anyone thinks, but we aren't going to worry about that right now. Right now, we're going to focus on one thing at a time. We can go to the hospital, the one over in Peachton, like you said, and get the kit done. You can do it. And after that, you'll take a shower, and try to rest. We'll worry about everything else later."

Delia bit her bottom lip. "Okay," she whispered.

We sat silent, huddled in the bed. The seconds ticked by, taking their sweet time, before I could bring myself to ask Delia the question that had been gnawing on the back of my mind.

I took her hand gently in mine. "Del?" I whispered, "Can you tell me what happened?"

"Isn't what you saw bad enough? You really going to make me tell you?" she asked, defeated. "Mama and Daddy keep trying to get me to talk. They're being gentle, but I can tell they're waiting, and honestly, I don't know if I'll ever be able to tell them."

"So let me. Tell me and I'll handle them for you."

Delia hesitated.

I didn't want to put her through reliving it, I really didn't. But I'd never feel as if she was safe until we'd caught the bastard who hurt her, and she might remember something, some tiny detail, that could be useful.

"Fine. But you have to promise me something first," she said. "I will not get Jack into trouble. Promise me, right now, that you won't say anything about him."

"Sure, Delia, but what does he have to do with anything?" I asked, more than a little confused.

"I was supposed to meet him. Uncle Gavin was going to let him go to town, and he was going to park a bit down the road. I was going to ride my bike to meet him as soon as I got the chance. We thought it would be easier to avoid getting caught," Delia said, staring at the empty spot of bedspread between us.

I didn't understand how sneaking on foot would be easier than ducking down in Jack's truck, but I kept my lips pressed together, dutifully quiet so she would continue.

"Daddy sent me to my room, and I waited a good hour before sneaking out. I didn't even really have to sneak. Mama was working on some craft and Daddy was zonked in front of the TV. Your door was shut, so I tiptoed through the back door. I had parked the bicycle behind the fruit stand. I only had to run down the drive without getting caught, and then peddle toward Brooklyn. Jack was supposed to be waiting on the side of the road no more than half a mile away. I pedaled and pedaled. I remember thinking how sweaty I was getting and that I should go home because I was going to be too gross to meet anyone, anyway. But I really wanted to go, you know? To do something normal. I should have known better." Her voice started to crack again, but she closed her eyes and breathed deep. She pulled herself up, straightening her spine, readying herself for the story she was about to tell.

"So I kept going. After what seemed like forever, I passed Blackbird Road. I thought 'I know that's more than a mile!' And I never saw Jack's truck. At this point, I was getting pissed off. But what was I supposed to do? By now, it was a long way back, and besides, I kept thinking that he would be parked a little further ahead, so I kept on. No one passed me on the road, until," she paused. "Until all of a sudden there were headlights right behind me. I slowed down, and got off the road, thinking they would pass me, but then they slowed down too. I was so scared, I couldn't have charmed him if I'd thought about it. Right when I was really starting to panic, they sped up and went around me. I should have turned back then. I should have hid in the woods. I should have turned around and went down Blackbird Road. I should have done something, anything, to get off that main road. But I convinced myself that I was overreacting." She wrung out her hands like you would squeeze the water from a washcloth.

I grabbed them and held them tight. "You don't have to tell me anymore if you don't want to."

She shook her head. "No. You're right. It's easier to tell you all of this than Mama and Daddy." After another deep breath, she continued, "So I told myself to shut up, and I kept on pedaling. By then I thought maybe Jack wasn't waiting for me, that he had got tired and left. I was thinking once I got into town, I would figure out how to get to the fair, find him, and give him a piece of my mind. My legs were burning, but I reasoned with myself that it would take longer to get back home than to go ahead into town. That I was almost there. Almost safe."

"I pedaled a little further and I thought I could make out a vehicle on the side of the road. I was so happy and angry at the same time, thinking that it was about damned time, but also glad to have a ride finally. I know it sounds so stupid, but I was tired, and it was pitch black."

Delia paused, and wiped her eyes with her palms. "I got off my bike, and left it sitting on the roadside, thinking I would make Jack go get it and throw it in the back of his truck, since he had made me pedal so far. All the riding had left my legs working about as well as gummy worms. I had to focus on walking, and I was almost all the way to the vehicle before it dawned on me that the outline was kind of short to be Jack's truck."

Her face scrunched into such a look of guilt that I almost asked her to stop, but she went on as I opened my mouth. "God, Tully, I was so stupid! When I realized it couldn't be Jack, I turned around and started back toward the bicycle, hoping that whoever was in that car hadn't noticed me. I made it no more than a few steps when I heard the door open. A man said, 'Oh no you don't, you stupid bitch!'" Her face contorted in that way that meant she was doing everything in her power not to cry.

"Tully, he said it just like that. Calling me a stupid bitch. Then he put a bag over my head and tied it around my throat until it was choking me. I couldn't breathe, or see anything but bright spots." Delia rubbed her neck where the bruises were already fading thanks to Grandma's magic.

"Then he kicked me hard in the back of the legs, knocking me down, and he kept kicking me over and over. It hurt so bad, and I…I laid there, trying to curl up, but he kept kicking me. Nothing happened for a few minutes. I thought he had left, so I tried to pull the bag off. That's when he jerked me up, twisting my arm behind my back until it popped." Delia burst into tears, her sobs guttural and deep. "I remember thinking, 'He's going to kill me!' He pulled me close to him and he told me, 'You can't magic your way out of this, devil bitch!' Then he put one arm around my throat, and he slid his other hand up my dress, and he. And he…"

My sister's face paled. Her breathing quickened and I squeezed her hand. "I started screaming and hitting and kicking. I remember thinking that this could not happen to me. He got my panties off before I caught him with my elbow. He cursed at me and started punching me. I must have passed out because I don't know what happened next. I woke up with the bag still on my head, and I could feel him on top of me, inside of me. I started to cry, and the bastard…he started laughing. He laughed. I tried so hard not to, but I vomited. I still had the bag on my head, Tully. He laughed even harder. I must have passed out again, because the next thing I remember is hearing you inside of my head, and then waking up here."

Delia's bruises and cuts were already fading. She was worse for the wear emotionally, but even in the time we had spent talking, Grandma's magic had been lingering and mending.

I understood why she was hesitant to go to the hospital. With the way Grandma's magic was healing her, no one would ever believe that she had been through the attack…unless they knew about our Gifts.

And if they knew about our Gifts, they would say it was her fault.

"God, Delia, I'm so sorry. Sister, I'm so, so sorry." There was nothing, absolutely nothing, I could have said to help her. Sorry was the only word that came close to expressing how I felt, but it seemed to belittle what she had been through.

I'm sorry I borrowed your sweater without asking and spilled Coke on it. I'm sorry you were attacked and raped.

But it wasn't important that law enforcement figured out who did it. It was important that we figured it out. We could bring our own kind of justice to the crime. I had to focus on why I'd made her relive this pain.

"Did you recognize the car?" I asked.

I hadn't, but Delia went into town whenever she could bum a ride from a family member, so there was the chance that she'd seen it around.

"No. I couldn't even see it. But there is something. This probably doesn't mean anything, but I remember thinking that the man smelled old. Like the cologne he was wearing was something men dad's or grandpa's age would wear. Probably useless, I know, but it stuck with me."

Her voice sounded so small and vulnerable that it cut right down to my heart.

"We will figure this out, Delia. He won't hurt you again," I said, vowing it was true. I would do anything to make it so.

As if on cue, a knock sounded and Grandma entered carrying hot tea. We sipped it from the tiny ecru cups, the same ones we had used to play tea party as little girls.

When we were done, Delia put on Grandma's fuzzy green robe and a pair of flip-flops that had been left by one of our cousins. I borrowed a sweatshirt from Grandma, then Mama, Daddy, Delia and me left for the hospital in Daddy's extended cab Chevy.

My stomach twisted with worry for Delia. The way her eyes darted about, catching on every shadow, made me afraid she might try to run at any moment. I had never seen that much fear in anyone, let alone my baby sister. And I was determined to do whatever it took to erase it.

Chapter Eight

The ride to the hospital felt at least twice as long as the forty-five minutes or so it actually took. Uncomfortable silence pressed heavily against us, making me squirm. Not because my head still throbbed, or because my legs ached and no matter how I sat. But because I felt like I should say *something*, but I had no idea what.

How was I to know what was okay to talk about on the way to having a rape kit done? I couldn't be happy and pretend it never happened, but I couldn't break down like I wanted to, because Delia needed me to be strong. And from their own awkward silence, I think maybe my parents needed me to be strong as well.

Daddy drove while me and Delia looked out of our windows.

The Peachton hospital was a big improvement over the small one in Brooklyn, which only had about twelve beds and an E.R. accustomed to treating snakebites and the occasional sports injury. But in its essence, Peachton Regional was still a small town hospital that didn't often have to deal with things as ugly as rape.

Mama took a deep breath. I caught her eye in the rearview mirror before turning my gaze back toward the passing landscape. "Delia, I know you said you don't want to talk about it right now, and honey that's okay, but more than likely there will be an officer that meets us at the hospital."

Delia's eyes flashed. "Why would there be an officer? I told you I can't talk to anyone right now. I can't. I-I won't."

Daddy rubbed a hand through his hair and glanced at Mama.

Mama turned back to look at Delia. "Baby, I called them from your Grandma's to let them know we were coming, and the hospital policy is to contact the Sherriff's Office whenever a rape kit is requested. They don't give them your name, and it's up to you to speak with the officer, but they arrange to have one meet you there as a way to keep you from having to drive all over the place. Honey, it's your choice. But you need to report this."

The leather seat creaked as Delia tried to sink backwards into it. "I'm eighteen years old. An adult. I may be treated like a child, but I am legal. And I told you I'm not ready to talk to anyone. I can't. Not right now. Besides, it wouldn't matter anyway. When they figure out who we are....who I am especially..." Despite her bold words, her voice sounded small and frightened. "Look. I'm going to have the kit done, but only because it will make you all feel better. Make no mistake, I don't expect it to accomplish anything. Face it, Mama. Everyone hates us and couldn't care less if I was raped. Hell, I could have been murdered and it wouldn't have mattered." The words rushed out of my sister, with none of the sadness and all of the rage from our earlier conversation.

My parents said nothing. Outside, rain fell in a solid roaring sheet, contrasting with the deafening silence inside the truck. Daddy pulled into the covered drop off area, letting Mama, me, and Delia out before going to park.

A nurse met us at the check in station of the hospital to take Delia straight back. Delia looked at Mama and told her that she wanted her to stay and for me to go with her instead. Mama's face drew together, pinched with pain, and her eyes shone.

I was growing weary of seeing those I loved hold back tears.

The nurse had a perfect helmet of hair colored a little too dark to be natural on anyone over the age of forty, and her face powder settled in the many creases and lines around her eyes and forehead.

"I'm Judy," she said, her voice affirming she had been working a long shift and did not have time for niceties, no matter why you happened to be in the ER in the middle of the night. "What we're going to do is have you change into a gown. Then we'll need to take samples from anywhere the suspect may have left a trace of D.N.A. We'll need to draw some blood and do a urinalysis, and take pictures of any physical damage such as redness or rash that was caused by the attack. I'll also need to ask you some questions and I need you to answer them honestly."

"How else would I answer them?" Delia snapped.

The nurse looked at my sister for a hard minute before shaking her head. "Please change into the gown so we can get started. Your sister can wait out here or be present for the kit. Whatever makes you the most comfortable."

With that, she turned and walked off. I followed Delia into the room where there was a green paper gown and a sheet folded onto an examining table, the kind with stirrups. A fluorescent spotlight hung directly above.

"Well, I guess Judy wants to get a good look, huh?" Delia said, grabbing the ugly gown from the table.

For all of her clinical attitude, the nurse was very gentle to my sister for the next two hours while she combed and clipped and swabbed. Delia closed her eyes and lay on the table, squeezing my hand. Judy stepped around me, working quickly and efficiently, only speaking to ask questions or to explain to Delia what she was doing.

"We're all done with this part of the exam. I'm going to leave and let you get dressed, and then we'll need to do some blood work as well as a urine test." Judy turned and handed me a white paper bag. "Have your sister put the clothes she was wearing in here to be preserved for evidence."

"She doesn't have them," I said.

"That's fine. When you get home, if they haven't been washed, put them in here and bring them back tomorrow."

"No. You don't understand. I was thrown into a ditch naked," Delia said, sitting up and looking Judy hard in the eye. "So you can see why it would be hard for me to find what I was wearing."

At the eye contact with Delia, Judy visibly softened. The tight line of her mouth drew into an expression of concern. "You poor girl," she muttered before hurrying out the door.

I raised an eyebrow at my sister.

"She totally deserved it," Delia snapped. She tied Grandma's green robe tightly over the paper gown, not bothering with the shirt and panties she had worn underneath. "That woman really has no business being a nurse. She seems like she would rather be anywhere else. I mean, does she think that this is where *I* want to be right now?"

Judy came back in, and after drawing some blood and handing Delia a cup to take to the bathroom, she pulled some papers from her lab coat pocket, as well as a plastic brown bottle. "You have some bruising and swelling, and will probably have a good rash. Using a cold pack should give you a little relief. I am giving you a prescription for some ointment, and one for some painkillers to be taken as needed. This is enough for a month, but when you feel like it, you can switch to ibuprofen. These two are for antibiotics. It's very important you finish all of these; they'll protect you from possibly developing a nasty sexually transmitted infection," Judy said with a newfound concern for my sister's wellbeing.

I couldn't blame Delia for charming Judy. The last thing any rape victim should have to deal with is a cold nurse. I wondered if she would have treated Delia differently if she had seen her right after the rape, before Delia spent time healing in my Grandma's presence.

"We did an H.I.V. test and will call you with those results, but you will need to come and be retested in three months, and then at six months. Try not to stress about it."

Delia was biting on her bottom lip hard, the way she always did when she didn't want to cry. I wanted to slap the nurse. What a stupid thing to tell someone! *Try not to worry about it?* Like that was possible.

"Now these," she shook the brown bottle of pills, "you want to start these right away. You take one now, and in twelve hours, take the next one. We give these to you and bill your insurance instead of having an assault victim being required to go and purchase them. Especially with so many pharmacies in this area not even carrying them," she said, shaking her head.

"What are they?" I asked.

"Emergency contraceptives. We strongly advise them for anyone who has the possibility of pregnancy from rape."

"But I, uh, I...was a virgin," Delia said. "I couldn't get pregnant from this!"

"Listen, hun. It only takes once. That is why these pills are so important. You probably aren't, but it will be better for you to take the pills and not worry about it. Put this behind you and move forward," Judy said, as nice and caring as anyone's mother, entirely different from the earlier version of herself.

"Wait. So these are the abortion pills that they talk about on the news? The ones that kill your baby?" Delia asked, horror written on her face.

"Oh, honey, no! It's not like that at all. That is a completely different pill. This keeps you from ever getting pregnant. It keeps your ovaries from releasing an egg. No egg, no pregnancy," Judy answered.

"Delia, you should take them," I added, thinking that the last thing Delia needed to worry about was pregnancy.

Delia looked at me, her eyebrows drawn together. "How can you tell me what I need to do?" she asked. "I'm sorry, but I don't believe that. There's no way I got pregnant from being raped, so there's no reason I would need those pills anyway. I'm done here." And with that, she pushed past Judy and left the room.

I left to follow her, when the nurse grabbed my elbow to stop me. She didn't say anything, only looked me in the eye, and pressed the small bottle of pills into my palm. I nodded, dropped them into the pocket of my borrowed athletic shorts and walked out.

I caught up with Delia in the hallway, and walked beside her to the waiting room to find our parents. They were sitting in the corner, talking with a redheaded man in light blue and navy uniform. His sleeve held the insignia for the Iberdene County Sheriff's Department.

"I cannot believe this," Delia whispered. She caught my Dad's eye, and hurried across the lobby, through the automatic doors to the parking lot. My parents stood up, said a few words to the policeman, and followed her into the rain.

The police officer came over to where I was left standing.

"I don't think she's ready to talk about it," I said in the officer's general direction. I got the feeling he expected me to say something, but I had no idea what.

"It's all right. From what I got from your Mama and Dad, your sister has been through a lot," he responded. "Besides, since the, err, incident technically happened in Brooklyn limits, we would likely send the report to them. She would have to retell it to someone on that police force anyway." His ruddy pink cheeks betrayed his discomfort. His smooth complexion and rounded face made it hard to guess his age, but I would have been surprised if he was even four years older than me.

The fact that he would not say what Delia had been through, no matter how uncomfortable it made him, angered me. How uncomfortable did he think it made Delia, after all?

"Incidents like what exactly? My sister was raped. That's not exactly what I would call an incident. More like a catastrophe. More like pure evil enacted toward a woman." I croaked out the words, surprised, but proud even as they passed through my lips. I stood to my full height, which was about even with the policeman, and made myself look straight into his eyes.

I wasn't going to use my Gift on him, I wouldn't dare. It was just that my anger had to go somewhere, and into words was my only option at that moment.

"Gee, um. I'm sorry. It's…I'm new and I've never handled a rape case before. Hell, I haven't handled too much of anything, except paperwork."

"Well, why would they send you?" I asked, appalled. My sister was traumatized and they wanted her to relive the moment aloud to this rookie? "No offense, but why wouldn't they send someone with more experience? Why didn't they at least send a woman?"

"Our only female officer is on maternity leave. And only two of us were able to answer the call, and quite honestly ma'am, you would much rather me than Coop. He…Uh, well, let's say he isn't the most sensitive guy on the planet." He looked down and rubbed the back of his pale, freckled neck.

"Well, why bother? Why send anyone at all? Why not tell us to wait and report it in Brooklyn?"

"It's hospital policy to contact us. The honest truth is though, in the past five years, there's only been one other time where we have been called about a rape, and that was a whole different situation. A man and his wife."

We stood silent for a minute. "I'm officer Dirk, by the way." He smiled, almost shyly. "This is my card. If you think of anything, or need to talk to somebody…You know, to talk, call me." He handed me the crisp white rectangle. I didn't know that police officers had business cards.

"Thanks," I said.

The card said Peter Dirkus in bold black letters with a phone number in slightly smaller script underneath. There was nothing to give away that the card belonged to a policeman, making me wonder if he'd ordered them online himself. I folded the card and shoved it in my pocket with Delia's pills.

"I gotta go," I mumbled. I turned and jogged through the lobby, toward the automatic doors, but paused before leaving. "There was one thing," I said, turning to face the officer. "A red hatchback. That's all I got."

Before the man could ask me any questions, I made it through the exit. Daddy had the truck waiting for me under the patient drop-off section. Beyond the glow of the hospital, the rainy night loomed like a net filled with hidden horrors, trying to swallow me up. The night had never looked threatening before, but now, I wasn't sure it would ever look safe again.

Chapter Nine

The next morning I awoke to a spot on my upper thigh prickling with the numbness of a limb fallen asleep. I rolled over onto my back and rubbed my leg, realizing what had caused the weird sensation. I had fallen asleep in my clothes, and the pill bottle had spent the night sandwiched between my leg and the mattress.

I pulled it from my pocket and stared at the plain brown container. It didn't say what the pills did, only listed a generic name and the directions for use. I twisted off the childproof cap and shook the two pills into my palm.

The tiny white disc could have been aspirin or any number of remedies. Instead, their creation caused a hotbed of political and social unrest in our state. There had even been a picket line at one of the chain drugstores in Peachton when they started carrying them. The congregation of the Holiness church had stood outside the business for days, rain or shine, holding signs and passing out leaflets. It'd made the Jackson newspaper. The headline read, "Peachton Conservatives Say No to Plan B."

"Babies should be a blessing," Grandma had remarked when the article came out, but that was the extent anyone in my family had acknowledged it, at least around me. We didn't talk about things like birth control.

I guess I understood how Delia felt about the pills. Truthfully, if someone were to ask me, I would have said the same thing. That I would never, ever take something like that. But that was before last night. I put the pills back in their bottle and pressed the lid closed. If these would help her move on and get better, then she needed to take them, I decided, forcing myself to be okay with that decision. I wouldn't think on what the pills did or didn't do. I would focus on helping Delia get healthy and happy again.

I swung my feet out of bed and walked over to my dresser. With only a moment's hesitation, I tossed the pill bottle inside of the small top drawer where I kept things like pictures and hairbands.

I shucked off my dirty clothes and kicked them under my bed before pulling on a clean t-shirt and sweat pants.

Voices from the dining room downstairs drifted up to me. *It must be close to lunchtime.* My stomach growled in response. Halfway down the stairs it dawned on me that I didn't recognize one of the voices. I turned around to go back to my room and put on a bra, when I heard a shout.

"Damn it, Chief!" Daddy's voice boomed. I could tell by the tone he was working hard to control his temper. I turned and sat on the middle step, forgetting about lunch and the bra. "Don't give me that shit! You will do something! You have to. This family has been a part of this town since before there was even a town here! We have never asked for anything. We have never caused trouble. I demand justice!"

"Calm down, Jepson. I'm not saying we ain't going to do anything. I'm just telling you how these things work. Since you say your daughter didn't see anything or say anything, well, there ain't much we *can* do. I'm being honest with you. You do want me to be honest, right?" I could practically hear the smirk in his voice. "Hell, if Delia refuses to give any kind of statement, how do I know this even happened?"

Chief Rucker's good old boy demeanor grated on my nerves. For all of the concern in his voice, he could have been talking about finding someone's lost kitten.

"Besides," he continued. "The fair was in town. I'm guessing if it did happen, it was probably one of those traveling carnie fellas. And they done packed up and left for Mobile first thing this morning. I guess I could call down to the Mobile police and give them a heads up, if it'll make you feel better. But we both know the best thing ya'll could do is to let it go. Move on. Hell, maybe get better control over your kids, Jepson. It could have been worse, you know."

There was a long pause. I started to wonder if somehow the men had gone outside without me hearing the door open, when Daddy spoke. I could barely make out the low growl of his words.

"Leslie, you will treat this like the crime it is. I promise you whoever did this will be brought to justice, if not by you than by me."

There was another pause.

"Now don't you go doing anything stupid. You know this is a small town. And I'd be lying if I didn't say there are more than a few folks who would like to see ya'll up and leave." The exaggerated slowness that usually coated the Chief's words disappeared. "So don't threaten me, Jepson Caibre. You won't like what it gets you."

Heavy footsteps tread across the dining room floor, before I heard the whine of the screen door being pushed open.

"I'll be in touch," the Chief called to Daddy, his slow accent pulled back into place. The screen door snapped shut. A second later, it pushed open again. "And if you ever call me Leslie again, I'll find something to arrest you for, I promise. You call me Chief." This time he let the screen slam closed behind him.

I sat, too shocked to move. After a few moments, I pulled myself up and padded down the stairs.

Daddy sat at the kitchen table, staring into his coffee cup.

"Daddy?"

He lifted his gaze from the cup. Fury twisted his handsome face into something truly frightening. "Did you hear that?"

"Yes sir," I said, sliding into a chair at the table.

"I'm sorry sweetheart," he tightened his grip around the mug, "you shouldn't have."

"They're really not going to do anything?" I asked.

"Don't worry. Whoever did this will pay. It's not your problem to worry about."

Daddy took a long pull from his coffee.

"Tallulah, baby, I need you to work the fruit stand today. Delia is supposed to, but—"

"Don't worry about it. I'll do it," I interrupted.

"Thanks, sweetheart. I can always count on my sweet Tully," he said, rising out of his chair and planting a kiss on top of my head. "I got to go. I have a meeting with Larry about his girls." Daddy managed to fake a smile. "They've been causing trouble with the rain again. Larry thinks it's about time for me to work with them on their control."

"Give them a hug from me." I loved the twins. They were walking, talking, seven-year-old balls of energy that happened to be able to cause it to rain.

"Of course," Daddy replied. "You should give Larry and Wanda a call later. They were at your Grandma's last night. I sent them home before you came to. I know they'll want to hear from you or Delia today."

"Ok," I said, even though the last thing I felt like doing was giving a replay of the previous night.

I ate a bowl of cereal, and then headed upstairs to shower and get ready for the day ahead.

Delia's bedroom door was open.

Well, it's now or never. I went into my bedroom, and grabbed the little brown bottle.

"Knock knock," I said, tapping on Delia's doorframe. "You feel like talking?" I stepped into her room without waiting for an answer.

"Hey Tully. What's up?" She was still in her pajamas, lying on her bed.

"How are you feeling today?"

Delia shrugged. "Ok, I guess. I'm trying not to think about it. Mama or Grandma or Daddy keep coming in to check on me. Jack called. So did Aunt Donna. And Bertie. They're all fake smiles and upbeat attitudes. Hell, Mama even brought me these," she said, rolling her eyes and gesturing to the pile of magazines that sat next to her. Mama hated gossip magazines. "But I know they're uncomfortable. It's bizarre. I wish they would either act normal or ask me whatever it is they want to know."

I didn't know what to say.

She looked at me skeptically. "Tully, really?"

I hadn't realized I had a grin plastered on my face.

"Sorry. It's not you. Well. I mean, technically, it is you, but it's not about what happened." I stumbled over my words.

"What are you talking about?" Delia asked.

"I mean, I get like this when I'm nervous, but you aren't making me nervous. Delia, I-I just need to talk to you."

"Well, hell. Talk to me! We talk every single day and you never act like this, so can you please be normal? For me? Please? I didn't do anything and I don't like everyone acting like they're scared of me, or scared I'm going to break or something. I'm fine. I promise."

"You're right. I'm sorry. It's just, Delia, did you take the medicine that the nurse gave you?"

"Yeah. Daddy picked it up from the pharmacy this morning. I've taken a dose of the antibiotic and I've used the cream, even though the rash is all but gone. Why?"

I tried to get my bearings. "The thing is, well, the nurse gave me these after you left and I 've been really thinking about it. Del, you need to take them. To be safe."

I held out the plastic brown cylinder to my sister. Delia looked at me, and then at the container before taking the bottle from my hand.

"Good," I breathed out a sign of relief. "It really is better to be safe. You don't want to chance something like that. And it's more than the pregnancy. What about our Gifts? How would that even work, you know? I mean, how would the baby be? Gifted? Not Gifted?" I rambled, unable to shut up.

My sister stared at me for a moment before getting up and walking out of the room. Clueless, I followed her into the small bathroom she and I shared. Without saying a word, Delia popped off the childproof cap, dumped the pills into the toilet, and flushed them away. She refastened the lid and handed the empty bottle back to me.

"I love you sister, but this didn't happen to you. It's not your decision. If you love me, you won't bring it up again. You will not mention it to our parents, and you will let it be," Delia said, her voice flat.

"Delia. How could..." I started before noticing the unshed tears pooling in her eyes. I had made things worse for her. *I should have known better.*

"Delia, I am sorry," I started again.

"It's ok, Tully. I know you want to help me, but I want to be left alone about it. I want to move forward. To feel better. Daddy wants me to give a statement to the police. Mama left a pamphlet about rape crisis counseling on my nightstand. You bring me the pills. I want to stop thinking about it. That's all."

I squeezed her in a hug. We were nearly the exact same height. Delia was maybe an inch shorter. And while we had the same hair and similar features, somehow we managed to look like night and day.

"Done, then. I won't talk about it anymore."

"Good," Delia said.

I knew that she was going to need help, but right now, if she needed me to leave her alone, then that's what I'd do. There would be plenty of time for us to figure out what came next, later.

Chapter Ten

By the time I reached the fruit stand, it was humid enough to drown a fish. The heavy wetness made it hard to breathe. Nearby banana shrubs bloomed, their fragrant white flowers tinting the air with a headache inducing sweetness. Bees landed on one plant and then the next as they lazily carried out their daily chore of collecting pollen. Every so often, a car would zoom down the road, breaking the speed limit by at least fifteen miles per hour.

It was the same scene I had lived at least three times a week for the past six years, and though I knew better, part of me was amazed everything kept moving normally, even after such a tragic night. I didn't know what I expected, but the fact that everything seemed the same...*bothered* me. In hindsight, I couldn't believe Daddy asked me to work.

Jack had opened for business, but we crossed paths on the driveway, me coming and him going. I would be the only one working. Suffering the heat was bad enough, especially when I was already irritated, but now it would be coupled with the stagnant boredom that came with sitting and sweating all by myself.

I sat in the folding chair, propped my feet up on the plywood counter, and opened my paperback. Mama had gotten me an e-reader last Christmas, but it sat in my bedroom, practically unused. I preferred the feel and smell of actual books. This one was about a telepathic barmaid who felt like an outcast because of her power. Boy, could I commiserate.

Barely half a chapter later, I put down the book. The heat made it impossible to lose myself in the pages.

Three crows perched on a beam on the open side of the structure, looking as bored as me, while their peering eyes recorded my every movement. They had always annoyed me, but now I had a true dislike for the intrusive little boogers. *Where had they been when I actually needed them?* I chucked an apple at them and they scattered, before circling in the sky and landing, this time spreading out. I didn't know if it was possible for a bird to look smug, but I swear those crows were giddy I'd given them a reason to tattle. Like a twelve-year-old at recess, I stuck my middle finger up and waved it in the air, and then turned the back of my chair to them.

If I was going to have a babysitter, why shouldn't I act childish?

So this is what my life has come too? Flipping the bird to a bunch of birds? The thought made me chuckle.

In an entire hour, only one customer visited. Well, a family really. According to the small talk they threw my way, they were getting ready to have a barbeque and wanted a watermelon. The mom thumped a few before picking out the perfect one, and then her husband handed me a ten. They loaded back into their SUV and left.

By six, no one else had come and I debated whether to close shop an hour early. Saturdays were normally a busy day for us, but in the summer heat, things were sometimes touch and go. Even the crows had abandoned ship. The mosquitoes had started their ambush early, and soon I was slapping them from my arms and legs, sounding like a human drum keeping tempo with the choir of bullfrogs that sang somewhere in the distance. Between the boredom, the slapping, and the droning frog-song, I felt I would go insane.

Rings of sweat circled the neck and armpits of my t-shirt, despite my deodorant and the industrial sized fan blowing on me from only a few feet away. I had given up on my book entirely, deciding to wait and read it in my air conditioned room where I could enjoy it without feeling like I was sticking to the pages. That meant I had nothing to distract me from thoughts of my sister, the monster who'd hurt her, and what I'd like to do to him if I got the chance.

In a word, I was miserable.

"Forget this," I grumbled aloud.

I started loading the baskets of fruits and veggies inside the storeroom section of the fruit stand, when a small black pickup truck pulled into the makeshift gravel lot. Tensing and doing my best not to be obvious about ignoring the vehicle while watching it out of the corner of my eye, I kept loading things up. If it was a customer, I hoped they would take the hint when they saw me packing it in for the day. If it were anyone else...well, I didn't think Delia's attacker would be stupid enough to show up here of all places. Still, if he did, I planned to heave a watermelon at him and take off down the driveway in a full sprint. Silly, but it was the best I could come up with in that split second.

"Oh good! You're here," a deep, familiar voice said to my back.

The tension drained out of me in a rush. I set down the basket of tomatoes looped over my arm and turned round. Logan, the guy from the diner, stood there smiling as if him showing up was the most natural thing in the world. I'd began to think I'd imagined the feeling at Myrtle's, the slight pull of electricity and excitement, the kind of anticipation that prickled the skin.

The logical part of my mind reminded me that I didn't know this guy. I'd only kind-of sort-of met him for like ten minutes, and the pull was probably excitement over the *idea* of something new and forbidden. But the rest of me—my heart, my stomach, and the butterflies that took up residence whenever Logan was around—they knew better. It wasn't only the giddy feeling either. It was how, for some unknown reason, being next to him banished the tension that had threatened to settle permanently in my shoulders. And how I could breathe, really breathe. Like I had been doing it wrong my entire life until I met him.

The feeling, though exciting, was also unnerving. And if I was honest with myself, it scared me to react so strongly to someone I didn't know. Someone off limits.

It also struck me that he was a stranger passing through. Not knowing who had attacked Delia, I should have been suspicious of him. But then, no one in their right mind would stick around after doing such a thing. More than that, I didn't believe the Chief's lame accusation that it had probably been a carnie or someone else from out of town. If anyone wanted to hurt my sister, it was someone from Brooklyn. Someone who knew us. It being this guy, Logan, didn't feel right, and not because I didn't want it to be him.

"Can I help you?" I asked, this time at least managing not to stammer.

That smile. Those lips. I blinked. *Dang it. Couldn't he have at least one crooked tooth? Or a birth mark. Or something.*

"It's me, Logan, from the diner? We met yesterday. Sort of. I was told this was the only place to get fresh produce around here."

"Well, I'm sorry. I was about to close up." I inclined my head toward the mostly emptied fruit stand. "But if you tell me what you want, I can grab it for you real quick and check you out. I've already loaded some of the baskets into the building."

I was suddenly well aware of how much I had been sweating. Trying to be inconspicuous, I sniffed the air around me. *Good.* At least I didn't stink. Pit sweat and a ratty, slick backed ponytail were bad enough, but if I had B.O., I would have melted straight into the ground.

"Oh. Ok. I only need…," he scanned the baskets that remained outside of the closed building, "a tomato."

"Only a tomato?" I asked. "You could have got that at the Pig over in town." Why was I trying to talk him into going somewhere else? *Shut up, Tallulah!*

"Well. I really like tomatoes and I want a good one." The way he spoke made it sound like the most intelligent reason on the planet. Or it could have been his dimples. Either way, I wasn't complaining.

"Well, ok then," I said smiling. "Here ya go! On the house." I tossed him a plump beefcake tomato from the top of the basket. Seemed like an appropriate choice.

"I can't take it for free." He caught it easily. "How much?"

"For one tomato? The scale is already put up. So really. Just take it." I waved at him to keep it.

"How about I pay you a dollar and we call it even?"

"If you want,." I shrugged.

"I'll have to write a check, though."

I raised my eyebrows, wondering if it were possible for a person to exist who was that good looking, but also dumb as a box of bricks. It would figure. He seemed too perfect. *It would serve me right for thinking I'm falling for someone without even having a conversation with them first.*

"Um. Sure. Whatever."

I imagined what Daddy would say when he saw the check for a dollar in the moneybag. Probably it would bounce. Probably I would have to pay the dang dollar. I mean, why else would someone write a check for a dollar, unless he was playing a joke or something?

Logan scribbled the check and tore it loudly out of the plastic checkbook.

"Here you go! The phone number at the top is my cell. You should give me a call sometime. Your name is Tallulah, right? That sleazy woman at the diner, Loretta? She told me."

I stared at him, puzzled. *He'd asked for my name? From Loretta? Lord, there is no telling what else that floozy told him.*

"Yeah. Sure is," I blurted. "That's my name. I mean, my name is Tallulah." *Yep, kind of want to melt into that puddle now.*

"Ok then, Tallulah. Nice to meet you. Oh, and don't forget about my number," Logan said as he turned and jogged to his truck.

I shook my head. *What in the world just happened?*

I started to load up the rest of the baskets. The whole exchange was odd. I wasn't an expert on men by no means, but I was an expert at peddling produce, and that had to have been the weirdest tomato sell in the history of ever.

"I'm sorry."

I spun on my heels, startled. Logan stood not far behind me.

"Hey. Look. I'm sorry about that." He shrugged his shoulders slightly and looked down at his sneakers.

"You need another tomato?" I asked, crossing my arms.

Logan's mouth twitched into an almost-smile. "Listen. I never do that. I mean. That whole thing was dumb. I'll give you a dollar for the tomato." He pulled a wallet out of the back pocket of his jeans.

His faded, perfect fitting jeans slung low enough on his hips. Damn.

"The truth is I don't even need the tomato. I asked around about you and was told you worked over here. I thought the check thing would be funny, but you didn't laugh and after thinking about it, I guess it's kind of creepy. Or weird. Or worse."

Why is he rambling? Is he nervous? Am I making him nervous? Is that even possible? He's standing here in his crisp t-shirt and jeans that can only be described as divine, while I'm drenched in sweat...and he's nervous? No way.

"Are you serious?" I asked, interrupting him. The electricity that had danced between us earlier didn't disappear, exactly, but almost. It waned enough that I could convince myself it was all in my head.

"Excuse me?" he paused.

"I mean, did you really come down here to talk to me?" I frowned. It would be nice to believe that this good-looking stranger had tracked me down because he wanted to meet me, but there had to be a catch. He was doing this as a joke, or because someone in the town told him we could do something crazy, like grant wishes. Well. I wouldn't be a punch line.

And I was no genie.

I crossed my arms and looked him straight in the eye. *His beautiful green eyes.* "You know I can't grant wishes?" I asked, deadpan.

"Huh?"

"Nothing. Forget I said that." On the off chance he was telling the truth, I had probably ruined it with the genie comment. If he had been from Brooklyn, it wouldn't have seemed such a strange thing for me to say, but if he had been from Brooklyn, he wouldn't have come to talk to me, either.

"It's...Are you trying to play some kind of joke? Because if so, you shouldn't. We've been through a lot recently, and I'm not in the joking mood. I am sure my Daddy isn't either."

I tried not to cringe outwardly even as the words left my mouth. *Nice.* If the genie comment wasn't bad enough, now I was threatening him with my Daddy.

"Look. I can tell I've touched a nerve. But I promise I only wanted to talk to you. I felt really bad, hearing what that waitress at the diner was saying. You sounded like you could use a friend," he dug his shoe in the dirt, "and I wanted to let you know that since I heard her threaten you, I'll back up your story."

"You will?" I stared at him. "But you don't even know me."

Yesterday, I wouldn't have thought it possible for me to forget about the incident at Myrtle's, but finding Delia in the ditch had wiped the confrontation clean from my mind, until now.

The warmth of his smile and the adorable way he kept rubbing the back of his neck put me at ease. And unless I was crazy, there was still the faintest tug of that strange connection between us. It was barely noticeable, but it was there.

"Well, I know you're definitely interesting. And nice. And I know you love your family," he said.

"So you liked what you heard," I raised a brow, "while you were eavesdropping?"

I am not good at this. Maybe having dates arranged is the best thing that can happen to me.

He took a few steps towards me. "How about this." Another step. "What if told you I know that you're pretty?"

My stomach knotted. I felt like I should run away. Or kiss him. Or faint. Or all three.

"I know you have the most amazing eyes I have ever seen."

He now stood directly in front of me, close enough I could smell the minty scent of his mouthwash.

Logan touched my arm, sending a current pulsing through me. I shuddered, staring up at him. Everyone that I met was so careful to avoid eye contact that the act of a simple shared gaze felt bold and intimate. Deeply intimate, like he wasn't staring at me, but into me, and could see my secrets and fears. My heart sped.

"Well," I said, panicking, "I would say you probably shouldn't have used that check line." I took a step back, sliding away from Logan's hand, and looked down, letting the intensity that had erupted between us dissipate. I wanted him to touch me, but everything that came out of my mouth was saying the opposite. I was so used to having my guard up around outsiders; switching off my defense mode was easier said than done.

"And how did you find out where I worked?" I asked him, knowing it wouldn't be hard to track down the crazy (at best), or evil (depending on who you asked) family that ran the fruit stand.

"The waitress mentioned a produce stand. This is the only one I've seen. I did a drive by this morning and a guy was working here. I was going to call it quits, but decided to do one more loop. I'm glad that I did."

I smiled at his words. I couldn't remember anyone ever saying they were glad to see me before. At least not anyone I wasn't related to.

"Because I really needed a tomato," he added.

My mouth dropped open.

"Tallulah? I'm joking." He laughed. "I thought we covered the tomato already?"

"I knew that."

He wasn't good at jokes, but the easy happiness of his words made it all right. It was like, he knew he was bad at them, and since it didn't bother him, he didn't expect it to bother anyone else. It worked, because the anger I'd felt for the millisecond I thought he was playing a trick on me evaporated.

"So. Since we've established I tracked you down to meet you and not buy fruit, do you wanna go grab something to eat?"

God, he was beautiful. And sweet. And he tried to be funny, bless his heart. And I couldn't go on a date with him. No matter how much I wanted to.

"I can't, Logan. Things are complicated for me. Even more so right now," I stared down at my flips flops, wishing I had let Delia paint my toenails.

Logan didn't say anything.

"It's that…my family won't let me date you. I can't. I mean, I want to." The need to fill the uncomfortable silence pushed the words from my mouth before I could think. *Did I really tell him I wanted to date him? Please kill me now.*

Logan squeezed his lips closed and raised his eyebrows in a look of understanding.

"It's fine," he said, turning to walk away. "I get it. This is south Mississippi after all."

"What?" I asked, confused. What did south Mississippi have to do with anything?

"I said I get it. I'm not the white country boy your parents would have picked for you. That's fine. I should have known." He headed toward his truck.

I watched him go, puzzled. His hand was on the door handle before it dawned on me what he thought this was about. "Logan, wait! Please wait!" I called. "I seriously doubt you know why my parents wouldn't want me to go to dinner with you."

"What else could it be, Tallulah?" His voice didn't carry any anger. Instead, it was the voice of someone who was talking about an old hurt. "I've dealt with this before. It's been a while, but I guess I should have known, since I'm back here in the good ole rural deep south."

"But it's not that at all! It's not. My parents don't care what color your skin is. Lord, if anyone can understand prejudice, it's us!"

"Then tell me, Tallulah, what is it?"

"Look. How much did you hear at the diner yesterday?" I twisted at the knuckle on my index finger.

"Most of it."

"Wow. And you still tracked me down?"

Logan crossed his arms, waiting for me to get to the point.

"So you heard me tell Myrtle about not being able to date?" My eyes widened. "That was true! My family is...We're different. And my parents are strict about who they approve of me dating. It wouldn't matter if you were white as an egg, it would still be a no-go. On top of that, we're kind of in crisis mode. If there was even a small chance before, Daddy would shut it down now in one second flat."

It sounded so lame. I was twenty-one, telling a hot guy that my parents wouldn't let me date him. Oh, well. At least I would have the memory of being asked out. That was something. I guess.

"So you weren't making that up? About the dating? What about the other stuff?" He cocked his head to the side. "There's no way that all of that's true. I thought you were jerking that lady around for being such a brat."

"I know it probably sounds crazy. But everyone around here knows we are, um, different. That's a big reason they aren't so friendly."

"But you work here, right? All the time?" he asked.

"Most of the time I work two or three days a week, but I'll be here a lot more for a while."

"Will you be here tomorrow?"

I thought for a minute. "Well. Yeah, probably. Why?"

"I might need another tomato." His grin shot from ear to ear. "What time will you get here?"

I knew I shouldn't tell him. There was really no point in seeing him. It couldn't lead anywhere good, and if he came asking about me while someone else was working, I would have to listen to a lecture about the rules. *The damned rules.* But there was that strange pull. *Like I'm supposed to know him.* Did that even matter, really? *What am I hoping for?*

I opened my mouth with the sole purpose of telling him there was no way, and instead heard myself say, "I'll be here in the morning at 8:30."

This cannot end well.

"Well then, I will see you in the morning. You can help me pick another perfect tomato." He winked at me, opening the door to his truck.

"Then you'd better bring cash!"

I had a date. Sort of.

And I'm getting better at flirting…I think.

Chapter Eleven

The moment something magical sparks, those precious minutes in the morning when you haven't yet left your dreams behind, that moment has always been the best part of my days. With the sun streaming in through the cracks of the plantation blinds, and reflecting off the pale pink of my bedroom walls, it gave me a sense of peace. The rays set everything in a rosy hue, while the dust motes danced in the sunshine. I always felt happy.

Until the thought of Logan slammed into me like a semi without brakes. Remembering what laid ahead filled me with that strange, dangerous kind of happiness. The kind that, if I were honest, had undertones of pure dread.

The numbers on my alarm clock blinked obnoxiously. 7:30. I was going to see him in an hour! An hour! What had possessed me to tell him it was okay to show up? If Daddy found out, I would get a lecture, but Logan would get more than he bargained for. I didn't think Daddy would hurt him, but he could make him miserable without causing an inkling of true harm. And for all of the talk about me being able to have the final say in who I picked to wed, I knew I would be married off within the year if certain members of my family thought I was fooling around with someone unGifted.

I'd have to tell Logan that it would never work. That I appreciated him being nice to me, and for his offer of backing up the fact that Myrtle was lying, if it ever came to that. But I couldn't see him anymore.

Not as friends. Not as anything.

Besides. This wasn't a time for me to be selfish. I had more important things to focus on than perfect hair and muscular arms. *I wonder what those arms would feel like wrapped around me?* I shook the thought from my head. It didn't matter.

Delia needed me. I needed to be there for her and help her recover. And to find the bastard who'd tried to break her.

But none of it changed the truth, I would see Logan today. I had to. There wasn't any way around it. *And since I have to see him, there's no harm in maybe dressing a little nicer, right?*

I crawled out of bed and went to knock on Delia's door. I needed her help.

***

Thirty minutes later, after placing myself in my sister's very capable hands, I was ready to face the day. The dread-filled happiness I had been harboring started to resemble something more like true happiness.

Getting Delia to make me over—something she was always pestering me to let her do—had brought her out of her room, where she'd isolated herself in a fortress of blankets, movies, and coffee, delivered to her door by Mama whenever she hollered.

I had actually almost gotten a smile from her. Of course, I didn't tell her why I was dressing nice and doing my hair. I couldn't. It felt wrong to be excited when she was so depressed, however, the way she kept narrowing her eyes at me and biting her bottom lip made me think she suspected something was up. Even if Logan was a no-show, I would be glad of the morning we'd spent together.

Daddy stopped me on my way out the door. If he noticed that I was dressed different, he didn't mention it. "I've been thinking. No more working alone. It's too dangerous," he said, his voice an octave deeper than normal. It was what my sister referred to as his Daddy voice. Never mind I had worked alone yesterday, or for the most part, the six years before that. There was no arguing with the Daddy voice.

When I got to the end of the drive, I was relieved to see my working partner was Jack. I trusted Jack to keep my secret meeting, well, a secret. But more importantly, I needed to talk to him about Delia.

He wouldn't have disappeared on her like that. Not on purpose. Not ever. But I needed to know what happened. At the very least, he had some explaining to do. *Where was he? Where had he been when she needed him?*

When I asked Delia, she'd shut down, saying only that she wouldn't get Jack in trouble, and I wasn't about to press her for answers.

At 8:25am on the nose we finished unloading baskets of oranges, apples, and pears onto the folding tables set up to be visible from the road. We worked in silence. Unspoken words weighed heavy between us. Jack had avoided eye contact as we had plowed through our opening duties: stacking a few watermelons on the ground in front of the table, arranging the smaller containers of strawberries, blackberries, and muscadine into neat rows. We kept the prettier fruits out front to attract people passing through. Bright fresh berries and ripe watermelon were much more tempting to passers-by than a bushel of potatoes or peas.

We dragged the piece of plywood with the word "OPEN" spray painted in neon orange and propped it against the two poles been fixed into the ground for that purpose. And then, we were done.

Our prep work took us all of twenty minutes, and as soon as it was done, we parked our butts in folding chairs and sat in front of the fan, still not speaking.

I caught Jack watching me with a strange look.

We stared at each other a moment. He wanted to tell me something, but needed me to ask. *Fine.*

"Jack, where were you?" I demanded. "Delia said you were supposed to meet her, but you weren't there."

Jack sunk low into his chair. "I was hoping I could talk to her first and explain. But Tully, you gotta believe me. I was there. I thought she had flaked on me. She does that all the time, you know, and it's never a big deal. But I waited. I waited forever." His eyes darted from the ground to me and back again. "Finally, a cop stopped and told me to move along. Someone had seen my truck and thought that I had broken down or something and called 911. The cop said that if I didn't get going I was going to get a ticket."

"So you left? Why didn't you drive back home and check on her?" Something else was nagging at me. "And what do you mean she flakes on you all the time?" I had to force my voice to stay even. Thinking about what happened to Delia was enough to make me hot with rage.

"Well. We, uh, we kind of go into town all the time. Delia said we couldn't invite you because it would be like bringing Aunt Jenny." He kept his gaze on the ground, but peeked at me from the corner.

I tensed at the comparison to my mother. It was Delia's favorite insult for when I wouldn't go along with one of her little schemes. It always upset me. Every. Single. Time. I loved my Mama, but we were nothing alike.

"I am not like Mama!" I seethed. But even as the words left my mouth, I knew I would never have let my sister sneak out, much less went with her.

"I'm sorry, Tully, but you, uh, I don't think you would've had much fun with us anyway," he mumbled.

"You mean like all the fun Delia had the other night? Yeah, it looked so fun in that ditch!" I regretted the words the moment they left my mouth. I knew I wasn't being fair. Jack had always been the follower to Delia's leader.

"I'm so sorry," he rasped. He wiped his eyes with his palms, and I looked away, embarrassed I had made my cousin cry.

"Jack, no, I'm sorry. It wasn't your fault at all. I just get so angry."

"You're right, though, I shouldn't have left." Jack turned to stare at the road. "But this wasn't the only time she didn't show. The other times she had made new plans without telling me. I was used to waiting. She always told me, if she were thirty minutes late to go ahead and we would meet up later. And we always did."

"What? Who was she riding with?"

"Tully, me and Delia both understand better than you think about wanting to meet other people. You aren't the only one who doesn't want to trust your future to Aunt Trudy."

"You mean, Delia has been sneaking around to meet boys?" I asked. Sneaking out sounded like Delia, but actually managing to do it without getting caught, did not. "There's no way. She can't have a conversation about going into town without pushing Daddy too far and ending up in her room for the night."

Jack crossed his arms. "Yeah, well. That kind of helped her out."

"You mean…" The truth slapped me across the face. I was an idiot.

"Yep," Jack nodded, "Every time. She said she would always bring it up on the off chance Uncle Jepson would give in, but really, it made it easier to leave unnoticed when everyone thought she was in bed early for the night."

I couldn't believe Delia had been pulling this off. If she had said she was going to bed early, everyone would have known something was up, but getting yelled at and then storming off to her room…well, she could count on our parents keeping to themselves for the rest of the night, and if her light was off, I sure didn't bother her.

And she never told me. Not once.

"What about you?" I asked my cousin.

Jack shrugged. "My parents don't care if I go into town, but I couldn't do it without Delia. If I go alone I end up cruising around, either bored out of my mind, or angry at myself for being too chicken shit to do anything. Delia, though, she's fearless. You should see her, Tully, she makes friends so easy! And she doesn't even use her Gift." His voice was thick with the kind of hero worship usually reserved for small kids talking about their much older siblings. "We go to Peachton because it's easier to make up a story and blend in. You'd be surprised how many people don't recognize our eyes unless they have a reason. The first time we went, we were so nervous we ended up going to Sonic. We were going to go right home afterwards but Delia said there was no way she had risked being grounded for eternity just to get a too sweet slush and a bad burger. She got out of the truck, and by the time we were ready to leave, we had met so many people our age. It was so great to hang out and not be a freak."

The way he said it, with his eyes glowing green, touched every nerve. That experience, that mundane action of sitting with a group of people and simply being, it was something I had always wanted, yearned for even, but had never thought could happen. It was hard to believe Jack and Delia had been living a secret, normal life, while I dreamt of one. And…it hurt.

I had always known Jack's Mama and Daddy—my Aunt Brenda and Uncle Gavin—pretty much let him do what he wanted as long as he didn't cause trouble. But I never imagined that what he wanted was the same thing as me.

Delia and I had grown up daydreaming about the kinds of things normal kids got to do, things like going to football games or sleepovers with friends. It had been years since I had indulged in any of those old fantasies. I had assumed Delia had left them behind also, accepting the way things were was how it was supposed to be.

Our games of 'If we were normal' had never interested Jack, though. He was always so content. Like his daddy. Uncle Gavin was the laid back twin. The perfect balance to my sometimes-wound-too-tight Mama. And Aunt Brenda had grown up in Maine, where her family kept their tiny Gifts a closely guarded secret. My Uncle's chill outlook on life, and my Aunt's mostly normal upbringing, meant that Jack got a lot more rope in his leash than the rest of us. That he had the opportunity to get away and blend in wasn't that surprising, but the fact that he wanted to, was.

I wondered when he had changed.

"It sounds amazing, Jack," I said, meaning every word.

We both sat staring at the road in front of us, watching the cars drive by.

I pulled a borrowed compact sized mirror from the pocket of my (also borrowed) linen shorts and frowned at my reflection. The hair product Delia had applied had mixed with sweat and turned to glue. I also had black smudges under each eye, and every time I wiped beads of perspiration from my face, my hand came away streaked in the Cover Girl shade of "creamy natural."

"Oh well," I sighed, and pulled my hair into a knot on top of my head with the elastic band I always kept on my wrist.

Jack raised his eyebrows like he couldn't believe what he was seeing. "Now can I ask you a question, Tully?"

"Shoot," I said.

He gestured toward my outfit. "What in the hell has gotten into you?"

"Why?" I worried. "Do I look stupid?" I'd let Delia dress me like a human doll, without so much as one complaint, and in the full-length mirror in her bedroom, the outcome had seemed perfect. Now, with my ruined hair and running makeup, as well as the gold sandals that were a half size too small cutting into my ankle, I wasn't so sure. The feather light material of Delia's cream-colored tank top had felt expensive and chic, but now it clung to my perspiring body. I felt exposed as I looked down at the clear-as-day outline of my bra. At least the shorts were still fine.

"No. Not stupid. You look like a clone of Delia, though." Jack grinned.

I pulled off the dangling clip-on earrings my sister had picked for me and stuffed them in my pocket. It was just as well. The constant pinching on my ears gave me a headache.

"Tully. Relax. You look good. I only mean, why are you so dressed up? I've seen you almost every day of my life, and this is a big departure from your normal clothes." Jack motioned at my outfit. "I mean, not that there's anything wrong with the whole free t-shirt and cutoff jeans look, but this isn't you."

"Ok. Listen. You have to swear not to say anything. Especially since everybody is so tense right now. I'm handling it."

"Tully, what are you handling?" Jack's forehead creased deep as his thick eyebrows pinched together. "Is there something you need help with?"

"I'm fine. Chill," I said. "Someone is coming to see me, is all. Nothing big. I'm going to talk to him and tell him I can't see him anymore and that will be it."

"Is that all?" Jack breathed a sigh of relief. "Good grief, Tully, you had me worried. You sounded like something big was going on! And after everything, well, I couldn't handle it if something happened to you too!"

"So I can count on you to keep your mouth shut?"

Jack grinned, and then pretended to zip his lips, and toss the key over his shoulder.

A truck crunched onto the gravel parking area, bringing us back to reality. The door of the small truck opened, and Logan unfolded himself out and stretched before walking over. His lopsided smile had the same effect on me as yesterday, sending my heart on a sprint.

Panicked, I looked over at Jack.

"That's him?"

I nodded, too fast.

"Relax, Tully. He's buying some fruit. It's not illegal. Hell, selling fruit is what we do."

Logan walked into the covered area of the little shack, and seeing Jack, started looking around, eyeballing the onions.

"Uh, Logan? This is my cousin Jack," I said. "He's okay."

"Oh, good!" Relief was evident in his voice. "After our talk yesterday, you had me scared that if I spoke to you in front of anyone I'd get thrown out and you'd get dragged away!" He laughed.

Jack and I glanced at each other. "Ha-ha," I forced a chuckle. "Well. I don't think I'd really get dragged away, but you did right. Jack's good. So is my sister, Delia. But anyone else…"

"Seriously?" he asked.

I looked down at the counter; this was already getting awkward.

"Tully, you need a drink? I think I'm going to get a coke. You can handle one customer by yourself, right?" Jack asked. "Good to meet you Logan." Jack hopped out of his chair. "Be back in a minute." He scooted around the large ice chest that held plenty of cold drinks, jogging off in the direction of his house.

"That wasn't obvious," I mumbled.

Logan laughed. "It's fine!"

He walked behind the plywood counter, and sat in Jack's chair. "So. Tully, huh? I like that nickname. It really suits you."

"Yeah," I shrugged. "When my little sister, Delia, was little, she couldn't say Tallulah. She's only two and a half years younger than me, so really I have been Tully for as long as I can remember."

"I always used to want a nickname," Logan said. "But unless you're five, you can't really give yourself one. And you can't really shorten Logan."

"You could be Lo-Lo," I said, smiling. "Lo-Lo…What is your last name?"

"Hosteen. But I guess what I should've said was, I always wanted a cool nickname." Logan leaned toward me, resting his elbows on his knees and still smiling his ridiculous smile. "Listen, I was still hoping maybe we could grab a bite to eat or see a movie or something."

I opened my mouth to give him my rehearsed list of reasons on why

I couldn't see him anymore. "Log—"

Logan lifted his index finger and placed it across my lips. The gentle touch sparked heat through my body, making me forget everything except how much I wanted him to keep his finger right where it was. The ardent feeling that his one finger pulled through me, made me wonder what might happen if the touch grew more intense. <y face heated up as I realized I wanted to find out.

Stop it, Tallulah. You know what you have to do.

"Now, before you say anything, listen. You say that you can't. But you already said yesterday that you wanted to." He grinned.

Dang it. I had hoped he hadn't caught that.

"It's dinner, not a proposal. I would never be so forward, but I think you need to cut yourself some slack. Do something fun. From what I hear, you don't really leave your, err, area too much."

So he had been asking around again. *Great.*

"You'd better be careful asking people around here about me." I sucked in the humid air. "You might not like what you hear."

"I don't care about those people," Logan answered. "Most of them seem half crazy themselves, so I sure don't need their advice on who I should ask out. Besides," he paused and shrugged, "there's something about you, Tallulah Caibre. I need to get to know you better."

"Logan, I can't. Even if I could have before, it's like I told you yesterday, things are complicated at my house. I won't risk sneaking off. My parents would have a heart attack if I got caught."

"Tallulah, I am twenty-four. I am not asking you to lie to your parents. I think you should tell them. I can't believe that they wouldn't let you have dinner with a friend. Do you like Italian? Let's eat at Marco's in Peachton. There's no way I'm going back to Myrtle's." He sounded confident in the way that good-looking people, even the nice ones, are. So sure that he would get his way that the opposite never entered his mind.

On the road, a car stopped, waiting for an oncoming truck to pass, and then gave its signal to turn into the gravel lot. Logan was less than a foot from me, and I wanted to say yes to him more than I had ever wanted anything in my life. But the worry about being caught so close to a man, was enough to burst my bubble.

"Logan, I can't. And you gotta move," I said quickly.

He smirked. "Come on Tully. One date. That's it."

The black car pulled in and parked on the opposite side of Logan's truck.

Logan grabbed my hand, and if a single finger across my lips had been a spark, his grasp was pure, burning blue heat. The feeling was so shocking that my first reaction was to pull my hand away from the flame, but Logan held tight.

"Logan...you don't understand."

The car door opened and shut with a thump.

"Oh, I understand. I think *you* don't understand. It's so easy to go along with the way things are planned, but the truth is, you're scared." He ran his thumb over our joined hands. "You've been hidden away over here, never really having to think about what you wanted to do because things have always been laid out for you. Isn't that what you told Myrtle? This is dinner, Tully, nothing to be scared of. But it could be more, and that's what terrifies you." He looked straight into my eyes as if seeing my soul. "Say yes."

I tried to pull my hand lose from his hold, and had to bite back a smile when he didn't let go. I had to say no. I really, really had to. But...

"This is blackmail, you know," I whispered.

"Say yes. Dinner. As friends. That's all," he said, still squeezing my palm in his.

Footsteps crunched up the gravel, coming around Logan's truck. Any second the person making them would be in plain sight. Damn.

"Fine."

"Great! I'll pick you up next Friday at seven?" he asked, his hold easing as he stood.

"No. I'll meet you there at eight-thirty. Now get over there and look at some vegetables!" I hissed. He dropped my hand and hopped over the counter, picking up a tomato, as a squat bearded man walked into the fruit stand.

And like that, my light, happy heart sank.

"Excuse me, Miss," Logan said, exaggerating his voice like a stage actor. "I do believe I'm ready to check out! Although all of your wares are quite lovely, I'll be needing this single tomato." He twisted his arms into a windmill swoop before bowing deep and placing the tomato onto the table.

The poor guy really wasn't good at jokes.

Reverend Armstrong watched from the corner of the open aired room, scowling behind his beard. I really hoped Jack would get back before Logan left.

"Um, if this is all you want, it'll be one dollar," I said.

"Excellent, excellent!" Logan was still acting as though he were performing Shakespeare. He reached into his back pocket, making a show of turning around, clearly enjoying the sour look he was receiving from his audience of one.

"Please tell me that you accept checks?" he asked, pulling out his checkbook and setting it on the table next to the tomato.

I raised my eyebrows and stared at him. "Um, sure?"

Okay. Maybe Logan was a little funny, but Reverend Armstrong sucked any happiness from the room, like some kind of emotional sponge. He stood with his arms crossed, not even pretending to shop, and stared at Logan with his beady black pig eyes.

God Jack, hurry up!

I didn't think the old preacher was dangerous exactly, but he let everyone know how he felt about my family. Those feelings made me nervous. I mean, what the hell was he even doing here? I had seen him in passing around Brooklyn, but I was always careful to keep my distance. For him to come to the fruit stand...it was unheard of.

Logan scribbled the check for a dollar, and ripped it loudly from the book with dramatic flair. "Good day, ma'am," he said, again bowing deep before turning to leave. He stopped in front of Reverend Armstrong and tipped an imaginary hat, and then waltzed out the door, pausing long enough to call, "Friday," over his shoulder before disappearing and leaving me alone with the crazy preacher.

Forgetting that I was wearing Delia's shorts, I wiped my sweaty palms down the front of the linen fabric, leaving a faint brown streak from the grime that had rubbed off the table. "Shit," I muttered. "This keeps getting better."

Standing at eye level with me, Reverend Armstrong wasn't a large man, but his presence filled the room, and had the ability to turn your stomach in anticipation of something bad. If Delia felt like Christmas, this man felt like rot.

But the scariest thing was the gun he always wore holstered at his waist. In south Mississippi, we're not shy about our firearms. Most people, even in my family, hunt. And according to the flyers that paper the corkboard over at the truck stop, Brooklyn was home to a thriving chapter of the NRA. Yet despite what the national news tried to project about southerners, we weren't a bunch of dingbats running around shooting off rounds into the air at the slightest provocation. My family, at least, stored our guns in a safe. And except for the time a few years ago when town councilmen Leon Merchant made state headlines by falling out of his tree stand and bringing his cocked shotgun down with him, I didn't know of anyone in our area ever being shot. Even councilman Merchant's death didn't turn anyone anti-gun. Instead, it was viewed as a warning to the importance of regular deer stand maintenance.

Reverend Armstrong was the only person I had ever seen openly wear a gun in public, totally unconcealed. It wasn't any gun either. With its pearl colored handle and the detailed maze of engravings that crisscrossed the nickel colored metal of the revolver, it resembled a relic left over from the civil war. But relic or not, any kind of weapon in the hands of a crazy person was disturbing. And from the deep wrinkles of his permanent scowl to the way his top lip twitched any time he looked at any of my kin, it was clear this man was all kinds of crazy.

It was common knowledge around Brooklyn not to question the preacher about the side arm, lest you get yourself on his church's shit list. A list my family had topped for as long as Embers of the Righteous Fire had been in Brooklyn.

I swallowed hard, forcing the lump down and out of my throat. "Can I help you?" I croaked. I wasn't in the habit of talking with crazy cult leaders, if I could at all help it.

"I thought you all's big thing was that you kept to yourselves," the Reverend said, stretching each vowel to the breaking point.

His arms stayed folded across his chest in disapproval, but he was careful to keep his eyes on my lips or forehead, never making eye contact.

Crap. How much had he heard? I slumped forward in my chair, wishing he would leave.

"Um. We do?" I said evenly, trying to sound braver than I felt. I didn't need this man to know how much he disturbed me.

"Huh. I didn't know that keeping to yourselves meant catting around and then crying rape," he sneered. "I heard your Jezebel sister used that depraved wickedness that lives inside of every one of you all to snare a man in her trap, and when he didn't give her whatever it was she demanded, she said he raped her."

Hate seared through me like a hot blade, slicing away the fear and leaving in its place only anger. How dare this man come here and say those things? How dare he call Delia a Jezebel?

I gazed into the old man's face, searching for his eyes. He said that he "had heard."

"What did you hear? From who?"

His graying eyebrows rested on top of his lids. Combined with his full beard, it gave the impression of a face covered with hair with enough room for two tiny accusing eyes to peep through. My attempt at eye contact made the Reverend go rigid.

Good. Let him be scared. If he was going to hate me, then at least let him fear me.

I was suddenly glad that, besides a few exceptions, the town's people didn't know the extent of our individual power. The Reverend, in his righteous indignation, would be a lot less afraid if he knew how little of a threat I actually posed.

"You know who raped my sister?" I asked. "Tell me!"

He snorted. "Girl, you don't seem to understand what I said. I don't think nobody raped that whore sister of yours. She bespelled someone and got exactly what was coming to her. But if you're asking me if I know who she fornicated with, then no, I can't say that I do. And, I don't reckon that whoever it was would be coming forward. Your sister may be playing the victim, but make no mistake, we know she's the predator." He spat on the floor. "Like the rest of you witches."

Sneering, he looked into my eyes, then realizing his mistake, turned his hateful stare back to my forehead. He crossed the room, stopping in front of me. The gaudy revolver knocked against the cheap plywood as he leaned across the counter, his hands splayed palms down in front of him.

"Mister, you need to leave or I'm going to get my father," I said, my voice cracking on the last word.

The hope of finding out who had hurt Delia evaporated along with my bravery. I wanted him to leave. He had to leave, or I was going to run. Fruit and vegetables be damned! I would not stay in the room with this psycho and his gun.

"Can we help you, Reverend?" Jack's voice a welcome reprieve. His bright smile was frozen into place. I knew from his rigid stance that he was as nervous about the man as I was, only better at hiding it. A week ago, the Reverend would have only made us uncomfortable, but everything had changed. Delia had been hurt, and somehow that made the hate real. Suddenly snide remarks and sneering glances could mean more than prejudice, they could mean danger.

Reverend Armstrong turned in Jack's direction, again careful to avoid eye contact. He slid his palms from the counter, and his face twisted into something between a grimace and a smile.

"I'm glad you're here, boy. You need to hear this too. This message is for all of you. And you go tell your Daddy, little girl. Tell him what a man of God has said."

He paused and the saliva that had collected in the corners of his mouth threatened to dribble down his beard. "You'll stay away from the town! Your filth and your evil will not defile the rest of us! Keep to your kind or there will be hell to pay! Thus saith the Lord, Because of the whoredoms and harlots, the mistresses of witchcrafts! I will cast abominable filth on thee and make thee vile, and set thee as gazing stock!" Reverend Armstrong paused, looking from Jack, to me, and then back to Jack. "You are vile in the sight of God and the good people have had enough. Things will get ugly for you if you don't keep to your kind." The tiny bits of spittle freed themselves and flew through the air.

Armstrong turned to leave, lumbering to his car at the pace of the old man that he was, when Jack hollered to his back, "We ain't the evil ones! We ain't done nothing!" The preacher stopped walking, but Jack continued to yell, "You can jumble up scripture to mean what you want and you can fool a lot of people who are looking for some guidance. But guess what? That makes YOU evil. What about love one another? What about that?"

I took three steps to where Jack was standing and put my hand on his shoulder. "Jack, please. That's enough."

"I ain't scared of him," Jack said through his clenched teeth. "People like him are why we have to live like we do. He has no idea how much we hold back." Jack's eyes flashed a dangerous green.

"And one more thing, Reverend," Jack said, spitting the title out of his mouth like old milk. "I didn't use my Gift on you. I could have. Easy. I could have had you under my control. Falling over yourself to make me happy. So maybe there will be hell to pay for us, but you would do good to remember that. Remember that we hold back because we want to be here. Don't make us not care."

I grabbed Jack's arm, digging my nails into his flesh. "Jack, stop it! You're going to make it worse," I hissed at him.

We had all thought the exact same thing at some point or another, but those words were the reality that made the people of Brooklyn hate us. It was what scared them and made them keep their distance. It was what made them easy prey for people like Joshua Armstrong. If we started advertising what they already thought in their hearts, the fragile balance that existed between them and our family for so many generations would shatter. Then it would get ugly. It wasn't perfect. Sure, we felt like freaks now, but even I knew that things could go downhill fast.

I thought of Delia, broken and bloodied, and I realized things were already tumbling downhill at breakneck speed.

"I can't make it any worse than it is. Than it has been," Jack said, as if he could read my thoughts.

At least he had stopped yelling.

"Well, think about if our parents hear! Maybe you don't care what Joshua Armstrong thinks, but think how hard our family has worked to keep things peaceful. Please. Hush!" I whispered.

Jack looked at me and then at the Reverend.

"I know it hurts. Delia was raped and that man calls *us* evil, but we're the ones that have everything to lose. They want a reason, Jack, that's why he's here. Don't let him win."

Joshua Armstrong stood for another minute with his back to us before finally climbing inside of his black Lincoln. I exhaled, not knowing at what point I had started to hold my breath. Jack said nothing, but a little while later, the faint tinges of Christmas started to fill the air again, and his eyes were their usual, bright green without the glowing flash of magic begging to be released. His Charm might not be as strong as Delia's, but it was still nothing to mess with.

We both sat a while, neither saying much before deciding to pack it in for an early lunch. We pulled the crates into the lockable area and put out the "be back in an hour" sign, and then headed down the driveway together.

"Listen, Tully," Jack said, keeping his eyes trained on the path in front of us. "I don't want to pressure you into feeling like you have to lie, but back there, my temper got the best of me. That lunatic twisting around the Bible and acting like we are the evil ones...I snapped."

I threw an arm around Jack and rested my palm on his shoulder, the way I had been doing since we were little. At eighteen, he was only three inches taller than me, an even six foot. "Jack, its fine. I'm glad you came back when you did. That man is scary."

"Yeah, me too." Jack took a deep breath. "Look, like I said, no pressure, but can we keep that between us? I don't want my parents to know I lost it." He ran a hand through his dark hair.

I hadn't even thought if I was going to tell or not. I mean, I figured I would, with everything that had happened to Delia, but if Jack didn't want me too...

"I think Mom and Dad know that I knew Delia was sneaking out. I don't want them to be even more disappointed in me. If you think you need to tell, though—"

I interrupted him. "My lips are sealed."

We stopped in front of my porch steps.

"You want to eat at my house?" I asked him. "I'm sure it's just sandwiches but you're welcome to come hang out."

"Nah. I need to run or something. I'm a little keyed up," he said, already starting to jog toward the path to Grandma's.

"Believe me. I understand."

My appetite had been destroyed by the run-in with the Reverend, however, the idea of going back to the fruit stand to sit for the rest of the day gave me chills. I intended to drag out my lunch as long as possible.

I trudged up the front steps, pausing as the door opened and my second—or third, I'm not sure—cousin Bertie came outside. She shut the door behind her.

"Oh good! Your Mama is waiting on you," the older woman said.

"Why is that?" I asked, worried that Mama had already discovered the confrontation at the fruit stand. I was pretty sure any crows that might have been hanging around had all scattered before Logan had made his appearance. Much less Reverend Armstrong.

"Oh, you'll see," my cousin smirked.

Truthfully, I had never liked the busybody.

Bertie slid by me and onto the driveway, heading—I guessed— toward her own house. "Good luuuuck!" she called over her shoulder in a singsong voice.

I pulled at the screen, pushed open the heavy front door, and walked into the room. The conversation within instantly stopped, and Mama and Grandma looked at me, guilt written all over their faces.

Chapter Twelve

Mama stood behind Grandma's chair, both of them smiling at me with the wide-eyed grins worn by those who got caught, but weren't ashamed. A lady sat across from them, hunched over a steaming cup of coffee, despite the ninety-degree weather outside. The woman was ancient with shoulders that rounded forward from the weight of breasts that had finally given up and taken a seat in her lap. The severe tautness of her bun didn't come close to lifting even one of the many wrinkles that decorated her face with old age, but her lips, however, had managed to keep most of the fullness that had likely made them beautiful in her youth. And underneath her hooded lids, her eyes shone with the green ethereal magic we all possessed.

"Oh Shit!" I said aloud before I could stop myself. Turning around and going straight back to the fruit stand suddenly seemed like the best idea in the world.

Grandma giggled and reached across the table to squeeze the old lady, her sister's, hand. For a second they resembled Delia and me. Different as night and day, but partners in crime all the same.

"Talullah! Language, please!" Mama said, warning me with her eyes to be nice.

She wore one of her bright colored sweaters with a knee-length denim skirt. The woman had sweaters in every color, and they were always baggy and always worn with a denim skirt. Delia called Mama's look Sunday school teacher chic. Mama did teach the children's Sunday school class, but I, along with everyone else who knew her, knew that Jenny Elisabeth Somersby Caibre was a woman who meant business. A wonderful mother and friend, but a person who demanded respect. So I snapped my mouth shut and gave a sheepish "sorry" to my great aunt.

"Aunt Trudy wants to talk to you! Here, you come sit next to her while I fix you some lunch. Is ham and cheese okay?" she asked, smiling.

Mama also knew you caught more flies with honey than vinegar. She had been sweet-talking my Daddy for as long as I could remember, but she was not fooling me. I knew exactly what was going on. It was the time of day when Mama was normally at work, teaching the little cousins, but instead, she was having a meeting with my Grandma and my flipping Aunt Trudy, a woman who hardly ever left her house and certainly never popped over for lunch. This meant one thing, and one thing only. An image of Logan flashed into my mind and I sighed. *Oh well, I guess it had been doomed from the start.*

I slunk into the chair next to the lady who would be deciding my future.

"Hello Tallulah," she rasped, pulling her hand from Grandma's grip and reaching over to hold mine instead.

Palsy, brought on by age and living for so long outside the health of her sister's Vigour, had made her movements sharp and jerkish, and it took a minute for her shaky fingers to find my hand. I knew I was being a brat by not meeting her halfway, or even smiling, but dang it, as a grown woman with no control over her own future, I earned the right to be a little bratty.

"I've been meaning to come talk to you. You are twenty-one, now, right?" she asked, her voice crackling.

"You know I am." My response earned a sharp look from Grandma. "I mean, yes, ma'am."

I knew I shouldn't be rude, but just because I was accepting my fate, didn't mean I happy about it.

"Well, your mama and Evelyn told me they've been talking to you. Telling you that soon it would be time for you to start courting. I've had a matchmaker from a Family in east Texas contact me with a young man they want to match. Sent me a picture. He's easy on the eyes," she said, glancing from me to Grandma.

Grandma winked at me and nodded to Trudy, nudging her to finish. "I need to sit with you a minute so I can get a read on you. Know if this would be a good first match or not. Now, I haven't met this boy, and so I have to go off of what they tell me about him, but I can give you a better read after I meet him."

I didn't say a word.

Aunt Trudy squeezed my hand. "There child. It's okay. Nothing to be scared of." She mistook my silence for fear. She reached around with her other hand and rubbed the back of my arm. "Don't you want to ask me some questions about him?"

I shook my head "no," and continued to sit, tightlipped.

Mama sat a paper plate with a ham sandwich and chips in front of me. "Really, Tallulah, aren't you a little excited?"

I looked from her to Grandma. They wore identical, hopeful expressions.

Dang it. They were so eager for me to enjoy this rite of passage, and if this would make them happy after all of the hurt we had endured…

I let out a long sigh. "Sure," I said, forcing a smile.

I took a deep breath and mentally pushed away the bitchiness that had taken over my mood. Mama reached down to squeeze my shoulders in a sideways hug.

"Yay! You're going to have fun. You'll see! Meeting your matches can be one of the best times in a girl's life. And Thomas really is a looker," she said.

"His name is Thomas?" I asked, doing my best to sound interested.

"Yes. He's twenty-three and has been working on an oil rig on and off, saving his money. His family lives like ours for the most part, but they don't have a Vigour, so I made sure he's open to moving," Aunt Trudy declared.

Moving? I thought this was a first match and no big deal. Who's moving? Ugh.

"Can I see the picture?" I asked. I had no intention of there ever being a second date, but it couldn't hurt to see at least what he looked like, since it would make them happy.

"Of course, child." Aunt Trudy nodded at Grandma.

Grandma slid a snap shot across the table to me. I leaned over to study it. It was of a young man wearing jeans and a camouflage t-shirt, smiling and standing in front of a four-wheeler that had what appeared to be fishing gear laid across the back. He was broad through the shoulders but lean at the waist with shaggy reddish brown hair that fell across his forehead. He was muscular, but without the blockiness of someone who spent a lot of time lifting weights. The overall effect was nice. He was handsome in an outdoorsy way. I picked up the photograph so I could get a better look at his face. His grin bordered on silly, which I liked. His eyes were the familiar green. My Mama hadn't been wrong when she said he was a looker.

Logan possessed the kind of unique looks that could almost be described as beauty, where Thomas was rugged. They were sugar and salt. So different that you couldn't really say one was better than the other. It came down to a matter of taste. And besides, I had to give him a chance, for my family's sake.

"How tall is he?" I asked.

Mama rolled her eyes.

Aunt Trudy laughed. "Well, he's 6'1. I may be old, but I know how girls think. You're a tall girl. You don't want to dwarf your date," she motioned to my feet, "With him, you can even wear heels."

I had to give her some credit; she seemed to be good at her job. "So now what?" I asked. As much as I hated to admit it, I was kind of warming up to the idea of meeting Thomas.

"You'll be going on a date with him on Saturday. He's going to call you and set it up," Aunt Trudy said, as if it were law. "Wear something nice, and try to smile and be yourself."

I looked at my Aunt in disbelief. It was odd enough that the antiquated woman was in charge of my future love life. It was odder still she seemed to know what she was doing, but the fact that she was giving me dating advice was almost too much. I picked up my sandwich and took a big bite to keep myself from saying something that might not go over so well. I chewed and swallowed before speaking.

"Great," I said.

Something heavy bumped into the window. Aunt Trudy jumped, but Grandma only glanced over, used to it. Birds had been bombarding Mama since she was five.

Mama walked over and opened the window. She rolled her eyes as the fat blackbird started squawking before turning and flying away. Mama shook her head and mumbled something about putting a net over the house.

"One thing, though," I said, an idea forming. "If I'm old enough to be matched, I'm old enough to not have a babysitter tagging along."

Mama said nothing, leaning against the countertop. I expected her to squash the request like she had so many times before.

After a moment, she said, "You know, fair enough. If you're meeting your potential match, you're old enough to do it alone."

"Really? You aren't just saying that?"

"No. You're absolutely right. No crows. Before your sister was attacked, I hadn't been letting them follow you as much anyway, if you haven't noticed, but I guess it's time to call them off all together. Now, they do like to gossip and I can't help what they do on their own." She grinned.

Aunt Trudy rose from her chair at a pace that would have made a sloth grow impatient. "I gotta get back. My soaps are on," she said, shuffling to the door where her walker was waiting.

Grandma jumped up. "I'll drive you back on my golf cart, Trudy," she told her sister. "I'll see ya'll later. Tully, baby, you let me know how that phone call goes, now." She smiled and helped Aunt Trudy out the door.

Watching them, I understood why my great aunt had asked Thomas's family about having a Vigour, and if he would be willing to move. Her husband, my Great-Uncle Vern, was from Tennessee. They had lived with his people until he passed away, when I was still a baby. The time she had spent outside her sister's Vigour had not treated her well, and now Trudy looked like Grandma's mother instead of her older sister. I couldn't help but wonder if she regretted moving away for so long. It made me think of Logan, and of the life I would live if I chose to defy my family and be with him. Sickness, injury, aging, and eventually death after my body had fallen apart. Was one guy even worth all that?

Chapter Thirteen

"You shouldn't tell them. That would be dating suicide! Now be still so I don't poke your eye out," Delia said. One of her hands was pressed against my forehead while her other hand clutched a pink and green tube of jet-black eyelash goop.

"I am being still. You try not flinching while someone comes toward your eyeball with a sharp object."

We were on the old oak bed in my Grandma's spare room. The same one in which Delia had laid next to Grandma on what we now referred to as "that night." I had told her about my plans to sneak out and catch a ride with Jack for my date with Logan. She had insisted that it would be easier if I spent the night with Grandma and left after she went to bed. Grandma didn't take nighttime clients on the weekends. She may have been younger than me, but no doubt, Delia was the expert.

"Then you won't have to sneak, simply walk out the door. With me here to cover for you, Jack can come pick you up," she'd laid out the plan. "Besides, you need me to help you get ready. And I want the scoop when you get back."

What lay between us, unsaid, was that sneaking out of our own home felt too much like what Delia had done "that night." I didn't tell her that I had already planned to leave from Grandma's house, because she was having too much fun playing the part that was seldom hers to play—advice giver.

This newfound role also included dating advice, and lots of it. I wasn't sure where she got her information from, or even if she knew what she was talking about, but sometimes seeming like you know something can be as effective as actually knowing it. In any case, her confidence was good enough for me. I was outclassed on the topic.

"If you had any kind of relationship with either of the guys, then yeah, you would need to tell them that you were also dating someone else. But this is only a night out. No more. No less. An opportunity for you to be normal. Don't ruin it by talking to him like you're hearing wedding bells." Delia continued to slap the goop on my eyelashes. "And you already know that this isn't going to go anywhere, so what's the harm? Enjoy the date."

That sounded good, but I wasn't even sure if there was going to be a date. I had not talked to Logan since he had asked me out. I had his number on the check, but there was no way I was going to risk calling him.

"Del? What if he doesn't show?" I asked, doubt creeping in.

"He'll show. All that effort he put into getting you to say yes? He would be the stupidest man on earth if he didn't turn up," she answered. She finished working on my face and smiled, handing over a plastic hand mirror. "And if he doesn't, then you have a fun night out with Jack. He'll enjoy all of the attention that you'll get him."

I rolled my eyes at my sister and took the mirror.

"No. I mean it, Tully. Look at yourself. You're gorgeous!"

I looked at my reflection through the grimy film of hairspray that coated the mirror.

Last time Delia made me over, I had come away looking like a taller version of her. This time, I looked like myself, only a little…different. Better different. I knew that I had makeup on. I had set for an hour while my sister rubbed and powdered and brushed and sprayed different products from different bottles and tubes and tubs onto my face. But looking at my reflection, I didn't look made up at all. My eyes looked bigger, and their color seemed almost fake, but there were no obvious lines of shadow or liner. My skin was also smooth and silky, without any telltale tan lines from sunshades or splotchiness from lack of sleep. I was me, but a better-rested, digital color version of myself.

"Wow," I said. "I can't believe you did this. I can't believe I look like this!" I touched my dewy cheeks with my fingertips. "You are really good, Del. Heck, this is as much a Gift as anything. You could be a makeup artist."

Delia swatted my hand from my cheek. "Thanks!" A smile crossed her face for half a second before turning dark. "There's no way anyone in Brooklyn would ever let me touch them. But it means something to hear you say that."

"Yikes!" I gasped, looking at the clock. "I gotta throw on my clothes! Jack will be waiting on me."

I turned and pulled my navy duffel bag closer to where I was sitting. I unzipped it and took out my favorite pair of jeans and a white tank. It wasn't dressy, but I knew that it looked good on me, making my tanned skin glow. Delia raised an eyebrow at the outfit.

"What?" I asked. But I knew what. She didn't have to say it. She didn't like what I had picked out to wear. "We aren't going anywhere fancy. Marco's, is all," I said, feeling defensive. I considered it my "nice" outfit because the jeans weren't too faded and the crisp whiteness of the tank still looked fresh and not worn out.

"It's not that anything's wrong with that outfit," Delia said, her voice taking on the affected squeaky tone she got when she was trying not to hurt my feelings. "In fact, that tank and jeans look great on you."

"So what's the problem?"

"Well. That's something you would wear on a third or fourth date. Or hanging out with a boyfriend. You need to wear something hot tonight."

"Well. This will have to do unless you think I should wear my Scooby Doo pajama pants, because that's the only other thing in my bag." I knew where this was going. The look on Delia's face as she slid off the bed and headed toward her zebra striped suitcase, told me everything I needed to know. She had planned on dressing me from the beginning.

I sighed.

"Good thing you have me! I have the perfect outfit," she exclaimed, pulling out a tiny turquoise swatch of material.

"What is that?" The garment in my sister's hands didn't look like enough fabric to cover my butt.

"Don't be dramatic. It's a sundress. I got it forever ago when Rebecca took me shopping in Jackson. I never got the chance to wear it. Besides, it's kind of long on me. I think with your extra inch, it'll hit you right. And I have the heels to go with it," my sister said in a way that a superhero would say, "it was nothing ma'am. All in a day's work."

I slid out of my shorts and t-shirt and pulled Delia's tiny frock over my head. "Jeez! Delia! You can see my bra!"

"Good grief, Tully. You aren't supposed to wear one. It's not like you have huge knockers."

I hesitated, and then I unhooked my bra. With a maneuver that required the kind of acrobatics seen at the circus, I removed it without having to take off the dress. I picked back up the handheld mirror and angled it so I could look myself up and down. I had to admit. I did look good. Really good, in fact.

"What do you think?" I asked my sister, striking a pose.

"Now you're ready for a first date with a hunk." She winked.

I rubbed the thin material of the sundress, a little concerned about going braless, and hoping it wouldn't be cold in the restaurant. I grabbed my Ole Miss hoodie from the back of the rocking chair and slipped it over my shoulders.

Delia shook her head. "Hopeless."

***

Fifty-five minutes later, Jack and I were pulling into the parking lot at Marco's in Peachton. The sun had set an hour before, but the crowded parking lot was well lit as both couples and families scuttled to and from their cars. Marco's was a local favorite in a town that didn't boast many decent restaurants.

I hope Logan called ahead so we aren't stuck standing around, making awkward conversation while waiting on a table.

"Can you make one more loop around the lot?" I asked Jack, clutching the door handle of the truck, not yet ready to open it.

At the last minute I had begged Delia to ride with us to drop me off, but she had insisted on staying at Grandma's so she could cover for me on the off chance my grandparents woke up. I'd given in because of the panic I had seen hiding in her eyes. She hadn't gone any farther than a relative's house since the attack and that look had told me she was nowhere near ready. I had been a little worried about going out at night myself. But the only time I'd be alone would be the short walk from Jack's truck to the always crowded restaurant. *Even then, my cousin would have eyes on me.*

"Sure," Jack said. He stopped to let a family cross in front of the truck. "Tully, listen, if you don't want to go, that's fine. If anyone understands being nervous, it's me. Hell, the only time I don't think I'm nervous is when I'm pissed about something. But you gotta know, you look beautiful. If you don't go for it, then in a year or two when Trudy and co. have you married off to some Poindexter, you'll always wonder. You don't have to get out of the truck." He smiled at me. "But you really should."

I leaned over to hug him. "Thanks Jack. I really needed to hear that." I took a deep breath, opened the door, and hopped out. I adjusted Delia's turquoise dress, straightened my shoulders, and started walking to the door with a death grip on my purse. Half way to the entrance, doubt seeped in, and I turned and ran back to the truck.

"Don't leave until I come back and wave to you," I said. I turned to leave again, this time making it only three steps before another thought invaded, sending me back. "Also, I know that—"

"Tallulah," Jack interrupted, "turn and march your tail into that restaurant!"

"Right." I shut the truck door, and this time managed to make it into Marco's.

A quick scan of the eatery told me that Logan sat at a corner table, so I waved to Jack and with a quick "beep beep" on the horn, he pulled away.

Marco's was a staple in Peachton, and I had been here with my family a handful of times, mostly for lunch. It was smallish with low ceilings that pulled off the ambiance of intimacy rather than feeling cramped. The tables were all covered with red checkered tablecloths and designed to seat four people at the most. In the center of every table rested an old wine bottle, some holding an arrangement of dusty, fake flowers, while others a single candle.

I made my way toward where Logan sat in the corner, thankful that

Delia had given in and let me wear flats. I was scared of passing out anyway, and the strappy heels she'd insisted "made" the outfit wouldn't have bode well.

Logan was fidgeting with what looked like some kind of MP3 device. *That guy loves music*, I thought, remembering the first time I saw him at Myrtle's.

He had still not looked up when I pulled my chair out to sit down. EEEEEK, the wooden legs scraped against the concrete floors.

Logan, along with everyone else in Marco's, jerked toward the sound, while I blushed hot with embarrassment underneath my sister's handiwork.

"Sorry," I mumbled. Logan jumped up and stepped behind my chair, pushing it in as I sat down.

"Wow," he said quietly, looking into my eyes. Something I wasn't sure I could ever get used to. "You look amazing."

"Thanks," I managed.

Logan looked pretty amazing himself. He wore jeans and flip-flops, but his black V-neck tee was fitted, showing off the cut and curve of lean muscle. His chin length hair was loose and parted in the middle, falling in shiny, dark waves that framed sharp cheekbones.

"So. Here we are," I said, fighting the urge to bite my lip or drum my fingers on the table.

"Don't be nervous," Logan said. He reached across the table and touched the back of my hands. "Relax. Friends having dinner. That's all. Nothing you'll get in trouble for."

He had no idea.

I frowned. "Logan, I wish that were true. You don't understand," I sighed. "And I can't expect you to."

"I want to. Why don't you help me? Start from the beginning," he waved at me to tell my tale.

I considered it for a minute, and Delia's advice ran through my mind. "Why don't you tell me about yourself first," I suggested.

"Well, what do you want to know?"

"I don't know. What do you do? Where are you from? That sort of thing, I guess." I slumped forward a little in my chair.

"Good start." He smiled. "I teach music—musical history and

guitar, over at the arts school about an hour away in Brookhaven. I rent an apartment here in Peachton because it's an hour closer to where my mom lives in New Orleans. My family moved a few times while I was growing up, but we lived in New Orleans longer than anywhere else, so it's home."

"That must be amazing."

"Yeah. New Orleans is awesome. Especially if you're a musician," he beamed.

"No. I meant to move around. I'm sure New Orleans is great too, but I've always lived in the same place. Nothing ever changes," I said, and then added, "for the better, anyway."

"Well, you know, you can change that. Go see the world. Hell, it doesn't have to be permanent. Go off to college or join a volunteer group or something."

"Gosh no!" I blurted out. The way his brow scrunched made me add, "I mean, I'm enrolled to start classes over at the community college in the fall. But leave? No. I couldn't do that."

True, I had always dreamed of leaving. Of taking off, but it was called a dream for a reason. I knew it would never really happen. Leaving the safety of Vigour terrified me. The thought of being sick…Or worse.

I shuddered.

Logan raised his eyebrows. "You know, I don't understand why you wouldn't want to leave. From what I gather, everybody in that crappy town treats ya'll like dirt. That's no way to live."

"Why should *we* leave? We've been there as long as they have." My Pawpaw's words ran from my mouth. "Longer even!"

"I don't mean everyone. I'm talking about you. The world, hell, the state, is a big place. And most people are nice, believe it or not. I'm saying why stay in a place that has nothing good for you."

"I don't expect you to understand," I said, bringing the conversation back to its beginning. "It's complicated." I looked down. "Very complicated."

"You keep saying that. Why don't you try me? I can't understand if you don't give me a chance." He paused. "But if you don't want to, that's okay. I was only hoping to know you better."

I thought for a moment. I had always chosen my words carefully the few times I talked with an outsider concerning family business. But Logan wasn't Myrtle Delacroix, and the thought of having someone to unburden myself with was as enticing as it was terrifying.

"Ok," I said. "You want to know? I'll fill you in. If you keep asking around, you're going to hear a lot of garbage, anyway, so I guess it's better to get it straight from the source. Um. I've never really had to talk about this before, so cut me a little slack."

"I upset you," Logan said frowning.

"No. It's not you. You're right. I keep saying it's complicated. There's no telling what you think." I eyed him warily. "Like I've said, I've never talked to anyone outside of my family about this and it feels kind of like I'm betraying their trust. I know that's dumb, but it's how I feel and I can't help it."

"I don't want to start out by asking you to do something wrong. If there is even a chance of something starting here, I don't want it to begin by upsetting your family," Logan said. He rubbed the back of my hands with his thumb, the simple gesture sending shocks.

"See. It's not even that simple." I sighed. "Being here. Eating dinner. Not being at home in bed, that's enough to betray them. I'm not supposed to do any of this." I gestured to the surrounding room and frowned.

"Tallulah, you're twenty-one years old, right? What are you guys? Like a cult or something?" he asked.

His words stung.

"That's still too simple," I snapped.

"Ok, then," Logan leaned back in his seat.

We sat awkwardly, sipping our glasses of water and nibbling on pieces of garlic bread from the basket on the table.

"Look," I said, making a decision, "I'm going to fill you in on everything. All of it. You can take it, leave it, or not believe it."

Logan looked at me, eyebrows raised and mouth held in a tight line. I didn't blame him for not saying anything. This first date could probably win an award for the most drama ever.

I was relieved when at that moment, a scrawny, tow-headed waiter came to take our order. I took a deep breath and pretended to look at the menu. I had always gotten the same thing the handful of times I'd eaten at Marco's, but I wanted tonight to be different, even if it was only one night. Logan asked about the shrimp scampi so I went wild and ordered it as well. The gangly waiter jotted down our order onto his note pad and disappeared.

"Ok," I took another deep breath and started again. "My family is Gifted. Not like, smart kids gifted, but we can do things. And there are others too. Not near as many as there are normal people, but still, there are a good number of us scattered across the country."

Logan opened his mouth to speak, but it was my turn to shush him. I held a finger in the air. "Let me finish, then if you want, you can run off screaming about the crazy lady," I stuck my chin out, motioning to the door, "Lord knows, no one would blame you."

He nodded and closed his mouth.

"Our Gifts are why everyone treats us like crap. It's why we don't go to normal school, or go away to college. It's also why we don't date. Well, we don't date normal people. We're set up to court others who are Gifted. It's odd, I know. That part is odd even to me!"

Elbows on the table, hands steepled under his chin, he leaned in. "Ok. Wow," Logan said evenly. "So tell me about these 'Gifts'."

I had expected him to laugh. Smirk. At least smile or something. Maybe even attempt one of his terrible jokes. I had prepared myself for these reactions.

My breathing hitched in my chest. Part of me had wanted him to think me insane. To get up and leave me sitting alone at the table while he made a run for it. It would have made things simpler. I knew how to handle being the "crazy" woman, and it wasn't half as terrifying as the idea of putting my trust in him.

"Well," I cringed, hating what I was about to say, "it's kind of like, for lack of a better word, magic."

Again, I waited for the laughter. Instead, Logan nodded, encouraging me to continue, and I realized that while part of me may have wanted him to bolt, mostly I really, really wanted to trust him.

I took a sip of my water to wet my dry throat. "So there's my Grandma. Hers is the most important Gift. It's called Vigour, and it's pretty rare. Death and sickness are slower in her presence. She even ages slower. It drives my Mama crazy that Grandma has fewer wrinkles than she does. She's also why our fruit trees are able to produce all year, and why our produce stand never has to close for the season."

I plunged ahead, afraid that if I gave Logan one second of a chance, I'd get that laugh or snide comment I'd been waiting on earlier. "Speaking of Mama, she can talk to birds. Crows are the chattiest, always gossiping and getting on her nerves. Daddy can call down the weather. He's been known to shield the town from a few close calls with tornados. My sister Delia, and also my cousin Jack, are Charmers. With a little eye contact they can convince anybody of anything." I paused, looking down to my hands and smiling. "When we were little, Delia was always stealing candy. If a store clerk saw her, she'd smile at them straight in the eye, and they would smile back, letting her take whatever she wanted. It's also the reason Myrtle is so scared of her, but that's a story for another time. I have a cousin who can see two minutes into your future simply by touching you, and an Aunt who can—"

I stopped talking, suddenly aware that Logan was staring at me, open-mouthed. "Look, I know it sounds crazy. I do. But I swear I'm telling you the truth."

He nodded.

Here it comes, I thought, suddenly aware of how much his rejection would sting. I'd shared too much. Now it felt personal.

"I didn't say that I think you're lying. It's…It's a lot. What about you? What's your Gift, Tallulah?" He asked, straight-faced. The look made me suspicious, fearful the skepticism was coming.

I sighed.

"Mine isn't that clear cut. But it's another reason on quite a long list of why this has to be our one and only date."

Logan narrowed his eyes. "That I don't understand. If I said that I believe what you're saying, then why couldn't we at least have a chance at getting to know each other? Let's say that I bought into all this," he swept his hand around the table, "That I believe you come from some kind of motley band of rural superheroes, then why would I need to stay away? I would know what I was signing up for."

I smiled. *Motley band of rural superheroes…*

"You believe me?" I asked. The possibility never occurred to me, not really. I had never, not once even imagined he would believe me at face value. I mean, I'd hoped it. *Really hoped.* And I knew he would hear the rumors, but to an outsider they would sound like small town legend. It was actually something my family had counted on over the years. One of the ways we remained hidden in plain sight.

Logan shrugged. "I think I do," he paused. "What if I told you I had my own secret? That there was something I never really talked about because it made *me* sound crazy?"

I stared at him, my eyes narrowing. What could he possibly have to say, after hearing about my family, that he wouldn't want to say for fear of sounding crazy? I think I had covered enough crazy for the both us.

His eyes widened a bit and he rubbed the back of his neck with one hand, a habit I was starting to find endearing. "With you, it's like it's out of my control. Like I'm being pulled toward you, like we're opposite poles on two magnets. And the crazy part is, I don't even care. It feels right and I want it more than anything. Don't get me wrong, I don't think it's because of your Gift, or anything like that. It's something I've lived with my entire life, this feeling, but it's never pulled me toward another person, before." He reached across the table and laced his fingers through mine. "I hope that doesn't sound creepy."

I froze. This was the best—and worst—possible thing he could ever say to me. That he wanted me. That he was pulled toward me and it was out of his control.

Because maybe it was.

I should have gotten up and left. In good conscious, it was the only option I had. Because if Logan didn't have a choice, if he was wrong and I was calling out to him, tethering him to me through Suggestion, or maybe even Reflection, then that made Reverend Armstrong's accusations true. If I held onto this man by means of my Gift, I was a monster. Evil, and deserving of the reputation that clung to my family. *Never use your Gifts against outsiders.* The most important rule. I wouldn't break it. Not on Logan.

Like everyone else in the Somersby Caibre clan, after my birth I'd been swaddled and carried to see our Familiar. My Grandma's brother, Great-Uncle Louis, had held my tiny body in his calloused hands and called out to my Gift where it lay hidden, soft as a whisper, deep inside my brand new soul.

"Suggestion," he'd said. "It's not the easiest Gift. Many unknowns, but it's hers just the same."

And he hadn't been lying. In my twenty-one years, there hadn't been one time my Gift had proved useful. And now, when I wanted...no, needed something to be real, Suggestion was deciding to make its appearance. Slipping out and uncurling inside of the first man that ever cared to know me.

No. I couldn't be with Logan if it was based on my Gift.

I wouldn't.

"This..." I sighed and pulled my fingers away from his, instantly grieving the loss of his touch. "This is a bad idea."

"But why? You still haven't answered my question. At least do that," he pleaded. "If your Gift is the reason that we can't be together, shouldn't I at least be allowed to know what it is?"

"I guess maybe you should," I said. "It's called Suggestion. I can put an idea in someone's head and help it take root. It takes a while to work, supposedly. But I don't know for sure, since I haven't had a lot of practice using it. My Daddy is strict about us using our Gifts on outsiders. It's a huge no-no. But I think that maybe, somehow...if you feel like we are tied together..."

Logan grinned. It was the reaction I had expected all along, for him to think I was a nut job or pulling his leg. But that didn't mean it didn't hurt. It did.

"It's true, Logan! I know what it sounds like, I do, but I am not lying!"

"That's not why I'm smiling, Tallulah. I'm not laughing at you. It's that...you. You think the reason I like you is because you somehow bewitched me. And on some level maybe you have, but not in the way you think." He again grabbed my hands, this time lifting them to his lips.

"Then how else could you explain it? You said you felt like you were being pulled to me. Like you couldn't help it."

"I also said that I didn't care."

"But how do I know that isn't because of my Gift? What if it wears off and one day you resent me because this whole time you were trapped!"

Logan chuckled. "First off, take a breath. Second, what I'm about to tell you I've never talked about with anyone. Well, anyone other than my Gram or sister. It's crazy, but somehow, I think you'll understand."

I sighed. "Ok." I knew that whatever he was going to say wouldn't matter, but at the same time, I prayed somehow it would. That he had some secret miracle he was about to impart on me that would make everything better. Because even though I had only known Logan a short while, I knew that pull he was talking about. There was no reason on Earth I should feel as strongly about someone I had only just met, especially when it was the same old Romeo and Juliet song and dance. Forbidden love never worked out well for anyone involved. Not really.

"I grew up mostly in New Orleans, like I told you. But my Dad took off when I was young, leaving my Mother, Gramm, and me and my little sister alone. Mother worked all the time to keep food on the table and clothes on all of us. She waitressed at two places and cleaned offices on Sundays. Gramm watched me and Sheila and did some ironing for people. There wasn't any extra, but there was always enough, even when on paper there shouldn't have been. Gramm said we were blessed with Chans. It means 'chance' or 'luck' in her Haitian Creole."

I cleared my throat and said, "Your Mom and Gramm sound like amazing hard working women."

"They are. But that's not it."

I edged slightly forward in my seat, eager for Logan to continue his story.

"Lots of people make do with what they have, right? But we always managed to do a little better than we should have. My Gramm was able to get us a decent place in our almost-non-existent price range in New Orleans. Later, me and Sheila got scholarships to Catholic school, and let's say that my little sister has never been a straight A student. There was always enough for Christmas gifts and medical bills. But I was a kid and didn't think much of it. Later, when I moved out, is when I noticed things didn't work out for everyone like they did for us. Most people in our situation had struggled a lot more. Later, we realized that our lucky charm, whatever it was, liked me, in particular."

Chans. I thought, rolling my mind around the word as Logan continued.

"It started when I had to pick a college. My grades in high school were good but not great. Between working part time to help out and playing little weekend gigs, I didn't devote a lot of time to the books. I was totally prepared to go to a community college first, but something kept nagging me to apply to Loyola's music program. I ignored it, but it wouldn't leave me alone. So I filled out the application and then put it out of my head. Two weeks later when they called me for an audition, and after that, accepted me into their program, I was a little surprised. But when they offered me scholarship for tuition, plus room and board, I knew there had to be more to the Chans than my crazy old Gramm telling stories. After that I made sure and pay attention to that feeling. It was like a little tug, pulling me along. It guided me through what professors to take and what jobs to apply for. Hell, after graduation, I was pulled to apply for the teaching job at the arts school. They never take first year teachers, ever. But I followed the Chans, even though I was certain it was a mistake. Needless to say, I got the job and have been happy there ever since."

My stomach fluttered with his news. It wasn't that I thought he was Gifted or anything, no way, but maybe there was something there. Some tiny spark that could offer an explanation as to why I felt like I was supposed to know this man. A reason that I was compelled to risk hurting the people who loved me more than anything by sneaking out, even though tragedy had landed in our laps only days before. Why this sudden attraction didn't scare me more than it did.

I realized the look on my face must have betrayed what I was thinking, and tried to tone it down.

Logan shrugged. "I wish I could explain it better. That I could say I came from some family that had powers or my Gramm was some kind of voodoo priestess, or that I had fallen in Holy Water when I was a kid, but I got nothing. All I can tell you is, every single time I have followed that feeling, the Chans, things have worked out for the best."

The flicker of hope again tried to light within me, but I wouldn't let it. Even though I wanted too. *Really wanted too.* I couldn't. "But you're not one of us. You don't have the eyes, the feel." It came out sounding harsher than I had meant.

"No, maybe not. But my whole life I've been guided. Led. Drawn to certain things. That's not exactly normal, is it? I may not have some hocus pocus lineage, but that doesn't mean that what I'm telling you isn't real. Believe me, Tallulah...please." Logan squeezed my hands and looked me in the eyes. "It's why I stopped in at that god-forsaken diner in the first place. I was speeding down the highway, heading home after a faculty meeting, and I felt the tug. And then I met you and I knew you were the reason. The pull was instant. The thing is, Tallulah, I may have been led my entire life, but never, not once, has the Chans drew me to another person." He paused, and then whispered, "So you see, I know I was meant to find you. It's not your Gift, Tallulah, but mine. It may not be a Gift like what your family has. It may not be anything but dumb luck, but for me, it's enough."

Heat crept up my neck as we sat in silence for a moment. My mind spun at the possibilities. *What is he saying?* The feeling he was talking about, the Chans, it sounded like as much a Gift as anything. But there was no way...*was there?* My kind was accounted for. Even though I'd never seen them, I knew there were books, and now hard drives, devoted to keeping track of who belonged to what family and who was born with what Gift. *But just because I've never heard of a Gift like the Chans, doesn't mean it isn't a Gift...does it?* It was too much, the idea that there may be people like us that we didn't know about. I took a deep breath and steadied my thoughts.

Do I really believe that Logan is Gifted? No. I can't. But if what he said was true, he wasn't exactly normal, either.

I suddenly realized I had been staring at Logan with my mouth hanging open.

"What are you thinking?" he asked.

"I'm not sure. I mean, I believe you." I forced a nervous chuckle. "I guess maybe I'm not used to being on the receiving end of that kind of news."

Logan nodded, pushed his chair back, and stood up. He walked around the small table and pulled me to my feet. I glanced quickly around the eatery but no one seemed to be watching us. I was used to snide remarks and sideways stares; it was hard to shake off the feeling of being the center of unwanted attention.

"I hope I didn't freak you out." He laced his arms around my waist. Without thinking, I leaned into the slight embrace.

"No. I hope I didn't freak *you* out," I answered.

In response, he pulled me closer.

"Tully. You're not going to run me off. The town's people are not going to run me off. The only way that I am out, is if you absolutely want me to be." He tightened his hold around my waist. My head fit nicely under his chin as he squeezed me. He slid his arms from my waist to my hair and I looked up to see him looking down at me.

"Tully?"

"Hmm?" I murmured.

"What's wrong? You're shaking like a leaf," he whispered.

"Nothing. Nothing at all," I said. I meant it, because in that moment, everything felt right. My family, our town, the guy I would be meeting the next evening thanks to Aunt Trudy, none of it mattered.

"So…May I kiss you?"

His hand wound through my hair, twirling my strands through his fingers. The smile on his face turned devilish.

My heart raced. Did I want him to kiss me? *Yes.* The idea of his lips on mine turned my insides to putty. But I was twenty-one years old and had never been kissed, a milestone most girls got out of the way before junior high. So while I wanted him too—really wanted him too, in fact—I was terrified. Again my eyes skittered around the room. It was getting closer to closing time, and the few people still scattered throughout the restaurant were nowhere near us, and engrossed in their own conversations.

"Um. Okay," I whispered. I nodded my head, pulling my hair on the twirls and loops that spun through Logan's fingers. "Ow!"

"Oh! I'm sorry," Logan said. "Here. Let me…" He worked to untangle his hand, pulling my hair even more. I reached back to help remove my now knotted strands. He pulled his fingers free and I rubbed my sore head.

"That's what I get for trying to be smooth." Logan tone turned sheepish.

"Ahem…Excuse me." A shrill voice interrupted us just in time. Our waiter had returned with our food.

I sat down and pulled the hairband off my wrist. I wound my hair into a ponytail, glad for something to do while I gathered my thoughts and willed away the hot blush from my face. Plates clinked down onto the table between us, the mouthwatering aromas of seafood, white sauce, and pasta drifting up from them.

"This looks great," Logan noted.

"Do ya'll need anything else?" The waiter squeaked.

"I think we're good."

With a quick nod of his head, the waiter scurried away.

"So," I said.

I had bared my soul to Logan and he had confessed things to me that anyone else would think were crazy. The moment had been tender and intimate. Now, with heaping plates of steaming pasta in front of us, I had no idea what to say.

"So," Logan answered.

He wiggled his eyebrows and took a big bite of his pasta.

I scrambled to think of something to fill the silence. "You said your Gramm is from Haiti?"

"Ah, you caught that. Yes. Gramm was born in Haiti. She moved to the States when she was eleven."

I chased a shrimp around my plate with my fork, kind of wishing I'd gotten the ravioli. *What if he tries to kiss me again? I'll have shrimp breath. Please let there still be some gum left in the pack.*

"That's really cool," I said.

"You know Tallulah. It's okay if you ask me."

"Ask you what?"

"You know," he said. "Or if you want to guess, then that's okay too." He rested his chin on his hands, turning from some kind of romance-novel-sex-god into the mischievous boy who had written a check for a single tomato.

"Um. I really don't." Thoughts raced through my head. *Had I said something to cause the conversation to take a left turn?* Because I was lost as a goose.

"My Gramm is from Haiti. But I'm not black. I'm not white either. It's fine for you to ask. It kind of cracks me up that people get so nervous and tiptoe around it. I've heard the question phrased so many different ways. 'What's your ethnicity? What race do you belong to? What's your heritage?' Everyone means well, but they're so worried about offending me. Why should I be offended by who I am? My personal favorite is asked by kindergarteners and little old ladies alike. The simple, but effective, 'What color are you?'" He laughed, putting me at ease.

It was true that with his black hair, light brown skin, and green almond shaped eyes he could blend in with any number of groups of people.

And it *had* crossed my mind, even if for only for a brief second.

"Ok," I hesitated, "If you really want me too. Then I will have to go with…What's your ethnicity?"

Logan grabbed his heart and threw his head back. "I'm crushed!" he cried. "You could have gone with my favorite!"

The few remaining couples in the restaurant looked over to our table, and without thinking, I slouched down in my chair. "Ok, ok. Fine," I said. "What color are you? And you'd better not say purple or orange or something because that's not funny, Logan!"

"You're cute when you're embarrassed," he said. "My Dad was…is Navajo. I haven't seen him since I was a kid, but I don't think he's dead. Mother's biracial. You know my Gramm is from Haiti, and her husband was blonde with freckles. I never knew him. He died when Mother was a baby. But Gramm says that I have his eyes."

"That must have been hard for your grandparents. To be a mixed race couple back then," I said.

"I guess. They were adults and they loved each other. They made it work. I think Mom had a harder time of it when she was growing up. It wasn't like it is now. I don't think she had many friends as a kid. She told me before that when she was little, she never felt like she really fit in with any particular group." His look turned serious. "It's a big reason why I got so offended when I thought your parents wouldn't let you date me because of my skin color. It's an old hurt. Not for me, but for my Mom. And nothing cuts you deeper than a slight against your mother."

I nodded. I understood hate and not fitting in, albeit in a different way.

Prejudice was an ugly thing, and unfortunately, it was still alive and well. I'd been fighting it my entire life, only for me, it wasn't based on the amount of melanin in my skin, or what country my ancestors came from. Being magic, especially in Brooklyn, Mississippi, was more than good enough reason for a healthy dose of good old-fashioned discrimination.

We finished our meal without any more deep discussion. Logan paid our waiter and we walked hand in hand through the parking lot. We were standing beside Jack's truck when I had an idea.

"I want to try something," I said.

Logan raised one eyebrow at me and smirked.

"No!" I said, instantly embarrassed, "Nothing like...no, not that!"

Logan threw his head back and laughed. "I'm playing with you. I don't think I've ever met someone who blushes so easily."

"I knew that!" I fished to the bottom of my purse and pulled out the half-used pack of Kleenex. "You want to see our Gifts in action?"

"Um, sure. But I already told you I believe you. You don't have to prove anything to me."

"I know. But I think this might help you understand a little better."

"Okay, then."

"Great," I said. "Now, whatever you do, don't give these to Jack. No matter what he says or how he asks, you hang on to them."

Logan shrugged. "If you say so, Tully."

He slid the packet into the front pocket of his jeans. I turned to open the truck door and start my little experiment, when Logan grabbed my hand. He slid his arm around my waist, pulling me in close. Before I could panic, before I could get nervous, and even before my heart had time to race off into the sprint that Logan's touch usually sent it on, he leaned down and pressed his lips to mine.

Surprised, my body went rigid before relaxing into the embrace.

Logan pulled away and looked at me, his face full of question.

I smiled and with the slightest motion, nodded my head. He again pressed his lips to mine, this time using his mouth to coax open my own, kissing me in a way I had only read about in the romance novels I kept hidden in the top of my closet. I closed my eyes, letting what felt natural take over.

The shrill "beep" of Jack's truck horn pulled us apart. My first—and second—kiss was over. I cleared my throat and smiled up at Logan, feeling clumsy as the outside world rushed to fill the vacuum we had briefly created.

I took the last few steps to the truck and pulled open the door.

"Heeeey you two! I guess the date went well," Jack said, his arms crossed over his chest. He was smiling like someone who had the power to embarrass. Which he totally did.

"Shut it, Jack!" I said, to which Jack waggled his eyebrows up and down.

"Hey. I'm just the chauffer. Don't mind me." He still wore the stupid grin, and I knew the teasing wouldn't stop anytime soon. But it was so worth it.

"Listen, Jack," I added, ready to change the subject, "I told Logan that whatever he did to not give you what was in his pocket. He needs a little proof, I think."

"You sure, Tully?" Jack asked, but I knew he loved an opportunity to show off. My cousin was a living contraindication. Shy unless he was mad. Reserved, unless a moment arose that he could really ham it up.

"Yeah. Go ahead." I nodded.

I stood to the side, so Logan could see my cousin. And more importantly, so my cousin could see him. Jack caught Logan's eye.

"Hey man! We met at the fruit stand, remember?" Jack asked.

The intoxicating feeling of good rolled off him, and I closed my eyes, letting the magic wash over me. Jack and Delia were both Christmas. They both lived in their own clouds of good tidings and cheer, but they were each unique in their magic. Delia's was sweet gingerbread and pies, baking and carols. Jack was fresh cut Christmas trees, crisp air, and a fire crackling in the fireplace. I took a deep breath, enjoying the sensation. Even though I wasn't looking in his eyes, I could feel the run-off of his magic as it permeated the air. It wasn't overpowering, like it would be for the person caught in his gaze, instead it was slight. Nice.

I held my breath for a few seconds before letting it out. I looked over at my date, who was standing relaxed, with his shoulders slightly rounded, and leaning minutely toward Jack.

"Yeah. Hey!" Logan said. "Thanks for giving Tully a ride. I really like your cousin."

His words made me smile, even though I knew the second part was probably meant for me to hear.

"Listen, man. I need a favor," Jack said. "Can you give me whatever it is you have in your pocket right there? That would really help me out."

"Um, I don't know," Logan said.

His face scrunched up, brows pulling together. I could tell he really wanted to make Jack happy, but for some reason he knew he shouldn't.

Jack leaned in a little closer. "Come on, dude." His gaze was doing its thing, reaching into Logan's eyes and massaging his mind.

Logan sighed and pulled out the tissues. He held them in his hand for a moment, and then tossed them to my cousin.

"Thanks Jack!" I said, slamming the truck door, and severing the tie Jack had created.

I turned to Logan, arms crossed and eyebrows raised.

"That is the weirdest thing that has ever happened to me," Logan mumbled. "And one time at Mardi Gras I got mugged by a cross-dresser in a pirate costume—so that's saying a lot." He shook his head, clearing the fog.

I would have to remember to ask him about the pirate.

"Now do you understand? Exactly what we are and what we can do? It's more than a feeling for my kind." My doubt about Logan's ability crept into my words. I hoped he hadn't caught it. *If he can believe me, then I'll believe him.*

Logan touched the side of my face, carefully. "I'm good with that. It doesn't scare me. Go out with me again. Tomorrow?"

"I can't." I wanted to. I wanted to more than anything, but I had my date with the match.

"Why not?" Logan asked.

I sighed. "Like I said in the beginning. It's complicated." I opened the door and jumped into the truck. "Come and see me at the fruit stand on Monday and we'll figure something out."

Shutting the door for me, he grinned and nodded. I put my hand on the windowsill and his fingers brushed across the top of mine, the simple touch sending sparks through me. My eyes locked onto his as we began to pull away.

As Jack drove us toward home, my mind wandered to ways I could get out of meeting my match, and I daydreamed not of escaping to a new place, but of living in a world where Logan and I could be together. One where it wouldn't be impossible to have him *and* my family.

"Be careful," Jack said next to me.

I turned to face my cousin, who glanced in my direction every few seconds.

"Oh. Why's that?" I inquired.

"Because I know that look, Tully. And I don't want anyone else to get hurt."

Chapter Fourteen

The next night, the same ritual of primping took place, only this time Mama, Grandma, and Aunt Trudy came to our house to "help" Delia get me ready. They were all buzzing around with enough excitement to camouflage my unhappiness.

Delia leaned close to my ear. "You're not cheating on Logan. You went on one date with the guy. Who's to say this one won't be even better?" she whispered to me as she yanked a flat iron through my already straight hair.

I tried to force a smile. Delia had listened eagerly the night before as I had filled her in on every detail of my date with Logan. I'd spent the night tossing and turning and second-guessing myself, as was evident by the amount of gunk Delia thought necessary to cover the raccoon circles under my eyes.

Since this date was approved—hell, it was provided— there would be no flirty little dresses. Delia shook her head, but said nothing when I pulled on my white tank and jeans.

"You aren't going to wear a skirt? Or sleeves?" Aunt Trudy croaked, appalled at the naked state of my shoulders.

"Nah. I'm good. This is supposed to be a match, right? Well, this is a nice outfit for me. Might as well be myself," I said, smiling because I knew neither Aunt Trudy nor Mama could argue with that. Grandma only chuckled. They were lucky I was wearing my "good" outfit. I had no desire to impress this guy.

I checked myself over in the dresser mirror. I looked good. Same make up as the night before, only tonight instead of letting my tresses hang loose, I pulled them into a high ponytail.

"You could have told me you were going to do that before I spent so much time on it," Delia complained.

I grinned. "Are you kidding? You made it so it falls perfectly, and my bangs look awesome."

She smiled back and shrugged as if it had been nothing. But it had been everything. The way she lit up and chatted while doing it was almost like the old Del. Seeing her happy made the entire night worth it.

I slid my feet into my flip-flops and led the group downstairs to wait for my match.

Fifteen long minutes later, Thomas's white pickup pulled in front of our house. Mama, Grandma, and Aunt Trudy crowded the window, falling over each other to peek through the blinds. Despite how I felt about the whole situation, I found I was peeking from a distance. When Thomas knocked, he gave them a wave, unfazed by the crazy vibes no doubt wafting to him from underneath our front door.

"Great, he's nice," I whispered to Delia, frowning. Blowing him off would have been much easier if he was a jerk. And blowing him off was exactly what I planned to do.

Delia poked me in the ribs. "Try and have a good time."

Mama opened the door, and there Thomas stood as relaxed as if he were visiting an old friend, instead of meeting the girl his family would have him marry. He was as handsome as his photo. His light brown hair curled over the tops of his ears, and carefully controlled magic danced in his eyes. A baby blue button-down showed off his broad shoulders, and tucked nicely into the trim waist of his boot cut jeans.

My feelings hadn't changed, and I didn't want to impress him; however, I couldn't help but think that maybe I should have listened to Delia and at least worn some jewelry.

Once inside, Thomas made little time in dazzling Mama and Grandma. His country boy smile worked wonders on them, and the fact that he thought Ole Miss football was better than State, "any day of the week," set him up as a good guy in Daddy's eyes.

"He's from Texas. What does he care about Ole Miss?" I muttered to Mama, rolling my eyes.

"Be nice," she said around her own toothy smile. "Your Daddy is from Oklahoma and he's an Ole Miss fan."

Yeah, but Daddy has lived here for as long as forever.

When Aunt Trudy grasped Thomas's large, rough hands in her own tiny wrinkled ones, he smiled at her and asked "You reading me?" Then added, "Well, I hope you like what you find," setting her at ease.

In the corner, I noticed Delia staring at him. When he looked over to where she sat, her cheeks reddened in a very un-Delia like way. She smiled a tiny, close-lipped smile and kept her eyes downcast. My sister was a lot of things, but shy had never been one of them.

"I'm Thomas," he said, walking past me and thrusting his hand out to shake hers. She tucked her hair behind her ears before offering her own hand.

"Delia," she mumbled. I simply stood there, recognizing the expression on my sister's face for what it was, certain I had worn a similar expression the night before.

This could be interesting.

Thomas held Delia's hand a moment too long. Before it could get awkward for either of them, I piped in, "Well. Ready to go Thomas?"

It took a while for his eyes to move from my sister to me. He smiled, but the tight line of his lips told me it was a little forced. So was his enthusiasm as he offered me his arm. "Sure thing."

***

The forty-five minutes it took us to drive to the Peachton Tinsel Time was spent in silence. I rolled around the idea of how to bring up the notion he and Delia would make a better pair, a fact I was certain he would agree on. The way his eyes lit up when he had crossed the room, passing me by to shake my sister's hand, had made it obvious. Delia had tried to hide it by averting her gaze, but the moment their hands touched, I knew there had to be the same electricity that sparked whenever I touched Logan. I *wanted* there to be sparks between them, if I was honest. Delia deserved that happiness, and it certainly didn't hurt my feelings. The second I met Thomas, I knew Logan was the one for me. There was no comparison. Sugar and salt.

We arrived at the theater, and Thomas went to get popcorn while I was tasked with finding us good seats. The movie we'd chosen was a comedy, which was perfect to me. No awkward romantic scenes or scary ones where I might accidentally grab onto him. Laughter was good. Laughter lightened the mood.

I chose two seats next to each other in the middle of the theater, not in the front where our necks would hurt, or in the back where he might think I wanted more privacy.

"I wasn't sure what kind you liked," Thomas said, returning with two large popcorns, two drinks, and four boxes of candy. I took my coke, a popcorn, and a box of Raisinettes.

"Wow, thanks," I said.

The lights dimmed and the movie started, taking away the pressure to talk. The theater had filled almost to capacity with a few random empty seats scattered around. Two next to each other remained in the middle of our row, so of course when a couple came in fifteen minutes after the movie began, that's where they decided to sit.

I don't know why, but this always bugged me. I had been to the movies maybe seven times in my life, and it always seemed like after it started, I ended up having to stand up to let someone shuffle in front of me. I sighed as they made their way up the steps to our row in the dim glow of the screen. It wasn't until I was face to face with the man in the couple, that I realized who it was. My stomach dropped.

"Tully?" Logan said, sounding as surprised as I felt. Everyone in the theater gave a loud, "SHH" in response.

"Hey Logan," I whispered, snapping my head from him to his date. Delia was right; we had only been out once. I mean, I was here with another person too, so I had no right to be upset. *Then why do I feel like someone punched me in the gut?*

Logan's date was petite, with the kind of cute, curvy figure that made me feel like a gangly ostrich. She had the same creamy light brown skin as Logan with dark curly hair that touched her waist. The girl was a knock out.

Logan glanced over to Thomas, who had stood up to let him and his date pass.

"Who is this?" Logan asked, getting evil stares from the moviegoers who wanted their money's worth without interruption.

Tears stung my eyes, and the truth, the unavoidable truth, sat in front of me. I was a joke. The fool with the weirdo family who actually thought a guy like Logan would want anything to do with me. I had even let him kiss me. That was probably what it had all been about. A bet to see how far he could get with the prude girl from the freak family. Everything he'd told me was probably a lie and I'd fallen for it. His girlfriend, the girl he really liked, was this perfect girl who was the physical opposite of me in every way.

I felt ill.

My eyes narrowed at him. "That's my date," I said, giving my words a good coating of the venom that was brewing inside of me.

Thomas stuck out his hand. "Nice to meet you," he whispered. Logan glared at the outstretched hand without taking it, and then back at me.

"Who is she?" I asked.

"She is Sheila. My sister. She stopped in for a surprise visit on her drive to see our mother in Louisiana," he answered. "Looks like it isn't so complicated after all, huh Tully?" he said, squeezing down the row to his seat.

His sister? I gasped and mumbled to Thomas, "I'm sorry. I need to leave." I shoved my extra-large container of popcorn into his arms, grabbed my purse from under my seat, and bolted from the theater. I needed fresh air. Fast.

I made it out of the heavy glass and metal doors into the parking lot before the tears came. Leaning against the front of the building, not caring what I looked like or who was watching, I sobbed. Big, real sobs.

His sister! His flipping sister.

I hated that I was so bad at this, so inexperienced. I should have known better. But now I had ruined everything.

An older couple walked by and the wife asked, "Is everything alright, darling? Was the movie that sad?"

I wiped my cheeks and ignored them.

"I told you that movie was going to be a tear jerker, Bill. That's the one I want to see! I could use a good cry," the tiny woman said to her husband as they walked away.

Thomas came out of the doors shortly after. *Great*, I sniffled, *I am such an ugly crier. He's going to think he hit the damned jackpot tonight!*

I pulled a tissue from the pack in my purse and as I blew my nose, it occurred to me that I was bad at first dates. Really bad.

"Are you all right?" he asked.

I shrugged. "Can you just take me home, please?"

"Sure." He turned to walk away, before hesitating and turning back to me. He opened his mouth to say something, but changing his mind, closed it, and turned to leave a second time.

I continued to stare at the ground in a heaping, crying mess.

***

On the ride home, I tried to keep my tears quiet. Thomas, God bless him, sat in silence, not knowing what was going on, and too much of a gentleman to ask outright.

"Look, Tallulah," he said finally. "It's none of my business, but really. Are you okay? One minute we're going to see a movie, the next you're running out crying. Who was that guy anyway?"

I stifled a hiccup. "That was Logan. That's the guy that I went out with last night. Now he thinks I'm a complete bitch."

"Oh. Ok." Thomas said. "Can I ask you why you came with me tonight? Seems to me you really like that guy."

"I did. I mean, I do. He isn't Gifted. My parents don't know anything about him. God, this is so screwed up." I threw my hands in the air.

"I see. Well, what am I then?"

"You're my match."

Thomas nodded.

Now I sounded like a double bitch.

Logan was a lost cause, but maybe there was something I could do to make it up to Thomas. If I wasn't going to be happy, maybe I could at least help Delia to be. God knows, she needed a bit of happiness even worse than I did. I took a deep breath to calm myself and thought, *Screw it! The night can't get any worse.*

"Thomas? What do you think about my sister, Delia? I saw the way you looked at her. And if you knew my sister, you would know she never gets tongue-tied. Ever. Maybe you two should go out." I hoped I had not mistaken and added insult to injury. *I don't like you so why don't you go for my sister instead?* No. That wasn't what I meant.

To my relief, his eyes lit up.

"You think she likes me?" he asked. "But she isn't even twenty. There's no way your Daddy would go for it."

I thought for a minute. "I think she does. And her happiness means a lot to me. What if I get her to come to the produce stand with me tomorrow? You come to see 'me' and it'll give ya'll a chance to talk. Ya'll can decide for yourselves what you want to do. I'll fill her in so she knows what is going on." I thought about the plan. "We let out of church at ten, so don't come before that."

"You would do that?" Thomas asked.

He was smiling the goofy grin from his match photograph. It appeared much better on him than the polite smile he had been wearing when he'd walked through the front door to pick me up.

"Sure."

"You're kind of awesome, Tallulah. And again, it's none of my business, but you should talk to that Logan fella. Tell him what's going on. It was a misunderstanding is all. Maybe I could help you explain."

I glanced over at Thomas, who was staring straight ahead as he drove. Maybe I was crazy for passing him over, but one look at his smile told me that, in his eyes, I could never hold a candle to Delia. And in my heart, I knew he would never be right for me either. He had every quality that, on paper, I could want. He understood my family. He was handsome. He was polite. He was a hard worker. But he wasn't Logan. And I wasn't Delia. I knew I was making the right decision.

We sat for a while, listening to George Strait sing about his wife's problem with Tequila and losing her clothes. When the song ended, a horrible country-rap combo started playing.

"Gross," I said at the same moment that Thomas muttered, "terrible," and switched off the radio.

I giggled.

"So, I hear ya'll ain't treated too kindly out here," he said, changing the subject.

I shrugged.

"At least ya'll have Vigour. So that's something," he kept his hands firm on the wheel as he spoke.

"Yeah. It's my Grandma's Gift. I've never known anything else. It's my normal, I guess."

Thomas nodded. "Living near a Vigour would be great. I can't even imagine it," he said in his east Texas drawl.

"How do ya'll get on over in Orange Texas?" It was nice to talk about family with someone and not have to convince them I wasn't a liar, crazy, or evil. And not have to worry about what the consequences would be. Talking about such things with your match was expected. It's kind of the whole point, really.

"Just fine, I reckon," Thomas replied. "In a lot of ways we live the same as you all do."

"What do you mean?"

"Well, for one, we all live near each other. Not on the same piece of property, but within walking distance, or at the most a short drive away. My uncle, our matchmaker, said that ya'll homeschool. We do that, too. Through elementary anyway. I played football in junior high and high school at the Baptist academy." His eyes lit up. "Best time of my life."

"I bet that was awesome." I tried to picture that life. "But I can't believe a church school let you attend. Most of the churches around here don't care for us. They aren't all outspoken about it, but still, I don't think they would go out of their way to invite us into their congregation. And they'd probably have a conniption if we tried to show up for Sunday service." I thought for a moment. "It's like they think we have any kind of say in being Gifted. Like we're in cahoots with the devil because of the way we're born."

"I guess that would be one of our main differences, then," Thomas said.

"What?" I asked.

"We aren't 'out' to everyone."

"How's that work?"

"Pretty good. I admit it's not ideal, but I've never had to experience the kind of ugliness you're forced to deal with. And we learn control early on. We have to, or else we don't get to enroll in the junior high, so that's a pretty big motivator." He smiled. "And on account of the public schools in the area being shit, we aren't even seen as the crazy home schooling family. It's kind of the normal thing to do."

"That does sound great," I said wistfully. "Can I ask you something else?"

"Shoot," he said.

"How come your family stays together if you don't have a Vigour? What's the benefit? It sounds like you could do whatever you wanted."

Thomas' jaw tightened as if he were chewing on his tongue, thinking. "I suppose staying together is what we want. Our family had a Vigour generations back, so that may be why everyone put down roots near each another, originally. But now, we live close because we like each other, you know?" His puppy-dog grin widened. "It's *our* normal. Why? Would you leave if you could?"

"That's just it. I have no idea. I like to imagine I would, but living outside of Grandma's Gift even for a little while…" I shuddered. "The idea scares me."

"I think I can understand that. It's like Vigour is the ultimate Gift, but also a little like a curse. You can have a healthy life, but the trade-off is that you can never leave." He paused. "Unless."

"Unless what?"

"Unless you loaded up Granny and took her with you," he said with a laugh.

"Ha!" I snickered. "But then everyone's crops would die and my family would go broke! No thanks. I'm not going to be the girl that kidnaps her Grandma and causes her family to plummet into ruin!"

"See," Thomas said. "Curse."

We lapsed again into silence as the truck bumped down the road, taking us closer to home. Thomas clicked on the radio.

I clicked it off. "One more question."

"Go ahead."

"What about matching? And your family?"

"What about them?"

"Well, you're being matched, so ya'll must keep the traditions. But then again, you're twenty-three and you work off shore, so ya'll must not be as strict. Do you all pick and choose? I mean, how does that even work?" Again I tried to imagine his life, a different life.

Thomas laughed. "There's no big conspiracy, Tallulah! We keep the marriage traditions because it's easier. We're expected to be matched in our twenties; however, you can take time out for college, or in my case, to work. My sister Lynn, she's in medical school in Alabama. And if you want to know the truth, I think she works so hard because she wants to be left alone. It works too, because the idea of having a doctor in the family is enough to appease most of my relatives. But not Mama. Lynn is almost twenty-nine and my Mama is convinced there's no hope for her now." He chuckled. He was so easy to laugh. I liked that about him, especially since it sounded so genuine now that he had relaxed.

"And for the most part, we all have normal jobs too. Mama owns a home décor shop. Dad's a welder over at the refinery. Of course, his natural ability at shaping metal sure hasn't hurt his career any."

"Wow. Sounds like ya'll are pretty laid back about it," I said in awe. I was intrigued with this perfect fusion of a normal life and the old customs. "What about your sister?" I asked. "What's Lynn's Gift?"

"Birds. Same as your Mama's."

"You've researched us!" My mouth dropped open.

"Of course. I was coming to meet the girl I might've married."

I gulped and turned my face to the window. "Sorry about that."

"Naw. It's fine," he paused, "You really think Delia likes me?"

"All I can say is I've never seen her act like that before." *And after what had happened, I was scared I never would,* I added silently.

"Well now. This might be a good trip after all." Thomas pulled onto the road that ran to my driveway.

"How does your sister like it?" I asked. "The talking to birds, I mean?"

He grinned. "She lives right in driving distance of the beach, but she never goes because she says the gulls drive her bat-shit crazy!"

We both laughed. "That's horrible!"

Thomas flipped on his blinker, waiting for a car to pass, and then turned onto my gravel driveway. The rocks crunched under the tires of the lifted truck.

"This is good," he said. "I'm glad you're going to be walking in laughing. I hear that your Daddy can call lightening and I gotta say I wasn't looking forward to dropping you off all mopey and crying."

He parked in front of my house and we opened the truck doors at the same time.

"I wouldn't have let you take the blame," I assured him.

"Yeah. But still. This is better. Although we are, like, two whole hours early."

I shrugged. "Yeah, well, we couldn't help that the movie I wanted to see was sold out," I said smiling. "And that poor pitiful lil' me got all nervous about my very first date. You were a perfect gentleman and brought me right home." I opened my eyes wide and clasped my hands under my chin.

Thomas grinned. "You know something? You are one cool chic, Tallulah Caibre."

"Thanks."

We shuffled slowly toward the door. My "date" may not have been a real date, but I wasn't eager for it to end. It was fun to be out with someone new, even if it was just a friend.

The air was quiet and I realized Mama had kept her word about the crows. Light shown through cracks in the curtains, but no one was peering through, spying on us from inside the house, although I knew I would be quizzed the second I walked inside.

"One more question before we go in?" I asked.

"I wouldn't expect anything less."

"What about *your* Gift? What can Thomas from Texas do?"

He thought for a minute. "Don't move," he said, taking a few steps back, "and watch this."

I stood across from him in the semi-darkness as he clapped his hands and made a motion like he was throwing an invisible ball into the air. A second later, there was a bright orange and red circle of fire floating above his hand. He clapped four more times, and made a juggling motion, sending the fireballs in a circle. His tongue stuck out slightly from the side of his mouth as he concentrated.

"Wow." The fireballs glowed deep orange and beautiful against the darkness, never quite touching Thomas' hands.

"That's nothing," he boasted. "Get ready for the big finish."

Thomas continued his juggling act, and then, one at a time tossed the fireballs into the air. They flew high, and when the last one seemed to disappear into the night sky, he clasped his hands behind his back. Looking up, he opened his mouth, and one by one, the flames dropped from the sky and down his throat, disappearing with puffs of smoke. When he had swallowed the last one, he stretched his arms wide and bowed deep.

"Amazing!" I clapped my hands. "I've never met anyone that could control fire like that."

"Not all fire. I can make these little fireballs, and then absorb them back into myself. I can't walk through regular flames, or anything like that. It's kind of useless, but it makes for a neat trick."

"Better than mine."

"You got Suggestion, right?"

I nodded.

"That's not useless! I have a cousin with Suggestion. It might be slow going, but it really helps her with her business. She sells cars. Has a record year, every year."

"I guess that does work out good for her, but we don't use our Gifts on other people, so I have to keep it bottled up. I'm not even real sure what I would do with it, or even how I could use it."

"Yeah. Well, that's the problem. It's not your Gift, it's that you don't get to practice." He snapped his fingers.

"Maybe." Thomas walked me up the steps and to the door.

"Trust me, Tully, you're not useless. Only unpracticed is all." He placed a hand on my shoulder and squeezed. The touch didn't ignite the flames I had experienced from a single brush of Logan's finger, but instead, it filled me with a comforting warmth. The kind you get from being near a trusted friend.

I wrapped my arms around him in a big hug, like one I would give Jack or Daddy, and without hesitating, Thomas squeezed me back.

"Thanks for understanding," I said, "You know. About everything." I opened the door and led us inside.

It occurred to me later that hugging Thomas probably should have been at least a little awkward, as I'm not a hugger. But it wasn't. It felt natural. Maybe there was something to Aunt Trudy reading and matching people. Maybe me and Thomas fit each other fine, but not in the way that was planned.

Chapter Fifteen

That night, after everyone fell asleep, I went into my sister's room, and crawled into her bed. It was a ritual that had been common once upon a time in our childhood.

"Del, you asleep?" I whispered.

She rolled over, eyes wide open and shining. "So how did it go? You know, really?"

I frowned into the darkness. Everyone had plenty of questions for me when I had come home hours early, and I hadn't the opportunity to tell Delia the truth about the date. Me and Thomas had used my excuse about my nerves and the movie being sold out. I kind of think Grandma knew it was a lie, but she let it alone. When Thomas left, and the barrage of questions started, my answers had consisted mostly of "fine" and "it went well" or "he is very nice."

"Good and bad." I could feel tears sneaking into my eyes. "We ran into Logan. I thought he had a date with someone else. I was so bitchy to him, Delia, and it turns out it was his sister. So now *he* thinks I was on a date with someone else. The bad thing is I *was* on a date with someone else!" The tears started to fall. "I should have told him yesterday."

"I'm sorry, Tully. It's all my fault, huh?" Her voice was heavy.

"No. No, it's not. I asked for your advice," I swiped at my eye, "And I'm a big girl. I could have told him if I'd wanted."

"How was Thomas?" she asked, her tone hesitant.

"A real nice guy. Took all of my craziness in stride. He said he would even talk to Logan for me," I responded with a smile. "And he is so cute. Don't you think so?"

"Yeah. He's definitely good looking." Her rosy cheeks hinted at her true feelings.

"Delia, I had a talk with him. He's coming to the fruit stand on Monday morning."

"That's nice."

"Yeah. I told him it was the perfect time to get to know you better."

She sat up straighter. "What? What are you talking about?"

"Oh Delia, come off it! I saw it the minute you guys noticed each other. And then *kept* noticing each other. I don't think he would have dropped your hand if I hadn't chimed in," I rolled my eyes, "So please, come talk to him. You should have seen his face light up when I brought up the idea. He's got a crush, Del."

"But I was wearing leggings and a ratty sweatshirt. There's no way he's interested in me."

"Trust me. He most definitely is. So you going to come?"

"I want to. But...I can't," she squeaked.

"Why not? He's a really good guy. I'm probably crazy for not attempting to get to know him, but I can tell already I would never compare to you, not in his eyes. And he doesn't even know you yet. It could be love at first sight or something!"

"No. I *really* can't. He won't want me," Delia whispered.

"Are you crazy? Did you listen to a thing I said?"

"NO! I mean yes, but I can't. He won't want me." Her sharp inhale set my teeth on edge. She exhaled slowly. "Tully, I'm pregnant."

"What? No you're not!" I shot up in the bed and switched on the purple lamp that rested on Delia's nightstand.

The soft light of the forty-watt bulb enveloped us in a highlighted cave that cast a ghostly glow on my sister.

"Delia, you can't be pregnant. It has to be a mistake. It hasn't been long enough to even know," I babbled.

For all of our rules about dating and waiting, our Mama was very thorough when she gave us, "the talk." We never discussed sex in any form except for the sterile, clinical way you might read in a public school science textbook. And, at the time, it had been horrible. She had explained fact after humiliating fact to our eleven and thirteen-year-old selves, using words like vulva, penis, and insert. Words that would make any tween blush. She didn't just cover sex either. Because of the in-depth discussion—and several equally embarrassing follow up discussions—I knew you couldn't know for sure if you were pregnant until four weeks after finishing the deed.

So this had to be a mistake. It was simple as that.

Delia's shoulders shook as she sobbed silently.

There have been so, so many tears, I thought dully.

"No, Tully. I definitely am," she said casting a meaningful glance at her belly. "I was pregnant before I was raped."

I stared at my sister, wanting to hug her, but an agonizing numbness stole my ability to move.

"Before?" I asked. "But….with who?"

"This guy I met at a bar in Peachton," she waved it off. "And before you say anything, it's not like what it sounds. We had been seeing each other for over a month. And he was Gifted." She scrunched her face in distaste at the memory. "We noticed each other's eyes straight away. It's why we started talking. He could absorb sunlight to see in the dark later. Really weird gift, if you ask me. Said he was down visiting some friends. I should have known that was a lie."

"Does he know?" I asked, quickly followed by, "You went to a Bar?!"

"SHHH!!! Yeah, he knows." Anger spilled across her face. "As soon as I told him, I think he started planning on going back to Tennessee. Our next date after he found out, he told me he had talked to his Dad and been matched. That he was going home." She sighed. "I don't even think I have his real name, the creep. And it wasn't a *real* bar. It was Big Bob's Steaks and Ale. You know that cheesy restaurant? It's got a bar in the back."

My insides twisted at her story. "Who else knows?"

"Well, besides you, only Grandma."

Of course. Grandma would have known even before Delia.

"She understood me wanting to figure things out before telling Mama and Daddy. And then... Then I was raped. Geez. My life is so messed up!" Delia wrapped her arms around her legs and rested her chin on her knees.

I scooted toward her, and not knowing what to say, slid my arms over her shoulders. Things made sense, now. Her refusal to take the pills at the hospital, the baggy shirts and loose dresses she had been wearing, her not feeling well enough to work the fruit stand. It all seemed obvious, except that things like this didn't happen in my family, so it hadn't been obvious at all.

"Del, I wish I could make it better. I do," I whispered into her ear while she cried. I hated seeing my sister like this. She had always been a happy person, and now it was as if life was trying to break her.

When there were no tears left, she pulled away and sat in front of me. Wiping her eyes on the hem of her nightshirt, she said, "I feel so much better, just telling you about it, Tully. You have no idea how it has been, carrying that around with me."

I wondered how long Delia must have been faking her happiness, walking around all smiles, but miserable on the inside, like a shiny piece of fruit with a worm at its core. It broke my heart to think of her that way. To know she was hurting and I hadn't even noticed. And that she didn't feel like she could confide in me.

Sitting here, with her face scrubbed clean and her hair pulled back, Delia barely passed for her eighteen, but she was living with very adult problems. After everything she'd been through, if anyone deserved to be young and to have some fun, it was her.

"You know, Delia, you could still come talk to Thomas. It's like you told me, you don't have to tell him everything right now. Or ever if you don't want. It would probably be good for you, you know, to hang out." I tapped her lightly on the shoulder and pulled a face. "It can be a day goofing off."

Delia laughed. "Yeah, well, you see how well my advice worked for you."

She did have a point.

"I think you could use a little fun, is all," I offered. "What can it hurt?"

"Maybe you're right," she said slowly. "I think maybe I will. It would be nice to be around people and pretend like nothing bad or

crazy has happened. A day hanging out. No pressure. No expectations."
She pulled the covers to her chin. "He doesn't know I was raped,
though, right? I know it's nothing I should be ashamed about because it
wasn't my fault. But if I'm going to pretend everything is normal and
sane, I don't think that would be possible if he knows. Even Mama and
Daddy treat me different, Tully. It's like I'm cracked and everyone is
waiting for me to break into a million little pieces."

Since the attack, my parents had been walking on eggshells around
my sister. When I'd filled them in on the details, they'd only gotten
worse. Even I noticed it. They did it out of love, sure, but it made
pretending things were normal a lot harder. And normalcy was what
Delia craved more than anything.

She wanted one sane day in a month of craziness.

"No. I didn't tell him anything about you. Only that I thought you
might like him."

I smiled at Delia. *This will be good for her.*

"And Thomas said he would talk to Logan for me." The prospect
of a good day for Delia made me feel better about my own situation.

"Maybe I'll call him and see if he'll meet us and let me explain." I
bit my lip wondering how that would go. "I guess I don't have anything
to lose." I still had one of Logan's dollar checks with his phone number
scrawled across it tossed in my dresser drawer. I could sneak home and
call him while everyone was having church. If he came to the fruit stand
when Delia was there with Thomas, he would have to believe me. I
hoped.

"You definitely should. It's settled. I'm going to meet Thomas and
you're going to fix things with Logan, and starting tomorrow,
everything is going to be better for everyone," Delia said, scooting
further under the covers.

For the first time since the attack, she sounded like the sister I'd
grown up with. I clicked off the lamp, and the faintest trickle of Charm
teased through the air, giving me hope things could be good again.

Chapter Sixteen

On Sunday it only took the smallest bit of coaxing for Daddy to let Delia work the fruit stand again. We still had to take Jack with us, but after Daddy's initial refusal, I could tell he was relieved Delia wanted to leave the house and actually do something. He was a goner the first time she said, "Please Daddy? I think it'll do me some good."

In a very short, very curt phone call, Logan also had agreed to meet me. I think it helped that he knew I hadn't outright lied about my family. Even though he seemed open to believing me because of the Chans in his own family, I was still worried his acceptance was because he had convinced himself that he was *supposed* to like me. Having Jack prove our Gifts to him had been a good thing.

No sooner had we set the display of berries and dragged out crates of melons, Thomas's giant white truck pulled up.

"How do I look?" Delia asked.

"Fine," Jack and I said in unison.

Delia had put even more time than usual into getting ready. Her hair was sprayed into big curls, and her fingers and toenails were painted a trendy shade of navy to match her shorts. She looked like she always had, a brunette Barbie and it was great to see her that way again.

The only difference was the shirt she wore, a white peasant top, looser than anything she'd have chosen a few months ago. She wasn't showing, exactly, but instead of her usual, razor sharp hipbones, there was now a soft roundness to her. No one who didn't know better would have noticed, and the weight looked good on her. But I knew Delia's vanity kept her from that realization.

Thomas sauntered over, wearing a Southern Marsh button down, and his goofy, Labrador-puppy-grin.

"Thomas, you remember my sister, Delia?" I asked.

"How could I forget?" he said with a tip of his head.

His hair curled from the edges of his Mossy Oak baseball cap that added to his laid-back charm. He and my sister looked like a matching set. Equal parts country and preppy.

"Pleasure," Delia drawled, sticking out her hand, beaming. "So you're from Texas? I love Texas!"

I made a face at Jack. He smiled and rolled his eyes. If Delia was in a good mood, she *loved* things. It never mattered if she'd ever seen or been to the place, she *loved* it. The habit had always annoyed the crap out of me, but right then, it was good to see her acting like her old self, even if her loose peasant top was concealing a secret.

"Uh, Thomas? I think I left my purse in your truck last night."

Thomas raised his eyebrows, but didn't take his gaze away from Delia. "I don't think so, Tallulah. I would have noticed. Maybe you left it at the theater?"

"No. I'm sure I left it over in your truck. *Way over there.* Jack, why don't you come help me look for it," I nudged him in the ribs with my elbow, "*Over there.* In the truck."

A look of understanding dawned on Thomas's face. "Oh. Ok. It's unlocked. Go ahead," he offered.

Jack smacked his forehead with his palm, and rolled his eyes again.

"Come on, let's give them a little room to talk," I whispered as we trudged toward Thomas's vehicle to search for my purse, which I happened to know was hanging on the back of the desk chair in my room.

After ten minutes of "searching" that really consisted of us sitting in the car, and Jack snooping through the glove box, we headed back to the fruit stand.

"Guess you were right," I said, shrugging my shoulders.

Delia smiled. "Would you mind if we ran into Brooklyn real quick. We won't be gone long. I want to ride in Thomas's new truck."

"Go ahead," I replied, happy she was enjoying herself.

The fruit stand had gone from busy to extra slow since the night of Delia's rape. I guess the people of Brooklyn were buying into the hatred that Armstrong was, no doubt, spewing. For the first time ever, we had actually had to throw out some of the gentler fruits because of rot.

"Thanks Tully!" Delia beamed.

"Hey, Tallulah, don't forget, I don't mind talking to Logan. He doesn't deserve you if he doesn't give you a chance to explain," Thomas said.

"Thank you. He'll be here later. Maybe you can talk to him when ya'll get back,." I did my best to sound cheerful.

Thomas smiled at me, and then he and Delia linked arms and walked off.

I sighed. I really hoped Logan showed. I didn't have to worry for long.

Thomas and Delia pulled onto the main road, heading in the direction of Brooklyn, and were still in sight when they passed a small black truck. My heart started to beat faster. The truck slowed and parked in the gravel area next to the stand.

The driver's door opened and Logan got out.

"Do you want me to stick around or do you want some privacy?" Jack asked.

"Privacy, for now, if you don't mind." I tried to stifle the butterflies taking flight in my stomach.

"Ok. If you're sure, I'm going for a run." He bent at the waist, taking a good stretch.

"Thanks, Jack," I said, as he pulled off his white t-shirt and tossed it onto the folding chair. He trotted off with the easy grace of someone with natural talent.

Unlike me, Jack was a runner. If we had lived in another life, he would have been a star athlete. At five foot ten inches, he was only an inch taller than me and almost as lean, except for the long ropey muscles that ran up and down his lanky frame. Where my legs had all the appeal of those seen on a stork, Jack's calves bunched and stretched in ways that drew the gaze of any woman he passed, despite our reputation. This always made Jack smirk. He was as vain as Delia, but with the decency to try and hide it.

Logan stood with his back to me, facing his truck for a few minutes before making his way toward me. His pace held all the eagerness of a man going to the electric chair. Guilt stabbed through me like a bayonet, ragged and rough. I had to focus to keep from falling from my seat on the counter.

That morning, I had gone over and over what I should say to him, but now I could not think of two words to stitch together.

How could I have been such a jerk?

"Hey," I said lamely.

"Hey," he whispered.

"I'm sorry," I blurted out.

His hard eyes found mine. "If you didn't like me, you should have told me. You didn't have to feed me all of that crap about how your 'family won't let you date and its complicated' stuff."

The way that he gazed into my eyes, as if he could see my thoughts, still unnerved me. It was like, inside I was this tightly wound ball of yarn, but with one look, he found the loose thread and everything started to unravel. I should have been anxious, or upset, but instead I felt lighter. Relieved. Like, I *should* be worried, but things didn't matter that much. Even now, when I had no right to feel anything but guilt, that look was somehow setting me both at ease, and on edge. *Was this Chans? Was this the feeling he had been talking about?*

"I feel like such an asshole!" Logan said. "I believed everything you said about Gifts and powers and everyone hating you. Not to mention you let me go on and on about my family. About Chans. You let me make a complete fool of myself! Why, Tully?"

"But all of that is true!" I cried. "That guy I was with? His name is Thomas. I had to go out with him. He's the guy my family found for me to date, my match! It wasn't really my choice to go out with him. He knows I like you—and he likes Delia. In fact, he's with her now. They'll be back in a minute and you can ask him!"

If he didn't want to see me anymore because of all of the baggage I was born into, that was one thing, but I needed him to understand that I wasn't a liar.

The irony wasn't lost on me. I had spent my whole life wishing I was like normal people, and now here I was, with someone I really liked, desperate to prove that we were different.

"And I showed you! With Jack. That wasn't a trick. That was real. That's our life. How else could you explain it?"

Logan was the first person I had met who completely accepted who I was. I had been loved my entire life. I knew I was important to Mama and Daddy, even if I wasn't the most important. But I had never known the kind of unconditional acceptance I had experienced in the little time I had known Logan. My path had always been laid out for me, with little room for variation. I was accepted—as long as I was who I was expected to be. When Logan touched me, I knew what it was like for someone to want me as I was.

I couldn't give that up.

Logan stared at his shoes. When he met my eyes again, the smallest smile flashed on his face. "I don't know. I can't figure out what happened. The power of persuasion, maybe?"

He hopped onto the counter and sat next to me, not touching, but almost. His scent, the smell of fabric softener and sunshine, gave me butterflies.

"Look, Tully. I know we're just getting to know each other, but I like you. A lot. I don't normally make a complete jackass of myself to get a woman to go out with me. That's all for you. Hell, it's only for you. I told you, the way we're pulled together…it's different. I don't understand it and I don't care. All I know is that it's good." He paused. "So you have to understand, Saturday night threw me."

"I know. I feel the same way. I saw you with your sister, and I thought I had only been someone you were playing around with. It hurt," I admitted. "Like, 'Watch me mess with the town freak,' and it…I don't know." I watched the floor, unable to believe what I was about to admit to him. "You were my first kiss." Heat crept into my face. Out of the corner of my eye, I could see Logan staring at me. *At least he has the courtesy not to let his mouth hang open.* I was officially humiliated.

"But you're twenty-one years old!" he said.

I swallowed. "Who would I have kissed? I didn't go to a normal school. We don't even go to a normal church. We go to Brooklyn to shop or eat and people treat us as if we're pariahs. The same people who buy from us or contract our services won't talk to us. And almost every time I've been to Peachton has been with my parents. Geez. To kiss someone I would have to actually know them for more than five minutes."

Logan scooted over and put his arm around my shoulders.

"Now you think I'm some kind of charity case," I moaned, leaning away from him.

"Stop telling me what I think," he said, again pulling me near. "Actually, I am honored."

He dropped his arm from my shoulders and cupped my face in his hands. My stomach clenched as I gazed into his eyes and leaned forward, ever so slightly. Logan bent down, and smiling, kissed me on the forehead. I raised my eyebrows in question. He laughed and pulled away.

I gave him the stink eye, and pulled my legs onto the table, sliding onto my knees. Again, I leaned into him, and without thinking, kissed him. When I pulled back, we sat, breathing the same air, Logan not saying anything, only staring at me in a way I couldn't comprehend.

He hated it.

"I'm…" I started to apologize, when Logan pressed his lips to mine and coaxed open my mouth. He put his hand on the back of my neck, drawing me deeper into the kiss. He used his other hand to pick my arm up, and wrap it around his neck. I took the hint and twined both of my hands around him, twisting his smooth hair through my fingers, careful to avoid knots.

His hands moved slowly around my back, giving me goose bumps down the entire length of my body. I scooted forward on my knees to close the minute space left between us. Getting close enough to satisfy my need to touch and be touched was impossible. We could have been pressed together into one being, it still wouldn't have been enough.

Logan pulled away from me first, breathing heavy. "Tully, we need to stop," he said.

"Why?" I asked. Heat ran rampant through my body, pumped throughout with every nervous heartbeat. Stopping sounded like the worst idea ever.

"If you just had your first kiss...We have time. I'm not going anywhere and I want everything to be perfect for you. No regrets." He kissed me again on the forehead.

"Logan, I'm an adult," I breathed. "This is what I want. Unless...you don't?" I searched his eyes. I was tired of living like I was twelve. This was what I wanted.

Logan's lips brushed mine in response. The kiss was light and sweet, but charged with that wonderful electricity that danced between us whenever we were close.

"You wanna take a walk?" I asked, nodding toward the dense cover of trees that bordered our property.

"Do I want to? YES. Are you sure you want to? What if Jack comes back?" he asked.

I had forgotten about Jack. And Delia. And Thomas.

"Tallulah, you're incredibly sexy. But, damn it. Your first kiss was a couple of days ago. If we go off. Alone..." he hesitated. "I don't want to take advantage of you."

Even as he spoke, his body never moved away from mine. His hand never stopped moving up and down my back in soft, slow circles. Logan could use whatever words he wanted, but I knew he wanted me, and the feeling gave me an intoxicating courage. I kissed him hard. We fell into a rhythm that felt both familiar and new. Safe and exciting. The kiss lingered, and when I finally pulled away, I was dizzy. I looked at the woods and then back at Logan.

"Now?" I asked.

He didn't hesitate this time. "Yes."

I hopped down from the counter. Logan followed behind, our fingers linking us together, carrying as strong a current as any power line.

"Oops. I almost forgot." I grabbed the green zip bag that held the money, and we walked toward the thick grove of trees.

When we were far enough into the cover that we could no longer see the fruit stand or road, Logan pulled me close and tilted my chin upward.

"Just a minute," I whispered. I walked in a wide circle searching the branches overhead. When you have gardens and fruit trees nearby, there will always be birds, but most birds wouldn't tattle to Mama, and would only speak with her if she sought them out. Crows, on the other hand, would run back to gain her favor, and there was nothing I could think of more humiliating than having her or Daddy come tearing into the trees while Logan and I were together.

Logan watched me, a smirk playing on his mouth. *His perfect mouth.*

"Tully. I'm sure you have a reason, but what are you doing?" he asked.

"Remember at Marco's when I told you about our Gifts and how my Mama can talk to birds? Well, crows love to blab." I scrunched my nose at their nosiness.

He nodded and looked up. "I think we're safe."

I continued pacing in the circle, searching the trees.

"I gotta be sur…" Logan ran behind me and picked me up bride and groom thresh-hold style. "What are you doing?"

"I am trying to get you to relax a little," he said, spinning us around in circles. We spun around and around, before falling to the leaf-covered ground in a laughing tangle of arms and legs.

My confidence from the heated moments at the fruit stand decided to abandon me while I was searching for crows, and familiar insecurities were beginning to settle into place. My feelings hadn't changed. I wanted to be as close to Logan as possible. But now that we were in the woods, alone, my inexperience sat between us, as solid and real as the pine trees that towered overhead.

I breathed in the woodsy scent of damp leaves and pine straw to calm my nerves. Somewhere in the branches, a frog was calling to its mate. If I strained to hear over my own heartbeat, I could make out the far away song of a mockingbird. The outdoor sounds and smells worked their own type of magic, casting a spell that relaxed me.

Logan rolled onto his side, facing me. I smiled, a tiny closed smile, as he traced the outline of my mouth with his fingers, his touch banishing what was left of my jitters and all but erasing my fear. I was filled with longing, and there was no room left for self-doubt.

"You have no idea what you do to me, Tallulah Caibre," he said.

I caught his finger in my teeth.

"Hey." He pretended the nip had hurt.

I grabbed his hand and kissed first his finger, and then his lips. And it was as if we had never stopped. His arms wrapped around me as desire seared its path, white hot and pushing aside any lingering embarrassment, until it took me over fully. The bravery that had earlier abandoned me, returned. I slid my hands under his t-shirt and ran my fingers over his tight stomach.

Logan worked his lips from my mouth to my neck, kissing behind my ear and down to my collarbone. Every touch left a trail of scorching pleasure. I pushed up his shirt, and taking my cue, he pulled it off and tossed it aside in a single motion. His lips picked up where they were interrupted, continuing their hot trace across my body.

His hand moved to my stomach, inching its way toward my bra, and sliding up my shirt. I lifted my arms for him to pull the cumbersome piece of clothing off me.

"You sure?" he hesitated.

I smiled slyly, unsnapping his jeans, and then lifted my arms back over my head.

He smiled back at me with his own sly grin and peeled off my shirt. Logan slid his hand under the thin cotton of my bra, his touch making me gasp and pulling an even deeper need from me.

It felt good. And with Logan, it felt right. I knew I could never regret it. A shiver of pleasure raced over me as he again kissed my neck, working his way lower and lower at a painstaking pace that left me almost unable to move with frustrating anticipation.

And that was when we heard it.

***

The explosion echoed through the trees, sending the few birds that were around scattering across the sky. We both jumped up at the same time. I grabbed my shirt and started pulling it on, taking off at a run toward the fruit stand.

Oh, no. I would never forgive myself if Jack or Delia were hurt. It didn't occur to me to wonder what happened. I grew up knowing that most people didn't like us, and ever since Delia's attacker had spotted me, pointing and shaking his finger as if I would be next, I carried it around in the back part of my mind. A fear that the bad things were not over. That they would keep happening.

I should be looking for the bastard that hurt my sister, not sneaking around chasing romance. I was being selfish and look what's happened.

I ran harder.

Being with Logan had allowed me to forget, but the explosion brought the terror and hurt back to the surface. I burst from the woods to see the fruit stand wrapped in flames and a deep black smoke. Dread bubbled up and settled over me as I witnessed the destruction of a part of my life that had been a constant since childhood. I almost fell down with relief upon seeing an empty parking lot. Delia and Thomas weren't back yet. They were safe.

Logan broke from the woods behind me, dressed, and holding the discarded moneybag in his hand.

"Oh my god," he said staring at the building, his mouth hanging open. "Tully, what if you had been in there?"

"I think that might have been the plan." I had not wanted to tell Logan about Delia being raped. I felt like it was not my story to share, but things were escalating. It wouldn't be right to have a relationship with him and keep him in the dark. Not when our attacker was willing to go to such lengths. *Not when being with me may put his life at stake.*

My legs finally gave out and I sat down hard on the grass. Logan dropped to the ground beside me, pulling my hand into his lap. I turned to look into his moss colored eyes, searching them for the courage and comfort I knew they would hold.

If I were going to fill him in, now would be my only chance.

"Logan," I began, "I have to tell you something. I should have told you before, but I felt like it wasn't my place to say anything. But if you really like me, and mean what you say, that you want to be together, then you should know."

Logan said nothing, but squeezed my hand in his.

"I told you that most of the town hates us. It's been like that for a long time. The other day, the night after I met you in Myrtle's, Delia, my sister, snuck out and someone abducted her and raped her. I walked up on the man dumping her in a ditch, and I know he saw me. I am pretty sure he saw my face, even though I couldn't see his," I finished, holding back tears, remembering.

"Did ya'll report it? Somebody has to do something. It's the law," he said, not bothering to hide the anger in his words.

"The police don't care. Besides. You know about us. What we're capable of. I can promise you justice will be served, one way or another." As I said the words aloud, I realized how much I meant them. I would do anything to help my sister, and it was obvious we wouldn't be safe until the man who hurt her was caught.

Logan eyed me, and then nodded slowly. "Yeah. I can understand you feeling that way, but you should have at least told the cops about it. Get it recorded."

"Delia didn't want to at the hospital, but I walked in on Daddy talking to Chief Rucker. The Chief was pretty much blowing it off, saying it was probably one of the carnival workers, even though that makes no sense! How would a carnival worker know where to find my sister?" My hands fisted at my sides. "And if he really thought it was a carni, it's not like that makes it any better! Logan, the man all but shrugged it off."

"That guy is a prick," Logan agreed. "The first time I was driving through, he pulled me over for doing a forty-seven in a forty-five. When he saw I was from New Orleans, it was like he was trying to find something on me. I think that I didn't even have an unpaid parking ticket pissed him off." He shook his head. "He's a real jerk. But still, all that aside, he is bound by law to do *something*."

In a place like New Orleans, there were probably consequences for cops who didn't do their jobs. But here, we were off the grid. If there *were* consequences for a cop not following protocol, who was going to enforce them? Chief Rucker had grown up as the town golden-boy, and now he was their caretaker. He could do no wrong. His word against ours, and he would win, every single time.

"In fact, why aren't we calling the police right now?" Logan pulled a phone from his back pocket. He looked down and cursed. "How on Earth is it possible there is still a spot in this country that doesn't get a cell signal!"

Maybe it was from hysteria, but that made me smile. *New Orleans boy must think towers circle the planet.*

Thomas's truck wheeled into the gravel lot as far away from the flames as he could get. He, Delia, and Jack tumbled from it, and ran toward the burning shed. I stuck my fingers in my mouth and let out an ear-piercing whistle. When the trio saw me and Logan safe on the grass, they relaxed.

Thomas stared at the flames wide-eyed, mouth gaping. Jack's lips were pulled back from his teeth and I could barely see his eyes through the deep creases between and above his brow.

Delia stood hunched, eyes on the ground, arms hugging herself so tight that her fingers had gone white. Seeing her like that, especially after she had been so happy earlier, turned me cold from the inside out, even though a fire roared only yards away. I rubbed the gooseflesh from my arms. I wanted the person who'd done this to feel how we felt.

Logan and I pulled ourselves from the ground and started jogging toward them.

"Are ya'll okay?" Jack asked, quickly followed by, "What happened?"

"We were taking a walk," I said. Technically that was true. "Thank God none of us were in there."

"We heard the explosion all the way down by the crossroads." Thomas shook his head. "We hauled butt back in this direction, and when we saw Jack running full tilt this way, we picked him up."

"Geez Tully! I was so scared you were hurt!" Delia cried, her tears running in black, staining streaks down her face. We pulled each other into a tight hug, needing the contact to make absolutely sure the other really was unharmed.

Gravel flew as Daddy's pick-up tore down the driveway with Uncle Drew (Mama's older brother), and Uncle Frankie (Mama's little sister's husband) riding in the back. Before it had even stopped, both men jumped free of the bed and ran full sprint towards us. Daddy and Uncle Gavin barreled out and followed them, leaving the doors hanging open.

I tried to smooth the wrinkles from my clothes, and ran my hands through my hair, removing any telling leaves I might have picked up from the forest floor.

"Thank God," Daddy boomed when they reached us. "Oh thank you God!" He squeezed me and Delia into a hug, kissing the tops of our heads.

Uncle Gavin had both of his hands on Jack's shoulders, looking him over like a parent checks a toddler that has fallen off the swings. The wind shifted and I coughed at the smoke-filled air. Daddy released us and turned to the fruit stand, before registering for the first time we weren't alone. Uncle Drew stood cross-armed, glaring at the boys, while Uncle Frankie stared at the flames.

Thomas stuck his hand out to my Daddy, who first stared at the outstretched appendage without touching it, and then at the man who had been hanging unsupervised with his daughters. My sister and I may be adults on paper, but in our family, the rules were the rules. Daddy knew Thomas. He liked Thomas. And he wasn't shaking his hand. Things were not going to be good for Logan.

"What in the hell happened?" Daddy rumbled. Unspoken questions hung in the air like moss from a live oak. *Did ya'll do this? Did someone do this to ya'll? Why in the hell are there boys here?*

"I'm, uh, I'm going to call the police," Thomas said.

"Good luck," muttered Logan. "There isn't any cell service out here."

Thomas said something about having a satellite emergency button in his car that could connect him to 911. I could tell by the way his eyes lingered on Delia, he wanted her to walk with him, but his gaze flicked to Daddy and he closed his mouth, jogging to his truck alone.

"We don't know. We went for a walk. When we heard the explosion we came right back here." I wasn't lying, but I knew Daddy would expect a better answer after things calmed down.

Daddy glared at Logan. He opened his mouth to say something, but Thomas called, "The dispatcher said that they're backed up. That it'll be a while. Can you believe that?"

"Oh I believe it," Daddy muttered under his breath, his eyes flashing.

The telltale sound of thunder boomed in the distance, making Logan jump. Without thinking, I reached over and squeezed his hand at the same time Daddy shifted his gaze back to us.

"I see," he said too evenly.

"Do you want me to call the fire department?" Thomas shouted from his truck.

"No. I'll handle it." Daddy's voice boomed louder, more frightening than thunder ever could be.

The truth was Brooklyn only had a volunteer fire department and most of the guys that worked at it went to Armstrong's church. They weren't going to come here, plain and simple. And Daddy could handle it before the bigger fire squad from Peachton would arrive.

A succession of booms filled the air, like cannon fire in the distance, as Daddy's eyes morphed into the bottomless shade of green-black that meant power. He breathed in deep and raised his hands into the air, his palms facing flat to the sky. Wind started to blow, gentle at first, and then harder. I was scared it would blow the fire and cause it to grow and spread, but I should have known better. The wind started to twist, forming a vacuum around the burning shed, twirling and shifting, but never actually blowing the flames.

Logan's hair whipped around his face as the wind picked up speed. His eyes were wide. It's one thing to hear about our Gifts, it is a completely different matter to experience them.

Especially Daddy's.

Daddy turned dark red, and the vein that always made an appearance when he and Delia had one of their fights, throbbed across his forehead in full force. His lips moved in silent repetition, chanting a verse only he could hear.

The eastern horizon crowded with angry nimbus clouds. They sailed across the sky, an ominous fleet, ready to carry out Daddy's bidding. When they were overhead, Daddy stopped chanting and jerked his arms down to his sides in a single stiff motion. Sheets of water, too thick to be called rain, fell from the sky, soaking everyone, and smothering the flames. The vacuum of air that had surrounded the burning fruit stand disappeared, its job done.

Daddy looked at me and then to Delia. My Uncles stood back, watching, but no one said a word. Daddy turned, and started walking down the long driveway to our house, leaving behind his truck, and us, standing in the rain. I stared after him.

Uncle Gavin got in the driver's seat of Daddy's truck. "Let's go, Jack! Now!" he called out the window.

Uncle Drew inhaled and gently blew, causing the wind to push the clouds back in the direction they came. Unlike Daddy, he couldn't manipulate the weather entirely, but he could make the wind blow. He came over to where I stood, never even glancing at Logan as he passed. "Tully, you and Delia need to go home. Your Mama and Grandma are worried sick. Me and Frankie are going to search around."

"I could help," Logan offered.

Uncle Drew pointed to where the two trucks were parked. "You need to leave. Now."

I didn't pull away when Logan grabbed my hand. The cat was out of the bag anyway.

"I'll try to call you tomorrow if I can find a way," I whispered.

He pulled me to him, wrapping me in a bear hug. "Tully, you be safe," he whispered back, before kissing me on the forehead.

When I passed Uncle Frankie, he stopped me and gave me a small smile. "I'm glad ya'll weren't in there. I don't care what you kids were doing. Anything is better than being burnt to a crisp."

He poked me in the ribs with his pointer finger, using his Gift to zap me with a playful shock of cold. He gave me a wink, and then left to investigate the smoking rubble with Uncle Drew.

Delia had made her way to the front of Thomas's truck where the pair were completely absorbed in each other's company, smiling as if our lives had not almost ended. Thomas reached to tuck a wet tangle behind Delia's ear, and her back stiffened. Fear flickered over her face causing her eyes to flash bright before she regained her expert control. Her beauty queen smile never faltered, and when Thomas bent to kiss her goodbye, only a sister could have recognized the panic in her eyes.

Chapter Seventeen

Delia jogged down the driveway in her soppy clothes and gladiator sandals.

"Wait up, Tully," she called.

I slowed my pace so she could catch up.

"Geez. That is crazy," she said, sucking in lungful of air between each word and trailing a step behind me.

"Yeah, crazy," I said.

The phrase didn't do justice to what had happened. Someone had bombed us. For real *bombed* us. It was a fluke no one was sitting behind the dusty old counter. The only reason I was still alive was because I'd hidden away to be with Logan. *Maybe it wasn't a fluke at all. Maybe…maybe it was Logan's Chans.* The thought stopped me in my tracks, causing Delia to bump into me. *I can't think about that right now.*

"Sorry," I mumbled to Delia as we again started walking, falling into step with each other.

A member of my family had been posted in the shack every day since before I was born. The post included my older cousins who brought their toddlers or preschoolers with them to play at their feet while they helped customers. I shuddered at the realization that one of my baby cousins could have been burned up in the fire before their little lives even had a chance to get started. Whoever had done this was evil, pure and simple.

"First the explosion…and then…I had no idea that Daddy could do that," Delia said, between deep breaths.

"Me neither."

Daddy's reputation had spread far among Gifted families. He was known to be powerful, and not someone to mess with, but as his daughter, I had only seen my mild mannered father use his power for mundane things, a far cry from the precise control I had witnessed today.

I'd heard that he'd held tornadoes at bay, but I hadn't actually seen it. Today, he had guided the winds with perfect discipline, keeping the flames from being spread to the nearby woods, all while calling bloated clouds to drench the fire. The day had been sunny and warm, with clear skies, so his reach had to be far. Real far.

I thought about the crack of lightening that had lit up the dark sky on the night Delia was attacked, making it bright as noonday, and what it meant that Daddy had the power to control something so magnificent. Or when he had been paid to call in snow flurries. At the time, I hadn't thought about the control needed to bring snow to Mississippi in the summer months, but it must be great.

But could he lose that control? Besides a few exceptions, he never really used his Gift for anything grander than blowing in a light sprinkle for the garden, or making rainbows on our birthdays. Maybe that was why he worked so hard to keep a calm, even attitude, never arguing with anyone except for Delia. Maybe he knew that he had the power to be destructive on an unhuman level.

Strangely, the thought comforted me. Whoever was trying to hurt us had no idea what they were messing with. Yeah, we grew fruit, smelled like Christmas, and could let you know if you were pregnant, but we could also unleash a world of hurt.

As if on some kind of cue, thunder bellowed, and I knew it was Daddy. The clouds were gone, the sun was back, but up ahead, the sky rumbled a low powerful groan, like all hell was going to break loose. Me and Delia looked at each other, and without a word, quickened our pace.

We neared the end of the drive when Baron and Deidra "beep-beeped" at us as they flew past in their Prius, or as Uncle Drew called it, his son's "hippy-dippy car." Pawpaw followed in his pick-up and Uncle

Louis rolled by in his rusty El Camino. A few seconds later two more trucks passed, slinging gravel as they hurried. No doubt, the show of power had been witnessed from afar by everyone on the property. I imagined most of the family would be making their way to the burned remains to get a glimpse at the disaster.

Another growl of thunder vibrated through the air as me and Delia bounded onto the raised front porch. Crows perched along the porch rail, crowding themselves onto the structure until the wood seemed to wiggle and writhe with their movement. I resisted the urge to run my hand down the row and knock the little boogers into the grass.

I ran into the house with Delia on my heels. Mama and Grandma were sitting at the dining room table, across from Uncle Gavin, who had his back to us. Jack was seated at one end of the small rectangle, and when we walked in, his large green eyes clouded with guilt. Or maybe it was sympathy. Daddy had been pacing the floor, leaving wet footprints across the dining room and kitchen. He choked the cordless phone in his giant fist.

"Sit down," he said, not bothering to place a hand over the receiver.

Jack glanced at us again, before looking to the table. Mama stared at Daddy, worry creasing her pretty face. Grandma was the only one who appeared herself. She jumped up and ran to hug us, whispering in our ears as she bent close, "It's going to be okay. Have a seat. We're trying to figure everything out."

I slid into the chair at the other end of the rectangle, across from Jack, and Delia took the seat on the corner, between me and Uncle Gavin. Grandma sat back down, folding her hands neatly on the table.

"What do you mean you aren't coming?" Daddy roared into the phone. "My girls could have been killed. Somebody better get their sorry ass down here NOW!" he barked, before throwing the phone through the open window over the sink.

Outside the sky rumbled, and a burst of black birds flew into the air, noisily squawking as the phone sailed through the middle of their assembly. Daddy turned his back to us, and breathed deep. He was calmer a second later when he turned around.

"No one is going to come. They're not going to send one damn cop here," he said, his voice raspy. He was talking to everyone, but he was looking at Mama. "It's happened. It has finally happened. The line's been drawn in the sand." He paused. "If they want to ignore us, fine. If they want to whisper and point, fine. But this? This will not be TOLERATED!" His voice rose with every word, ending in a boom. "My girls! They tried to hurt my girls!"

"I agree," Uncle Gavin said. "We need to have a meeting. Tonight. We can't let this go on. I don't know who's behind this but—"

"You don't know who is behind this?" Daddy interrupted. "I can tell you who's behind this. That damned cult is behind this. That crazy preacher has Chief Rucker in his pocket. This whole damned town is evil, but that so-called church, that 'CHURCH' is nothing but pure hate. I bet there hasn't been any talk of God or religion from Armstrong except to say how much God hates us!"

I remembered Joshua Armstrong threatening me at the fruit stand. *I should have told. Why didn't I tell?* Well, I could tell now. I opened my mouth to explain. Before any words came, Mama caught my eye, her own wide with warning, and she gave her head an almost unperceivable shake. I shut my mouth.

"If one of my girls would have been killed, I would have wiped out that whole godforsaken town! I would have leveled every last home. I would have shown them the 'evil' they so badly want to see,'" Daddy raged.

His gaze shifted from Delia, to me, and then back to Delia, before his eyes came to rest on Jack, who instantly looked down. That's when I understood Daddy knew why we weren't in the fruit stand. I couldn't blame Jack for telling. What was he supposed to do? If he had made up some story, Daddy would have known it wasn't true the second he asked me or Delia about it.

"And what in the hell were you girls thinking anyway? Delia was raped and ya'll want to go off with some boys you don't even know? Like a couple of whores?"

Mama rose, slapping one hand against the wooden table before pointing the other straight in Daddy's face. "Jepson Caibre, you better shut your mouth or you're going to regret what you're saying! These are your daughters and a word spoken can never be taken back!"

I'd never seen her so mad. Sure, she probably thought we were beyond stupid to be out with guys, and we would probably catch it from her later, but no one was allowed to call us names. Not even Daddy.

Grandma nodded in agreement.

But Mama was right. Something spoken couldn't be taken back, and my eyes clouded with tears at the sting of Daddy's words. I had spent my entire life being good. Doing what I was supposed to do, letting the life I dreamed of pass me by, and now I was being called a whore? For what? For doing something that most teenagers had done, being with someone I really liked? Who liked me? I tried to swallow the tears, but they slipped silently from my eyes and down my cheeks.

"We're not whores," I whispered.

"Of course you aren't, sweetheart," Mama said, walking around the table to stand behind me. "Of course you aren't."

Daddy was still red, and shaking with anger, but the words that had spilled out of his mouth had shocked even him. "I'm sorry," he said. "I truly am. I didn't mean that. But you girls…what were you doing? What were you thinking, going off with those boys? Do you know how dangerous that is? We still don't know who attacked Delia."

"Dangerous?" Delia said from her spot at the table. She had been sitting with her hands folded in her lap, looking down and had not even flinched when Daddy called us the horrible name.

"Riding around in a truck listening to music isn't dangerous. Going for a walk with a man you like isn't dangerous, Daddy! You ought to be calling and thanking Thomas and Logan. They saved our lives!" Her words grew louder as she gained momentum. "Heck Daddy, it seems like the most dangerous place we can be is here! The fruit stand got BLOWN UP!" She tossed her hands into the air for emphasis. "I can't believe you're lecturing us. Calling us names, instead of being HAPPY that we're ALIVE!"

Daddy stared at Delia, not speaking. His face softened, and I knew she had gotten through to him. He walked to the chair Mama had vacated and sank into the padded seat. "I don't know what to do," he whispered. "I don't know. I should be able to keep you safe. I can rule the weather. I can summon tornados, and lightening, but I can't… I can't even keep my family safe."

Everyone sat in miserable silence, the seconds stretching forever.

"Logan?" Daddy asked, looking up at me after a while. "Is that the dummy that wrote us a check for a dollar?"

I must have left one of the dollar checks in the moneybag on accident. I smiled. "He wanted an excuse to talk to me is all."

Across the table, Grandma was almost grinning. "I think it's sweet."

Daddy frowned. "I know it doesn't seem fair, but you have to understand, Tallulah, we do things a certain way for a reason. I know you think you like this guy, but honey, it can't happen," he declared. He turned to my sister. "And you. You aren't old enough. You'll have your turn. After everything you've been through…You shouldn't even be thinking of boys right now."

Delia looked into my Daddy's eyes, narrowing her gaze, her voice low and even. "Daddy, I'm pregnant."

"You're what?"

"I'm. Pregnant. I'm going to have a baby."

Uncle Gavin cleared his throat and glanced at Jack. He stood to leave, motioning with his hand for Jack to do the same.

"No," Delia said, staring Uncle Gavin in the eye. "I appreciate you trying to give me some privacy. But you might as well stay. God knows everyone in the family is going to know soon enough." She took a deep breath. "And I know you and Jack…ya'll will take up for me."

"Of course," my Uncle said quietly, sinking back into his chair.

Daddy never turned his sight from Delia. "But. But you were attacked recently. There's no way to know yet. You aren't pregnant." There was no anger in his words, only disbelief, as if he was waiting for Delia to tell him she was joking.

"Yes, I am. I'm several months along."

Daddy raised his eyebrows. "Several months? It hasn't been several months." The lines in his face softened when my sister's words sank in. "You mean, you were already pregnant. How?"

Delia shifted in her seat. "The same way everyone gets pregnant."

"Who? Who did this to you?" Daddy's voice stayed quiet. "You tell me whose it is."

"I'll tell you whose it is," my sister hollered. "It's mine!" She raised a shaking hand to wipe her eyes. "The guy, he," Delia paused. "He left.

He was Gifted. He said he was from Tennessee and when I told him, he said he had to go home because he was being matched! I know I should have known better, but I swear Daddy, it was an accident!"

"You," Daddy said, pointing to Jack. "You had something to do with this, didn't you? How else could she get out and get pregnant?" Then, he lit into Uncle Gavin. "I've been telling you that you needed to get a handle on your boy! Now look what he's done!"

Uncle Gavin stood and met Daddy's stare with one almost as cold. "You leave Jack out of this! He hasn't done anything. If he gave Delia a ride, it was better than her trying to walk or hitch into town. For heaven's sake, Jepson, have you stopped to think that maybe if the girls had an inkling of normalcy in their lives, none of this would have happened?"

"Well, that'll be enough of that!" Grandma said, matter of fact. "We aren't going to turn this into a contest to see who has the biggest stones."

My mouth dropped open at Grandma's brazen declaration. Delia slapped a hand across her own mouth, trying unsuccessfully to hold back a giggle.

"Mother!" Mama said.

"Ha! Grandma said stones!" Jack said, at the same time.

"Jack, that's enough," Uncle Gavin shook his head.

Daddy scratched his neck, eyes down at the table, and looked embarrassed my Grandma, his mother-in-law, had talked about him and "stones" in the same sentence.

"Besides, a baby is always a good thing. So what if it gets here a little different than we're used to? She's going to be such a blessing!" Grandma reached across the table to take my sister's hand.

"She?" Delia asked, smiling.

"Yes, deary, she." Grandma's eyes sparkled.

Daddy exhaled, and stared hard at Delia and then Grandma, before walking out of the kitchen. He turned at the last minute, back to Uncle Gavin. "Tell everybody we're meeting tonight. Nine o'clock in the barn."

Uncle Gavin nodded, and Daddy was gone fast as a summer wind. Outside it was quiet except for the squawk of crows, who could tell something exciting had happened and were nosy to find out what.

But it didn't thunder.

That was a good sign.

After the shock wore off, Mama and Grandma hugged my sister.

"I can't believe I'm going to be a grandma! And to a sweet little girl!" Mama gushed.

Uncle Gavin hugged Delia too, and Jack beamed at her. I had the suspicion he had already known for a while. I didn't care if Delia had said that only me and Grandma knew, she and Jack had never been able to keep secrets from each other.

At the end of the table, Delia wore a look of relief as she endured the embraces from Mama and Grandma with a half-smile. Bad as this day was, it had taken pressure off my baby sister. But it had done something else too; it had proven that whoever was behind the attacks on our family was getting desperate. And desperate people made mistakes. I was going to have to poke around the stand once the timbers cooled.

Chapter Eighteen

While Delia napped, and Daddy and Mama arranged the meeting, I took the opportunity to sneak back to the end of our driveway alone. Charred beams smoldered, still too hot to touch. The metal fan stood, its base warped and its blades blackened. Everything else was gone.

I don't know what I was expecting, a piece of a bomb, unexplained tire marks, weird footprints. But I found nothing that couldn't be explained by Uncles' own investigation. I should have known Daddy's Gift would do a number on the scene, but part of me had believed something would jump out at me like in the novels. Apparently, that only happened in books.

Defeated and freaked by every sound that came from the nearby woods, the same woods where I'd lain with Logan earlier, I made my way to the barn before the rest of the family started showing up.

The barn wasn't really a barn at all. It was actually a metal, multipurpose building. The kind you order prefabricated and then assemble on your own property. It had folding tables and chairs, a concrete floor, and a table with a couple of neglected computers set up in the back. They were bought for use with the homeschool program Mama ran for my school aged cousins. The computers didn't get used as much as they should on account the high-speed internet hadn't made it to the Mississippi boonies yet. We still suffered dial up, believe it or not. There'd been talk about looking into the satellite service, but no one had ever followed through with it. My parents weren't exactly the kind of people who were in on the latest tech trends.

Not only had I gone to "school" in this building for most of my childhood—having been purchased and assembled when I was eight—but it was also where we had church services and any kind of family party.

Lately, the only time I ever darkened its doors were on Sunday mornings to listen to Uncle Frankie preach for an hour. Last year, in an attempt to get out of working at the fruit stand, I tried to help Mama teach. It did not end well. Turns out, I don't like teaching homeschool any more than I liked attending homeschool. I goofed off with Delia and Jack for most of the day, before Mama threw her hands up and sent me back to work at the end of the driveway.

Today, the barn had a somber feel to it despite all the family that milled about. Or maybe because of it. Everyone knew why we were meeting, and their nervous tension gripped the room.

Delia and I pulled two metal folding chairs to the back, to set near the exit. Delia had told Daddy she felt rattled, and he had agreed that, in her condition, it would be fine to slip out early to rest. But we had to make an appearance so everyone could set eyes on us and know we were okay.

The scent of fresh baked cookies wafted to me, drawing my eye to the back of the barn. Bertie and her two tween daughters were laying baked goods and punch on a table in the corner.

Lord, I thought. *Who thinks, "Oh, we're having a family meeting to discuss rape and attempted murder, why don't you have some sherbet melted into a bowl of ginger ale and a break-and-bake cookie?"* I mean, it wasn't a damn party, after all.

But that was Bertie in a nutshell, I guess.

Darkness began to fall outside as the last few cousins squeezed into the building, some with babies on their hips and some dragging cranky children behind them. All in all, about twenty-five adults, and a passel of tots, toddlers, kids, and tweens ran around. Even ancient Aunt Trudy had scooted through the door, the tennis balls on the end of her walker sliding soundlessly on the concrete floor.

Delia and I kept our heads down, waiting for the meeting to start so we could make our escape. Our plan was to call Logan and Thomas, and arrange for them to meet us later that night to talk. Thomas's family might not have to put up with this kind of drama, but at least he kind of understood what we were going through.

Logan on the other hand... Well. If he stuck around after today, I would know he meant it when he said nothing would scare him off.

Everyone in our family had heard the explosion and knew we had been bombed. Most had stopped by during the day to see Daddy, or check on me and Delia. The meeting was more about planning. I wasn't sure what Daddy and Uncle Gavin had in mind, but things were getting serious.

Daddy stood up and the talking died down instantly. The hostile energy spread thick, feeling off and wrong in the space where we met to worship God and, once a year, open Christmas gifts.

"By now, everyone knows what happened at the fruit stand today," he began. "The fact that somehow, someone was able to bomb our property, intending to kill our children, proves the time for peace and trust is over. It is time for action. We must react! The police have made it clear they will not help us."

Daddy's words stirred the anger already boiling through the crowd, and everyone started talking at once.

"Quiet! Everybody!" Uncle Gavin hollered.

The talking died down, slower this time.

"Now, thank God the girls are fine; however, this attack makes me think that what happened to Delia may somehow be connected," Daddy said, unable to bring himself to say the word "rape" in a room full of children.

Of course they're related. How could they not be?

Delia half-shrugged her shoulders and stared at the floor as everyone gave her sideways glances. A few of my older relatives shifted to stare at her straight on. No one would dare outright blame my sister for what happened to her, but I had overheard a conversation between one of my cousins and his wife about why Delia wouldn't tell them where she was that night and how she managed to get abducted in the first place. At the time I was shocked our own family would question Delia. Now I wondered how many people in this room thought the same thing.

"I think it's pretty needless to say any help or assistance we normally give to the townspeople stops right now. No more favors," Daddy continued, "paid or otherwise."

Again, the noise grew as everyone chewed over what was said.

Daddy raised his voice above it, the sounds echoing through the barn like thunder. "I also think it's important we don't appear afraid. In the past, we have kept to ourselves while in Brooklyn. I say, no more. Everyone may now openly practice their Gift at home, and those of you over the age of twenty have permission to use your discretion while in Brooklyn. If you need your Gift, then do what you must. Only, don't break the law," he cautioned. "Our intent is to show them we will not take this anymore, that they should be scared, but not give them a legal way to lock us up. And be smart. Cameras are everywhere. Be mindful not to get photographed or recorded."

More than a few gasps traveled through the room, but for the most part, the heads of each family had known this was coming. They had spent the day in our kitchen discussing it.

"And the last thing, before we open the floor to discussion, if you are attacked, protect yourself. Do not be a victim. Do whatever it takes to get free, no matter what that entails."

Again, chatter erupted. This was huge. In normal families, this may mean fighting back, but Daddy was talking to a room full of people with abilities ranging from heating objects to the point of catching fire, to blowing down trees by manipulating the wind. Everyone had always been instructed to never, ever use their Gifts to harm under any circumstances.

That ban had been lifted, granting my family a freedom most of us had never known.

Amidst the chaos of a million discussions, Delia and I slipped outside.

***

At a quarter to midnight, Delia and I tiptoed out the front door, careful to ease the squeaky screen shut. I clutched the closed pocketknife I had taken from Daddy's desk drawer so tight, I could feel the engraving in the handle. I'd never been scared of the dark, not even as a child. But I'd never before had a reason to be afraid. Now the fear of who lay out of sight, watching us unseen, made my skin crawl. And while the closed knife would be next to useless if we were attacked, the weight of it in my hand made me feel better.

Once we were at a safe distance from the house, Delia snickered. "What are you planning on doing with that thing, Tully? Throwing it at someone?"

"It's better than nothing," I whispered back.

As we neared the remains of the fruit stand that had been such a huge part of our lives, I saw the silhouettes of three men. Moonlight played across Logan's handsome features.

"I'm so glad that you came," I said, throwing my arms around his neck.

"Of course I came," he whispered into my ear.

The moon was bright and clear, and the five of our faces all wore matching worried masks. Behind us the beams of the stand stood up like charred bones. It was weird it was gone. I couldn't say I would miss sitting in a hard chair, being bored to tears, but the fruit stand had stood at the end of our gravel drive, always looking the worse for wear, since before I was born. And now, it simply wasn't.

"So," Jack said. His thumbs were hooked through his belt loops and he rocked from heel to toe on his tennis shoes. "What now?"

"What do you mean?" Thomas asked.

"Well, there's no fruit stand to work at, anyone over the age of twenty has been given permission to use their gifts and go into town as they wish, but I'm sure that means everyone over the age of twenty, except for Tully. *My* dad was even acting weird when I told him I wanted to run to town tonight, and he's never had a problem with it before. I get the feeling they're waiting for something to happen," Jack shrugged, "But in the meantime, they're going to watch us like hawks."

"You mean crows," Delia offered. "Watch us like crows."

"Hmph," I snorted at Delia's joke.

"So what I'm saying is, I think we're going to be on lockdown. I might be the only one here not matched with someone," he continued, using the term that made me cringe. "But I don't like the idea of being a prisoner any more than you all do." Jack motioned from Logan to Thomas. "So what next? We got to figure out what the hell is going on

before something bad happens, again. And in the meantime, there has
to be a way for us to have a little freedom."

"We know who's behind this," Delia said. "Joshua Armstrong has
had it out for us for a long time. Tully told me about what he said the
other night. He pretty much confessed he was going to attack us."

Jack bit his bottom lip.

"It's not your fault, Jack," Delia added.

"But why now?" I asked. "And why would they attack you,
specifically?"

Delia hugged herself and kept her eyes toward the ground. Crap. I
had opened my big mouth, forgetting that she hadn't told Thomas
about the rape.

Jack walked put his arm around Delia's shoulder in the protective
way he'd done their entire lives.

"I don't know," my sister mumbled. Thomas, who had been
standing on the other side of Delia, took her hand.

"What does Tallulah mean? What happened to you?" he asked. He
leaned closer to Delia, like she was the only one around.

"I'm sorry, Del," I said, hoping I wasn't making things worse.

"It's fine," Delia whispered, her face set defiant and hard.

She gave Thomas the full weight of her gaze. "I was raped. About
two weeks before I met you. We don't know who it was. They left me
unconscious. In that ditch," she pointed to the place she had been
tossed, "I was blindfolded the entire time. I kept blacking out." Her
eyes were steely with no more tears left for the subject.

I held my breath, worried about how Thomas would reply. Delia
was acting tough, but she wasn't. She was more fragile now than she
had ever been. I could see it in the way she shook, bottom lip quivering
as she waited for Thomas to react. Again, I kicked myself for my folly.

Thomas didn't say a word, instead he pulled Delia close to him,
wrapping her in his arms, and held her. Jack let her go but didn't move
away.

Delia's spine straightened at the embrace. Her hands balled into
tight fists, and she pulled her brightest smile onto her face like a
Halloween mask. But I knew she was struggling with the close contact.
I knew she wanted to be okay. To move on. But she wasn't there yet.

When Thomas released her, Delia's smile was replaced with a look of relief. She took a deep breath before saying, "I don't know who did it. And honestly, I don't think I want to know. Right now, he's a faceless monster. He's someone I can put from my mind. But God. If it was Joshua Armstrong..." she shivered.

I thought I understood what she meant.

Armstrong hated us. He viewed us as dogs. The thought of him even touching me made me sick to my stomach, so the idea he might have violated my sister had to make Delia ill on a level I couldn't grasp. *Could someone who claimed to be a man of God really do such a thing, though?* I had a bad feeling Armstrong wouldn't blink at the idea of bombing us. Part of me wanted to storm over to his house right now and demand answers. He was a bad man, for sure, but a rapist? It didn't feel right.

"Even if Armstrong was the one who bombed us, why now? Why after all these years, would he finally drive his cult into trying to take us out? It's no secret to anybody in Brooklyn that we have powers, even if they don't fully understand what those powers are," I mused. "Shoot, Grandma and Aunt Trudy grew up on this same plot of land. So what happened to set this off now?"

There had to be a reason. Brooklyn might be prejudiced, but the crime rate was almost nonexistent. And all of sudden we were getting raped and bombed? It didn't make sense.

"I don't know if Delia and Tully have noticed," Jack chimed in, "but it seems like the overall atmosphere in town has been more hostile this past month or so."

I thought back to the first day I'd ever met Logan, and how Myrtle had attacked me, accusing Daddy of incest. I had eaten there for years, and while I would have never called her a friend, that day she had blindsided me with her threats. *Could it really be a coincidence?*

"I say, we need to all be on the lookout. Be careful. Because whoever is doing this obviously isn't scared of getting caught. I still can't believe they threw a freaking bomb in broad daylight," Jack said.

They either weren't worried about getting caught, or were getting careless. Either way, it meant we had a better chance of finding out who they were. "Do you remember seeing any cars drive by?" I asked Jack. I had tried and tried to remember if I had heard a passing car while I was in the woods with Logan, but no matter how hard I thought, I couldn't be sure.

"Now that you say that, I don't." Jack scratched his head. "I guess maybe there could have been, but nothing stands out, and I was running right down the side of the road. Why didn't I think of it before?"

"So what does that mean?" Delia asked.

"It means, whoever did it must have planted the bomb here the night before, and they must have put it somewhere we wouldn't have found it," I stated.

"If it was on a timer, then they were trying to kill us, and not just scare us. It was dumb luck none of us were in there. Or anyone else for that matter." Jack visibly recoiled. "And who in hell knows how to make a freaking timed bomb?"

All five of us were silent as we contemplated what it meant. Someone wanted us dead. I hugged myself tightly and leaned into Logan.

"So. How are we going to continue to have some small semblance of a life?" Delia inquired.

God bless her for changing the subject so obviously.

"You must mean you and Jack when you say continue," I mumbled.

My lack of any kind of life had been bearable when I thought we were all suffering the same fate. Now that I knew Delia and Jack had both been doing whatever they wanted for the past year, it made me feel even more like a naïve girl who had been afraid to live her own life. A coward.

Jack shrugged. "I guess we have to play it by ear. I say we let everyone kind of calm down, and then start meeting up in town. I don't think sneaking out is going to work. I bet my Dad is sitting on the porch waiting for me right now."

I hoped not. If Uncle Gavin knew Jack was here, that meant our parents would check on us, and I really didn't feel up to another fight.

"Jack, what did you tell Daddy that me and Delia were doing when the bomb went off?" I asked.

Jack blushed at the question. "I'm sorry, Tully, but I couldn't lie to him. You know how he is."

"I'm not mad. But really, what did you tell him? I think I have an idea." I wriggled my brows.

"I told him you went for a walk and that me and Delia went for a ride. He said he noticed my truck wasn't anywhere around so I had to tell him we rode with Thomas. He kind of pieced the rest together." Jack frowned.

"So you didn't outright tell him anything about Delia and Thomas?"

"No. I guess not. Why? What does that matter now?"

"Because. Thomas was my match. The man that was picked for me by Aunt Trudy. If they don't think anything is going on between Delia and Thomas, then they could be convinced you two were distracting Thomas for me so I could be with Logan," I said, waiting for the idea to sink in. Instead, they stared at me with wide, uncomprehending eyes.

"So?" asked my sister, not following.

"So, then Thomas can come and pick me up for a date. You can come along as our chaperone." I scrunched my fingers into air quotes as I said the words date and chaperone. "And then ya'll can drop me off with Logan. Thomas can pick me back up and bring us home and no one is the wiser," I pronounced, proud of my idea.

"That's a great plan, Tully, but it doesn't really fix things. It's like putting a Band-Aid on a broken arm," Jack slapped his forearm for emphasis, "We need to figure a way to get things *at least* to normal."

He was right. I had already decided to have a look around Armstrong's property. I just hadn't planned on mentioning it until I'd had a chance to talk to Logan. I also hadn't planned on explaining everything in front of Delia either. I didn't want my pregnant sister sneaking around, trying to help. Jack might come. I could definitely use his charm. And I was braver with Logan around. His Chans might actually prove useful too. I still had the suspicion it had something to do with getting us out of the produce stand before the explosion.

"Well. Now you mention it, I was thinking I might need to go have a look around Armstrong's house to check on a few things."

Delia shook her head. "No, I don't want you anywhere near that crazy Preacher!"

I patted her arm and gave her my best innocent look. "I won't go anywhere near him. I only want to check out his house, and the church, see what I can find."

Like maybe a red hatchback. Even if he didn't own one, I was willing to bet someone in his congregation did.

"I won't do anything reckless, no one will see us, and besides, Logan will be with me," I assured her, hoping the last part was true.

Eyebrows rising, Jack crossed his arms. "You're going to break into the man's house?"

"No!" I exclaimed. "Just have a look around outside, that's all."

Jack nodded. "That could work."

Next to him, my sister bit her bottom lip, and then added, "But you have to promise to be careful. Look from a distance, then leave."

Holding one hand up like I was swearing an oath, I crossed my heart with the other.

The entire time I was laying out my plan, Logan stood quietly behind me. He hadn't said the idea was crazy, but he hadn't exactly jumped in to say he would help either.

I spun around to face him. "What do you think?" I asked.

"I think I really like you. And of course I want to help catch whoever is doing this to ya'll. But I wish there was a way without lying to your parents. I don't want to start out on your Dad's bad side."

I wiggled away from him, frustrated. *Not this again.* "Logan, we already talked about this, and after what happened today, things will only be harder."

"I know. But I'm twenty-three. I have a full time job. I want to date you. There's nothing wrong with any of that so I don't know why we have to lie. We're adults," he motioned from him to me. "I can kind of understand not telling your Dad about searching for clues, because why cause him to worry? But as far as us being together, I don't understand what the big deal is..." His voice trailed off.

I implored Delia, Jack, and Thomas for help. "Can't ya'll please tell him that I'm not exaggerating. As if it weren't obvious by the fact I had to sneak out for this little shin-dig?"

"Look, I know how you feel," Thomas said. "I've worked off shore on an oil rig for the last couple of years. I live in the world where people don't even know our kind exists. If the guys knew I couldn't really be serious with anyone unless my great Uncle Lloyd set it up, I would be laughed out of the ocean. I've an older sister whose spent most of her twenties away at college to avoid being matched. When she's done with school, she'll be qualified to deliver babies, but not pick her own husband." He ran a hand through his hair. "So yeah, it kind of sucks, but that's how it is for us. And really, under regular circumstances, I'd agree that maybe ya'll should push for a change. Hell, we all could. But after all of this," Thomas gestured toward the burned ground. "Families like ours aren't going to be even considering doing things differently in the matching department for a while. Your best bet is to keep it a secret." He shrugged his shoulders. "That's my two cents anyway."

"He's right. It sucks. But he's right," Jack added.

Delia only nodded.

"If it's the only way I can see you, then I guess that's how it has to be," Logan conceded, raising his hands in defeat. "For now."

I smiled. I hated lying to my parents too, but I would do anything to see Logan, and I was glad to know he felt the same.

"So you come pick me up and we act like all is going good with the match," I said to Thomas. "Mama probably won't say anything. I don't know with Daddy. Since it's an approved match, he might be fine, but he did see me with Logan, so he might see right through it."

Thomas's eyebrows drew together, no doubt the memory of Daddy, eyes green-black while controlling wind and rain, playing through his mind.

"Why don't we give it a little time first," Thomas offered. "Like let's wait until next week. I'm staying in Peachton at the Ramada. It's comfortable, and I'm good with staying longer. I'll call my Uncle Lloyd and tell him we hit it off. He'll probably say something to your Aunt and that might make it easier. Besides, whoever did this will expect your family to come looking. If we wait, I think we might have a better chance of them slipping up."

I had to fight back my protective instinct. Waiting was the last thing I wanted to do, but he was right. It was too dangerous right now. "That makes sense. So a week then. Call the house some this week to talk to me. That'll make it more believable."

"Good plan," Thomas agreed.

After a nod to me, he and Delia walked a few feet away, heads together.

Logan pulled me closer to him, wrapping his arms tight around my waist. He surprised me with a kiss. I fell into it, wanting his lips to linger as long as possible. We didn't separate until spots danced on the edge of my vision from lack of air. Even then, I didn't want to.

"Next week?" I gasped.

"The longest week of my life."

Jack rolled his eyes. I'd forgotten he was standing there. *That's not creepy at all, Jack.*

After far too brief goodbyes, Logan and Thomas loaded into their trucks and headed toward their homes, or in Thomas's case, the Ramada. Jack, Delia, and me linked arms and headed down the drive.

"Well, at least you two will have a life," Jack said.

I hadn't even thought about finding a way for Jack to come along. I mean, he had never really had the need to be sneaky before.

"I'm sure it'll be okay for you to tag along with us," I said.

"Yeah. And then what? Go on your date with you? No thanks." He snorted.

"Actually, I was kind of hoping you'd help me check Armstrong's? Charm would be useful, and no way am I letting Delia come."

To my surprise, my sister didn't protest at being told she couldn't do something. *Good. I didn't want to argue with her about this.*

"Good idea," Jack agreed. "Maybe while you and Logan are checking the church I can search the Reverend's place. Less chance of me getting caught alone. And don't worry, we'll figure this thing out." He sounded confident.

I squeezed his arm a little tighter. "You're the best, Jack."

He shrugged and said through a huge smirk, "I know."

We parted ways at our front door and Delia and I watched until we could no longer see Jack's silhouette in the moonlight. Thank God there were no crows.

Chapter Nineteen

Once Daddy lifted the ban on using our Gifts, there always seemed to be a nice breeze blowing, and the air was filled with the natural perfume of flowers in full bloom. Colors even seemed brighter. Delia and I lounged beneath the shade of a weeping willow and watched our first family picnic. My younger cousins played openly, practicing their control in a way I had never been allowed to. One of the younger girls, Dory, made bubbles using the moisture that hung so heavy in our southern air for another cousin to pop mid-flight with tiny jolts of static electricity.

My Uncle Frankie's little boy gave new meaning to the game "freeze-tag," chasing his playmates around and shocking them with zaps of icy-cold whenever they were caught. We laughed and encouraged them from our refuge in the shade. Others listened to the secrets told by butterflies and lizards and garden moles. Not far away in the orchard, a few of our pre-teen cousins danced with the wind, blowing juicy apples down from the treetops for the entire gaggle of children to enjoy.

No longer ordered to hide what we were capable of had taken a while to sink in, but after a few days, it was like everyone was happy for the first time.

The word whimsical didn't do it justice.

Del, Jack, Logan, Thomas, and I had managed to work our plan twice. Once with me and Logan driving down to check the cars at

Reverend Armstrong's church during one of their many weekly "prayer" meetings, while Jack drove past his house. We didn't see a red hatchback, or anything else suspicious for that matter. On his way to meet us on Sunday, Thomas drove by the Embers of the Righteous Fire Church to do a quick scan of the parking lot, but he didn't have any better luck than we did. The last time we managed to work our plan, Delia convinced us to take a break from investigating, and instead we got pizza in Peachton, convincing Jack to come along by promising no awkward kissing in front of him. Of course, I broke that promise, but what did Jack expect, really?

In that moment, I had been able, for at least a little while, to push away the misery that threatened to bubble to the surface from somewhere under my skin. I could pretend we were a normal group of friends hanging out. It was a good and much needed respite from the constant need that pulled at me. *I have to find the attacker.* I knew the only way I'd ever feel safe again was once the person that had attacked my sister, who'd attacked all of us, was put away—one way or another.

By the way Delia refused to talk about either the attack on her, or the fruit stand, I could tell she was trying to move forward, to forget. And I really couldn't blame her.

But that didn't mean I was ready to.

It wasn't only us and the younger cousins relishing in the distraction.

Even the older adults seemed a little more lighthearted than expected. Especially Mama.

That night as we helped her prepare dinner, she was a smiling, giggling ball of energy.

"Mama, what kind of a bee have you got in your bonnet?" Delia asked her.

Mama's eyes twinkled, not with magic, but mirth. "Well," Mama said, pausing dramatically. "You know that checker down at the Piggly Wiggly, the gray haired lady whose bun is pulled so tight it makes the corners of her eyes turn up?"

Delia wrinkled her nose. "Yeah. I know who you mean. That woman's skin looks like a piece of crumpled paper that's been opened and smoothed," she said, cutting potatoes into a large bowl. "Two words, lady: night cream. She should try it.'"

"Oh, you mean May?" I asked, remembering the red and white plastic nametag pinned to the terrible woman's apron. "Lord, she stinks. The smell of stale cigarettes hangs around her like a cloud. Like that dirty kid on the old Charlie Brown cartoons."

"You'd think someone would tell her," Delia added.

I nodded in agreement as I continued to put together a dinner salad.

Mama's bright eyes widened as she nodded. "Sounds like you girls know exactly who I'm talking about."

Again came a long, dramatic pause during which Delia and I leaned forward. How could we forget? May never smiled. Or even spoke, for that matter, except to tell us what we owed or to answer a direct question that couldn't be done justice by a snort or grunt or eye roll. All of these things would have even still been tolerable, except that with everyone else, she was pleasant. The checker would laugh and joke with customers ahead of us in line, but as soon as it was our turn, the woman soured.

Mama put down the spoon she had been stirring with and sat at the table. We joined her. "Well, I unloaded my groceries, same as always, a carton of milk, whatever meat was on sale, you know, the usual. May rung them up, and then I told her to hold on, that I had a coupon for the chicken." Mama's eyes glowed emerald with mischief. "That hussy told me it was too late. So, I told her it definitely was not too late, because I had not paid yet. So what did little miss May do? She crossed her bony arms over her chest, and told me she wasn't accepting my coupon and I needed to pay and get out."

"Really?" I asked, appalled. We had shopped at The Pig forever and May had always let it be known through her actions that she didn't like us, but she had never said anything before. That worried me more than a little.

"Really," Mom said, her glee growing with the smile she tried to hide. "Now listen, I am going to tell you what I did, but I don't want you repeating it. I wouldn't want to ruin anyone's reputation. No matter who they are."

I raised my eyebrows at Mama and nodded.

"Sure," Delia said, bobbing her head. "We'll keep it between us.

What did the checkout tramp do?"

I slapped playfully at Delia's hand for the comment, but couldn't help laughing.

"Well, I looked May straight in the eye and crossed my arms right back at her," Mama continued. "And I said, 'May, I think you're going to take my coupon and I think you're going to do it with the same smile you give everyone else.' She grunted at me and said, 'You think so, Huh? Why would I do that?' and so I told her, 'Well, maybe because *a little bird* told me how you like to entertain while your husband is off driving his rig across country.' That woman turned positively white!" Mama exclaimed.

Barely able to hold back her smile, Mama leaned in and continued, "And that's not even all. She asked me what I had heard exactly. I told her I knew all about how she loves to use Halloween costumes, especially a fuzzy dog costume in particular, to *please* her guests. I told her how I had heard that some of her guests wouldn't be too happy if word got out. Especially a certain bearded preacher."

"Mama, you didn't!" I laughed. "Wait. Eww. Gross! May does that!? With Reverend Armstrong?"

Delia laughed so hard she had to dab at her eyes.

God, it's good to hear her laugh like that again.

"Wow, Mom! I didn't know you had it in you! So what did freaky-May do?" Delia asked.

"I slapped my coupon on the counter. She grabbed it up, and scanned it without another word. I paid and left. Of course, I couldn't help but stopping at the door, though, to smile and tell her bye. Outside, when I was sure that she was watching me through the store window, I looked up and got several of my winged friends to fly down and land on my shoulders. You should have seen the look on her face when me and the little dears waved to her. She was terrified! Goodness! I know I shouldn't be proud because it is wrong, but it felt so good to finally teach that smug old biddy a lesson!"

Delia cackled in laughter again before jumping up from the table and sprinting toward the bathroom. "Mama! You're going to make me pee my pants!"

I wiped my eyes with the palms of my hands. It felt great to laugh, even if it was almost too much to think about the mean old checkout lady being a "Freaky May," as Delia had called her. What felt even better was hearing my baby sister laugh so hard and free. It made everything feel okay. Like how it used to be. Or at least, how I thought it used to be.

And even though I was happy with the laughter and gossip, a thought nagged the back of my mind. I wondered at why the woman had been so bold to speak out in the first place. It wasn't a good sign. Still, for Mama and Delia's sake, I pushed the speculation aside, determined to focus on the good. I wouldn't let the dark thoughts pollute my joy. I could worry about it later.

Chapter Twenty

I threw a piece of popcorn into the air and attempted to catch it in my mouth. It bounced off my forehead and joined its brothers on the floor next to the couch.

Delia laughed and threw another piece at me. It stuck in my hair. I pulled it free and popped it into my mouth.

"I talked to Jack yesterday," she said, rubbing the very tiny bulge of her belly, lounging back into the overstuffed sofa.

With the fruit stand gone, Daddy had yet to find us a new chore to fill our time. This meant our morning routine had morphed into hanging on the couch in our pajamas, reading or gossiping, until someone ran us either outside or to Grandma's house. Besides occasionally driving past Armstrong's house and church, or snooping around where the fruit stand had stood, most of my sleuthing was now in the form of me attempting to work things out in my mind, and keeping notes in an old composition book I stored in my desk drawer. I hadn't given up. Not at all.

But without anything new to go on, and Delia so uncomfortable talking about it, I had kind of hit a brick wall.

It's definitely time for another look around.

"So? You talk to Jack every day. I would be surprised if you didn't talk to Jack," I responded.

"Yeah. True. But he told me that somehow Aunt Brenda talked Uncle Gavin into letting him get a job! Isn't that great! Can you imagine?" She clapped her hands.

"Wow. That's cool," I said, the slightest bit of envy in my voice. "Where at?"

"He's going to Peachton today to fill out applications. He said he thinks he can get on at a feed store or maybe a nursery or something. He hasn't said so, but I know he isn't above using his Gift to get hired if it means he gets a little normal time."

"That's awesome." I sighed. "Has he decided if he's going to go to college next year or not?"

"I think he's planning on it." Delia smiled. "He goes back and forth. I think he likes the idea of it, but doesn't really see the point."

"I know exactly how he feels." I frowned. It felt like ages since I thought of the acceptance letter lying folded on my dresser. *So much has happened since then. Is going to school still a possibility? Do I even still want to go?* Yes. Definitely. *Could I really add more stress to my family?* Now that, I was unsure of. I shoved the thought away, not wanting to get depressed over the dream that had seemed in my grasp only months before.

The front door squeaked opened and Daddy walked in, his heavy footsteps rattling the house in a familiar way. "Girls."

"In here," we hollered in unison.

When you entered our house, you were in the dining room, facing the open doorway into the kitchen. The living room was through another open doorway on your left with the couch separating the entryway and the television. It was a quirky old house, whose floor plan didn't really make sense by today's standards, but Mama said she loved all of the character and that you could never get that in a modern home.

"I'm heading to Home Depot," Daddy said. He hardly ever went to Peachton. Home Depot was one of the few places he thought was worth the drive into the slightly bigger town. "Ya'll wanna ride?"

"Sure!" Delia answered at the same time I said, "Nah."

"Ya'll go. I'm going to stay around here," I said.

"You sure? I'll buy lunch," he declared, raising his eyebrows.

"I'm sure."

"Okay then," he said. "I'll bring you back something from wherever we decide to eat."

"Give me five minutes, Daddy." Delia hopped up. "I need to brush my teeth and throw on something decent."

Daddy shook his head. "I'll be waiting in the truck, sweetheart. Don't turn five minutes into forty-five minutes. Your Pawpaw and Uncle Gavin are waiting on us to pick them up."

Delia grinned, and said, "Who me?" before skipping out of the room toward the stairs.

Mama and Grandma were planning to clean the hardwood floors, and if I stuck around, I would get roped into helping. It was one of those chores that if you were in the house while it was being done, then you could count on what Mama called, "being put to good use."

That might explain Daddy's trip into Peachton, now that I thought about it. It was the kind of chore me and Delia had been dodging since we were thirteen. Today I had been planning to ride Delia's pregnancy coat tails. She couldn't help move heavy furniture, and there was no way they would make one of us help and not the other. But since she was going into town with Daddy, I would have to disappear for a while, and I knew what I wanted to do.

I had a phone call to make.

***

Fifteen minutes later, I slipped out as soon as I heard Daddy's truck circle in front of our house after picking up Pawpaw and heading down the gravel drive. Mama and Grandma were too busy fussing over the best method to get the living room floor to shine to even notice. I snuck into Grandma's empty house and called Logan.

"You aren't worried about getting found out?" Logan asked, surprised when I suggested the rendezvous.

"Why? You don't think I'm worth the risk?" I teased. Truth was, I was a little worried, but strange enough, it added to the thrill. I was beginning to understand the appeal that sneaking out had held for Jack and Delia.

"No. I definitely wanna meet you today. I knew you were going to call. Seeing you in person will be a great bonus."

"Really?" I asked, amused.

This wasn't the first time that Logan had known I was going to call. Sometimes, the urge to talk to him became overwhelming. I would sneak away to give him a call, and he would answer before the phone even rang. It happened too often for it to be chalked up to coincidence.

It was something neither of us controlled, and I was beginning truly to believe there was more to his Chans than I had originally given Logan credit for. It also seemed that the more time we spent together, the stronger the connection grew, pulling us closer, as if Logan were right. As if we were meant to be.

"I'll see you in our spot in the woods in forty-five minutes," he said.

"Great," And boy, I meant it. I grinned. *Our spot.*

I slipped Grandma's old dial phone onto the receiver and headed out the back. I was going to loop the long way around the driveway to kill some time, instead of cutting through the woods to my house. Mama had kept her word through it all, keeping the crows out of my business, and to anyone who may have seen me, it'd seem like I was going for a run.

***

I paused at the blackened earth where the fruit stand had stood. My Uncles had cleaned away the debris this week, after letting it stand for a while as an ugly monument to the evil that had been done. Grandma could have made the new grass grow, snuffing out the ugly spot and turning it as green as if nothing had happened. But no one wanted that, because something *did* happen. The stain of burned ground stayed as a reminder someone had wronged us. There would be no question to our patrons as to why we were no longer open for business. It was a sign we wouldn't forget. That we weren't scared.

Only that wasn't entirely true, because I *was* scared. Delia was scared. Not even the freedom to use my power could make me forget the sight of Delia's body being dumped in a ditch, of that finger pointing at me, of our fruit stand blazing. I couldn't imagine ever feeling truly, one hundred percent safe, again. But I was careful to keep that fear hidden.

I pretended to inspect the dead area of ground while working up my nerve to dash into the woods. I had been a little worried about sneaking off, that someone might be lying in wait, but the thought of seeing Logan made those fears seem worth it. He was going to park his truck at one of the many logging turn off gates that dotted all of rural Mississippi. Men often left their trucks in those spots while they made the trek to deer stands, and recently Delia had told me a lot of town kids used them as places to go "parking."

I counted to twenty-five and when a car didn't pass, and no one ran up the driveway looking for me, I spun on my heels to dash into the woods, but as I was making my turn, something silver winked at me from the ground. I redirected my run, midstride, and barely caught myself from falling.

What's this? Everything that hadn't been burned had already been cleaned up and moved off, and I knew besides my own investigations, Daddy and my uncles had searched over the area a dozen times. It seemed impossible anything could have been missed.

I picked up the metal object. It was a small rectangle, smooth on one side, but with two prongs coming out of the other side. I shoved the thing into my pocket, planning on giving it a closer look when I was sure no one was around. I took a deep breath, swallowed my fear, and sprinted into the woods to meet Logan.

"There you are," he said. "I thought maybe you'd changed your mind." He walked toward me, and slipped his arms around my waist.

"Well, I was hoping we could go check one of the Reverend's haunts," I said, looking up through my lashes at him.

"So that's the only reason?" He stared down at me, his eyes working their way through me, in that familiar, but unnerving way.

"There might be one more." I stood on my toes and gave him a quick kiss on the lips.

He closed his arms around me tighter, pulling me in. His dark hair hung straight around his face, changing his green eyes to look almost magic. He tugged the elastic band from my hair, letting my own dark brown tresses tumble across my shoulders.

"You are so beautiful," he whispered as he stroked my hair.

"I'm not. Delia is the pretty one," I said automatically.

Logan pulled away from me, shaking his head.

Why did I say that?

He held onto my arms, as they hung straight on either side of my body. "What are you talking about?"

"Nothing. Forget it. It was a stupid thing to say and I didn't even mean to say it out loud." My cheeks burned hot.

"But that's what you think, though, right? Even if you wouldn't have said it, that's what would have went through your head? That you aren't the 'pretty one'?"

I shrugged, staring down at his converse.

"Tully, look at me," he said, gently placing his hand under my chin. "You're beautiful. Just because your sister is pretty, doesn't that you aren't. I think you're the most beautiful thing I've ever laid eyes on."

"Shut up," I whispered. The hot blush that had prickled across my face spread down my neck.

"No. I won't. Any girl can put on makeup and all that junk on her face, but Tully, you don't need that. You're gorgeous and you don't even try. You're real."

My mind raced, alternating between what he was saying, how beautiful *he* was, and how he must be insane because there was no one, NO ONE on this planet that would say I was prettier than Delia. She was perfectly groomed, while I forget to tweeze my eyebrows. I looked away, the same eye contact that had made me brave, now felt intrusive. Logan frowned, dropping his hands.

"Tully, that's not good. You know how many people would kill to look like you? I had a senior class for homeroom last year. You should have seen the crap those girls painted their faces with to try and get some attention, and they still couldn't hold a candle to you. Yeah, Delia is really pretty, but she tries to be."

I didn't know where my feelings were coming from. I had always thought of Delia as the pretty one, but it had never bothered me, not really. Looks weren't something I had ever cared about, so why now, at the worst possible time, were these insecurities deciding to pop up?

I smiled at Logan. "That's really sweet. Thank you."

Thank you? I thought. *Really? Thank you?*

"I'm not saying it to be sweet. I'm saying it because it's true and you need to hear it," he laid a gentle hand on my shoulder, "When I met your sister, it didn't even cross my mind to compare her to you."

"Well, why did Thomas want to be with her instead of me?" I blurted out.

Logan froze. "What are you saying? That you wish Thomas was interested in you instead?" He paused. "Thanks Tallulah. Thanks a bunch. I'm standing here like an idiot telling you how beautiful I think you are and you're wishing I were Thomas. The truth is, he would probably drop her like she was on fire if he thought he had a chance with you. Why wouldn't he?" He shook his head. "But the fact that you care...That hurts." He stood there, arms crossed over his chest.

I felt like a complete and total brat. *Why did I say that?* I hadn't given Thomas two thoughts since the night I met him, other than to wonder how he was going to take my sister's "news." No, I didn't care about Thomas. Not like Logan. That's why I kept risking everything to be with him. *And now I'm throwing it all away by opening my big mouth.*

"Logan. No. It's not that. I don't care. I don't care about Thomas at all. It's just that he was my first match. The first one handpicked for me, and I could tell the instant he saw my sister he wished that I was her. I don't want to be with him, I guess it made me think there was something wrong with me is all."

The anger and hurt that had filled his eyes softened, and the corners of his perfect lips lifted into the tiniest, almost-smile. Then, he kissed me. Really kissed me. It was rough, and possessive, and wonderful. His hands felt their way under the back of my t-shirt, until the addictive, electric prickle of his touch buzzed across my lower back.

Dizzy, I pulled away. I gazed again into his eyes, and for once, thank goodness, had nothing to say.

"If you think you want to be with Thomas, even a tiny bit in the back of your mind, you should say so now. If not, I'm going to believe you and never think about it again," he tucked a loose piece of hair behind my ear, "You really are beautiful, and that you don't think so makes me crazy."

"So you get hot for pretty girls with low self-esteem?" I asked, trying to bring back the easy humor we usually shared.

Logan shook his head. "No. It doesn't make me *that* kind of crazy. Your skin makes me *that* kind of crazy. The way you smell," he said, pulling me in for another rough, delicious, kiss. "Makes me *that* kind of crazy. Your eyes," his lips lightly brushed my forehead, "Make me insane. Your body..." He didn't finish telling me what my body did to him. He didn't need to.

Logan kissed me in a neat row down my neck, leaving a trail of fire that pulsed and beat in time with my heart. My breath hitched as he unhooked my bra, and then slid his hand over my naked skin. The nervousness was nothing compared to the desire that drove my actions.

Do I want this? Now? The question flickered for half an instant through my consciousness, but it was enough for Logan to pick up on. He hesitated, not saying a word.

"Yes," I whispered, and as soon as the words left my lips, I knew that I meant them. That was all it took.

Yes. This was definitely what I wanted.

Chapter Twenty-One

I snuggled closer to Logan, his chin resting perfectly on top of my head, like two puzzle pieces snapped into place. His long muscular arms wrapped around me, shielding at least part of my nakedness from the world, while a warm breeze licked lazily over our skin. It stirred my hair from where it lay against his chest. Tired contentment hung in the air, a feeling that contrasted greatly with the frenzied anticipation of only moments before, but a feeling that was just as good.

Maybe.

I turned my head and kissed whatever I could reach, which happened to be his shoulder, and wiggled my hips, pressing against his bare thigh.

"Again, so soon?" I could hear the smile in his voice.

"Later. Another day. Soon," I said, the words coming out awkward and jumbled.

Logan laughed, and kissed the top of my head.

"I hate to say this, but I think we need to at least get dressed," he said after a few minutes. "As much as I would like nothing more than to keep you naked and laying near me, I can't shake the image of your Dad walking into the woods and striking me down with lightening."

I sat up. "Yeah. You're right. Not about Daddy striking you down, though. He's at the hardware store. In fact, most of my family is in town doing God knows what today. So I'm pretty sure you're safe."

Being naked in the woods and caught up in the heat of the moment was one thing, but the longer we laid there on the grass and leaves, the more I couldn't help but think that we were *naked*. In the *woods*. As much as I loved lying alone with Logan, soaking each other up, there were some places I didn't want to get bit by a mosquito.

I felt safe laying in Logan's arms, but the tiniest bit of fear had twisted inside me and refused to leave. I was determined not to let thoughts of what happened last time we were together in this spot ruin my perfect moment. Yet, I couldn't totally ignore the nagging feeling. It sat in the back of my mind, like a thief hiding in an alley, waiting for the perfect moment to attack.

I tried to shove the worry aside, gave Logan another kiss on the shoulder, and sat up.

We pulled apart and searched around for our clothes, shaking off the leaves and debris as we gathered them up. Logan claimed his white under shirt from a pine sapling, giving me a chance to see all of him. Every inch of his skin was flawless, even perfection across his body, without a single tan line or scar. His arms and legs were long, and cut with muscle in a way that said that he must do more than sit around and play his guitar all day, even if he wouldn't admit to hitting the gym. He stretched his arms high over his head and sighed, showing of a row of sculpted abs, with obliques that made it hard to look away and drew my eye down to his narrow hips.

He caught me staring. "What?"

"You," I teased. "I bet more than one of your students is hot for teacher."

I sauntered over to him, enjoying the way his eyes lingered on my bare breasts. Rising up on my toes, I gave him another long kiss. When he stepped back, he grinned and slapped me on the butt. I froze, shocked, and he started laughing.

"You know that's war, right? I'll get you back," I said, trying to see if there was a handprint on my backside.

"Is that a promise?" His eyes danced with glee. "Because it'll be worth it if it means I'm going to see you naked again."

We pulled on our clothes and picked the leaves from our hair.

"Well, I have to say, I don't feel much like investigating after that. Not that I'm complaining, at all." I smiled. "What now?"

I hadn't expected anything to come of checking up on Armstrong, but I did feel a bit selfish for spending the entire afternoon distracted. Too much time had passed with me unaccounted for to risk sneaking off now. We could hang for a little longer, but eventually I would have to head back toward home.

"Tully," Logan said, "I don't want you to think I came here…for this. I wanted to see you. This was a surprise. An amazing surprise. You're special to me."

"I know," I replied. "You're special to me, too."

Neither of us wanted to be the one who left first, so we sat, propped against a pecan tree, dragging each second out for as long as we could. I laid my head on his shoulder, wallowing in our togetherness.

"We haven't been in each other's life for that long, but it's like I told you that very first day in the diner, I feel like I know you. I feel like I have always known you." Logan rested his head lightly against mine. "And I know I never want there to be a time when I don't know you. Know what I mean?"

"That's a lot of knowing," I teased.

"Well. I know." He laughed, and then angled his head so our eyes met. "For real, I've fallen for you, Tallulah. I know that's about as cheesy as a person can get, but it is what it is."

"Almost as cheesy as writing a check for a dollar to get a girl's attention." I cocked a brow.

"Hey! It worked, didn't it?"

"Yeah. I guess it did. I like you too, Logan, a lot." I kissed him softly on the lips. "A lot, lot."

The way he made me feel was more than like, and I knew it. I liked ice cream. I liked lying in my hammock. He made me feel beautiful, and smart, and loved. Even though I knew it was true, and had for a little while, the "L" word still surprised me with the ease at which it popped into my mind. But it was the only word that could do justice to how I felt. Yet knowing it, and being the first one to say it, were two very different animals.

We continued to sit in comfortable silence, our fingers laced together. *This is my happy place,* I decided.

The few streams of light that managed to squeeze through the dense trees darkened as a cloud moved in front of the sun, before pushing to the other side. An odd chill danced along my skin, even though it was well over eighty degrees.

"That was weird," I said, and jumped to my feet.

The sound of birds shrieking broke through the trees and I realized what the strange cloud was. It was De Ja Vu. Hundreds of wings beat against the air, same as the night I'd blacked out with Delia in my arms. The birds' cries grew louder, drowning all other sound. I shielded my eyes with my hand and stared into the sky at the never ending cover of birds. Not letting my mind process what I feared most, I left Logan standing in the trees and ran for home as fast as my legs would go.

Chapter Twenty-Two

Birds blanketed the yard in a living, writhing tarp, and still the cloud continued overhead, endlessly bringing more and more of the flock. There wasn't a spot left to land, but still they came. Redbirds, robins, blue jays, hawks, and even hummingbirds. The birds, many of whom were natural enemies, laid aside their differences to commune on the house of their friend. My mother.

And of course, there were crows. They bullied their way to the spots nearest the front door, where they called, screaming loudest of all.

Oh God.

I tore through the yard, and the birds parted for me like the red sea for Moses. I made my way up the front steps, my worry turning me clumsy as I tried to open the screen door. I paused, taking a deep breath, and tried again, this time managing to get inside the house.

"Mama?" I called at the top of my lungs. "Where are you? Grandma? Someone answer me!" I ran into the dining room. It was empty, the floor polish still sitting in grocery bags on the table.

"MAMA! Dammit! Someone answer me!" I yelled again, rushing into the kitchen.

Empty.

I thought I heard footsteps and froze. "Mama?" I considered for the first time the possibility I was overreacting. I listened again for the footsteps, but the only noise I could hear was the squawking from outside, and my own heart working overtime. I ran into the living room doorway, and scanned the area. It was empty, and undisturbed.

I turned to leave the room to go upstairs, but paused. Something didn't feel right. Everything looked in place. The lamps stood on their end tables. Mama's afghan was draped across the back of the couch where Delia had left it. I turned around, gooseflesh breaking across my arms and working its way up my neck. I forced myself to suck in another breath to calm my nerves.

That was it. Something was wrong with the air. Under the scent of furniture polish and fried things, the usual smell of our home, was another, *very wrong*, smell.

It wasn't even a smell, really, but almost a taste. A metallic taste that clung to the back of my throat. It reminded me of the time when I was ten and Delia had dared me to swallow a penny. It was a memory I hadn't thought about in years, but the coppery lilt of the air had pulled it to the forefront, making me smile, before reality drug me back into my present state of panic.

I scanned over the room again, taking a mental inventory. Again, I found everything in place, and again, I turned to go, thinking I was overreacting, but unable to shake the very real fear that gripped my insides.

That's when I saw the small red trickle on the floor. It came from underneath the couch, like someone had spilled a glass of red wine or punch and wiped most of it up before it ran. But a tiny stream had managed to escape under the sofa and out the other side.

Only, I knew it wasn't punch. I flashed back to the night I had witnessed Delia, bloody and abused, being tossed into the ditch. The trickle had run down my sister's legs and face in the same shade. I'm sure that the smell of metal had coated the air that night as well, but my senses had been shocked, and I couldn't remember.

I walked around the sofa, my steps careful, not wanting to find what was on the other side. Not really. But I knew I didn't have a choice.

"NOOOO!" I screamed. "God, no!" I sank to my knees and the red stickiness grabbed me wherever it touched, hanging on and staying. I didn't care.

I was faintly aware of footsteps on the porch.

The front door opened. "Tallulah?" Logan called. "Tallulah, where are you?"

I opened my mouth to answer, but instead of words, a wail pierced the air. The sound pulled from deep inside, starting at my soul, and working their way free. It was pure feeling vocalized; an expression of the pain clutching me, threatening to squeeze me dry until there was nothing left but a husk of someone who had lost something very important, and died from the inside out. The type of pain that words could never touch, and from which a person could never really recover.

Mama and Grandma lay crumpled on the floor, their life force surrounding them in one conjoined pool. Mama was on her back, her arms splayed beside her in different directions. The front of her orange sweater had absorbed the blood from her chest and was now colored a deep red.

As horrible as it was to see Mama, Grandma was a million times worse. Someone had stabbed her over and over, mutilating her chest and abdomen, and even slashing her arms and legs.

I sobbed. I know I did because I heard the sounds that came from me, doubling me over. But tears never fell. I began to slip down and away, my mind unable to accept what lay in front of me, bringing the strange relief of incomprehension.

Where is all of the blood coming from? Why are Mama and Grandma on the floor? "Get up!" I demanded. "Get up now!"

Panic gripped me, hard.

Logan stepped into the room and froze. "Oh, Tully. Oh, baby. I'm so sorry."

I crawled closer to my Mama and curled beside her. I wrapped my arms around her, ignoring the tacky grab of her blood, as I squeezed her close. Logan stared at me, but I didn't care. I continued to slip. Terror invaded my body and drew me into near hysterics before I disappeared into a hollow, empty peacefulness. It enveloped me, replacing hurt with calm, and suddenly I knew everything was going to be okay. Mama was going to be okay. Grandma too. They needed me to lie with them. That was all. They needed me and I was going to be there. This time I wasn't going to let them down.

"Tallulah, baby, you should get up," Logan said, his voice tight with a forced calm.

"No, Logan. She needs me. THEY need me," I said, rubbing the hair away from Mama's face and kissing her on her forehead.

Why is he talking to me like that? Like I'm dumb. My Mama needs me! Doesn't he understand?

"I know, baby, but we need to call the police now. They're going to need pictures. Why don't you come sit over here? Or better yet, let's go outside. It's so nice out there. We can look at all the pretty birds. Come on! What do you say?" he said again, in the same, weird voice.

What's wrong with him? Mama hates having people over when things are a mess. And she'll never allow pictures while her floor looks like this. Never.

"Logan. Can you get me a dishtowel? They're in the drawer in the kitchen next to the sink. Mama never wants people to see her house like this," I said.

Logan's eyes grew wide, and sweat beaded across his forehead in tiny drops.

"Um. Ok. Why don't you come show me where they are? I don't want to dig around in your Mama's kitchen," he replied.

"Fine. I'll get it myself," I snapped. I stood, and walked around the couch toward the doorway. When I passed Logan, he reached out, grabbed my wrists, and pulled me to him, wrapping me in a bear hug that pinned my arms to my side.

"Hey! What're you doing? I gotta clean up!" I yelled. Logan held me tight and we stumbled with him half-dragging me to a chair in the dining area. We sat down hard, he in the chair and me in his lap. "Logan, let go of me!"

"Tallulah, I'm so, so sorry. Listen baby, let's sit here a minute. Let's just sit here and calm down a bit, ok?"

"No, Logan! Let go of me!" I hissed. "Maybe you should go. I gotta help Mama and Grandma clean up the floor. Besides, they aren't going to be happy when they notice you here."

"Tallulah, baby, they're dead. They're dead and we have to call the police so they can catch the bastard who did this, but for that to happen you have to stay out of there." He wiped stray hairs off my face. "I'm sorry. So, so sorry and I feel like a complete ass for this, but baby, you have to stay here. Right here, in this chair for now."

"Dead? What are you talking about?" I whispered. "Why would you say that? You're supposed to be my friend. My boyfriend. Why would you say that?"

"Baby, lets calm down and think. Look at this blood," He put my hand up to my face. "I'm so sorry, Tallulah," he said again, "But think, baby, where did this come from? Think about where your Mama and Grandma are."

I stared at the bright blood caked between my fingers and on my palms as what Logan was saying sank in.

Their wide, glossy eyes. All that blood. And they had been lying so still on the floor in broken heaps. Dead. They're dead. Admitting that hurt so bad I thought I might die too.

Logan slid from under me and sat me in the chair, arranging my hands in my lap. It hurt too bad to think, to make the connection between thought and movement. So I sat, motionless, laboring with each inhale and exhale. The peace that had enveloped me was gone, leaving behind only pain.

They are dead.

Logan walked into the kitchen and picked up the phone. Three little beeps somehow managed to echo over the sound of the screaming birds outside.

"Yes. We have an emergency..." I heard Logan say into the phone.

My mind drifted away.

Chapter Twenty-Three

The next time I was aware, Logan was sitting across from me, watching me. Someone had cleaned my hands and face, but my clothes were still sticky, covered with evidence that everything hadn't been some kind of terrible nightmare.

Men in uniforms milled around, violating our home. People were not murdered in our neck of the woods. It simply wasn't done. We were a world away from Jackson, and it seemed that anyone who could feign the authority to be at the scene in our house was there, regardless whether or not if they were needed.

The EMTs and coroner had shown up, and with harsh, jarring movements, were putting Mama and Grandma in body bags. It felt wrong. The two most important women in my life, the women who had raised me to be who I was, were being whisked away. It wasn't right. Didn't they know how incredible those women were? How special? They deserved better. They deserved to be handled with care. To be taken delicately. Not tagged and bagged like street criminals on a CSI rerun.

At some point, members of my family had arrived and were answering questions from the uniformed people. Several of the men I recognized from Brooklyn. Like a lot of positions that were held in town, I knew many of the people were probably volunteers who held other jobs, first responders, and others who couldn't wait to get a peek into the local freaky family's house. The expressions that decorated their faces ran the gamut from horrified to smug with only one person showing anything that resembled empathy.

He was dressed in slacks and a polo with the Quiet Pines Funeral Home insignia on the pocket. I sneered. I could picture the man setting in front of his mirror trying out expressions to make grieving families feel comfortable, working to find that perfect balance of sympathy and understanding that would be great for business. The thought made me hate him. I narrowed my eyes, watching as he stood talking to Mama's little sister, Aunt Kay, who herself was standing tightlipped, and looking like she was trying very hard to hold it together. Her skin was splotchy, and she hugged herself, rocking on the balls of her feet, as the funeral home man gave her information. I couldn't hear what they were saying, but Aunt Kay looked how I felt. I doubted very much that anything from the conversation was sinking in; however, I vowed we would not use Quiet Pines.

Heavy steps pounded across the front porch. "Well you're going to have to talk to her later. I told you, ain't nobody going near my niece right now. The poor girl just saw her Mama and her Grandmamma dead in her own house. Her Daddy ain't here yet, so YOU ARE GONNA HAVE TO WAIT!" Uncle Drew's deep voice boomed from outside. Seconds later, he stomped into the house and let the screen slam behind him.

"Dammit to hell, if that boy don't git to gittin' right now he's gonna wish he had!" he hollered.

"I'll go talk to him," Uncle Frankie said from the corner. He nodded to the man he was speaking with, the same man who had put my Mama into a body bag, and walked out the front door.

"And somebody do something about all these damn birds!" Uncle Drew hollered after him.

I closed my eyes. The image of my Mama and Grandma was there, waiting for me behind my eyelids.

My stomach turned violently at the memory, and I jerked my eyes open with epiphany. *Whoever did this must have known exactly what we were capable of.* Grandma was proof.

The person who'd killed her had really taken the time to make sure she was dead. To make sure that she couldn't heal herself. Inside me, something changed, and a hardness that had not been there before settled in.

I realized nothing could ever go back to how it was before. Without Mama or Grandma, a chapter of our lives was over. No more pretending things could be peaceful and that we were fine. The person who did this, the person who knew us and *still did this*, they would pay. I might not be strong, and I might still be learning a Gift that kind of sucked, but that didn't matter. One way or another, they were going to hurt.

The shrill ring of our house phone filled the room. I shook my head to clear away the scene that threatened to camp out permanently in my mind. I wanted to remember my Mama how she was. Beautiful, happy, a little bossy. Not the horrible, empty shell that had been broken and displayed on the floor.

When no one had picked up the phone by the fourth ring, I glanced at Logan. He nodded and went to look for the phone. I sat, numb and angry, wishing everyone would leave, but not ready to be alone, either.

Uncle Drew looked over from where he was standing with his hands in his pockets staring at the wall. The lines in his face had deepened, and there were new bags under his eyes. He looked old. Mama was his baby sister. Grandma was his Mama. It was strange to think that my big, rough uncle was in as much pain as me. Losing your baby sister and your mama had to be as bad as losing your Mama and Grandma. Maybe.

It was like he noticed that I was sitting at the table for the first time, even though I had been planted there, unmoving, since Logan had gotten me off the floor. Uncle Drew crossed the room in three strides and sat heavily in the seat Logan had occupied seconds earlier. He seemed like he wanted to tell me something, opening his mouth and then closing it when no words would come. Instead, he grabbed my hands and squeezed them, staring at me in the eye without blinking. He held the sorrowful stare for several seconds before getting up and walking back outside, again letting the screen door slam.

Mama hated it when we let the screen door slam.

Logan stepped back into the room with the phone, his hand covering the mouthpiece.

"Who is it?" I heard myself ask.

"Where's your Uncle Drew?"

"He went outside. But who is it, Logan?" I asked again.

He paused, his face scrunched and his mouth drew tight, like he tasted something terrible and wasn't able to spit it out.

"It's your Dad," he said.

For the briefest second I worried about how much trouble I was in with Daddy, since Logan had answered the phone. I realized how stupid that was as guilt burned through me, killing me. I was lower than low. *That doesn't matter. Nothing matters.* How could I forget? How could I already, even for a single second, forget? The coroner was still here and I was already selfishly allowing myself to escape the situation. *I'm a horrible person. Maybe if I had been here I could have stopped it. Maybe this happened because I broke the rules.*

"Tallulah?" Logan interrupted my thoughts again. "I'm going to be right back. I have to run this outside. Don't go anywhere."

Where would I go? I wanted to snap, but it wasn't Logan I was mad at, it was me. So I nodded as he turned and left to find my uncle.

The way Logan had looked at me with his face full of sorrow, reminded me of when Delia and I had rescued a bird fallen from its nest. It was bald, and ugly, and pitiful. I named him Beaker and put him in a shoebox that Delia decorated with Hello Kitty stickers and neon markers. We sat the box on the kitchen counter next to where Mama had been washing dishes, and told her Beaker was going to be our pet. I was so excited, knowing how birds loved Mama and I knew she would be so happy. Instead, she looked at us the same way Logan had. Her lips pressed tight, as if she was trying to decide how to tell me something she didn't want to say. The next morning Beaker was dead.

"Baby birds can't live without their mommies," Mama said to us while we were snuggled up on the couch, stricken with the kind of grief only little girls can experience over a dead bird.

"Well why did you let us keep him?" Delia had cried.

"Baby, I should have told you yesterday, but I didn't want to. It was sad news. But I still should have told you. I'm sorry," Mama had said, hugging us both tight, making everything right in the world.

Would everything always remind me of Mama? Every look or comment someone made. *Anytime I saw a bright ugly sweater or heard a bird sing? Anytime I caught the scent of cinnamon or saw flowers blooming, would it bring back memories of Grandma?* God, I hoped so. I couldn't forget anything. I needed to hang on to every small detail. Not only how they looked, but who they were and the way they made me feel. Their goodness. I deserved the image of them on the floor, but they deserved to be remembered as they had always been. Sweet and perfect.

True to his word, Logan was back inside within a minute. Instead of sitting back down, he stood in front of my chair and kneeled, grasping my heavy hands the same way Uncle Drew had minutes earlier. The electric fireworks Logan's touch usually brought were gone. I watched my fingers turn red and thought that he was probably holding on too tight. *It should probably hurt*, I thought, but I didn't say anything. I waited for whatever Logan needed to tell me. I couldn't imagine it would matter, but he was still gazing at me in the way that reminded me of the dead bird.

That reminded me of Mama.

"It's your Grandfather. Your Pawpaw, Tully," Logan said.

I didn't say anything. It hadn't occurred to me that Pawpaw or Daddy were not back yet, but of course, they weren't. There's no way Daddy or Delia would leave me at this table if they were here. They should have been back. The second this happened someone should have called them. I should have done it.

I keep letting my family down.

I closed my eyes and the image of my Mama and Grandma once again filled my head. I jerked my hands from Logan, jumped out of my seat, and ran to the door.

I barely made it through the screen, careful not to let it slam, before I lost my stomach over the side of the steps. I hung over the railing, wondering where all of the birds had gone, and heaved. Logan appeared seconds later with a glass of water. I swished it around in my mouth and spit it out, before setting the plastic cup on the rail and stepping into Logan's arms. I let him hold me. He squeezed me to him as I buried my face into the space between his neck and shoulders. He didn't say a word, and I loved him for it. What could he have said? Everything was NOT going to be okay, and I sure as hell didn't want to hear it would be. I didn't want him to try and make me feel better. I didn't want to feel better. I deserved my hurt.

I should have been here. I could have stopped this from happening. The more I thought about it, the more I was sure it was the truth. I could have called someone, or convinced the killer to stop, or maybe all it would have taken was one more person, me, to help fight off the murderer. If I hadn't broken the rules, if I hadn't been so selfish, I would still have them.

Logan holding me was more than I deserved. I deserved to crush under the weight of this burden, alone. But I was weak, so I squeezed him tighter and breathed him in, his presence both calming and shaming me.

Uncle Drew stood a few feet behind Logan, paused in front of the door. He caught my eye with his glare, giving a shake of his head before walking inside.

"Let's go in, Tully. I gotta tell you something. I hate to tell you, baby, but I have to." Logan's voice was heavy.

"Tell me here," I said, unable to deal with my Uncle's disapproval on top of everything else.

Logan hesitated.

"Ok," he said. "Your Pawpaw is at the hospital in Peachton. They think he had a heart attack at the appliance store. Your Dad, Uncle Gavin, and Delia are there with him, but that's all the information I have. Your Uncle Drew will know the rest."

That didn't make any sense. Pawpaw couldn't have a heart attack. He was the picture of perfect health, and not just for his age. I had never known of him getting anything more significant than a cold. Grandma's Vigour had always extended to cover him more than anyone.

I bit my lip until I could taste a salty prick of blood.

But Grandma isn't here anymore. So her Vigour couldn't protect him.

For the first time I realized the danger my family could be in. And for the second time, I understood the person who hurt us had to know exactly what they were doing.

"I need to go talk to my uncle. Thank you for everything Logan, but you should go. I will call you as soon as I can," I croaked.

I pulled away from him. My steps were mechanical, like a wind-up toy using its last bit of power, stiff and slow. I headed inside and shut the door before Logan could protest.

I knew it was cruel to shut him out, especially now, but I had no choice. There was no room in my life for someone like Logan. *If I hadn't been with him… If I'd only been at home…*

The EMTs had loaded my Mama and Grandma and driven away. The funeral guy had gone, as well as most of the other workers I couldn't place. Now, the room was crowded with familiar, sad faces with fierce glowing eyes. Everyone who'd been home, except those who had kids to care for, was crammed into the smallish dining room, circled around a lone deputy.

"Ok, folks, if any of you can think of anything, anything at all you feel we should know, please call us. I'm going to need to talk to Tallulah sometime within the week. Now, I know it's a hard time for you all, but the sooner I can get any information, the better off our chance is to catch the person who did this," the cop said, peering at his yellow legal pad.

Uncle Drew snorted. "Yeah. Ya'll are going to try real hard to solve this, huh? Kinda like ya'll tried so hard to get the person who blew up our property or how ya'll tried sooooo hard to find the pervert that hurt one of our girls? Deputy, I don't know you, but I know Chief Rucker and it'll be a cold day in hell before he gives a damn about anything that happens out here. Hell, he ain't even worried enough to come himself? And he didn't send anyone but you? How long have you even been a cop, boy?"

"Um," the deputy said, paling. "This is my first year."

"Hah! You're about as useful as a milk bucket under a bull, and you got the nerve to stand here, in my family's house, and act like this case takes any kind of priority?" His voice boomed. Outside the wind picked up as Uncle Drew's eyes started to flicker.

"I'm doing my job, sir," the deputy said, his voice cracking on the last word. His self-perceived importance deflated under my uncle's gaze. Uncle Drew had that effect on people under normal circumstances. The deputy didn't stand a chance.

"Your job," my uncle snorted. "Ain't no police officer that works for Leslie worried about helping us. You need to go ahead and get out of here. Our family needs some time together to talk." Uncle Drew eyes sparked more and more with each passing second. The crowded room jeered, repeating his sentiments. The temperature rose and fell as members of my family fought to keep control.

The last of the color drained from the deputy's face, causing his black eyebrows to stand out, garish against the chalk white of his skin. He had to be new because I had never seen him before, and being a small town, Brooklyn never employed more than a couple of cops. His smooth face was round, and plump as a toddler's, making him look young. Twenty at the oldest.

Uncle Drew was right; the police chief was not concerned about us. He had sent his greenest officer on his own to investigate a double murder. I knew this guy was following orders, and it wasn't his fault he worked for a jerk. I knew he would probably rather be anywhere else, and there was no telling what kind of bullshit Chief Rucker had filled his head with. I knew all of these things, but at that moment, I didn't care. My heart had hardened. It was us and them. And if they didn't give a damn about us, why should I care how they were treated? Why were they special?

They're not. Not like Mama. Not like Grandma.

Terror and pain swam around the room, glancing off the deputy, and washing over everyone as if it were liquid. Without thinking, or even understanding, I reached with my mind and stirred the emotions, feeling the ripple of my touch as if I'd dropped a stone into a puddle. It was natural, taking me over in a way I'd only heard the elders in my family talk about.

I continued to stir the emotions until they grew thick. I pulled them together and pressed them onto the young officer. Anyone could tell at this point he was scared shitless, but I wanted him to feel how I felt when I walked into my living room. I wanted him terrified.

I stared into the man's eyes, encapsulating that feeling of horror and worthlessness that had combined in me to create something altogether new and heinous; the feeling that had earlier paralyzed me, but now gave me power.

Goosebumps prickled my arms and I pictured the feelings floating as a green orb, across the room, and pressing into the man's forehead. Adrenaline laced panic slid from the deputy. I could feel his heart rate increase, and knew it was because of me. I continued to push my feelings onto him, smiling as small beads of perspiration gathered on his top lip. Energy thrummed through me and I felt alive. I was angry, hurt, and terrified and now he would be too.

The deputy's arms trembled, and I released his gaze. He looked around at us, one by one, and then at the door, his eyes growing wide at the realization we blocked the quickest exit. Reaching a shaky hand to his forehead, he pushed his sweat soaked bangs to the side. He continued to glance around the room, before resting his eyes on me. I opened my mouth, but Uncle Drew shouted at the man before I could say anything.

"GET OUT NOW!" he hollered, the wind howling behind his words, and pushing the door open with a bang.

The deputy ripped off the top page of his legal pad and thrust it to my Uncle as he made his way around us, stumbling toward the door.

"This is officially a crime scene and is sealed until you hear from the Chief. Ya'll should have the house back within the week. After that, call one of these numbers to get someone out here to clean up."

The door again slammed against the wall, sending a baby picture of Delia and me crashing to the floor.

"Now don't go and do anything stupid," the deputy called over his shoulder before running at a fast clip to his patrol car.

We watched from the doorway as the car peeled down the drive, the wind causing it to fishtail in the gravel. When he got to the end of the drive, the deputy turned right onto the main road toward Brooklyn, and the wind stopped.

Uncle Drew's arms were crossed over his chest. "Dumb ass," he sneered, his eyes back to their normal, natural dark green. He almost smiled at me. "Good job Tully-girl."

My family stared at me, wondering what I had done. I opened my mouth to explain, when Logan appeared in the doorway.

"I was going to leave, but it didn't feel right. I need to be here for Tully," he said, keeping eye contact with Uncle Drew.

My uncle narrowed his eyes.

"Look, I don't think you're a bad kid. But we got it now, so you can go ahead on home."

"No sir. I need to be here. I *want* to be here. I know Tully needs me, even if she doesn't realize it," Logan said, not buckling under the weight of my Uncle's presence.

"I don't think you understand. I thought we made it clear the day that the fruit stand got burned up you shouldn't come around Tallulah anymore. We have a way of doing things, and it doesn't include your kind." His words had bite. "Now, part of me wonders what you were doing with my niece when all this happened, but considering how much you helped her, I can let that slide. But that doesn't change things. We're her family. We're the people she needs and we'll be here for her. You can never understand our ways, and the best thing for you both is for you to go away."

Logan squared his shoulders and raised his chin. His shirt was streaked in my Mama's blood from when he'd helped me. "I don't think you're the one that understands. I'm going to be here for her. She needs me and I love her. I felt the wind that came through, and I saw that police officer hightail it out of here, but I'm not scared of you. I know you're hurt and worried, but I'm not the enemy," Logan said, then quietly added, "I would do anything for Tallulah."

Uncle Drew snorted. "You love her? How long have you known her? The answer is that you barely do." His eyes flashed with the telling sign his temper was heating up. Outside, the wind whistled.

Logan didn't flinch.

I loved him too, but that was the problem. I wanted him more than anything. I wanted us to be together and have a normal life. But my life could never be normal, and now, because I was selfish, because I had been off with a person with whom I could never have anything more than what we had right now, because of this, two people I loved had their lives cut short, and my entire family was in danger. I walked toward Logan, but instead of stopping, crossed through the doorway and onto the porch. For the first time that afternoon, I gazed out over our yard.

Anyone outside of the family wouldn't have noticed. Wouldn't have realized the significance, but it was laid before me like a crystal ball, offering a glimpse of our future. Things that were in season, the plants that would have grown no matter what, they were fine. But many flowers that had always been there, whose blossoms had been a permanent fixture in our landscape, now withered. Our prosperity was as linked to my Grandma's Vigour as were the plants—and the plants were dying.

I shivered. Sickness and death would be our reality now, and I didn't know if we were prepared for them. My family and Logan were watching me through the screen door, waiting to see what I would do. Overhead, a crow let out a squawk. I inclined my head toward the noise that had annoyed me for most of my life and again felt the pain of loss. The birds had gone. All of them, except for the crows. There were hundreds of them, their inky bodies blurring the branches, but I knew that without Mama, they would soon leave too. It was something I had always wished would happen, but never like this.

I stepped back inside and threw my arms around Logan.

"Tallulah, I forbid—" Uncle Drew started. I held up my hand to cut him off. Surprised, he closed is mouth.

"Logan, I love you too. But I can't be with you. Not right now. Not after all of this. I can't be with anyone."

Logan grasped my shoulders and held me in front of him. "You don't mean that," he whispered. He grabbed my hand and I let him lead me back outside, shutting the wooden door behind us.

"Logan, I do. I'll never forget you. I'm so grateful for you, but I can't…" I said, my voice cracking.

Logan dropped my hand, defeated. I thought back to our moment in the woods earlier today. It felt like years, not hours, since we had made love and lay their laughing and talking after. I had allowed myself to hope everything might work out. All I had worried about was that he loved me, and I had trusted him completely. That had seemed like enough.

I blinked back tears and smiled. "I love you. And today, for the first time in my adult life, I felt like things were right, and I was honestly happy. You made me happy. But Logan, I don't think I can ever be that happy girl again. If I wouldn't have been off, if I would have been here, with them…"

"You would have been killed too! Tully, none of this is your fault! None of it! There's a crazy person out there that did this and nothing you could have done would have mattered. You cannot blame yourself. You cannot blame us!" He reached for my hand again, but I pulled away.

"I can't. I…Not now," I repeated. "I can't sneak around anymore. My family needs me. If you really do love me, you'll understand. You'll go and not make this any harder than it already is."

"If that's what you want," Logan said, his entire body rigid. "But Tully. It's a mistake. You don't need to be alone. Not now, and when you see that I'm right, call me. Even if it's just to be your friend." He turned and left, going down the steps to the driveway.

I watched him, a not so small part of me wishing he would turn around, or at least look over his shoulder. Anything that had ever been any good in my life was gone.

"Where's he going? Where is his car?" Aunt Brenda opened the door and joined me on the porch.

"He parked on the side of the road," I said.

"Well, why would he do that?" she asked.

I stared at her, hoping she would stop asking me questions like our entire lives had not been turned inside out.

"Oh," she said, as the reason for Logan's parking choice dawned on her.

Aunt Brenda sighed, and wrapped her arms around me in a hug. Heat burned my back where her fingertips brushed against me.

I yelped, "Aunt Brenda!" and yanked away from her embrace. My Aunt looked as alarmed as I was, before realizing what happened.

"I. I'm sorry," she said, her shoulders slumping. "It was an accident, I swear. I'm having a difficult time holding it in. I have to focus really hard right now." A tear escaped down her cheek.

"It's okay," I told her.

But nothing was okay. I didn't see how anything would ever be okay again.

Chapter Twenty-Four

No one wanted to stay home, but eventually it was worked out that Aunt Trudy would keep the kids in the schoolroom with Uncle Drew staying behind to "help." Truth was, no one felt safe leaving their children and our elderly Aunt alone and unprotected, while the rest of us visited Pawpaw at the hospital.

Uncle Drew was worked up. Staying back would give him more time to calm down so when Daddy and Uncle Gavin came home for the night, he could take his turn at the hospital. When his wife, my Aunt Donna, commented about visiting hours, he mumbled something about hoping they tried to stop him from seeing his Paw.

Jack hadn't made it back yet, and part of me envied him that his world had not yet been shattered.

My aunts, Uncle Frankie, Rebecca, and I rode in Aunt Kay's suburban. It was nice being in the car with my cousin Rebecca. Finding peace in the midst of turmoil was a rare thing, but tranquility wafted from my cousin, more effective than any pill ever could be. Rebecca was going to be needed throughout the next few weeks while everyone adjusted, and not for the first time, I thought about how wonderful it would be to have such a deeply good and helpful Gift.

Delia met us at the front desk of the hospital, and it was impossible not to notice the change she had endured since I had last seen her that morning. My beautiful sister, whose only sign of the life growing in her belly had been the tiny bulge of her midsection, barely noticeable unless you knew better, now had a green tint to her complexion. Clusters of small bumps dotted her forehead and her hair hung limp and stringy. Random, tiny splotches stained the front of her white t-shirt, and she looked tired. Dog tired. Delia who had resembled a television version of pregnancy, complete with that glow you hear so much about, now looked like the haggard moms-to-be we saw when we were out getting groceries.

Grandma's Vigour had covered us in ways we had never realized. It was like a well-fed person not understanding the deep reach of hunger, until suddenly they ran out of food. We always were told Grandma's Gift was so important, but now I saw how mightily it had sheltered us, keeping even small things in check.

"You know?" I asked her, not having to say anymore. Delia's face crumpled, and she nodded. I threw my arms around her, hugging her while she let a few rouge tears escape.

"Uncle Drew told Daddy," Delia sobbed. "But I knew. I knew something was wrong, before anyone said anything." Her voice caught in her throat and she paused. "The baby. She...she started kicking me and didn't let up for over twenty minutes."

I rubbed her arm, knowing there were no words to make it better.

"Come on. I'll walk you up. Pawpaw is in a room. You aren't supposed to have more than three people visiting at a time, but I'll make sure it's not a problem."

Sure enough, no one said anything as our entire herd crammed into two elevators and made our way to Pawpaw's room. Delia held me aside as everyone else shuffled into the small, sterile space. When the last person was inside and the door was shut, she wrapped me in another hug, not saying anything.

"Are you okay?" I asked her. "You know, besides everything that's happened..." I knew the question didn't do justice to what we were going through, but it was all I could manage without breaking down.

"No. No, I'm not!" Delia said. "What is happening to us, Tully? *Why* is it happening?"

"I don't know," I answered, truthfully. "What about...you know," I moved my hands up and down, gesturing to her condition.

"Oh God, Tully, it's horrible. I don't want to complain. I don't.

Pawpaw is sick and Mama and Grandma are…" She paused, closing her eyes and taking a deep breath before continuing, "I need them so much right now. This is so hard. I've thrown up six times since I've been here. My face is a mess. My feet and back feel like they're gonna break and I don't know why I squeezed into these jean shorts this morning. But that's not even the worst part. When I asked a nurse if this was normal and could she give me something, do you know what she said to me?" Delia asked, her face scrunching in an effort to hold back more tears. "She told me this was just being pregnant. That I was *lucky* if this was the first time I was getting sick. LUCKY!"

"Yeah, we're lucky," I narrowed my eyes, "That's exactly how I would describe us. Did you get her name? We could do something. Report her, maybe."

"I thought about it, Tully. But I don't think she meant anything. Besides, that's not even the bad part. When I was in the bathroom, you know, being sick, another woman asked me who my doctor was. I told her I didn't have one, yet, and she looked at me like I was the devil! I'm used to it in Brooklyn because of who we are, but this was different. She looked at me as if I was doing something bad to my baby! I'm going to get a doctor, I am, really…." My sister said, letting the tears fall.

"Shhhh," I hugged her again, "I know you will. I'll go with you. We'll find you one this week." I wiped her face with my fingers and tucked her hair behind her ears. "Let's go see Pawpaw now."

We squeezed into the small room with the rest of my family. Papaw lay in the hospital bed, the tubes and tape that connected him to bags of liquid and beeping monitors made him look like fragile, old, and not the robust, man with the laughing eyes. The man he had always been.

He smiled when we came through the door. The bright fluorescent lights cast an ashen look to his usually pink skin.

"There's my girl," he said with some effort. "Come over here Tallulah. Ya'll let her in. I want to see her."

I squeezed around my aunts, uncles, and cousins and made my way toward my grandfather. He seemed so breakable. So frail.

"Hush now, Tully-girl. No tears for this old man. I'm fine. Besides, I'm sure you have cried yourself out today."

I wiped my tears on the backs of my hands. Leaning over the hospital bed railing, I laid my head on Pawpaw's shoulder. "I am so sorry!"

The familiar scent of his after-shave mingled with the antiseptic smell of the hospital. The smell was wrong. Pawpaw was never sick.

"For what, my girl? You didn't do anything," he said, reaching a shaky hand to pat the back of my head. He motioned over to Daddy, "I need a minute with Tallulah."

Even though they had been in the room for less than ten minutes, everyone filed out without complaint.

"You found your Mama and Grandma, today?" Pawpaw asked, his words raspy between his labored breaths.

"Yes sir. It was horrible. I can't get the image out of my mind. It's there. Waiting for me, whenever I shut my eyes," I whispered.

Pawpaw took in a couple of slow breaths.

"You know, Tallulah, I've never been able to forget anything. Good or bad, once I experience something, I have it forever. It could drive me crazy if I let it. A lifetime's worth of sadness and disappointments." He paused. "But I *choose* not to let it. I *choose* to turn my Gift into a blessing instead of allowing it to be a curse. Do you know how I do it?"

I shook my head no.

"I bring the good to the forefront. I find something happy and when the sadness threatens to take over, I fight it back with that happy memory. It's hard, but time and practice help."

I didn't say anything. Moving past today felt impossible.

"I know right now your heart is broken," Pawpaw said, his old eyes wet with tears. "But your Grandma and Mama loved you so much. They wouldn't want to be the cause of your heartbreak. And the funny thing about a broken heart is that it can lead to a bigger, stronger spirit."

"What do you mean?" I knew him better than to think he was going to give me some cliché about what doesn't kill you makes you stronger. Mama was worth more than a cliché.

"Have you ever seen those bodybuilders on the TV? The ones that have all those huge muscles bulging all over the place?" He grinned.

"Yes sir," I said, unsure of where he was going.

"Growing up, I had a cousin who was into that mess." He chuckled.

His laughter stole his air and he had to stop talking for a minute. I sat there, holding his hand, waiting on him to catch his breath. When he finally did, he continued, "Weird looking, if you ask me. Which he never did, so I guess to each his own, as they say. But Gerald, that was my cousin's name, he explained it to me one day. He said the way they build that muscle is by lifting weights that are too heavy. The strain causes tears in the muscles, and when they repair themselves, they grow bigger. Stronger."

My eyes widened.

"Tully girl, the heart's a muscle and no different. When you go through something hard, horrible even, and your heart breaks, it has the power with time to heal itself. Leaving you stronger with the ability to be a person that you never could have been otherwise." Pawpaw paused, and closed his eyes. His breaths were becoming shallower and I knew that all the talking was putting a strain on him. "The secret is, though, you can't let anger and sorrow fester inside you. It might feel justified. It might even seem to help you feel better, but it will only wither your soul."

I would have shrugged off advice from anyone else, angry they would dare try to understand how I felt, but Pawpaw was the man who could never forget. He had healed his soul from loss and heartbreak over and over again.

We took for granted time lessening hurt by taking the edge off bad memories. It was a luxury Pawpaw had never known. I realized for the first time how hard he must have had to work most of his life to stay happy. I hoped I had a little of him in me, and I could work through this, because I could not imagine ever feeling better. I hurt. And I wanted to make the person who did this hurt even more.

"You cannot let this change you, Tully girl," he whispered. "Not for the worse."

I kissed him again on the cheek, feeling guilty because it had already changed me. Pawpaw's eyes were sad, and for a fleeting moment, it felt like he saw my thoughts, and understood I had failed him already.

I knew that he was right. I knew I would have to move through this and grow, but I could never be the same. I could never go back to being the woman I was. That woman had died in my living room.

***

It was dusk by the time I left the hospital, riding home with Daddy and Delia. We pulled into our driveway, and there was Logan, sitting on the tailgate of his truck.

"Let me out," I said, and without a word, Daddy slowed to a stop.

His eyes weighed heavy on my back as I crossed in front of the truck and walked at a careful pace toward Logan.

I worked hard to muster up some of the fire that had been alive in me when I'd sent him away, but the surety of my actions was gone, and the only thing I felt when I saw him was relief. I wanted to be angry. To be that strong woman who only needed her indignation to make it through the bad times. And maybe I was her. Maybe I didn't *need* Logan. I don't know. But I sure *wanted* him, and I was happy he had come back. That he had not listened to what I said, but instead had known what I needed. He didn't need me to be strong. He didn't care if I changed or melted or fought. He wanted to be there for me.

Daddy rolled down his window, and I braced for what I was sure was going to be a replay of the incident with Uncle Drew.

"Tallulah, don't be long. I really don't want you out here late." Daddy paused and stared at Logan, considering his words.

Finally, he nodded and said, "Logan." With that simple acknowledgement, I knew that something had shifted.

I stared wide-eyed as Daddy eased away and drove the truck toward Pawpaw's house, where we would be staying. Even after our home was cleaned and released back to us, I could never imagine being at ease there again.

I walked closer toward where Logan was sitting on his tailgate and stood in front of him.

"I needed to see you," Logan said. "I've been thinking. I know today has been the worst day of your life, and that I am tied to that. But I can't leave you alone. Not right now. When they get the person who did this, if you want me to, I'll go. No complaints and no tears. But I can't do that right now, Tully. Please don't ask me to."

"Well," I sighed, "This was the stupidest thing you could have done. What if Uncle Drew had been the one to find you?" I put my hands on his knees and leaned into him, relaxing against his legs.

"I was kind of thinking he would be. I was prepared for the fight of my life."

I raised my eyebrows at him.

"Let me also add I was prepared to lose the fight of my life." He smiled.

"I am glad you have no delusions about winning. I am sure my eight-year-old cousin could take you. With my Uncle, it wouldn't have been a fight so much as an incident."

"Yeah, well. You're worth it."

"And Logan? I need to tell you something." My face burned through the numbness that had settled over me. "I don't know when, or even if, I'll be able to…do, you know, anything physical for a while," I whispered. "After today and finding Mama, I can't imagine ever wanting to."

Logan held my face in his hands, turning my chin up to look into his eyes. "Tully, Shhh," he rested his thumbs over my lips, "Like I said a minute ago, you're worth it. I'll be your friend, and only your friend, if that's what you need."

He paused.

"Of course, I can't say I won't miss our, uh, rendezvous, but I'm counting on my irresistible charms to bring you back around, eventually." His eyes danced.

I pretended to be angry and punched him in the leg. He slid his arms around my shoulders and pulled me close to him. I let him comfort me. I could feel guilty later, but now I hung on greedily to the sensation of not being alone, grateful there was a person that knew exactly what they were getting into by being with me, and still wanted me anyway.

"Have you thought about what you're going to do?" Logan asked. "It's escalating, Tallulah. I'm scared to think of what will happen next."

"What do you mean?"

"Have you thought of why? Or how you all can stop it?" Logan didn't lessen his grip around me. If anything, as he said the words, he squeezed me tighter, like talking about what happened put me in danger.

"I don't want to think about anything. Nothing. Right now, I want to *be*. That is hard enough."

But the truth was, everything he'd said had kept circling my mind since my conversation with Pawpaw. I would hurt whoever had done this, I knew that. But right now, there was too much to process.

"I want you to be safe. But you're right. We'll worry about that tomorrow. I should take you home now." He glanced toward the wood line, and then down the driveway. The sun had set, and the crickets were starting to sing. I'd always liked the gentle symphony of outside noises in the summertime, but now, when it felt like anyone could be watching from the darkness, the night song creeped me out. "It's probably not the best idea for you to be hanging around outside at night. Besides, I don't want to push it with your dad."

"Yeah. How about that?" I mused. "He seemed totally fine with you being here."

"Maybe he is."

Logan hugged me goodnight on the doorstep of my grandparent's house, kissed me on the forehead, and waited until I was inside before heading to his truck.

When I walked inside, Daddy was on the couch, sitting up, but fast asleep. The day had turned him into an old man. Dark circles hung under his eyes, and tiny red blood vessels that had not been noticeable before, now marked his nose. But it was more than just his appearance. The feeling of strength he had always given off wasn't there, and in its place was intense sadness.

I settled on the sofa beside him. He opened his eyes.

"Thank God you're safe." His calloused fingers scratched gently across my forehead as he pushed my bangs aside.

I was safe, but two people I loved were dead. *I should have been there for them.*

"Tallulah, you have nothing to feel guilty about," Daddy said, sighing. He knew, in the way only a father could, how to decode the expressions and silences I'd worn on and off throughout my life.

"I don't know where you were today. I'm assuming you were with that boy, but I'm thankful that you weren't at the house. There's no doubt in my mind that if you would've been helping your Mama clean, I would have lost you too, and I don't think that's something I could recover from."

"I might have stopped it," I breathed, saying the words that had been haunting me aloud.

"No. That's not something I would ever want to chance," Daddy said. "Losing your Mama and Grandma…" His voice cracked. "But if I had to bury you or your sister, my little girls, I couldn't."

Daddy squeezed me tight and we sat in silence for a bit. As it stretched on, he suddenly turned to me and asked, "Answer me this. Is he a good man? Is Logan a good person, and does he make you happy? You trust him?"

"Yes sir, I think so. I do trust him, but if it'll make things harder, then I can let him go." The words pained me even as I said them, and I didn't know if they were truthful.

Daddy paused, considering.

"No. You deserve to be happy. But be careful. Tomorrow we'll talk about everything. Right now, why don't you go check on your sister?"

I hated to leave him, but I knew he needed to be alone. To think and remember.

Delia was curled up in the middle of the bed she had lain in with Grandma to recover. She was in her same, vomit stained t-shirt, but now had on a pair of men's pajama pants. Probably Pawpaw's, since I knew no one had braved going back into our house yet, even for clothes. I was dressed in a borrowed pair of too-big khaki shorts and an extra-large "Eat at Joe's" t-shirt that Rebecca had lent me. The clothes swallowed me, but I was grateful to my older cousin just the same. I realized as I was pulling them off that my shoes and socks were still speckled with my mother's blood. I had to inhale deep to keep from losing it. I threw the socks into the wastebasket and the shoes into the corner and forced the idea from my mind.

I crawled across the feather bed to lie next to my sister. We had spent many nights in this bed growing up, telling each other stories and imagining who we would be when we were grown and what our husbands would be like. There was comfort here. The quilt still held Grandma's scent of cinnamon and outside things. I wiggled deeper, pulling the blanket up to my ears, and breathed in the familiar smells.

"I told him," Delia said next to me.

"Told who, what?" I asked her from my spot under the covers.

"I called Thomas and told him. Everything. About the rape, the guy before the rape, the pregnancy," she said softly. "I didn't tell him about today. I didn't want him to stay with me out of pity." Her voice was even, void of happiness or sadness, with the words spoken in the deliberate way someone used when they were trying very hard to keep it together.

"And?" I asked.

"I don't think he's going to stay here. I can't blame him. Not really. Even without the pregnancy, it would have been unfair to expect him to stick around," she hugged the pillow tighter, "So if I knew all of this, why does it hurt *so* bad, Tully? Why does it *still hurt* when people react exactly how you think they will? He isn't a bad person for it, but knowing that doesn't make it better. I think it makes it worse, actually. I feel ruined. Like I can't blame a good man for not wanting to have anything to do with me."

I thought about Logan. It wasn't fair that I had him, and Delia had no one. But if I had learned anything lately, it was that nothing was fair. No matter how promising things seemed, the bigger picture was always looming, desolate, and ready to mess up your reality.

"Maybe he needs time," I said. "You're still dealing with it yourself. Maybe it needs to sink in, you know?"

"Maybe."

"And you aren't ruined. Oh my gosh, Delia, you're the same person you've always been! Everyone loves you," I snuggled closer. "You're the beautiful one. The fun, happy one."

"Well. Everyone loves me because I make them. Or they have to because we're family. People don't *really* like me. And now, I'm not even pretty. And what if I'm not good for this kid? What if I'm a terrible Mom? I don't know how to be a parent, but at least I had Mama and Grandma. Now…Now I'm alone!" Delia cried. "Tully, what am I going to do?" Her shoulders shook softly as tears rolled down her cheeks without so much as a whimper.

"Delia, you're going to be great," I assured her. "Yeah, it would be easier with Mama and Grandma, but, well, they can't be here. And yeah, that sucks, but I know they would want us to be strong. That baby is going to have more love than it can stand. And you know how spoiled she'll be?" I smiled, thinking about my aunts, uncles, and cousins bringing little baby boots and things. "I probably haven't acted as excited as I should have, but trust me when I say that I have absolutely no doubt you're going to be the best mother."

"And if Thomas doesn't know how special you are, then he's an idiot," I added.

As much as she had matured, I knew Delia still needed the fuss. She *needed* someone to make a big deal over her. With all of the craziness, her pregnancy had been another thing to take in stride. We hadn't talked about names or clothes or anything. And now Thomas was leaving and we didn't have Mama or Grandma or Vigour, and my sister was terrified.

I decided to try something.

I twined my fingers through Delia's and focused on the happiness I felt at being an aunt. Again, the Reflection came as natural a thing as walking. Not something I was born knowing how to do, but something ingrained inside me, and then unlocked.

I waded through the lingering feelings and pushed aside any fear or sadness from the day, careful not to let it contaminate the pure goodness I felt over the new baby. I let the emotions collect into a pool, and instead of pushing them onto my sister, the way I had with the deputy, I let the joy wash lightly over her. It kissed her hands and cheeks and whispered in her ear and I knew the instant she felt it. Her brow relaxed and she smiled.

"Thanks Tully," she said. "That's amazing."

I smiled back at her, grateful I could help my sister. Secretly, I had been afraid my new power would be one that was only channeled through hate, and that was something I wanted no part of. I did not want to turn into the monster we had always been accused of being.

"And you know," she whispered. "I think you're right. This is a lot happening."

"I have an idea. Why don't we go shopping tomorrow?" I squeezed her shoulder, "We can buy some clothes. Grandma said you were having a girl, and she's never been wrong. Not once. So let's go get something tiny and pink."

"Sure. Okay. That sounds great. But I wish..." she paused, "I always imagined Mama would be with me, shopping for baby stuff. I already miss her so bad."

"Me too, Del. Me too."

Chapter Twenty-Five

Daddy was not comfortable with us going into town on our own the next day. Or the next. Or even the next, but after three days of Delia's moping, he crumbled.

"Be safe," he told us. "If anyone confronts you, or you feel threatened in any way, come straight home."

"Thanks Daddy!" we said in unison.

He handed Delia two one-hundred dollar bills. "Here. I can't have my first granddaughter dressing in rags." He winked at my sister. Delia beamed, and threw her arms around his neck. It was the first time either one of them had smiled in days.

As I followed my sister out the front door, Daddy gently grabbed my arm. He leaned close and said seriously, "Don't be afraid to use your Gifts if you need to, you hear?"

I nodded. I understood what Daddy was saying. *Protect your sister if you have to.* He had nothing to worry about. I wouldn't let anyone hurt us.

Without even discussing it, we drove to Peachton. Neither of us wanted anything to do with the town of Brooklyn, Mississippi. After shopping for two hours, Delia was ready to drop, so we loaded into our old truck and headed toward home. At the main red light in Brooklyn, we saw an old political sign that had been painted over to advertise a hair accessory shop with a big bow as their logo. Delia's eyes lit up.

I knew we shouldn't risk it, but seeing her excitement was too much for me to resist. "One more stop?" I suggested.

"Yes! I think that's what Jenevieve needs," Delia said. "Some frilly bows that are bigger than her head. Don't you love little girls that wear those huge bows?"

"You picked a name?" I asked.

"Oh. Yeah. I meant to tell you. I thought of it this morning. Jenevieve. You know, after Mama and Grandma. Jenny and Evelyn. Do you like it?" she asked.

"Del, I think it's precious!" I said, as I navigated the truck in a U-turn to head to the shop.

It was located on the edge of Brooklyn in a converted metal shed across the street from Brooklyn's only car wash. The sign read, "Babs' Beautiful Bows," painted in fuchsia onto a large sheet of white washed plywood propped against the front of the tiny building. When we opened the front door, a bell tinkled overhead.

"Come in!" a lady called from where she was sitting at a sewing machine behind the counter. "Excuse our sign. Our real one should be in sometime next week."

The voice didn't sound especially familiar, which was a good thing. Hopefully that meant we could get in and out without any of the locals noticing us. I didn't mind the idea of a confrontation. I kind of wanted one, in fact. But not while my pregnant baby sister was with me.

From the looks of things in the shop, Babs had been busy with her bows. They were everywhere, neatly arranged by size and color. Within ten minutes, Delia had picked three bows and a headband for Jenevieve, and we sat them on the counter to pay. The lady added our total on a pocket calculator.

"I'm going to order a real register if the business seems to do good," she said, pushing the small numbers with a pencil eraser. "Twenty-nine dollars even."

"Are you Babs? Your hair bows really are beautiful," Delia said.

"That would be me. And thank you," Babs smiled, "It was a hobby, and kind of turned into a business, you know?" Babs pursed her lips, as she squinted at Delia and me behind her tortoise shell frames. We stood, frozen in front of her, wearing awkward smiles and waiting for her to let go of our bag so that we could take the bows and go home.

"I'm sorry," she said. "You girls are Evelyn's granddaughters, aren't you?" She sounded sincere, even looked it, but my stomach still tightened.

She had to give us the bows. She had already taken our money and this was supposed to be a day for Delia to be happy. For both of us, actually.

"Yes," I said, steeling my nerves for whatever this woman felt the need to say.

Babs chewed her bottom lip and blinked her large eyes before taking off her bifocals, and wiping away tears with her pointer fingers, careful not to smear her mascara. "I knew your grandmother. I went to Evelyn with both of my pregnancies, gosh, thirty-five years ago. She was such a sweet woman. I'm so sorry about what happened. I can't even imagine that someone around here could be so evil."

Delia snorted. "I can."

I elbowed her in the arm. We had experienced more than our fair share of evil, but this woman was the first local to be so…so *nice* since everything had started to fall apart.

"Is there going to be a funeral? Can I send flowers?" Babs asked.

"Thank you so much, but we decided to have the funeral at home," I answered, fighting not to let the surprise show on my face.

I didn't know what to tell this woman. I had thought of a million retorts for people bent on being hateful, but I couldn't think of a single thing to say to someone who was sympathetic. I guess not everyone could be bad. I guess maybe the horrible people were also the loudest.

Babs nodded. "Yes. Yes, I can't say I blame you. Well, if you girls need anything, come by and let me know. Your grandmother was a good person. And nobody deserves what happened to her."

We walked to our truck, parked on the side of the building. There had been no one beside us in the gravel lot when we pulled in, but now the space was taken by a familiar black Lincoln. Reverend Armstrong leaned against his driver's side door, his piercing eyes recording our every move.

Delia and I glanced at each other, and marched purposely to our truck. A month ago we would have cowered inside of the store, waiting for the cult leader to give up and go away, but now, things were different. We had both had enough, and I planned on going to the truck and leaving without giving Armstrong the satisfaction of seeing me squirm. I opened my door and slid inside, waiting on Delia to do the same. Instead, my sister turned and faced the horrible man, her hands on her hips.

"What are you doing here?" Delia demanded.

I opened my door and got back out of the truck, watching the confrontation from across the hood.

I knew the smart thing would be to get Delia into the vehicle so we could leave, but I was done with being scared and backing down. I was done with "taking it" and done with being the bigger person. If Delia had something she needed to say to this snake, then I was going to have her back, dammit!

Crossing my arms over my chest, I watched, waiting to see what Delia had planned, assuming she had a plan.

"I own the car wash across the street. I saw your truck," Reverend Armstrong said simply.

"So. What? You're stalking us?" Delia hissed.

"Hardly. If I didn't feel called to speak with you, I would never sully my hands by coming near the likes of demon seed." He spat on the ground. His words fell slow and venomous, but his body was rigid, and his hawk-like eyes were planted on Delia's forehead, carefully avoiding eye contact. He tried to hide it, but the man was scared. Of us.

It seemed absurd, and at the same time, settled in my stomach like a stone. Scared people do stupid things. And of course, there was his gun. It looked ridiculous, but I bet a bullet from it could kill you as fast as getting shot with a more practical looking firearm. Delia almost grinned, and I realized she sensed his fear as well. But it wasn't making her cautious, it was making her brave, fueling her anger.

"Well. Go on. You're good and sullied. What is it you feel compelled to tell us?" Delia asked.

The Reverend clenched his jaw, causing the light green veins in his temples to pop against his pasty skin.

"I guess he takes being sullied pretty seriously." Delia drew her words free in a long singsong rhythm.

I snickered, despite myself. I knew provoking him was bad, but what could he do in a parking lot, in broad day light? If he were going to use that gun, this would be the last place he would do it.

"Harlots. Whores," he seethed. "I have been sent to tell you that if you do not cast off the demon magic you possess, and stay away from Brooklyn, even more bad things will be brought down on you."

His words sliced into me like a knife. He had said *even more*? Did that mean he had something to do with the "bad things" that had already happened?

"What do you mean 'more' bad things? Do you know who killed our Mama and Grandma?" I demanded.

Seeing our pain, the Reverend relaxed. His lips parted, and he smiled, enjoying his role in making us hurt.

I was sick and tired of people who wanted to cause my family pain. "Answer me!"

My cheeks grew prickly with heat as I was bombarded with images of Mama and Grandma sprawled lifeless across the floor.

Witnessing me on the verge of losing it, the Reverend, for a half second, dropped his gaze from my forehead, to look me in the eye. That small moment was all I needed. Reeling with the same pain I'd used to send the policeman running from my house in fear, I let my newly developed Gift slip over me. I gathered the loathing, siphoning off the hate that already filled the Reverend from his toes to the top of his head. I stretched it, willing the putrid emotion to grow, and then pushed it back into the Reverend.

Once I held his gaze, I was able to will him not to look away. *You don't want to look away,* I thought, pushing the idea deep into his mind, focusing intently on his beady eyes. *You need to answer my questions!*

"Tell me the truth. Now! Do you know who hurt my family?" My voice rose with every word. "Tell me. Who killed my Mama?" I imagined my questions as a seed, being planted inside of the Reverend with tiny tendrils slipping around his brain as the need to answer me took root in his mind.

He grabbed his ears as if a loud noise threatened to burst his eardrum, and bit his bottom lip so hard that two tiny droplets of blood slid down his chin and mingled with his ratty beard, but he could not look away.

The combination of the Reflected emotion, and being compelled to answer me, was too much.

I had him.

Delia realized what was happening. "Do you think he did it?" she asked me.

Without thinking, I glanced at my sister, breaking my gaze with Armstrong. He moved his hands to his eyes, and shook his head.

"Damn you, harlot! You will burn!" He shouted at me. "You will not control a man of God! You. Will. Burn. For your sins!"

The few customers at the car wash were now staring at us from across the street, trying to figure out what was happening.

Please, no, I panicked. This was what I didn't want. Another reason for people to hate us. An excuse to make our lives even harder than they already were. But the need to know if Reverend Armstrong was responsible overwhelmed me. It was more important than what anyone thought about us. *More important than anything.*

"Stop it!" my sister hissed at the Reverend. Before I knew what she was doing, she lunged at him, pulling at his arms, trying to uncover his eyes.

"Delia, STOP!" I cried. "You're pregnant! Please stop!"

Reverend Armstrong backhanded Delia across her cheek in a loud thud, and she fell backwards with a yelp. Armstrong froze, stunned. He looked from his hand to where my sister leaned against our truck. For a moment, he didn't look evil. Or menacing. He looked only like a scared old man that had realized he had done something bad.

But I didn't care.

"She's pregnant, you asshole!" I hissed at him, putting an arm around my sister. A whelp had blossomed bright red across Delia's cheek.

The Reverend said nothing, but continued to stare blankly at Delia, who decided to seize the opportunity. Brighter lines of green swirled through her eyes as she glared up at the old man.

"I would love it if you clapped your hands," she said, knowing that she had him.

Delia's power hung thick in the air, and Reverend Armstrong nodded his head and started clapping his hands.

The bell from the bow shop tinkled, and Babs stood on the walkway in front of her makeshift business.

"Everything okay out here? You girls okay? Reverend?" she said, clearly torn at who she thought could be at fault. We were grieving young women, but Armstrong was a preacher, even if he did have a reputation as a kook. "Should I call someone?"

"No!" I said too loudly. "I mean no. That's not necessary. Everything's fine." I forced a smile.

"Tell her everything is great," Delia hissed to the Reverend.

"We are all great!" he called, waving to Babs, but never looking away from Delia.

Babs stood, undecided as to what she should do, but eventually nodded and walked back into her shop. A few minutes later I noticed that the blinds facing us were opened, no doubt so the older woman could keep an eye on what was happening in her parking lot. I wasn't sure if she was watching out for us or for him. The realization that this was the first time I thought someone in this town might be looking out for our welfare, struck me something powerful. Suddenly I didn't want to give her any reason to think ill of us.

Delia's Gift was strong, but I had never known it to work so thoroughly. So completely. She had taken over Reverend Armstrong's will, leaving him at her mercy.

Charming meant that the person would do anything to make her happy, but this was total submissiveness. Delia slipped into the power like an old nightshirt, and if she had any nerves or reservations about what she was doing, she hid them well. Even though she was my little sister, it was scary as hell.

She smiled at the Reverend. "Ok, so, did you hurt my family?" she asked, calm as a hornet waiting to strike. Her eyes glowed now, giving her the kind of vicious beauty that could be found in the colorful markings of a snake, or the way a lion gracefully moved to take down its prey. It was that dangerous kind of beautiful.

The Reverend shook his head slightly, still unable to look away.

"Do you know who did?" she asked next.

I saw Babs through the open blinds with a phone pressed to her ear, her lips moving a mile a minute.

"Del," I said nodding toward the window.

Delia nodded her head in understanding, careful not to break eye contact.

"Who did it?" she asked again. "Answer me fast."

"I'm not sure," Armstrong said.

"Then what do you mean *more* bad things will happen to us?"

Even under Delia's spell, the Reverend's eyes narrowed at the words.

"You and your demon family anger the heavens. He will bring more bad down on you if you do not stop," Reverend Armstrong said, his tone matter of fact. He believed every word he said. The evil that held him, gripped him down to the deepest part of his humanity, owning him completely. There could be no hope for a person like that.

"But we aren't bad! We didn't DO anything to anyone," Delia said, her eyes beginning to water. She had wanted answers as desperately as I did, but there weren't any to be found here.

Reverend Armstrong stared at Delia.

"You are demon seed," he said, as if that explained everything.

"Delia, let's go," I said softly, touching my sister's arm.

She shook her head. "You get in your car and you drive to Peachton. Don't come back until you have been to, um, until you've been to Wal-Mart *and* Home Depot," she ordered the man, naming stores that were on opposite sides of town from each other.

The Reverend seemed to consider this before nodding his head and getting in his Lincoln.

We got in our own truck and headed home.

Delia leaned her head against the passenger window, frowning. "Dang it. I should have gotten him to get rid of that stupid gun while I had him."

***

We found Daddy slumped in Grandma's back porch swing. Pawpaw had built it for her when they had first gotten married, carving intricate designs of hearts and flowers throughout the cypress, with an ornate "R&E" as the crowning centerpiece. When I was little, I would rock in the swing and trace the designs with my fingers. I didn't know that R&E meant "Rex and Evelyn" until I was old enough to be embarrassed for not realizing it sooner. I had heard people call my Grandma by her name, but Pawpaw was Pawpaw, or Paw, if one of my uncles or aunts were talking to him. It was strange to think of him as Rex.

Daddy had his arm draped over the back of the swing the way he did when Mama had sat beside him, snuggled up and in love after so many years of marriage. Now he sat swinging, his face wistful, and the spot next to him painfully empty. I sat down next to the man who had always been invincible. Delia turned her mouth in an exaggerated frown.

"What about your favorite daughter?" she asked.

"His favorite daughter is already sitting beside him," I replied.

Daddy chuckled a deep, hiccupping sound, and slid over to make room for my sister on his other side.

"Did you get my grandbaby anything good?" Daddy asked, his cheerful words not quite able to hide his sorrow.

"Sure did," Delia grinned, "We got her a couple of outfits. One has a hot pink tutu." She rubbed her belly, and smiled.

Daddy raised his eyebrows. "A tutu?"

"Yeah. It's super cute," I said. "And then we went to a new little hair bow shop in Brooklyn. The owner knew Grandma. She wanted to send flowers."

Daddy tried to smile. "That's nice. It's good to know the entire town hasn't gone sour."

I glanced across him to where Delia was sitting, chewing her bottom lip.

"What? Did something happen?" Daddy asked, catching the look that passed between us. His easy tone vanished in an instant.

"Kind of. Yes. We saw Reverend Armstrong," I said.

"And? What did he say? Tell me exactly what happened," Daddy ordered.

"When we came out of the bow shop, he was waiting by his car. He had parked it next to our truck. We asked him why he was there and he said to give us a message," I began.

Delia picked up when I stopped. "And we thought that because of the way he worded it, that he might know something about, you know, what happened."

"What did you girls do? Please tell me you left him standing there," Daddy said. He had put his feet on the ground, stopping the swing.

"Well," I said. "We were going to, but it was like he was lording it over us, and we couldn't leave. Daddy, you gotta understand we thought he killed Mama." I looked straight at him. "We thought that if he had done it or knew something, that we should make him tell us."

"So what did you do?"

"We used our Gifts, but things got a little out of hand," Delia admitted.

"And then he hit Delia, and everything kept escalating. But we were careful, Daddy," I said.

"He hit Delia?" he asked me, and then turned to my sister. "He hit you? That grown man hit you? Where? Show me where?"

I could feel the magic rising out of him, even before I could see it in his eyes. The air buzzed with electricity, and sure enough, lightening cracked overhead.

Delia turned her cheek to show him where she had been struck. The place where the welt had been had all but faded, and a light pink mark was barely visible.

"That son of a bitch," Daddy roared. "I am going to kill him."

"Now Daddy, wait," Delia said, grabbing his arms. "It's okay. We scared him pretty good and we found out he was bluffing. He doesn't know anything, and I can guarantee he'll think twice before he comes around again."

"Yeah. And even better is that we aren't scared of him anymore. He's a mean old man looking for control. And he can't stand it that he can't control us," I added.

Daddy stared from me to Delia, before standing up and walking inside. Moments later we heard the front door open and shut, and his truck speed away.

I was in bed before I heard the door open and slam with his return.

Chapter Twenty-Six

My mind kept me awake most of the night, playing out the scene with the Reverend, and worrying about Daddy. When I finally dozed off, I slept through breakfast, not making it downstairs until the clock on the bedside table showed 10:30. Delia was snoring lightly beside me in the feather bed, so I tiptoed out of the room, careful not to disturb her.

I found Daddy back in the porch swing, this time a cup of coffee in his hand. He must have slept late too, because normally he was up and done with his coffee before me or Del made it out of bed at our usual time. I walked outside barefoot, in my new pair of navy pajamas, the one thing I had bought for myself on yesterday's ill-fated shopping trip.

The light breeze that filled the air was charged with the tiniest current of magic. It floated around us, uncurling, and so scant it was barely detectable. There was no rain, or thunder and lightning, just this sweet, lazy breeze that seemed to make the late morning perfect. It alleviated some of the sadness that crept its way into any quiet moment when our minds dared to drift and remember.

I sat beside Daddy in the same spot as the day before.

"You know," he said without looking over, "When I was courtin' your Mama, when we were being matched, your Pawpaw didn't really trust me to take his daughter off anywhere." He smiled. "Back then there wasn't that many places to eat, even in Peachton. And the only movie theater had been all the way over in Brookhaven. So we spent a lot of time swinging in this swing and talking. That's how I fell in love with her." He took a long sip of his coffee.

"And anytime we didn't see eye to eye or would hit a rough patch, we would always end up back over here, in this same swing. We always worked it out."

We sat in thoughtful silence while his mind drifted to somewhere in his past.

"Your Mama was such a good woman. Too good for a hardheaded man like me."

Daddy had never talked to me like this, so candidly of his relationship with Mama. I leaned into him, and laid my head on his big shoulder. The smell of rain and tobacco and after-shave comforted me. My heart ached as for the first time I considered how hard this had to be for him.

"I love you Daddy," I whispered.

"I love you, too, sweetheart. So did your Mama, you know. She had so many ideas and plans that she thought you could do. So much faith in you..." he trailed off.

"Faith in me for what?" I asked.

Since I had started growing up, I had been closer with Grandma. My love for Mama was unconditional, but I couldn't say she wasn't hard on me, and I would be lying if I didn't say at times our relationship was strained. The only plans she ever talked about for me included marrying my match and helping with the school kids.

"She imagined you could do anything. Go places. Change things," he said. "And I fought her on it. She wanted to make you go to college. To not match you until later. She wanted you to be happy, and I stopped her."

"But, that can't be right." My breath caught in my throat as I thought about the folded acceptance letter to the community college sitting in my room. I'd fretted over talking it over with my parents, positive that it would lead to a fight. I'd been so sure they'd say no or be disappointed in me even wanting to go, that I'd constantly put off the conversation. And now Daddy was saying Mama had *wanted* college for me? That going may have made her happy? It was too much.

"No. That can't be right," I said again. "She never said anything about me going to school and she was so excited for me to meet

Thomas."

Daddy sighed, sitting up and leaning his elbows onto the knees of his faded jeans. He held his now empty mug between his hands. I noticed it was the mug Mama had always used when we had breakfast at Grandma's. It was cream-colored, with redbirds flying around the rim.

"That's because I told her no. I told her things were fine. I wanted you here, matched with someone who could understand you, protected by your Grandmother's Gift.... And protected by me." He glanced at me.

"Why didn't she ever say anything?" I all but whispered.

"Oh, your Mama was loyal to a fault. She trusted me, but I should have given in more. Not just about that, but so many little things that didn't matter. She had her ways though," he said, the hint of a smile in his voice. "She kept you at the fruit stand hoping you would get sick of it and beg to go school. I think that's why she smothered you with her crows too, so you would want to escape."

I thought about what he was saying. It still didn't seem likely to me, but I knew better than to doubt my Daddy's words when it came to Mama. For all of my parents' faults, they had always seemed to have the perfect marriage: completely wild about each other.

I swallowed my sadness. "You know I applied to the community college? Got accepted too. I was so worried that ya'll would be mad that I never said anything. I was going to talk to you about it right before the semester started. But now...I don't know."

"Oh sweetheart," he said, squeezing my shoulder. "I had no idea." He stared into the yard. "Of course you should go. Your mama would have wanted it."

I sniffed and wiped away the tears that had puddled in my eyes before they could roll down my cheeks. We sat, rocking in silence, while I gathered my thoughts.

"I think I will," I said finally, surprised these words made me feel almost happy. Without even realizing it, I had given up on the idea of school. It hadn't seemed important, but now that I could go, and knew that it was what Mama would have wanted, the tiniest spark of joy lit my heart.

One thing didn't make sense to me though. "If Mama really wanted me to go to college, why had she been so gung-ho about Thomas?"

"Well, I know she met with Aunt Trudy a lot. You don't know this, but before Thomas, your Mama vetoed five other matches. She probably thought Thomas would be a good fit for you. He worked in the outside world, and she liked that about him. Maybe she thought he would want to go and see something of the world. And that you could go with him," Daddy said.

I knew my Mama, but this person Daddy was talking about, that was someone I had never known. The person who wanted freedom for her daughter, didn't seem like the same woman who had a snappy attitude and a thing for bright sweaters, liked to do crafts, and ran our homeschool group with an iron fist. But…she had gone off to college. She had lived on the outside, no matter how briefly. I wished with a hopeless yet intense desire that I had told her about the acceptance letter. But how could I have, when I'd never known that side of her existed?

"So…" Daddy let out a deep breath. "So that's why, if this Logan fellow means something to you, then I'm willing to give him a chance."

"Really?" I asked. Not running him off when he wanted to talk to me was one thing—actually, it was a big thing—but giving his blessing for me to date, that was something else altogether.

"Let me make sure that I understand. I can…*date* Logan?"

"Well…Yes. I mean, that doesn't mean I'm automatically going to like the guy. But I'll give him a chance. I know he helped you the day that you found…," he paused midway, "the day of the murders. So I think there has to be some good in him."

His eyebrows raised, he crossed his arms over his belly. "And I'm not stupid, Tully. I was young at one time, too. If you're going to see some boy, I would rather know him than have you sneak around. I told you that your Pawpaw didn't like me taking your Mama off…I didn't say we always followed his rules."

"Oh, Daddy…ew," I said laughing.

Daddy bellowed one of his old belly laughs. The sound did me more good than anything had in a while.

"Well, I know your Mama wanted you to have some more freedom, so I'm giving it to you. But be careful, Tallulah. Make sure you really know him."

"Oh, Daddy! He's a good guy. I think you're really going to like him. He teaches music at the arts high school, and he plays piano and guitar...And he is..."

Daddy held up his hand, stopping the rapid fire of information.

"Rest assured I know all about him, Tallulah." He smiled. "I *am* your father, and there's no way I would be okay with this if I hadn't checked him out first," he assured. "Gifted or otherwise."

I didn't want to know how he had checked up on Logan, but I didn't doubt him.

"Why don't we go to lunch today? All of us, you, your sister, me, and Logan. I think it would be good to meet him, and for him to meet me, in a normal situation," he proposed.

I couldn't help but think Daddy wanting to go out to eat with my non-Gifted boyfriend was about as abnormal as you could get, but I kept that to myself.

"I'll call him," I said, smiling. "What time? And where at?"

"Why don't you get him to meet us here, that way we can all ride together. We'll decide on a place then."

***

Daddy hesitated at the end of the driveway. "So. Do ya'll want to drive into Peachton to eat? The only place to get any real food in Brooklyn is Myrtle's, and it's always packed at lunch time."

Sitting in the passenger seat as he was, I couldn't see Logan's face, but he met my eyes in the rearview mirror.

Comfortable in the large back seat of Daddy's big extended cab Ford, Delia and I glanced at each other at the mention of Myrtle's. I had never told Daddy what had happened the last time I was there. If I never went back to that woman's place, that would be fine with me.

As if reading my mind, Logan said, "Yeah, and ya'll don't want to eat there after what happened with Tully."

"You mean Delia." Daddy said. "And that was years ago. I think enough time has passed."

Logan cringed, his gaze moving away from mine in the mirror.

"Um. No sir. Myrtle's is where I met Tully. And I was there when Myrtle said some pretty horrible things to her," he said.

I couldn't blame Logan for being honest. No one wants to get on the bad side of a man that controls lightning.

"What things?" Daddy asked. "Tallulah? What things?" Now Daddy met my eyes in the rearview mirror.

"Um. Well. I didn't want to tell you. It was pretty bad." I stared out the window.

Daddy gripped the steering wheel harder. "Tallulah, it's very important to tell me now. I am trying my best to figure out what is going on around here. The police don't care, what with the way they botched the crime scene and sent only that one new cop. I can't even get Leslie to answer his damn phone, so I need you to tell me everything that woman said. Any little piece of information could be important."

Logan was silent the rest of the ride as I repeated every vile accusation Myrtle had made. It was horrible, having to tell Daddy the lies she threatened to spread if I didn't tell her what she wanted to know.

Delia stayed quiet window while I talked. When I finished, she turned to look at me, and her eyes were glowing. Daddy said nothing, but instead of driving to Peachton, he turned his car onto the road to the diner.

I. Am. So. Sorry! Logan mouthed to me in the mirror.

I nodded and tried to smile. This was not going to go well.

The drive was silent and tense, but blessedly short. Cars filled the small parking lot. Myrtle's was the only offerings of a hot, sit down meal in our small town, and the entire Brooklyn workforce seemed to be crammed into the available booths and tables. We filed into the restaurant, Daddy in front, Delia second, and Logan and I side by side bringing up the rear.

I half expected the place to go quiet when we entered, but no one seemed to notice, and we seated ourselves in one of the few empty tables that were scattered throughout the floor. Somehow, the lack of attention disturbed me more.

Lorretta walked over to us, her hot pink smile showing a splotch of lipstick on her front tooth. Once she realized who she was about to wait on, the smile vanished. She put her hands on the hips, crinkling the horrible crinoline uniform.

"Whatcha want to drink?" she demanded.

"Nothing from you," Daddy said. "Get Myrtle. We want her as a waitress."

"But this is my section. Duh," Lorretta said, rolling her eyes. The woman was stupid, but she had guts.

"Oh, hey Logan!" she said, noticing him for the first time. She put one hand on the table in front of where my sister was sitting, ignoring her, and leaned across the table, closer to Logan.

"You never called me! And I really wanted to help you get settled in, too!" Lorretta pursed her lips.

Daddy's irises flickered and sparked. He took a breath and they calmed into their natural shade, but I knew he was working to control his Gift, as well as his anger. Beside me, Logan squirmed in his seat, not saying a thing. *Poor guy.*

Delia placed a hand on top of Lorretta's.

Lorretta jerked her eyes from Logan to my sister.

"You don't understand," Delia said, holding her gaze. "We will not tip you if you wait on us. Get Myrtle. You don't want to help us anyway."

"Fine," Lorretta said, the malice gone from her voice. "But it'll be a while. She's backed up at the counter."

"We'll wait," Delia assured her.

Lorretta sashayed off, shaking the ridiculous skirt from side to side. She looked over her shoulder and blew a kiss to Logan.

Logan's mouth hung open, his upper lip pulled high in disgust. "You know she is an idiot."

I smiled at him. "Everyone knows that, Logan. The girl gets around, and it must drive her crazy to see you here with me after that show she put on for you when ya'll met."

"You saw that?"

"Oh, yeah."

"She's scary," he said, making me giggle.

Daddy stared over my head to the booth behind me. I turned to see who had caught his eye.

Chief Rucker sat across from one of his deputies, bent forward, and talking in fast, hushed tones.

I shifted back around in my seat. "You okay, Daddy?" Raindrops started to pelt against the front door, and I hoped it was simply raining.

"I'm fine," he answered, not turning away.

The Chief must have felt the weight of Daddy's gaze, because a second later he was out of his booth and standing beside our table.

"Jepson. Just who I needed to see," he said smiling and sticking out his hand.

Daddy snarled at the outstretched hand. When it was obvious he wasn't going to shake, the Chief dropped it to his side.

"Any leads on the murders?" Daddy asked.

"We're on it. You know, Jepson, but in small towns like this, it takes time." His smiled never faltering. The man was a snake. "We don't have those big city resources."

Daddy glared at the Chief. The magic was back, dancing behind his eyes, as if itching for release.

"But there's something else I needed to talk to you about," the Chief said, grabbing an empty chair from the table next to us, where an elderly man sat eating alone. He dragged it to the end of our table, and plopped himself in the empty space between me and Daddy. "Seems like there was some strange weather out at Reverend Armstrong's church last night."

I froze and grabbed Logan's hand under the table.

"Weather can be a strange thing," Daddy replied.

"Yeah, especially this. The whole building is down. Looks like it was blown over. But there weren't any reports of tornadoes anywhere in the area last night," the Chief said evenly, "And it gets stranger. The trees around the church weren't touched."

Daddy continued to stare at the Chief, not saying anything.

"Yeah. And then it burned," he continued. "Fire department said it looks like it was struck by lightning. I know those boys are volunteers, but anyone can tell they're right. Must have been some kind of freak storm."

"Must have, Chief," Daddy said, a heavy note of warning in his tone. "Too bad you all don't have the *big city resources* to know for sure."

Outside the rain had picked up, beating fast against the roof and window.

Chief Rucker's jaw tightened.

"We know Reverend Armstrong hates ya'll. I never bought into his whole 'Righteous Fire' following, myself, but many a respected person in this town does. And then there was the incident with your girls yesterday." He motioned to Delia and me, dropping his snake-oil-salesman-grin, and staring back at Daddy. Both kept up the match, refusing to be the first to look away. Tension squeezed the air from the room, and outside lightening cracked. The police Chief flinched.

"I don't know why you're telling me this, Leslie." Daddy's voice was deceptively calm. "What exactly are you trying to say? No one can control a thing like the weather. That would be...," Daddy gave the Chief's grin right back to him, "Crazy. If you arrested someone for that, then I would imagine you'd be a laughing stock. It'll be hard enough for you to move up the ladder with that drug addicted son of yours dragging your reputation down. But if you start arresting people for something like controlling the weather, well, I don't think that would attract the kind of attention you want." He crossed his arms. "What's next? You going to start a task force to search for leprechauns every time there's a rainbow?"

Chief Rucker seethed, his face turning the same shade of red as the vinyl cloth covering the table.

"And I suggest you start using your time, and what resources you do have, to catch the murderer running free around this town," Daddy continued, his voice rising above the restaurant chatter. "You botched the whole damn crime scene, Leslie. People who had no business being there traipsed all through my home, and you sent only that one cop and haven't bothered to send anybody since!" He paused and glanced around the eatery. "Maybe it's not the resources that's the problem. Maybe you don't know how to do your job."

The Chief jumped up, nearly knocking over his chair. "Watch yourself, Jepson. I know what you're up to, and I'll find a way to keep you in line."

Chatter died down and people in the restaurant began to stare. Chief Rucker swept his gaze around, smiled, and then looked back down to where we were sitting. He nodded before walking back to his booth. I squeezed Logan's hand even tighter. That man was no good.

I raised my eyebrows at Daddy, wondering what exactly he'd done after he had stormed out the evening before. He raised his own eyebrows back at me, his lips twitching as he attempted to hide a smile. No one but me or my sister would have noticed, but it told me what I wanted to know. That Daddy had indeed flattened Armstrong's church, and he knew that he was right. The Chief's hands were tied.

Within a few seconds, Myrtle scurried toward our table. The woman was drawn to drama like a beetle to a porch light.

"Tully, after our last visit, I sure didn't expect to see you back here," she said, her voice all honey and sugar. "But I'm afraid I'm going to have to ask you all to leave. That little stunt with the Chief Rucker, well I can't be having that here. This is a *family* restaurant, after all."

She tried to hide it with a smile, but I could see in her eyes Myrtle was rattled. I had always been the safe one. The one that no one should be scared of, but Delia terrified her. And now there were rumors about Daddy and the so-called church.

"And what stunt are you talking about?" Daddy interrupted her. "We were having a friendly chat with the Police Chief."

Myrtle smiled, resembling a scared animal baring its teeth at a predator.

"Well now, the whole restaurant saw you all having words. And not to mention those rumors been going around," she said, eyeing me, so sure I had not told Daddy about her threats.

My hands trembled. Anger had sent me running before, but I was no longer that scared girl, and I silently vowed I would never run from this woman, or anyone else, again. I smiled back at her, and waited to see what Daddy would do. She flinched a little, and wicked as I knew it was, I enjoyed it.

Delia sat with her face propped in her hands, feigning boredom as she followed Myrtle with magic eyes. Myrtle avoided looking at my sister, glancing only from me to Daddy.

"What rumors would those be, Myrtle?" Daddy asked. He was going to make her say them. Out loud. In front of him.

Most people would have cowered, but Myrtle had years of practice in dealing with people who were pissed at her for spreading both truths and lies.

"Oh, they're so vile. I could never repeat them. But I'm sure Tallulah here has heard them." She turned toward me, smug, confident she would be able to cow me into walking out, forcing my Daddy and sister to follow.

I bit my bottom lip and counted from ten to one in my head before replying, "I haven't heard any rumors, Myrtle. Why don't you tell us what it is you're spreading around?"

"Come off it." The honey in her voice turned to vinegar. "You know exactly what rumors I'm talking about. And if they were to get around, I wouldn't be surprised if people started thinking your Daddy, here, had been involved in what happened to your Mama!" Myrtle clamped a hand over her mouth as soon as the words were out, eyes widening as they shot to my Daddy. Fear shone on her face, not theatrics, as if she truly hadn't meant for that last part to slip free.

Daddy opened his mouth to reply, but before he could, I stood up, balled my fist, and putting every last bit of anger I had for this despicable woman behind it, I connected with Myrtle's nose. The blood was instant. *Who said that getting even meant I had to use my Gift, anyway?*

"You little bitch!" she yelled. "Ya'll saw that! Ya'll saw it! She is evil! She hit me! I want her arrested. Chief Rucker, I want her arrested now!" She stomped her foot like an angry toddler. Then, turned her head up, and grabbing a napkin from the table, tried to staunch the blood.

Rising from his seat, Chief Rucker grinned at Daddy. "Well Jepson, you heard her. She's pressing charges, and with all of these witnesses, I'm going to have to take your daughter in, I'm sorry to say." He reached to grab my wrist, and in a flash Daddy came between us.

The busy noise from the restaurant disappeared. Every eye followed Daddy.

"If you ever touch my daughter," he said, pausing to glare at everyone in the room in turn, "If any of you ever touch either one of my daughters again, I will level this town."

Something smacked against the glass door, loud as gunfire. It happened again. And again. The sound continued, picking up speed. Someone yelled, "It's hailing outside." No sooner had the words been said than the ugly, painted-over window cracked and shattered. Balls of ice bounced into the restaurant. People in the surrounding booths fell over themselves to get away as baseball sized hail slid across the linoleum with the occasional thud of bigger clumps slapping the floor.

Daddy continued to stare down Chief Rucker.

Hate colored the Chief's face. He was furious at Daddy for embarrassing him, but he backed away.

Delia walked over to where Myrtle was still standing with her head turned back, upset her injury had been upstaged by some weather. My sister grabbed the woman's ears, and yanked her face down, forcing Myrtle to look into her eyes. She leaned in to where her nose was almost touching Myrtle's own, bleeding one.

"You will not press charges. Ever. And you will not spread those rumors. If I discover you do, I will make you pay in so many ways you will hate yourself for crossing me."

My pregnant baby sister was terrifying. Her eyes glowed, but the feeling of Christmas that was so closely tied to her Gift was absent. She let go of Myrtle's ears, grabbed Daddy's hand, and headed for the door. As soon as it was open, the hail stopped and the sun appeared.

Logan and I followed them into the parking lot, where the only cars damaged were the Chief's patrol car, and Myrtles ugly turquoise coupe. Their roofs were caved in, and their hoods dented so deep, you could make out the shape of the motor. They were totaled for sure.

Once we were in the truck and pulling onto the road, Daddy asked, "Do ya'll want me to go through a drive through?"

"No!" we answered in unison.

"Yeah. I'm not hungry anymore either," he said.

Chapter Twenty-Seven

Uncle Gavin rose from where he sat stooped on the front steps of our house and dusted himself off. "Where have you all been?" His usual smile was tight around the edges. His eyes widened when Logan hopped from Daddy's truck, but he kept any comments he had to himself.

"We went to eat lunch in town. You'll have to ask me how it went later," Daddy chuckled.

Eyes widening in shock, I looked over at Daddy. He seemed more at ease than he had in a long time, making me wonder how many years of pent up anger had been dispelled in a single afternoon.

"Gavin, this is Logan. Tallulah's, er, boyfriend." Daddy said the word boyfriend like he was trying to speak a foreign language. In a way, I guess he was. "Logan, this is Tallulah's Uncle Gavin. He's her Mama's little brother."

"Ha! Younger by eight minutes. And I believe that we've met a couple of times, only not officially," Uncle Gavin said. He grabbed the hand Logan had thrust in front of him and gave it a strong shake.

Logan nodded. "It's good to see you again, sir."

My uncle's eyes darted from me to Logan to Daddy as if he were silently trying to solve a puzzle, but was missing a key piece. Daddy crossed his arms and smiled. Still dazed from our afternoon at Myrtle's, it took me a moment to realize Delia was sagging against the truck as if it were all that held her up.

Logan was the one to break the silence. "I hate to run off, especially after everything that happened, but I have a faculty meeting this evening I need to prepare for. Our funding is about to be cut for the next school year, I'm afraid," he said, grabbing my hands.

I winced. That's what they don't show you on television. When you punch someone, you hurt your hand as much as you do the other person's face.

"Oops. I'm sorry," Logan apologized. He brought my wounded hand to his lips, and gave it a soft kiss.

"I'm not," I said, not daring to look at Daddy's reaction to the small show of affection.

"I'll call you later." His deep green eyes melted me from the inside out.

"Mr. Caibre. Thanks for such an educational lunch," Logan said, waving as he got into his vehicle. "Let's do it again sometime!" He gave me a wink before pulling his truck door closed.

Daddy chuckled again. "Well, Tully girl, that one has a sense of humor."

I shook my head. He had no idea.

Uncle Gavin shoved his hands into the pockets of his faded Levi's. He watched Logan's truck rattle down the driveway in no hurry to leave, waiting until he was completely out of sight before speaking. "Jepson. Tallulah. Delia," he began. Ribbons of tendon bunched under the skin of his neck, exposing the tension he was trying so hard to hide.

"What is it, Gavin?" Daddy prodded.

My uncle rubbed the back of his neck and kept his eyes trained on his boots. He was the laid back uncle. The yin to Mama's yang. The not-quite-as-strict parent that had caused me often to envy my cousin.

And he looked pained.

"I don't want to tell you this after everything you've been through. We have all been through a lot, but you and your girls, ya'll have caught the brunt of it. With what happened to Delia, and then Mama and Jenny..." Uncle Gavin said, his voice straining to hold up the weight of his words.

He cleared his throat and paused, staring over Daddy's shoulder at nothing in particular. "I will just say it. It's what I think and it wouldn't be right for me not to be honest with you, brother."

Daddy nodded slightly for Uncle Gavin to continue.

"When everyone was able to use their Gifts, it was like they were happy for the first time. Adults and children got to see what it was like be their true selves with no shame." He paused and met Daddy's eye. "Everyone was so…joyful. But the murders, they changed it. Now we, as a family, we're broken, Jepson. It's fresh and we're all still hurting. I know it will take a while for us to heal, but…"

Daddy leaned slightly toward Uncle Gavin, waiting for him to get to what he meant. My uncle hated confrontation, and Daddy, though he and Uncle Gavin were close friends, was not an easy person for anyone to confront. About anything.

"But you and I know there's more to it than that." Uncle Gavin's voice softened. "Without Mama's Vigour, why should anyone stay here? Without the security of health, without the surety that we'll have a crop every year no matter what, why would anyone think the right decision would be to cling to this god-forsaken town? What's the point of trying to make it work in a place that doesn't only hate us, but clearly doesn't want us here? Brenda is a nervous wreck all of the time. She's been talking to her sister. We're going to move to Maine, closer to her family, as soon as Paw is home and recovered."

Daddy stood silent. He breathed deeply through his nose, taking his time as he considered Uncle Gavin's words. "I can't disagree with you, Gavin. All I can tell you is that I'm not going. Jenny wouldn't have left. Wouldn't have heard of it. And Rex, we both know he ain't going to agree to move anywhere. You do what you have to do. I won't try and talk you out of it, but I'm staying because this place is ours. I'm not letting anyone take it from us. The Somersby family, your family, has been here for as long as anyone knows. The clan may have grown and shrunk and grown again, as families do, but the Somersbys have always been here. I know that I'm married in, but I am not letting this family be scared off from the only place it has ever known. Not on my watch."

Gavin drew back as if Daddy had struck him.

"I'm not blaming you for anything, Gavin. You were telling me how you felt, so I did the same. That's all. You have to do what's best for Brenda and Jack."

Uncle Gavin's shoulders rounded slightly as he relaxed, slipping back into his usual, easy stance.

"Is Jack going, too?" Delia asked.

My father and uncle jerked their heads to where Delia and I stood. It was clear that during the intense discussion, they'd forgotten we were there.

"I don't know. Your aunt is sick over it, but we decided to leave it up to him. He should be back from Peachton before too much longer. He said he was going to turn in some more job applications, but I kind of think he might have needed to get away for a bit. Either way, when he gets in I'll send him to find you two," Uncle Gavin said.

The phone rang from somewhere inside.

"I'll get it," I said with Delia trailing behind me into Pawpaw's house.

"Hello?" I answered into the receiver. "This is his daughter. That's great! Ok. Sure, yes, I will tell him! Thank you."

I hung up.

"Who was that?" Delia asked, resting a hand on her belly. It had really popped in the last week and a half, almost doubling in size—though still not very big as far as pregnant bellies go. I had a feeling it was a large part of why she had explained everything to Thomas.

"Well. It's not all bad news today," I said smiling. "That was Pawpaw's nurse. Unless something changes tonight, and she doesn't think it will, Pawpaw will be discharged tomorrow afternoon."

"That's great news!" Delia said.

We were well overdue for some good news. The fact that Jack may be moving away was icing on a cake made from the bad tidings.

I rubbed Delia's belly, and her smile changed from one of relief, to a smaller, mischievous grin. Her old grin.

"Can I tell you something, Tully?"

I nodded. "Always."

"I think I made a mistake. The guy who got me pregnant, well, the thing is, we had been sleeping together for a while before he bailed. I know I said I barely knew him, and really, that's the truth. But I was scared that if I said we had any kind of relationship Daddy would go looking for him or something. Anyway, I didn't have any symptoms, so

I was really surprised when I took the test and kind of assumed it had happened." The words spilled out of her mouth, running together.

I stared at my sister, not getting the point she was trying to make.

"With Grandma's Vigour, I kind of felt the same, even after I could feel the baby inside of me. I might have been a little more tired, but that was it."

I blinked, still not comprehending.

"What I'm trying to say is, it was easy, so I never had reason to research any symptoms or anything," she continued.

"Ok. And?"

"Well, without the Vigour, I kind of freaked out because, well let me tell you, this is completely different than before. So I started looking into it. Jack got me some books from the library, and I used Rebecca's dial up to research some stuff online, and Tully, childbirth does not look like any kind of miracle to me. It looks gross. Anyway. What I'm trying to say is, I think I might be further along than I thought."

"What? How much further?" I asked.

"Twenty seven weeks…," she bit her lip, "I think." Delia jumped from foot to foot, and clapped her hands.

I guess this was good news. It definitely wasn't bad news, but how could you be *that* off about how long you have been pregnant? "I don't understand. How could you not tell? And why didn't you tell me when we went shopping?"

"I don't know. You remember that show we used to watch about those women who didn't know they were pregnant until they gave birth on the toilet or the airplane or whatever? And they always would say that they didn't know?" she asked.

"Of course I remember. We made fun of those women." I blinked.

"That's why I didn't tell you! I was embarrassed, because, well, I *didn't know*. But I kind of think Grandma did. I guess she had to know, really. I mean why wouldn't she? She always knew with other women." Delia shrugged.

I shivered, remembering how much blood covered my sister's thighs. Grandma had known, but she had also known that everything was okay. That she had been able to heal Delia and that the baby hadn't been hurt. Without her Vigour, things could have turned out very differently.

"When did you figure it out?" I asked.

"Maybe a few days before Mama and Grandma died," she said.

She wrung her hands in front of her. I hated that anything could be linked in memory to such a horrible day. Hated how from now on, anything significant would be described, time wise, in relevance to how close it occurred to the deaths. *She was married the year after Mama died. Her birthday is the week before Grandma's death. He only lived for three more years after her death.* It made me queasy.

I hugged my sister tight. Her belly pushed ever-so-slightly between us, and we both laughed.

"Come on. Let's go tell Daddy," I said.

Delia looked at me as if I had sprouted another head, and I realized she thought I wanted to tell Daddy her pregnancy news.

"No!" I said. "I mean about Pawpaw!"

"Oh," she giggled. "Thank goodness. I am not talking conception and due dates with Daddy. Ew!"

The deepest conversations held between Delia and Daddy about the baby didn't stray from the subject of names or shopping trips. Delia got super embarrassed if the topic of actually giving birth managed to worm its way into the conversation. Daddy himself usually beat a hasty retreat if anything "female related" came up, so it was just as well.

"But I do think Daddy will figure it out when you, ya know, go into labor a couple of months earlier than expected," I said.

Delia frowned. "I know. But I need to wrap my own head around it first."

"Del, everything I said the other day. About how you are going to be a great mom, I meant every word. It's all going to work out."

Delia wrapped her arms around her tummy and sighed. "I hope you're right."

Chapter Twenty-Eight

We sat in front of the TV for the rest of the afternoon, flipping from one channel to the next, not settling on anything. Daddy had decided to stay with Pawpaw at the hospital to help get him discharged the next morning. He had made us promise to spend the night with our cousin Rebecca, and to get there before dark. We still had a few hours before we had to leave.

Delia yawned.

"I think I'm going to head on over to Rebecca's. That way if I fall asleep, I don't have to get back up," she said. "Do you care if I take the old truck? I don't think I have the energy to walk it."

I thought of how the people that had done all this were still out there and had to suppress a shudder. "Fine with me, I'd prefer you didn't walk. I think I'm going for a quick run, and then I'll be right over."

I hadn't run since the night of Delia's attack. The discovery that the Reverend had nothing to do with the attacks on our family still had me reeling. I'd been sure he was behind at least part of it. I needed to clear my head, so I could figure out what I was missing. *Running will help.*

But still. There was a murderer out there somewhere... *No one in their right mind would come back here, knowing we're on the lookout for them.* I reasoned my driveway—in full view of anyone who happened to be coming or going—was the safest place I could possibly be. Safer even, than being shut up in a house alone.

The clock on the wall said I had a good two and a half hours before dark. Even at my best, two hours was plenty of time to wear myself out. And I couldn't imagine running at night any time soon. *Maybe not ever.*

I strapped on the newly washed running shoes that Mama had gotten for me after my old ones had been splattered with Delia's blood. I had not even had to ask. My other ones had been tossed away, and there had been a new box in my closet soon after. My heart twisted at the memory.

My cousin Baron and his wife had braved our house to pack us a bag of clothes, and had dropped it by a couple of days ago. It was the type of bag someone packed for a person that they weren't that close to. Whatever jeans happened to be hanging in the closet, whatever underwear was on the very top in the drawer, and clean t-shirts and socks. There were no favorites, whatever was easily accessible, but I was thankful for the clean clothes, and I was more thankful that I could put off going home for a while longer.

Yesterday, I had overheard Uncle Drew tell Daddy that the crime scene was scheduled to be cleaned, and as soon as Pawpaw was out of the hospital, they needed to have the funeral. Mama and Grandma's bodies were being housed at the morgue in the basement of the tiny Brooklyn hospital, a thought that made me ill, but we couldn't lay them to rest without Pawpaw. The pain of not being able to say a final goodbye would never dull for him, and Mama and Grandma were in heaven, not in the empty bodies that lay in refrigerated, steel drawers. So we would wait.

I bent forward in a deep stretch, and then pushed through some lunges. The movements were stiff, making me feel old, aged years instead of months since my last run. I started at a slow pace, more like a bouncy walk than a true jog, forcing myself to pay attention only to my movements and breathing.

My steps landed awkward and rigid. I focused on relaxing my muscles, willing my body to find a comfortable rhythm.

My body wasn't having it. My shoulders continued to carry the tension I had been busy absorbing for too long, and my legs absolutely refused to play nice, but I would not give in. Dang it, I was going to make it down the stupid driveway and back at least one time. I could do this. Hell, I *had* done this. Many times.

"And I am going to enjoy it," I mumbled.

Half way down the drive, my lungs started burning. By the three quarter mark, the burning had graduated to feeling like my insides were being slashed with a fire poker. At least my gait improved. Instead of an awkward bouncy canter, I now fell somewhere between a toad and a duck. I slowed to a walk and sucked in deep breaths of air, but forced myself to keep moving. If I stopped, it would defeat the purpose. I couldn't let my mind go blank while standing, no matter how hard I tried. It was like trying to turn off thinking before bed. I could actually envision the words "don't think," but my brain would still carry me away, and right now, that was a trip I didn't want to go on.

I put one foot in front of the other, sucking in and blowing out.

Muscle memory....yeah right.

I tried to coax my calves into the duck trot that I had mastered, but they felt like heavy sacks of dead weight hanging from my knees.

"Well, crap it," I panted. Defeated, I stopped in the middle of the gravel and took breath after shallow breath, attempting to appease my angry lungs as sweat slid down my face in thick drops. The stillness of the afternoon surprised me. There was no breeze, and other than the raspy inhale-exhale of my breathing, it was completely quiet.

Peaceful. *A little eerie.*

Somewhere a crow cawed, slicing through the silence.

An image of Mama, the way I'd found her, flashed through my memory before I pushed it down and away, but not before grief mixed with intense anger washed over me. *I will find who did it. One way or another they will pay.*

I looked over the property than ran along next to the driveway. The field to my right had been green for as long as I had been alive, but now it was dotted with brown splotches where different plants couldn't make a go of it outside of their hardiness zones. Grandma's death was a game changer, and again the feeling crept through me that whoever had killed her had known exactly what it would mean.

It had been immediate in some areas, evidenced by the mottled brown condition of our gardens and orchards. Grandpa's heart attack had happened soon afterwards, if not at the exact same time, and the ease of Delia's pregnancy had evaporated and left her with a textbook list of symptoms that weren't dangerous, but sure didn't look fun either.

The lack of Vigour had affected everyone in some way or another, slowly curling around our family and leaving its fingerprint on all that had reaped the benefits of a mostly pain-free life. Several of my aunts and uncles had developed a noticeable amount of gray in their hair, and Jack, who had been as beautiful as Delia, now wore a patch of painful looking acne that ran along his jaw. Some of the babies developed milk allergies and Aunt Trudy had gradually stopped leaving her house altogether. There was even talk of bringing in a home health nurse. These were the everyday reminders that when Grandma's soul had slipped out of her body and made its way towards heaven, it had taken our safety net with it.

Maybe there was more to my body refusing to cooperate than poor muscle memory, and a serious lack of coordination.

This is the first time I've attempted to run since the murders, I thought. *Makes sense it would be harder.*

The realization did not make me feel any better.

What else is going to change? What else is going to turn from fun into work?

The pettiness of the thoughts were not lost on me, and disgusted with myself, I turned to head to Rebecca's, abandoning the idea of even a brisk walk.

Something moved in the field, startling me. I wiped the sweat from my eyes with the bottom of my t-shirt, and took a few steps, squinting to make out a form propped against a tree. It was a person, lanky with a head of short dark hair, and when he spotted me, he stretched his arms high over his head, waving like a castaway trying to catch the attention of a passing freightliner. I smiled and waved back, wondering how long Jack had been hiding.

***

I loped toward my cousin, my legs all but staging a mutiny. The sun was starting to slip into the horizon, not quite ready to set, but still taking away some of its heat as it prepared for the day's end.

"Hi," Jack said.

"Hi yourself," I responded, surprised at the sharpness in my voice. I had no reason to be mad at Jack. None of this was his fault, but my stomach clenched when I thought of him leaving us.

Jack deflated. "So, you talked to my Daddy, huh?"

"I can't believe they're moving to Maine." I was still not at terms with how they could possibly be abandoning us, now, when the killer was still around, planning God knows what.

We needed everyone, but without Vigour, I knew Uncle Gavin was right, and that they were only the first to admit openly they were going. We didn't have the produce stand anymore, and the townspeople who didn't hate us were too scared of us to actually come around and pay for any kind of service we might offer. Honestly, if anyone had cared to, they could have seen this coming ever since the explosion. Instead of one, solid unit, we were becoming separate smaller factions. Our family had cracked, and we were slowly splintering into pieces. The murders had been the final blow.

"Yeah, they're leaving. Daddy feels guilty, but Mama is excited," Jack said.

"What are you going to do?" I inquired. "Are you going to go with them?"

"No," he said flatly, staring over my shoulder.

"Great!"

He continued to look away.

I froze. "But...you aren't staying here either, are you?"

"I can't, Tallulah."

"Well, why the hell not? Things are going to get better, you'll see. Jack, you can't go. We need you here. Delia, needs you!" I exclaimed.

"Now that ain't fair, Tully!" Jack said, looking me straight in the eye. "Delia will be fine. She has you. And your Daddy ain't going anywhere. Pawpaw sure ain't leaving."

Jack rubbed the back of his neck with his long bony hand, seeming every bit as pained as Uncle Gavin had earlier while giving my Daddy the same news.

"This is something I got to do. And to be honest with you, it's something I've known I was going to do for a long time. Long before everything went to shit around here," he admitted.

"I don't understand."

That was a lie. I kind of did. Only I didn't want to. I didn't want his leaving to make sense. I wanted it to be irrational because that meant everything could go back to normal and he was overreacting.

"Look, I have to go somewhere where I can be alone and figure things out. There's no future for me here. Not one I want anyway." He kicked a clod of dirt and drew invisible circles in the dried grass with the toe of his sneaker.

"We all feel like that, Jack. None of us want things planned for us. I can't believe I'm saying this, but if anything good at all has come out of these last few weeks, it's that we're starting to have a little more control over our lives. I think Mama and Grandma would have wanted us to have something good after so much evil. And," I added weakly, "you can take classes at the community college. Be whatever you want…"

"It's not only that Tallulah. This ain't no place for someone like me."

"Someone like you? What are you talking about, 'someone like you?' You aren't any different than the rest of us, Jack Somersby."

I could forgive my cousin for taking a chance at a normal life, but how could he feel so entitled to it? We were the same. Blood-kin. He was no more special than the rest of us.

"Will you listen to me, Tallulah? This ain't easy! I'm trying to tell you that I could never stay here, not even if our last name was Smith and we were as normal and boring as anyone else in this town." He sucked in a breath, "Tallulah, I think I'm gay…"

"What, Jack? What does that even mean, you *think* you're gay?"

"Ok. So I *am* gay," he admitted.

"What…How do you even know?"

"How do you know that you aren't?" he replied, deadpan.

"What do you mean how do I know that I'm not?" I raised an eyebrow. "I DO, that's all."

"Exactly. I just know. And I also know that being from this family, I don't have a prayer of living a life that makes me happy if I stay around here."

"Have you told anyone else? Do your parents know?"

Jack paled. "No. No, and you can't tell them. I don't want them to know. Not yet."

"Jack, I would never tell anything that you didn't want me too! You should know that. Are you going to tell them, though?"

"One day. I want kind of to live for a little while first. Not be the boy from that family of whackos, but I also ain't ready to be 'our gay son, Jack', either," he said, mimicking his mother perfectly. "I want the opportunity to go somewhere and live and discover who I am. Tully, I have to."

I sighed, hating myself for the tiniest sliver of jealousy that still pierced my heart. "Where are you going to go?"

"I filled out college applications for a lot of places. I'd really like to go to the west coast. California. But I also put a few applications for some places up north, and one in for a school near Atlanta."

"Jack, why didn't you ever say anything? You know that Del and I are on your side, no matter what, like you have always been on ours!"

"I wanted to. There were lots of times I was going to. But it's hard! Then other times I kind of decided I would do what everyone does, be matched and try to go with it. Not disappoint anyone…" His words trailed off.

"And then everything started falling apart anyway," I said.

"Yeah. And I feel like a terrible person for saying this, and you know I would give anything in the world to have Grandma and Aunt Jenny back, but it's like you said. They would want us to find something good in all of this. I can escape. Besides—"

"Besides, what?"

Jack smiled. "Besides, I think Grandma knew. She never said anything, but I think she knew. And I'm not sure that I would have been able to fool old Trudy when it came time for her to read me."

I snorted. He was probably right about Aunt Trudy. She was old, but hadn't been as helpless as she seemed. And she was shrewd. She would have known the second she got her wrinkled hands on Jack. What she would have done with the information, that was a mystery.

"Well," I said.

"Well, what?"

"You better go somewhere worth visiting so me and Del won't be bored when we come and see you."

Jack smiled and wrapped his lanky arms around me. "Thanks, Tully."

"For what?"

"For listening to me. You don't know how relieved I am to have finally said that out loud."

As Jack walked me back to Pawpaw's house, I couldn't shake loose a thought that had managed to wind its way into my brain and bed down. I knew my cousin. I knew it couldn't be true. *But maybe.*

Myrtle had said something about the Chief Rucker's son and "one of us." At the time I had written it off as gossip, but what if the "one of us" was Jack? My gut told me no. There was no way my mild mannered cousin would give a good-for-nothing drug user like Jason Rucker the time of day. Gay or straight, it didn't matter. Bad people was bad people, and from what I had heard about Jason, he was about as cookie cutter perfect an example of bad people as you could hope for.

But what if Jack was tied up in something and needed help? *Hell, that would fit right in line with how everything was going lately, wouldn't it?*

"Jack. I know it's none of my business, but I heard a rumor, and I wanted to be sure that everything is okay," I began.

Jack's wide green eyes, so like my sister's own, narrowed. The acne that had spread across his jaw barely took anything away from his looks.

"Ok. What is it?" he asked.

I tried to think of a way to ask the question delicately, and decided there wasn't one.

"Oh. Hell. I'm just going to ask. You haven't been, uh, sleeping with the Chief's son, have you? There was a rumor he was caught at the Palm Tree Inn with a man who had magic eyes..."

"What? Jason Rucker? The meth head? No way! Tully! How could you even think that? Geez!"

I let go a deep breath, whistling between my teeth. "Oh thank goodness. I-I don't know. I mean, I didn't think it was you, but heck, I didn't know. You know how this town is. It probably didn't even happen." My face was scarlet with the guilt I had even thought it could possibly be my cousin. Of course, it wasn't him. He wasn't stupid.

"And besides. I, uh, wouldn't want my first time to be at the Palm Tree Inn," he said, his own cheeks starting to color.

"You mean, uh, you haven't?" I asked.

"Um. No." Jack said. "And ok. Let's not talk about this. Ever. How about the weather? Or Delia? Or anything?" he said, looking around, everywhere but at me. We were both burning up in our embarrassment.

"Agreed! That is a conversation we will never have. The weather. It's great. You know. Daddy's breezes are the best," the corner of my lip curled up, "they will blow you away."

I guess Logan wasn't the only one bad at jokes. Jack ducked his head.

"That's horrible, Tully, but if I don't laugh I might never be able to look you in the face again." His laughter loosened something inside of me and before I knew it, I was giggling like a child, right along with him.

Jack huffed and puffed, trying to catch his breath. My joke was terrible, but our laughter was contagious, and the borderline-delirious giggles felt amazing.

When we had both managed to pull ourselves together, he jerked his hand up in a wave. "Well bye," he said. "Look. Let's turn and walk in opposite directions. We will never talk about each other's sex lives again. Ever."

"Yeah. Agreed. See ya later." We both turned sharp on our heels and headed to our own destinations.

I thought of Jack as my brother. We had always been close, maybe not as close as he and Delia, but still, I had never considered there were subjects off limits between us.

Well, I had been wrong.

So Jack is gay, I thought. A few months ago, that would have been huge news. Now it really didn't seem like that big of a deal.

I imagined Pawpaw or Uncle Drew finding out, and slapped my hand over my mouth to cover another giggle. It wasn't funny. Really, it wasn't, but it seemed so…odd of a thing, either one of them talking about a person's sexual orientation. They knew that some people were gay. They weren't stupid, but people weren't open about such things in Brooklyn. *How would they react?* My old Pawpaw in his blue denim overalls and trucker hat would probably nod silently, like he did about everything. He was a gentle giant, and loved his grandkids deeply. I couldn't imagine him understanding why Jack liked men, exactly, but I equally doubted it would cause the smallest wrinkle in his relationship with his grandson.

Uncle Drew, on the other hand, well, who knew? Jack didn't have to worry about me telling, that was for sure. Uncle Drew didn't like me being with Logan. His head would pop clean off if Jack brought home a boyfriend.

I would love to see his reaction... *from a safe distance, of course.*

Jack had kept this secret ever since he had figured it out. Delia had been secretly sneaking off to meet boys. Mama had secretly wanted for me the very things I thought she was opposed to. I wondered who else in our family had a secret they guarded. *Was I the only boring one?* But I had Logan, so I guess I wasn't that boring either.

Maybe our family was the same as everyone else, we were just all too afraid of each other to show how we really felt.

Chapter Twenty-Nine

Me and Delia left Rebecca's right after pancakes the next morning. Visiting Rebecca was fun, but I was ready to get everything in line for Pawpaw's return home. Delia was anxious to nap in a real bed. Rebecca's couch had not been as comfortable as it looked, apparently. I'd slept on a pallet on the floor.

I made quick work of tidying up Pawpaw's bedroom. I had been jumpy all morning, and being alone, even in the familiar space, gave me the willies. *Stop being silly!* I cleaned faster. *Pawpaw deserves to come home to a nice clean room.*

Since Pawpaw had been stuck in the hospital and had not yet had the opportunity to sort through Grandma's belongings, I didn't feel comfortable throwing anything away, or even changing things too much. When I lifted pictures and knick-knacks to dust under them, I made sure I put them back in exactly the same spot. I did throw out a vase of withered flowers, knowing my Aunt Donna had sent a fresh bouquet of daisies to his hospital room. I vacuumed and changed the sheets, and decided to call it done, eager to join my sister in the living room.

Before leaving, I surveyed my handiwork, happy with the results. There was only one thing missing. Grandma had some television trays stored somewhere in the house that I, and my cousins, had used often when spending the night. I would have to remember to dig one out to put next to the bed for Pawpaw's meals. I turned to leave, at the last minute deciding to open the tiny bedroom window to let in some fresh air. The house was old, but the windows had been replaced when I was a girl. It slid smoothly on its track, letting in a little breeze, as well as the shrill, sweet song of the catbirds that always nested in the plum trees near the edge of my grandparents' yard. Now that most of the crows had moved on, the small gray songbirds had claimed the rest of the yard for themselves, and bravely moved closer to the house. Pawpaw would enjoy listening to them sing while he was recovering.

I considered briefly that maybe leaving the window open wasn't the smartest thing, but I assured myself it was a very small window, and high off the ground too. *If someone was going to sneak in through it,* I thought, *they'd definitely make enough noise for me and Delia to hear.* I'd never worried about someone breaking in on me while at my grandparents' house before, and it made me angry I had been robbed of my peace. That this place of comfort now felt violated as if I had to be as careful here as anywhere else.

I made my way to the living room. Delia had not managed to get to the feather bed; instead, she was snoring lightly on the old couch. *Poor thing. From one sofa to another.*

The silence began to get to me. I needed to talk, and to hear another person's voice. But after a night on the couch, I didn't want to wake my sister. I decided to call Logan. I considered using the rotary dial phone in the kitchen. I loved the ancient hand piece and the long, curly cord that I could wrap around my fingers for days while I chatted. But Grandma's bar stools were uncomfortable, and besides, I wanted to be free to move around the house while I talked. I got the cordless phone from its charger, punched in Logan's number, and slid onto the couch near Delia's feet, careful not to wake her.

"You have reached the voicemail of Logan Hosteen, teacher of guitar theory, music 101, and now offering private lessons on the second and fourth Saturdays of every month. Please leave a detailed message and I will get back to you as soon as I am able. Thank you."

I guess Chans is on hiatus today, huh Logan? I thought, smiling.

I hung up the phone, amazed at how…teach-ery Logan sounded. I knew that he taught music, but for some reason I had never thought about what that meant. He was in charge of teenagers on a daily basis. I could hardly believe he put up with my family's rules on dating. *Geez, I'm immature. I'm a grown woman and I have to get my Dad's permission to go on dates.*

No sooner had I hung up than the phone beeped in my hand.

"Hello?" I said, smiling.

"Tallulah?" Daddy said through the phone.

"Oh. Hey Daddy," I said, not bothering to hide my disappointment.

"Well, it's good to hear from you too, sweetheart," Daddy joked.

"Of course I'm glad to hear from you. I just thought you were…someone else," I said. Even though it was now a non-issue, it still felt strange to tell my Daddy I had been waiting on Logan to call.

"Listen, Tully, Your Pawpaw had an incident. He's fine, but they're going to take him back for surgery. I'm going to call your aunts and uncles and let them know so they can get to the hospital and see him before he goes into prep."

"Oh, no!" My stomach knotted. "What's wrong? What's the matter?"

"Nothing major. He's just an old man and the attack took more out of him than the doctors realized. They're doing a procedure to help increase the blood flow to the heart. The nurses are going to be prepping him here in a minute. They said it's nothing to worry about, but that we'll have to stay here another night, at least. I don't want you two to rush down here. I'll call you when he gets out and you can come then."

It didn't sound like such a small deal to me. In fact, heart surgery sounded like a very big deal. "Daddy, we want to come!"

Daddy sighed into the phone. "Wait, baby. Your aunts and uncles will be coming to see him and there isn't enough time for everybody. Besides, your sister doesn't need to rush and stress any more than she already has these past few days. Ya'll can come as soon as they bring him back to the room."

"Ok," I mumbled, feeling like the world's worst granddaughter.

"And listen, sweetheart, can you pack me a bag? I have some clothes in the dryer. You can stuff them all in an old grocery bag or pillowcase and bring them tonight. I thought we were leaving today so I didn't bring anything but a toothbrush."

"Sure Daddy."

"Thanks, sweetie. Love you. Oh, and don't forget to keep the door locked. I want ya'll to plan on staying another night at your cousin's."

"Sure thing, Daddy." I had already checked the doors three times this morning, but I didn't tell him that. I didn't want Daddy to worry about me being scared or jumpy while he needed to focus on Pawpaw.

"Love you, too. Bye." I hung up the phone, my good mood vanishing.

Delia was still sprawled out on the couch next to me, snoring away. For a brief second I considered waking her, but Daddy had been clear there was no point in us rushing to the hospital, and it would be pretty crappy to wake her up to give her bad news. I let her sleep.

I flipped through the television channels without stopping. After the third loop, I realized again how bad daytime TV was. I clicked off the old set, and picked up a book that had been sitting on the end table. It was one of my Grandma's Agatha Christie novels. I smiled, remembering how she always had a book tucked away somewhere, and how Miss Marple had been her go to choice. I thumbed through it for a second, unable to concentrate on the pages. Beside me, Delia had not moved. Her mouth was open wide and a tiny stream of spit had leaked from one corner as she sucked in and blew out, sounding like a pug. *I wish I had a recorder*, I thought. My sister was one of those people who refused to believe she snored.

After a minute, I got up to pack Daddy's overnight bag. *He has to be starving, too*, I thought, deciding to make him a sack lunch as well. As I walked into the kitchen, I stepped onto a loose floorboard. Its loud creak made me almost jump out of my skin.

Stop being a goober! I forced myself to laugh at how silly I was being. I'd spent time alone in this house many times. It was my other home. *Yeah. But I can't go to my real home right now, can I?*

I busied myself putting some eggs on to boil for tuna salad, and then went to get Daddy's clothes out of the dryer, not stopping long enough to allow myself to be get creeped out.

There's nothing for you to worry about. The doors are locked. The phones work. Your sister is here too. Stop freaking yourself out! No matter how many times I repeated this mantra, I wasn't able to convince myself to relax. Every groan of the house, every outside noise, left my hair on end. *Keep busy*, I sighed. *Keep busy and keep distracted.*

The laundry looked like it had been sitting a while. I sighed and pulled out the ironing board. It hit me then how much my Daddy had relied on Mama. It was amazing he had even known how to wash and dry a load of laundry.

An hour later, I had packed a bag of wrinkle-free clothes and a lunchbox of tuna sandwiches and potato chips. I washed the pot I had dirtied to kill five more minutes. I still had not heard from Logan, Daddy hadn't called back, and Delia was still asleep. I already knew there was nothing on T.V., and my mind was too scattered to focus on a book. Running was definitely out of the question. I could go to Rebecca's and use her internet, but then I would have to leave Delia here alone, and I was definitely not doing that.

I rummaged around, trying to find something else to keep my mind from turning every dark corner or random noise into an ambush, when I remembered the tray for Pawpaw's room.

My grandparents' house was a two story, with another bedroom and a half bath upstairs, but they had long stopped using the upper level for anything other than storage, and after searching through every closet and pantry downstairs, I decided that's where the trays must be.

The house was built in 1892, and like most old homes, it had been added to throughout the years, resulting in a rambling train of rooms whose use of space didn't make the most sense. The one set of stairs were tiny, and crammed into a small room near the back of the house, which Grandma had used for sewing. Like their bedroom, the sewing room had been untouched since Grandma's death. Mason jars sat along the windowsill, neatly holding shears and seam rippers, and other gadgets whose use I didn't know, while tomato colored pincushions rested among the different colored balls of yarn in a wicker basket that sat on a spindle chair in the corner. The green and blue floral material Grandma had been using to make drapes was spread out on a folding table, the lines etched and ready for cutting. Being in the untouched room was like seeing Grandma's ghost. Like she had left to fix lunch, but would be returning to her project at any moment. *I'd give anything for that to be true.*

I smiled sadly and ran my hand across the thick cotton fabric, the same way I had ran my hand over the material of the many Easter dresses Grandma had made for me over the years. The only girlie things I owned had been created in this room. I had always complained I would be happier in jeans, but Grandma would shake her head and tell me to be still so I wouldn't get stuck with a straight pin.

That part of my life was over. There would be no more dresses from Grandma. That she was truly gone in every possible way, cut me deeper than losing Vigour ever could. It hit me in the gut, and I dropped to my knees, willing the room to stop spinning around me. No tears came. Instead, anger again tore its familiar path through me, heating my insides, and the sour taste of hostility drew my lips together. Grandma had been my heart, and right then I wanted nothing more than to find the person who had stolen her from me, and…. *do what, exactly?*

Could I really hurt someone? I didn't know. When I had turned my Gift on the deputy, it had felt natural. Primal. It had not required thought. I had punched Myrtle, but that was in the heat of the moment. *But could I actually really hurt someone? Could I kill someone?* The memory of finding my Mama and Grandma seared bright in my mind. Someone had taken their time. It was not a gunshot wound, but multiple stabbings. It was barbaric. And it had happened to the two people I loved more than anything.

Yes, I decided. If it was the person who had hurt my family, I absolutely could. I was sitting on the floor, thinking of what this said about me as a person, when the loud beep of the phone rang. I jumped, slamming my elbow into the wall. A painful tingle ran from my funny bone, down my arm, setting my fingers on fire.

"Dammit," I muttered, hopping up from the floor and dashing to answer the cordless before it woke my sister. The phone let free another series of loud beeps before I could get to it, and as I punched the talk button, Delia sat up, jerked from her sleep.

"Sorry," I said, my hand over the mouthpiece.

Delia wiped her eyes with her palms. "No big," she said through a yawn, before grabbing the remote and clicking on the television.

"Hello?" I said into the phone.

"Hey, baby." Logan's voice made me smile.

"How's it going?" I asked, knowing that Logan had been worried about his meeting at work.

"Not great," he replied. "But, could be worse, I guess. You would think that with it being an arts school they wouldn't consider doing away with music."

It's one of the things I really liked about Logan. He truly loved his job. Going to work and exposing kids to different types of music made him happier than almost anything else. He was convinced the next Clapton or Hendrix was going to pass through his classroom.

"Oh, I'm sorry." I propped against the back of the couch.

"Well, I get to keep my job, so that's good. The bad news is that you're now dating the entire music department," he said. "I still can't believe an arts school would cut music funding. But it was either us or the dance department, and since the woman who teaches modern ballet has a husband on the board, well...We lost."

"Yikes. Well, I'm afraid I have bad news too."

"What is it? Is your Pawpaw alright?"

"Well, yes and no. Daddy said he was fine, but that he had to have surgery and won't be coming home tonight."

"That's too bad, Tully. I wish you guys could catch a break," Logan replied.

I glanced over to where my sister sat, eavesdropping. Her eyebrows were raised into two questioning arches, as she waited for me to get off the phone and fill her in.

"Me and Delia are going to the hospital later, so I guess I won't see you tonight."

"If ya'll aren't leaving until later, then I could ride with you."

"Really? I don't know. I don't want to cause any more stress for Pawpaw, and you know my Uncle Drew."

"I don't have to go into the room. I can stay in the waiting area. Let me be there for you, Tully."

I didn't know if it was the smartest decision or not. But Daddy knew we were dating and was okay with it. I doubted very much Pawpaw would care one way or the other, so Uncle Drew would have to get over it.

"Yeah. Ok. That should be fine," I said.

"Great! I'll finish up here and head toward your place. It shouldn't take me more than twenty minutes before I leave, so I guess that will put me to your house in about an hour and fifteen minutes."

We said goodbye and hung up.

"So you heard everything?" I asked Delia.

She nodded. "Daddy said everything sounded okay, though?"

Delia, after everything she had been through, still had the ability to believe everything would always work out.

"Yeah. He said everything was fine. He's going to call me when Pawpaw is out of surgery." I looked at the digital clock on the phone. "It's been a little over an hour since I talked to him. But its Saturday, so who knows how long it took them to get to Pawpaw after we hung up."

I didn't have a lot of experience with hospitals, but everything I had ever read or seen on TV had made it seem like they were always late. Plus, they were working on a man that had practically zero medical history to go on. It made sense to me it would take longer.

"You okay here?" I asked my sister. I explained what I had been doing upstairs.

"Yeah. Great," she said, "I'm just tired. If you don't care, I'm going to lay here until it's time to go."

I headed back to the sewing room, not stopping until I was on the stairs. Halfway up, the doorbell chimed.

"I got it," Delia called.

"Wait!" I called down, my heart pounding in my chest. "Check out the window first."

"Yes ma'am! Anymore advice?" Delia teased. "It's Chief Rucker."

Ugh. Next to Reverend Armstrong, the Brooklyn Chief of Police was the last person I wanted to see…ever. But at least we weren't in any danger. The Chief was probably looking for Daddy. I hoped Delia could get rid of him before I had to come back down.

No such luck.

"Tully! I need you to come down for a minute," Delia called in the singsong voice she adopted when forcing herself to be pleasant.

I muttered some choice words under my breath, annoyed that I still hadn't managed to get the trays down, but mostly aggravated I was about to have to listen to whatever BS the Chief felt like dishing out.

"Coming!" I called, mimicking Delia's tone.

I stomped down the stairs a little harder than necessary. The Chief's broad frame darkened our doorway.

"Chief Rucker. How can we help you?" I asked. After Myrtle's, I couldn't believe the had the nerve to come around here. Unless it was to deliver bad news. He would enjoy that.

"The crime scene cleaners called and said they're coming tomorrow. They called to make sure the scene wasn't sealed anymore. I need to go over a few more things over there, and since your Daddy isn't here, I need you girls to let me into the property." There was no sign of the smile he reserved for his adoring public. In fact, he seemed relaxed. Almost normal, not like the slimy hate monger that I knew he was. It made me a touch nervous.

"Shouldn't you have a key?" I asked.

He ducked his head, looking down and then back at me.

"Well, I do. But I left it at the office. Look, I thought about what your Daddy said, about solving this case, and that's what I'm trying to do here. I sent my deputy down last time, but I want to get a good look at things before the cleanup crew comes," the Chief said.

I didn't buy it. Daddy had traded insults with this man, not had a heart to heart. And he had tried to arrest me, for crying aloud. He may not be any kind of physical threat, but his sudden profession of being a changed man didn't sit right. I looked hard at the Chief. On the outside, with his combed hair and starched uniform, he reminded me of a character from one of my grandparents' favorite shows. A sheriff from a town called Mayberry.

"I'm not buying it," I said. Delia stood quietly beside the door, watching the exchange with her hands on her hips.

"Pardon?" Chief Rucker asked.

"I said that I am not buying it. What is it that you want? Why are you here?" I asked again.

Chief Rucker straightened his spine, changing from the forgetful cop of the boonies, to a rigid, power hungry man on a mission. His mouth twisted into the familiar sneer he reserved for those of us that did not meet his standards as human beings.

"Stupid girl. I am trying to help you," he said.

"Ok, then. Why? Why now?"

His gaze lingered on me, feeling as if he was sizing me up. I didn't flinch, and after a moment, he nodded.

"You want the truth? Fine. I'm here to solve this case. But not because of you and your backwards family. I'm going to run for office next year, and this has potential to win the thing for me. Murders don't happen around here, and if I solve this one, it's bound to get some state-wide exposure."

That I could believe.

"But, there's nothing wrong with us both getting something from it. You want to find the person who did this, and I want the publicity. There's no losing side," he added.

I considered what he was saying. I did want to find the killer. Did it really matter who was working the case or why? And we hadn't been able to turn up anything on our own. The closest thing I had to a clue was the funny piece of metal I had found where the fruit stand had burned, but that didn't even count. When I had shown it to Jack, he thought it looked like part of an old dog collar that had probably fallen off of one of the many lost hunting dogs that sometimes wandered up. And as far as I knew, Daddy hadn't turned up anything new in his search either.

"You should know I have jurisdiction to work it anyway," the Chief said. "There's nothing you can do, but if you play nice and help me, I can paint a good picture of you and your people. Seems like ya'll could use that nowadays. But if you make this hard, it will come out that I solved a white trash murder. It wouldn't take much to convince everyone in the surrounding area of what the good people of Brooklyn already know, how demented ya'll are." His fat lips parted in a grin, showing as much of his gums as teeth.

My skin crawled. I didn't care what everyone thought. I didn't care if we were painted as white trash or hicks or anything else. What I did care about was my family. If the person who was out to get us were put away, then things would be safer for everyone. I thought of my young cousins, as well as soon to arrive baby Jenevieve.

Delia still stood by the door, unreadable, in deep thought. Her eyes flashed green and then settled to the faintest glow. She looked at me, and I shook my head "no," hoping she understood that I was telling her to calm her powers.

I hated this man. I truly, truly did. But if I didn't accept his help, the case could go unsolved forever.

"Fine," I said. "I have my keys, let's go."

"Good. I have some questions for you both. Delia? Are you coming? You can help?" the Chief asked.

"I wasn't there that day," Delia said.

"Oh. That's right."

He brushed past my sister, and out the front door. Delia stiffened, but didn't move. I glanced at her raising my eyebrows, but she only stared back, blank.

"Why don't you lie back down?" I suggested. "I'll be back in a minute."

"Ok," she mumbled.

Her haunted gaze remained on the man a moment longer before she turned away.

Chapter Thirty

I followed Chief Rucker onto the front porch, where the air was wet and smelled of rain. It licked my skin and even though I'd showered that morning, I felt like I needed a bath. Dark bloated clouds sailed overhead, covering the sun, and casting the yard with a drab, gray light. I remembered the open window in Pawpaw's room, and hoped the weather would hold until I got back.

"I left my car at ya'll's house and walked over. It might be quicker to cut through these trees, though," Chief Rucker said.

I checked the sky and then nodded. I knew that the man wouldn't give me a ride back, which meant I was going to get soaked.

Chief Rucker followed me as we picked our way through the sickly fruit trees without talking. With no obnoxious squawking, or rustling wings, the orchard that I had spent so much time in growing up felt spooky and unfamiliar. The apples that had always hung onto branches for dear life now littered the ground, wormy and rotting in the summer heat. And the constant hum of bees was frenzied and threatening unlike the soothing song I'd always known. The orchard, my childhood playground, was another casualty of the murderer who'd set us in his crosshairs. And if I had to work with the Chief to catch the sonofabitch, it was a small price for me to pay.

My heart sped as we crossed out of the orchard and neared my house. No part of me was ready to face the room Mama had died in, but I would do anything to catch her killer. I straightened my back and marched up the steps, keys held firmly in hand. I would answer Chief Rucker's questions because it would help solve the case, but I would not let him have the joy of seeing me upset.

I squared my shoulders and slid the key into the lock.

I could not shake the feeling that something didn't make sense. The possibility that I was missing something important, pulled at the back of my mind.

I turned the key, cracking the door, and that's when it hit me.

"Where's your car?" I asked. "You said you parked over here?"

I turned to look at Chief Rucker behind me, and let out a yelp, startled at the lack of space between us. He had followed me up the steps, close enough for me to catch the sour scent of his breath. I scrambled to think of a joke about personal space, when he fisted his hand through my hair, and pressed his body hard into my back. He jerked his hand, and I could feel the tiny hairs near my neck snap, pulling out of my scalp with little shocks that brought tears to my eyes.

"What are you doing?" I panicked.

"Get inside and shut up!" The Chief spat. He shoved me hard through the door, and I fell, the linoleum bruising my knees and palms as I caught myself.

My heart thumped in my ears. *What is happening? Was this because of what happened at Myrtles?*

I knew one thing for certain. I had to get out of that house and away from that man. He was the closest thing that Brooklyn had to a town hero. He could do whatever he wanted to me, and short of a video of it happening, no one would ever think to accuse him, or believe me if I did. Everyone knew he didn't like us, sure. He gave us shit and wrote us tickets as much as he could get away with it. He was always threatening to arrest someone in my family, but I'd never truly believed he was capable of physically hurting anyone.

Chief Rucker stepped over the threshold, and I scrambled across the floor, pressing my back into the row of cabinets next to the doorway that led to the kitchen. I didn't dare stand. He was taller than me and at least a hundred pounds heavier, but he was also older. I had a better chance of escaping him if he had to bend over to catch me.

"Ask me again," he ordered. A snarl pulled tight at the pink flesh around his mouth. The fat of his cheeks bunched, the size and color of two over ripe persimmons almost covering his eyes.

"Ask me where my car is."

I couldn't say anything. In a swift, single movement, he pulled a revolver from the back waistband of his uniform pants and aimed it right at me. The hammer made a loud click as he pulled it back. The silver gun was too gaudy to be practical, and since he hadn't pulled it from the holster at his side, I knew it wasn't his duty weapon. It sent chills through me.

Besides, I would have recognized that gun anywhere.

"Where did you get Reverend Armstrong's gun?" I asked.

"I. said. Ask me about my car!" Chief Rucker bellowed.

The Reverend's revolver had always seemed intimidating at best, and at other times almost comical, but it turned out to be scary as hell when pointed at my head.

"Okay. Where. Where's your car?" I stammered.

"I parked it down the road," the Chief said through a horrible smirk. "In the same place I parked it when I killed your Mama!"

His heavy boot connected with my chin, sending me sideways onto the floor. Stars erupted, blocking my vision. I grabbed at the place he had kicked me. Bright red blood spilled into my mouth and down the front of my t-shirt.

I sat dazed as pressure gathered in my head. I could feel the magic glowing in my eyes, and couldn't stop it. And this time, I didn't want to. My Gift pressed hard inside of my mind, begging to be set free. The magic hummed as it grew, and I stared up at the psychotic man in front of me, willing him to look down.

He was stronger than me and had years of training. He even had the revolver, but if I could get him to look me in the eye, even for a brief moment, the playing field would be leveled. Eye contact could be the equalizer.

"Uh, uh, uh!" Chief Rucker said. "Now you know better than that! Keep your eyes on the ground. We can do this fast or we can do it slow." He drew the gun back, threatening to hit me with it.

I lowered my eyes. I would have to be smart. I could wait.

He laughed. "Guess which way your Grandma took it? All those cuts. They kept healing so I had to keep a slicin'!" He slashed his finger through the air like a knife.

Outside, footsteps padded across the porch.

The Chief went still.

"Tallulah! Tallulah!" Delia's voice called.

"No," I whispered, the blood that had filled my mouth slurred my words. "Go away. Delia, go get help."

The Chief smiled at me.

Delia burst through the front door.

"It was him! He did it! I knew I recognized that smell!" Tears streamed down Delia's face. She froze when she saw me.

"No," she whispered. Low. Barely heard. Then on a breath, she screamed, "Nooo!"

"Yes, actually," Chief Rucker said, laughing and grabbing my sister by the arm, throwing her onto the floor next to me.

"You asshole!" I yelled. "She's pregnant!"

"Oh! Don't I know it!" he said. "It's all your slut sister's fault. She ruined everything." He gestured to Delia with the revolver.

"Eyes on the ground, both of you!"

"My fault? What do you mean my fault? It's your fault you dirty old bastard! You raped me!" Delia's eyes glowed as she yelled. "I know it was you! I'll never forget that smell as long as I live! When you squeezed by me in the house, it hit me, but I thought it couldn't be. You're a police officer...But, I know it was you!"

Chief Rucker brought the back of the gun across my sister's cheekbone, sending her face to the floor. She coughed and two small, bloody teeth bounced across the tile.

Delia's hand flew to her mouth.

"It's going to be okay," I whispered to my sister, keeping my eyes down and my voice even.

"You were not raped!" the Chief yelled. "You were not. My son? Now *he* was raped. By someone like *you*," he said, raising the gun directly toward Delia. "Some dirty, green eyed devil fag raped my poor boy! And now he's all confused thinking...thinking that he wants it. This is your kind's fault!"

Delia looked up, defiant. Her voice was calm, controlled as she insisted, "You raped me."

He raised his boot, and out of instinct I moved, but he caught Delia solidly in her belly. The color drained from her face and she doubled over.

Chief Rucker spat at Delia. "I said keep your eyes down, or next time I will shoot you!" he yelled. He trained the Reverend's gun at my sister's head.

Delia whimpered, and started to speak, but I quickly clamped my hand over her mouth.

"Don't argue with him," I whispered. She shook her head. "Delia, please."

Without sitting up, Delia spat out the blood still gathering in her mouth. "What your son does has nothing to do with me," she said, her voice weak, but even.

"It has everything to do with you. I know about you and your little 'power'. You make people want you. Same as that fag made my boy want him. You trick people and use people. And I watched you. Ever since you pulled that shit at Myrtle's a few years ago, oh, did I watch you. Sneaking out and riding your bike down the road or waiting at the end of the driveway. Dressed like a whore all painted and smelling like Christmas cookies." He breathed in deep, and licked his lips. "You wanted it. You were begging for it and all I had to do was wait for the right time. I knew you wouldn't be able to resist going to the fair. I gave you what you asked for. Exactly how you deserved it!" His words flowed out as if he couldn't tell us fast enough. He looked euphoric, as if he was getting off on revealing it to us. On making us relive it.

Delia hugged her belly tightly and pressed her mouth closed.

"I called in on the radio that someone was parking on the side of the road and looked suspicious. That's all it took for one of my boys to ask your idiot cousin to move, leaving you by yourself. I had you. I had you so good." His smile twisted into a grimace. "And then you said that you were raped. You were not raped!"

The Chief grabbed his head with his free hand, pulling at his hair. He took a deep breath, aimed the gun right at Delia, and walked toward her. The weapon settled three inches from her face.

"You had spent all that time asking for something. Making me want you. Well, when you got it, you. You…" He lowered the gun, and again grabbed his hair with his free hand. His face scrunched and contorted and he beat the revolver on his leg. The fit lasted less than ten seconds, before he calmed and again trained the gun on Delia. "I gave you what you had been asking for, and you said I raped you."

I sat on my knees still as stone. I had to think of something. He had taken everything from us. He was not taking our lives too. And I would not let him touch Delia again.

Logan, I thought. He was coming to pick us up, and he would know something was up if we weren't at my grandparents' house. He would come looking for us. *He had to!*

Please hurry Logan! I projected the thought. *I need you. I need you right now!* I repeated over and over in my mind, hoping against hope that Logan had been right. He'd said we were connected. That we were linked by an invisible thread. It had been funny when Chans had meant phone tag and kisses in the woods. Now I needed it to be more than that. More than anything, I needed for Logan's words to be true. I focused on that need, hoping it could somehow pluck the string that guided Logan to where he needed to be. I hoped he was right, that we were connected, and the connection was strong enough for him to feel my distress. *Please, Logan! Hurry!*

In the meantime, I had to keep Chief Rucker from killing us. When Logan got here, the two of us would take him.

Keep him talking.

"How did you get that gun?" I asked again.

By the ugly smirk he wore, he was obviously proud. Bat shit crazy. Sadistic. And proud.

The Chief spun the gun toward me. "You won't let it alone, will you?" His voice was angry, but the same twisted smile crept onto his face. It made me sick to see how much he was enjoying himself.

"How hard do you think it was for me to get this gun? I'm a cop. Hell, I'm *the* cop. I took the gun when I was at Armstrong's house talking to him about his church burning down. He left the room, I took it. Easy as pie. I should probably thank your Daddy for giving me a good reason to go see the old kook." He laughed. "Investigating that fire was a hell of a lot better than anything I could have come up with."

Chief Rucker scratched his chin with his free hand. "But you two. Ya'll ain't too bright. You think this just happened? No. I've been planning this for a while. I wasn't lying earlier. I'm going to be running for office, and I'll be a shoo-in when I solve these murders and lock up the Reverend. Everybody suspects he's a little off, and that little spat ya'll had with him the other day? Well, that don't hurt none, either. When I discover his gun at the crime scene, that'll be all she wrote, as they say."

Next to me, Delia let out a moan, her body went rigid, and then relaxed. I reached over and grabbed her hand, keeping my movements slow and my eyes trained on the floor. Chief Rucker still had the gun pointed at us, and I didn't want to give him a reason to use it. We didn't have much longer and Logan would be here. He had to be. Delia whimpered again, a low, almost unconscious sound.

"Shut her up! Shut your sister up!" the Chief yelled.

I glared at the floor, the magic still pulsing in my mind, begging for release. *Hurry Logan. Please hurry!*

I stroked the back of Delia's hand. "Shhhh…" I leaned over, like I was going to kiss her head, and whispered in her ear, "A little longer. Logan will be here. Just hold on a little longer." I gripped her hand tighter. She squeezed back.

"I think…I think that the baby might try to come," she wheezed.

No, I thought. *Not now.*

"Hang on a little longer," I whispered.

Hurry Logan…

Delia squeezed her eyes shut, and breathed hard through her nose.

I chanced a look at Chief Rucker. The twisted charge of lust mixed with hate rolled off the man. He licked his fat, bottom lip, and narrowed his eyes at me.

I stared back at the ground, a new fear knotting itself in my stomach.

"You know, I always knew you would be the easy one, ever since I caught you watching me get rid of your sister. Did you try to help? No. You sat there. Now, your sister, when she wasn't all big, she put up a fight. Not you. You came right on in here and sat on the floor. Maybe you need someone to bring out the fire in you."

Fighting to keep my gaze settled on the ground in front of me, I breathed deep, hoping to calm my magic. I had never felt it so strongly before, but if the Chief thought I was trying to use my Gift, he would shoot me without another thought, and then, he would shoot my sister. The only reason we were still here was because he believed what he was saying. He had a weak girl and a pregnant girl. We were no match for the mighty police chief. He might as well take his time and enjoy the moment. With my posture and demeanor I let him think that. Hell, I wanted him to think that.

"Now," he rubbed the barrel of the gun against his chin, "What am I going to do with you two? You and I both know, ya'll ain't leaving. This would be where I would have a little fun, but I don't want to buy what you two are selling." He chuckled at his joke.

"You girls are disgusting, you know that? One of you all pregnant. The other, screwing a colored boy." He paused, like he was considering some big decision. "But it can't hurt to have a look now, can it?"

Without thinking, I jerked my head up. "No."

He laughed. "Well, now, I don't see how you really have a choice. Unless you want to do it the hard way. Or as I like to call it, the fun way."

Delia whimpered and squeezed my hand tighter.

"It's going to be ok. I promise, we're going to be okay."

Logan where are you?

"Oh I wouldn't go making promises now." In two quick strides, the Chief was next to me, jerking me up by my hair. My scalp screamed.

"Get up," he said, giving my hair another yank.

"Ok. Ok," I whimpered. My stomach turned and I swallowed hard.

I stood, shaky, but upright and the Chief backed away again.

"Now that's better. Don't be shy. Go ahead. Let's take off that shirt," he shook the gun at me. "But keep those eyes down. Don't try anything stupid. You might get yourself killed. Wait! Too late! That's happening!" he howled.

I would bide my time, but I would not let this scumbag touch me. I would rather be shot. The only reason I had not fought back so far, was my sister laying on the floor, unable to help herself. I wouldn't let him hurt her again, no matter what it took.

I don't know how, but he will pay. I will make him pay.

"Come on, now." He pointed the ugly gun at my head. "Get on with it."

I pulled my blood stained t-shirt over my head, trying not to let the fabric catch my sore chin. The shirt dropped to the floor, and I squared my shoulders. I would not let him see my embarrassment or fear. I stood with my hands at my sides, unmoving.

"Uh-uh! You aren't done," he said, wagging the gun at me. "The bra, too."

The familiar prickle of scarlet burned my cheeks. Silently, I cursed, willing the embarrassment to turn into anger. *I will not be shamed by this man. He will not see me squirm.*

On the floor, Delia's whimpers turned into sobs.

"You better get your sister to shut up or I'm going to straight shoot her now. I did have some reservations about killing a pregnant woman, especially one that might be carrying my child, but I figure I'll be doing a service, taking out a demon baby," he snapped.

So he thought he had gotten Delia pregnant when he raped her. No wonder he wanted her dead. He could deny accusations all day long, but if there was a kid running around with his DNA, then he'd think we had all the proof we needed. But why had he killed Mama? And Grandma?

I prayed silently, asking God to save us, and also thanking him that Chief Rucker hadn't fathered my unborn niece.

Delia clamped a hand over her mouth, muffling her own cries. I slid my arms out of the straps of my white cotton bra and unhooked it, letting it fall to the floor. I stared at the wall, focusing on the small lines in the painted-over wood paneling. I was going to have to do something. Fast. Logan might not get here soon enough.

And I am not going to let this man touch me.

"Ohhh weee! That's nice! A little flat, but that's never been a deal breaker as far as I know. Makes me almost glad I didn't get you with my bomb." He reached down and adjusted his crotch. "Almost."

I shuddered, causing goose bumps to break over my naked flesh. The Chief noticed, and again his vile tongue darted across his lips in sick appreciation.

He circled me slowly, dragging the tip of the barrel across my shoulder blades and collarbone. I ground my teeth together and tensed, refusing to flinch. Better the gun than his hand.

"Yep. That would have been a waste. I thought I had already seen the pretty one, but you ain't half bad hidden under those baggy clothes. What I don't understand," he walked in front of me, the cold metal of the gun leaving a light scratch as it dragged along my skin. "Is why," he leveled the barrel and pressed it into my chest, "you would want to mess around with a colored boy!" He shoved me hard with the gun barrel.

I stumbled backwards, but didn't fall.

"You…you've been watching us?" I stammered. What private details had he witnessed? I thought of all of the sweet kisses shared between me and Logan. Had they been corrupted by Chief Rucker's eyes?

"How do you think I managed to show up today, sweetheart? It's my duty to keep you all in line," he said. "Can't have you hurting any innocent people. No sir, not on my watch."

"And you're the one who blew up the fruit stand."

"Well aren't you a little Einstein! I already told you that. I couldn't very well chance her remembering anything, now could I?" He pointed toward my sister with the pistol. "The bomb delayed. You two were supposed to be in that fire."

I crossed my arms over my naked breasts.

"But that doesn't matter now," he said, pressing the barrel over my heart. "It's been fun, girls, but this party is about over!"

"Wait! Wait. First. Tell me. How did you set off a bomb? There wasn't anything left at the stand after it burned. There would have had to be some pipe of something," I said, praying his ego would keep him from realizing that I was stalling, and more importantly, why.

He smiled and lowered the gun.

"Well, that's actually a good question. It was simple really." He sounded proud of himself. "I used c4 and a dog training collar. All I had to do was plant the explosive and collar in the stand, and when I turned on the detector and moved it out of range, the collar would deliver a shock and KABLOOEY!" He threw his empty hand into the air. "Evidence gone!"

Jack was right, the piece I'd found was part of a collar. The nylon or leather would have burned into ash, and no one thought twice about my tiny find.

"What. What happened then? If it was so simple?" I had to keep things moving. We could not afford to give the man a minute to realize that maybe it would be better if he stopped talking and shot us.

"Well, sweetheart, as best I can tell, it delayed. But don't you worry your little tits about that. This is more fun, anyhow."

He brought the back of his free hand, smacking across my cheek and jerking my face to the side. Everything swayed, and I slipped down. The cold floor pressed against my belly, and it took me a moment to register I had fallen. My stomach exploded as the Chief delivered a kick into my gut. I curled up, coughing, the pain too intense to even bring tears to my eyes. It felt as if someone had peeled away my outsides and took a hammer directly to my organs. I swallowed back the bile that threatened to bubble out of my throat.

"Stop it!" Delia's voice screeched through the room. "Just stop!"

Chief Rucker looked back and forth between me and Delia.

"Your Mama put up more of a fight than you two." He shook his head in disappointment and jerked me up by my arms, dragging me across the room. "Did I tell you about your Mama?" He threw me down, sticking the gun in my face. "It's a shame I had to kill her. She was actually a decent woman." He chuckled. "But it sure was a lot of fun, and besides, what choice did I have? May told me that she could talk to birds. You know May? Works down at the Pig? That little stunt Jenny pulled scared ole May out of her mind! Now hold still a minute." He jammed the gun into my throat as he sat heavy on my hips, pinning my arms with his weight.

I panicked, jerking my head from side to side, ignoring the gun. I had bought us about all the time we had.

Where is Logan?

"I said be still," he roared. He slammed my head into the floor with his palm. Everything faded to gray as yellow spots danced in front of my eyes. I lay stunned.

"Now. That's a good girl," he pushed the gun further down my throat, "So you see why I had to kill your Mama. Too big of a risk that she'd hear something from one of her feathered friends. But Evelyn, now, she was a bonus! I was sure Jenny was here alone. Your Daddy and sister left, and you snuck off to whore around."

He paused.

"Jenny now, she fought, but when it came down to it she was pretty quick to die. But Evelyn, what a treat! All those wounds healing, keeping her from bleeding out. I would stab and the wound would close," he said, reveling in the memory. "It took her a while, but eventually, she gave up too. I gotta say, she was probably my favorite! But don't be jealous. I'm not saying that you aren't going to be good." He took the barrel out of my both and pushed it into my side, dragging his other hand over my breast.

I tensed, every sliver of my being wanting to get away.

A noise erupted from somewhere in the room. It was feral and raw, more growl than scream.

Delia came at the Chief with everything she had, slamming her body into his side. The blow surprised him, giving me enough leeway to slither out from under his unyielding weight. My sister was pure energy, her eyes bright green as she clawed and bit anything that she could catch.

As soon as I was loose, I jumped onto the Chief, teeth bared. I grabbed his shooting arm and bit down, hard. He yelled and jerked away, sending the gun flying through the air.

I turned and went after it.

Chief Rucker realized his mistake, and stumbled over my sister, trying to get to his feet and come after me. Delia twined herself around his legs, slowing him down. He reached down and grabbed Delia by the hair.

"You crazy bitch!" he growled. He yanked Delia's hair and punched her in the side of head. She fell limp.

The gun skidded to a stop under the dining room table. I picked it up and held it with shaking hands. Chief Rucker stopped in his tracks, eight feet from where I stood.

"What are you going to do? You aren't going to shoot me." He took another slow step in my direction and I raised the pistol and pointed it at his chest.

"Get back!" I said.

He paused, raising his hands, smiling.

I glanced down at where Delia lay. "What did you do?" I screamed at the man.

Chief Rucker smirked as he inched closer.

"Back! I mean it!"

"Ok. Now, no need to fuss."

I wanted to run to where my sister was crumpled on the floor. To check for a heartbeat, but I couldn't lower the gun, not for a second.

Delia's delicate cheekbone was swelling, and the side of her face was turning a sickly shade of purple-blue. I searched for the phone, keeping the gun pointed straight ahead at the chief of police.

"What's your plan, sweetheart? After you shoot me, then what? You gonna call the cops?" He snorted. "You go ahead and do that!"

I backed toward the kitchen doorway, reached into the room and pressed the locate button on the phone charger. Three high-pitched beeps sounded from the living room. If we were going to make it, I had to get that phone.

"Sit down. Right there at the table," I said.

The Chief stared at me, careful to avoid eye contact, and slowly scraped the wooden legs of a dining chair against the cheery yellow linoleum.

All I had to do was back into the room, get the phone, and we were saved. *I could do this.*

The Chief let out a deep roar, and in the next second, the dining chair was hurtling in the air toward me. Instinctively, I threw my hands in front of my face, dropping the gun. He plowed into me like a linebacker, sending me crashing into the floor. I scoured around for the pistol, and before I could move, he pounded his fist into my cheek. Everything went hazy, as the blows kept coming.

The Chief froze as I heard the muffled sound of a car door slam. My shoulders dropped to the ground when he released me and retrieved the gun. He pressed himself close to the wall near the door where he would be hidden from view from whoever was entering.

I was a silent lump, broken and unable to call out a warning. Feet pounded up the steps and I waited, horrified, and useless.

"Tully, I'm here! I'm here, baby!" Logan burst through the door, and right away, he saw me. "Tully?" he said, terror settling on his face.

I struggled to shake my head no. He had to run. To get away and get help. I looked to where the Chief was hiding, wishing Logan to follow my gaze, but it was too late. Chief Rucker winked at me, and then raised the gun, and without so much as a second of hesitation, he fired.

Chapter Thirty-One

Chief Rucker howled with laughter. "Well this keeps getting better, now don't it?"

Logan crumpled and fell to the floor, grabbing his side. I tried to scream, but instead the sound came out as a groan.

Chief Rucker crossed the room in long strides, stepping over Logan, and coming to a stop over me. I stared past his boots to where the only man I'd ever loved lay bleeding. I willed Logan to move. To roll over. Move his head. His arm. Something, anything to let me know he wasn't dead.

"Stare all you want, little lady, but that boy is gone." Chief Rucker laughed. "Of course, you ain't long behind him, so don't be too sad." He pointed the ugly war replica at me.

I had failed. I was going to die. Then, he would kill Delia, and her baby would die too.

"I'm sorry," I whispered to my sister, knowing there was no way she could hear me.

This couldn't be the end. It couldn't. There had to be a way to get help. I had called everyone once, on the night I had found Delia. I'd managed to reach everyone in my family, and they'd all came to my rescue.

But it hadn't been on purpose. It hadn't been anything I'd done. The day I'd stumbled upon Mama and Grandma, I'd escaped the pain, disappearing into myself. Who knows how long I'd have lain on that floor if Logan hadn't been with me?

The night Delia was attacked, the terror and pain had ripped through me, desperate to find a way out. I'd screamed without thinking, over and over, shredding my vocal cords. The pain had kept coming and pulsed through my mind so hard it eventually left me unconscious. I had somehow reached everyone, but I was useless.

Could I take that risk now? With a gun in my face? Could I risk the screams? Could I risk blacking out and leaving Delia to fend for herself and Logan to bleed out?

No. There has to be another way.

A small smear of blood trailed across the room. I followed the path with my eyes to where my sister had disappeared into the living room, and was now making her way silently towards me with a table lamp. She was holding it like a baseball bat in two hands. Her face was contorted, twisted, and red with fury and pain, and each step was costing her.

But, slowly, she inched her way closer.

Step by painful step.

The Chief said something I couldn't understand. When I didn't react, he spat at me, the glob hitting me squarely on the cheek.

Still, Delia moved toward us, Mama's favorite lamp raised over her head.

Chief Rucker pulled the hammer back on the revolver, and I smiled. Anger flashed across his face, and he realized I was looking behind him.

"Whatthehel…" he started, and Delia brought the lamp down in an explosion of ceramic and glass. The Chief fell forward, catching himself by putting his hands on his knees. Once again, the gun hit the ground. It landed with a boom, missing everyone, but blowing a hole in the paneling.

I didn't hesitate. I was hurt, barely able to move, but I knew that if we were going to live, I had to act. With every bit of strength left inside me, I dragged myself to my feet, and lunged at the man, knocking him back. Both of us fell hard to the floor, me landing on top of him. I had only seconds before he regained his senses and went for the gun to finish us off.

"What do you think you're going to do? Stop now and I'll make it quick," he smirked, his eyes going from my forehead to my naked chest.

He still did not consider me a threat, but that was fine. That was going to save us. I leaned forward and grabbed his ears, pulling his head up a few inches. I would have to catch his eyes fast, or he would be up and it would all be over. I drew close, and he started to chuckle again, before he realized what I was doing. He tried to throw me off, bucking from side to side, but I wrapped my legs around his body and hung on. I pressed my forehead against his, and in his panic, he made the mistake.

He lowered his gaze.

That second was all I needed.

I imagined that everything I had been through, the pain, the anger, the trauma as a ball of fire, burning in the center of my body. I gathered everything I had been carrying around since the night I found my sister crumpled and abused in the ditch, and I pushed it into that little fireball, making it glow hotter and hotter.

Yellow dots danced at the edge of my vision with every sudden movement, but I didn't let up. Chief Rucker stopped thrashing, but if I looked away, he could still free himself.

My head was swimming, and my eyes wanted to close with each throbbing heartbeat that sounded in my ears, but the little fireball I had gathered in my chest kept me focused. I took it all and pushed it into him. The magic surged, glad to be free finally. I kept pushing, deep into his mind. My Gift filled every crevice of his skull with fear and hate and agony. It twisted through his grey matter, consuming his thoughts and slicing his synapses. I felt every inch of its progress and it was both wonderful and terrible.

"Stop!" he wailed, unable to look away. "Stop!"

But I was beyond letting go. I held my gaze, and imagined the fire spreading through him, searing and burning and destroying him from the inside out. He had hurt so many. Had snuffed out the light of people I loved. Now, I would make him feel every hurt, every gut-wrenching heartbreak. He would know the pain and fear he had so gladly heaped onto the lives of my family. I pushed harder, forcing more emotion, raw and savage, into him. When he was full, I kept pushing.

There was a shriek, like the high-pitched scream of a teakettle, and bright red blood leaked from Chief Rucker's nose. But I held on. He began to tremble underneath me, his body twitching from side to side.

There was a wet sounding "pop" and then silence. The Chief went limp, but his eyes, bleeding and empty, were still unable to look away.

Chapter Thirty-Two

I slid onto the floor, and lay next to the corpse. I had killed a man.

The cold linoleum felt good against my throbbing cheek. My head was pulsing in time with my heartbeat, which pounded in my ears like a base drum. My stomach and ribs felt like they might snap if I tried to sit up. I closed my eyes and didn't move.

It's over. We are safe.

A sour odor cut through my thoughts and burned the back of my throat. I coughed and opened my eyes.

The Chief stared blankly as blood ran from his mouth and nose into a small puddle next to him on the floor. I gagged at the other bodily fluids that seeped from him, and rolled onto my other side, putting him behind me.

Now that he was gone, my adrenaline ebbed, and pain started edging back through me in a sharp, stabbing way. Around me, the room shifted. I didn't know if it was the result of my weak legs, blood loss, or from being hit in the head, but I managed to make my way to Logan and sat down beside him.

The wound had not stopped bleeding, and the loss was turning his rich complexion to the waxy white color of the moon. I had never had a first aid class, but I did know to check for a heartbeat. I lay my head onto his chest. The faint, sporadic thump filled me with joy.

"Logan?" I whispered.

I held my palms on either side of his face, and pressed a kiss into his forehead.

"Hang on, Logan. Don't go. Help will be here." I pushed myself to my feet to look for the phone. I found it in the living room and dialed 9-1-1. We had a dead police officer in our house, and I knew where the blame would fall, but the only thing that mattered was saving two people I loved.

"9-1-1, state your emergency please." The woman's voice was calm. Too calm for the situation.

Delia moaned from across the room.

"My boyfriend has been shot and my sister is hurt and unconscious." I worked to keep the panic from my voice.

"Are you safe, ma'am?"

"Yes. The shooter...I...He's dead," I managed. "But my sister is pregnant. We need an ambulance right now." I gave her my address. If she recognized it, she didn't let on.

"I'm sending help now. Are the victims breathing?"

"Yes. My sister is unconscious, but my boyfriend is barely breathing. He's bleeding. A lot." I tried to keep the tears from my eyes.

"Where's the injury?"

"It's in his side. There is so much blood."

Panic threatened to overtake me. "Tell me what to do. Now. What do I need to do?"

The operator gave me instructions, and on wobbly legs, I stumbled into the kitchen and grabbed every dishtowel we owned from the drawer, pressing them against the hole near the right side of Logan's belly.

"Is he cold to the touch?" the woman asked.

I pressed my cheek to his clammy forehead.

"Yes," I answered.

"We need to keep him from going into shock. Do you have a blanket or towel?"

"Yes. Upstairs," I said.

"Cover him with it. Then continue to apply pressure. Help will arrive soon," she assured.

I made it upstairs, falling every couple of steps, and pulling myself forward on the banister. I went into my room, and yanked hard on my comforter, but it didn't budge. My strength was waning. I pulled hard a second time, a third time, and finally, it slid off. I gathered it as best I could, and headed back downstairs, stopping every few seconds to keep from blacking out.

I threw the blanket over Logan, pulled it to his chin, and pressed over the cover again to apply pressure. Blood seeped through, first as a tiny red flaw spotting the pink fabric, and then opening into a scarlet bloom, a deadly flower draining the life from his veins.

"Hang on, baby. Hang on," I whispered.

Across the room, Delia moaned.

The dispatcher stayed on the phone with me, but I was focused on the movements of Logan's chest, every time it fell, silently willing, praying, it would rise again.

"Tallulah?" Delia yelled from across the room. "Tallulah, please. I think I need help."

I had been so fixated on Logan that I had no idea how long she had been awake. I crawled across the floor to where she had managed to prop her back on the bank of cabinets.

"I think I'm going to have the baby," she said. Her left eye was wide with fear. The right one had swollen shut.

"It's ok. It's all right. An ambulance is coming," I told her, hoping I sounded calmer than I felt.

"Tallulah, it's too early," she cried.

"Shhh. It will be okay," I said, holding her hand.

"Ma'am?" the operator snapped me back to attention.

"It's my sister. She's awake. She thinks she's having her baby," I spoke into the phone.

Delia screamed, and clenched my hand hard enough to turn my fingers blue.

"She's coming!" she said through her teeth. Her muscles went rigid as a spasm seized her body before she collapsed.

"The baby is coming," I told the operator, "But...but it's too soon."

"We need to get your sister through this, and help is almost there. I'm going to tell you step by step what to do, but I need you to be prepared for your sister in case there are complications. How far along is she?"

"Twenty seven or twenty eight weeks, we think," I answered.

"That's viable, but still very early. In a hospital, the baby would be fine, but we're going to do our very best with what we have. You ready?" the woman asked. The calm authority in her voice shifted to a warmer, maternal tone.

I followed her instructions, getting Delia out of her shorts and underwear. I put a towel under her and talked her through breaths, trying to delay the birth until the ambulance arrived, but it was soon obvious Jenivieve was going to make her appearance.

Delia tensed, and with a hard push, the baby entered the world, wailing loudly, letting everyone know she had arrived. I followed the dispatcher's directions, picked up my tiny, wrinkled niece, and sat her on my sister's chest, careful not to pull the still-attached chord.

"She's…she's beautiful," my sister said, between breaths.

"She's perfect," I agreed.

She was the smallest baby I had ever seen with wrinkled, pinkish purple skin, and a head covered in thick dark hair. Her lungs seemed to be working fine if the noise she made was any indication.

I silently thanked God, and prayed that the ambulance would hurry. The dispatch was across Brooklyn, on the edge of the far side of town. We lived in the boonies, so they could be anywhere.

"Tallulah," Delia whispered. "Tallulah, my face is feeling better." Delia's eye grew wide. "It's the same type of feeling I got whenever I was hurt and visited Grandma," she said. Delia chewed her bottom lip. I clicked off the phone without thinking, and sat it beside me on the floor.

"What do you mean?" I asked.

Delia turned her head to show me her already fading bruises.

"You don't think?" I asked her.

There was no way this tiny person could possess Vigour. Even if she did, Gifts didn't usually kick in until a kid was older, two or three at least.

But it made sense. She was early, but seemed to be doing well. Real well, actually. And the birth had happened so quick, so easy.

I stood on my knees and leaned in to examine Delia's face closer.

The swelling had lessened and the new dark purple was fading to the green color of an old bruise.

Delia stroked the crying baby's back softly. We had slid her shirt off, so the baby could lie skin to skin, draping the discarded clothing over her legs to cover the parts that needed covering.

"Your face is looking better," I cried in shock.

I had not allowed my mind to go to Logan while I was helping my sister, but now that Delia was in the clear, an idea was forming.

"Delia. If she does have Vigour that could fix everything," I whispered, scared that if I said the words too loudly I would jinx them.

Hope was a strong thing, and for the first time it was replacing the dread and fear that had intruded on our home. I had been relieved when I killed the Chief, and again when Jenivieve was born, but this was the first time I had let myself actually hope that everything would be okay.

"I don't know if I would want to put that on her. That's a lot for a little girl to grow up carrying," she said. And she was right. I could never expect this tiny baby to hold the burden of keeping our family together and safe. But that wasn't what I meant.

"I don't mean things like the fruit stand," I replied, looking over to where Logan was still on the floor.

Please hang on.

Delia followed my gaze, picking up on what I meant. She rubbed Jenivieve's back, and nodded.

Down the road, I could hear the distant squeal of sirens. The ambulance was finally coming. If we were going to try this, it would have to be before the medics arrived. There would be no way to justify placing a premature infant into the arms of a dying man.

I reached for Delia to hand me the baby, and realized my mistake. The operator had instructed me, under no circumstances, to cut the cord. My sister still had to deliver the placenta, and the more that we let the medics do, the safer it was for her. Jenivieve was still tethered to her mother.

Delia was spent. After being beaten and giving birth, she was in no condition for even the short walk across the room. Even with the healing power of her daughter, she had still been through more than most people would survive.

The sound of the sirens grew closer to our driveway.

I was going to have to bring Logan to the baby. I crawled back across the floor and leaned beside him, not daring to check for a heartbeat. I tapped the side of his face, hoping for a miracle. He didn't move.

I couldn't pick him up, even if I wasn't hurt.

I'm going to have to drag him. I cringed. His wound was in his side, and if I grabbed his legs and yanked, the bleeding could worsen. If we were mistaken and the baby wasn't yet Gifted, it would mean a death sentence for Logan.

I had to think. And fast.

I paced in a circle around where he lay tucked under my comforter. The same comforter that Delia and me had used for "carriage" rides when we were younger, one of us lying on the blanket while the other ran around the kitchen, holding onto the corners and pulling the blanket behind her.

That's what I could do.

Logan shook when I pulled off the cover and lay it beside him. Looping my arms under his armpits as delicately as I could, I inched him over onto the blanket. I did the same with his feet, moving carefully, so as not damage him any worse. My arms and back screamed in protest every time I lifted, but I couldn't stop. I wouldn't.

Once he was on the blanket, I grabbed the bottom corners, and pulled as hard as I could, trying to slide him across the slick linoleum.

The tendons and muscles of my arms cursed at me, my knees threatened revolt, but foot by foot, we slid across the floor. Finally, we reached Delia's side. I knelt next to him and placed my head on his chest. His heart was faint, and it seemed like an eternity passed between each beat.

The sirens were turning into our driveway. We had minutes. Maybe seconds. I unbuttoned Logan's shirt. The skin on his chest was the same waxy color as his face. Jenivieve wailed in protest when I lifted her off her mother's chest and slid her onto Logan's.

The gravel crunched loudly as the ambulance barreled closer, down the drive.

I held my breath, waiting for something to happen.

Jenivieve cried out, but Logan didn't move.

"Tallulah, she's scared," Delia said gently.

"I know. One more second," I begged.

I watched Logan's face as I rubbed the baby's tiny back.

Outside, the ambulance slid to a stop.

"No," I said. "No." Tears filled my eyes, and I lifted Jenivieve and placed her back with her mother.

"Tallulah. I'm sorry, Tallulah," Delia cried, cradling tiny Jenevieve.

The front door crashed open and a large, busty woman barreled in. A second later, her partner, a smallish man with a mustache that took up most of his face, followed suit. They froze when they saw us beaten and huddled together. The police chief lay dead next to the dining room table. Blood crisscrossed in trails through the room, and the smell of gunpowder still hung in the air. In the middle of everything, my sister was sprawled against the wall, covered only by the t-shirt draped across her bottom, with an infant still attached.

The uniformed man and woman looked horrified. I imagined that most of the emergency calls around town were from car wrecks and elderly people who had fallen in the shower.

"Shit, Gilda. I told you it was the same house," the mustached man said to his partner. Gilda grunted in response, running a large palm over her salt and pepper buzz cut.

"Well let's get to it, then," the man pronounced, pulling himself together.

I huddled next to Logan while the mismatched team saw to my sister and the baby.

"I tried, Logan. I promise I did," I whispered, sliding my hand over his dark hair.

I was hollow. Broken and hollow. Logan lay on the floor. He would have been fine if he had never met me. I had killed the man who had done this, but it didn't matter, because in a way I had killed Logan too.

I struggled to catch my breath while tears fell, running down my face and landing in fat drops onto my jean shorts, one after the other. I sniffed and wiped my nose on the back of my hand. In the same day, I had caused the death of the person I hated more than anything, and the person that had made me the happiest I had ever been.

"Oh, Logan," I whispered again, and leaned over and kissed his forehead.

His eyes fluttered, opening into tiny slits.

"Hey, you," he mumbled, "Don't cry."

"Logan!" This time I shouted. "You're not dead!"

"Yeah. I just feel…weird," he said. "Nice shirt."

I looked down, remembering that I was topless from Chief Rucker's assault.

Logan's lips twitched into his lopsided smile I loved so much. Filled with love, and relief, my heart in my throat, I leaned forward and pressed my lips to his. His lips were dry and cold. He was lying flat on the floor, still weak and unable even to sit up, but that kiss was the best one we had ever shared.

Behind me, the male paramedic cleared his throat.

"Ma'am? I'm Clive. My partner is Gilda. Your sister is stable. So is the baby, amazingly enough. Another ambulance is in route, and I need to check over this man. I would appreciate it if you would sit over there and as soon as she is able, Gilda will come look you over.

Clive held out a folded white sheet. I took it and wrapped the crisp fabric over my shoulders.

"See you in a little bit," I whispered, and moved out of Clive's way.

Gilda had a chair waiting for me by the kitchen table, and as soon as she was done poking, prodding and determining that I was in no immediate danger, she left me to help Clive bandage Logan. The adrenaline had ran its course, and my eyelids were getting heavier. The cool wood of Mama's dining room table pressed solidly against my cheek. I let my eyes close, still determined not to give in to the exhaustion.

A whistle escaped someone's lips, and I heard Gilda say in her husky voice, "You're one very lucky man. There's absolutely no reason you should still be alive. The amount of blood you lost. What I don't understand is how the wound would stop bleeding. I hate to use the word, but this is the closest thing I've ever seen to a real miracle."

I smiled. Maybe it was a miracle. Maybe it was Jenivieve.

Maybe Jenivieve was a miracle.

Chapter Thirty-Three

When I opened my eyes again, I lay on the scratchy sheets of a hospital bed, fastened to a bag of fluids by a small tube connected to the back of my hand. The fluorescent light instantly made my skull ache, and I squeezed my eyes shut. That caused pain itself, the motion pulling tight against the skin in my cheek. I touched the spot where it felt tightest and discovered the place was covered with a thick, gauzy bandage.

The hospital air smelled like antiseptic mixed with something sweet, and surprisingly, it wasn't bad. I squinted enough to see through my heavy lids. On my bedside table sat a vase filled with white and red roses. My favorite.

"You're awake," Daddy's baritone voice rumbled from my other side.

"Yes. Can you turn out the lights? They're killing my head," I said.

"Oh. Yeah. Sorry, sweetheart." He reached above my bed and flipped a switch, turning off the overhead bulb. A soft glow coming from the opened bathroom door provided enough light to see, without making me feel as if my brain was in danger of leaking out my ears.

I started to slide over onto my side, to face Daddy, but the movement made the room swim.

"Don't worry about moving, sweetheart. It's okay. You're going to be fine, but you're pretty beat up," Daddy said.

"You should see the other guy," I quipped. I frowned as soon as the reply left my mouth, remembering there was another guy...and what he looked like.

To my surprise, Daddy chuckled.

"Don't laugh, Daddy," I said. "I killed him." The words felt funny on my tongue. I tried again, whispering, "I killed a man."

"No. No, you didn't. Don't think that way. You did what you had to do to survive. If you hadn't fought back, you would be dead." His voice grew husky. "So don't you for one second think that you're a killer. You saved not only yourself, but your sister and your niece. And Logan, too. Sweetheart, I wish I had been there. That I could have handled it so you didn't have to, but you did good. Real good, and I don't want you to ever, for one second, doubt that you're a hero."

"Daddy, my power. I think it may work differently than we thought," I said.

Daddy's face relaxed. "Yeah. I guess so. I have some ideas, but I don't want you to worry about that right now. As soon as Jack gets here, we're going to see your niece. That will help you feel better." He smiled.

"So she is…Vigour?" I asked. "But she's so young!"

"That's how Vigour works. It's strongest when you're new. The doctors and nurses are having a hard time accepting that she's doing so well. And your sister is better. Completely better."

"What about Logan?" I asked.

"He's stable. Delia told me about what you did. It's very likely that you saved his life, Tallulah."

There was a knock on the door, and Jack came in, pushing a wheel chair.

"You ready?" he asked.

"Sure, but they aren't going to let us go in there. Not with me like this." The room was still swimming when I kept my eyes open for too long. Getting in that chair was going to hurt, and I didn't want to go through it for nothing.

"Tallulah, Oh Ye of little faith. You let me handle that!" Jack winked at me. The comfort of charm filled the room, and out of habit, I inhaled, pulling the dregs of his magic into my lungs. I let the breath out and smiled.

"If you say so," I said.

I let Daddy and Jack lift me into the chair, carefully maneuvering the I.V. pole alongside it. True to his word, Jack had no trouble getting me to my sister's room. In the hallway, a nurse asked where we were heading. A quick answer and a smile from Jack, and she let us continue on our way.

Delia was sitting up in her bed, dressed in light green sweats, and holding baby Jenivieve close to her. I looked down to the threadbare hospital gown I wore. It was the only thing I wore. They must have given me some good medicine because I had not even thought to be embarrassed when Daddy and Jack were hauling me into the wheelchair.

"There is Aunt Tully!" Delia said, smiling.

"Hey," I managed.

My muscles continued to ache, and my head throbbed while everything danced and swam around me, but I knew immediately that Jenivieve was Gifted. Everything was a little better, and a light comfort eased over me, dulling the sharp edges of my injury.

"Can I have a minute with Tully?" Delia asked Daddy. "Aunt Brenda and Aunt Donna went to get something to eat, so they should be in the cafeteria. And I know Rebecca, and probably Bertie, are stopping by later, so I need alone time with my sister while I can get it."

"Sounds good to me," Jack said.

Daddy hesitated. "Are you sure that you girls are okay?"

"We're fine, Daddy," Delia assured him.

Daddy nodded, and he and Jack left to find my aunts.

Delia scooted to the side of her bed, my niece in her arms.

"They didn't want me to keep her in here," Delia nodded to her little girl. "And I would understand it if she were a normal preemie. But she's fine. I had to Charm them."

I nodded. My headache was continuing to improve.

"I just couldn't shake the idea of, what if someone wanted to find out why she was okay? You know? What if they wanted to do tests on her or something?" Delia eyes flashed green and she hugged her daughter.

I doubted that the Pediatrics doctors at Peachton Regional would subject our little Jenivieve to scientific testing, but I thought better of saying it. If Delia wanted to keep her in the room, she should be able to.

"Besides, I've been waiting for you to wake up and visit. It's easier for us to help if she's already in here." With that, she hopped off the bed, as if she had not been beaten by a grown man, and then given birth naturally on a dining room floor earlier today.

Or was it yesterday?

"How long have I been out?" I asked my sister.

"A day. Daddy was so worried about you, but the doctor told him that it looked worse than it was. Nothing was broken, you were just bruised up real bad."

I nodded. A day. That wasn't too bad, I guess. It was weird to think that so much time had passed without me knowing.

Delia sat Jenivieve in my arms, holding her there.

When I had been sick as a child, and visited Grandma to get better, her Vigour had felt like happiness and sunlight slowly making its way through my veins, healing and helping to restore my body to health. I had never been hurt like this before, but even so, Jenivieve's Vigour felt different. It was like giggles and freedom. I could feel each part of my sore body healing as I sat with her pressed to me.

I smiled down at my baby niece.

She lay, staring up at me with bright green eyes, content and serious. Did she know what she was doing? Could she feel her Gift like we could? I had never asked Grandma those questions because, well, she was my Grandma. She had been the same for as long as I was born, as constant and steadfast as a lighthouse. She was how she was. But now, with this new Vigour, I wondered exactly how it felt to use such a Gift.

You get what you get. I smiled as I thought of Grandma's old saying.

My head stopped hurting. I blinked rapidly as the tight feeling across the side of my face was relieved. Delia took the baby from my arms.

"We don't want you to heal up so much that the hospital starts asking questions me and Jack can't satisfy," she said, sliding back onto her bed. She smiled, revealing a gap where Chief Rucker had knocked two teeth from the left side of her mouth. "And Tully, I need to fill you in on what happened with the Chief. I'm sure an officer will be over to talk to you soon, now that you're up."

"Ok," I said. "What's our story?"

"I told them about Chief Rucker confessing and all he had said, you know, minus the part about our Gifts. They're going to run his DNA against what they got from me in the rape kit. I told them that he shot Logan and was beating you when I hit him over the head with the lamp. I said that it knocked him out." She took a breath. "They think that the blow to the head made him have some kind of stroke or seizure or something. Your Gift didn't leave anything real unusual. Well, nothing that could really be held against us anyway," she sucked in a breath, "I guess what I mean is, there aren't bullet holes or stab wounds, so I let them draw their own conclusions."

I nodded.

"Delia," I began, "If it comes down to it and they try to charge you with something, then I'll—"

"They won't," my sister said firmly. "They can't because there isn't any evidence. Daddy said to keep quiet and answer only the questions asked. We will get a lawyer, but I don't think it will come to that. The evidence from the rape kit will speak volumes."

I nodded again. There was no way I would let her take any blame, but I would worry about that later.

"What about Logan?" I asked, changing the subject. "Daddy said he's okay."

"He's in a room, stable. I am going to visit him with the baby as soon as we're discharged. If they don't release us in the next day or two, I guess I will have to sneak Jenivieve up there."

"I'm going to go see him, next, I think.". I didn't want poor Logan to be in a bed all alone while me and Delia were healing and surrounded by family.

Maybe I should get in touch with his family?

"He's a good one, Tully. You shouldn't let him get away." Delia smiled at the baby in her arms for a moment, lost in her thoughts. "You know," she said finally. "Daddy said that there was a voicemail on the phone for me from Thomas."

"Yeah? What did it say?" I didn't know how to feel about that.

"To call him when I get a chance. That he had been thinking and wanted to talk to me," she replied.

"Well, are you?" I had mixed feelings about Thomas, but Delia was a grown woman with a baby. I would have to be there for her no matter what she decided to do.

"At first I thought I would. But he up and left after finding out what had happened to me. I can forgive him for that because it would be a lot for anyone to take on. Not to mention he barely knows me." She paused. "But after thinking about it, probably not. If he can't handle my past, he doesn't deserve my future." She looked down again at her baby. "He doesn't deserve *our* future."

With that, I knew Delia was going to be okay. Maybe we all would be.

"I'm going to see Logan." I stood up from the chair to leave, carefully pulling my I.V. pole with me.

Delia giggled. "Um, Tully?"

I turned back around. "Yeah?"

"I know that you want to see him, but you might want to put on some pants first." She snickered and pointed a finger to my green, scratchy gown that was open in the back.

"Oh yeah," I said laughing, and trying to hold it closed behind me.

Delia's laughter was contagious, and soon my ribs were throbbing from shaking with deep belly laughs. When we finally started to calm down, Delia snorted, setting it off again. After all of the tears, the laughter felt good.

I sat next to my sister on her bed. She held Jenivieve against her chest, and when we were sure we were finished giggling, she moved the baby to where we could look into her tiny face.

I touched my little niece on the cheek and as she smiled her gummy, newborn, smile, any sadness that had lingered in me started to evaporate, and a feeling of pure, innocent, goodness filled the space it had occupied.

"Delia," I said. "I think we're going to be fine."

Chapter Thirty-Four

Logan was on good medicine, sleeping peacefully when I finally made it to see him, my backside now modestly covered with an extra robe from the closet of Delia's room. The hotel feel of the maternity ward was worlds away from the medicinal environment that was the rest of Peachton Regional.

Holding and kissing my tiny niece had done wonders, and even though I still looked very close to a corpse, I felt a lot better. The swollen stiffness that held my movements captive during my wheelchair ride to Delia's room had eased, and transformed into the kind of dull ache that happens following the first long run after a time of laziness. It was amazing.

I wrote a note for Logan, not wanting to wake him, especially before Delia could sneak the baby in for a visit.

Call me when you feel like it! Room 312.

Xoxo-

Tully.

After everything that we had been through, it felt incredibly simple, girlish even, to write *xoxo* and leave a note for my boyfriend. I smiled, realizing that this might be our future. Love notes and date nights. Normal stuff.

Well, after he healed from his gunshot wound and my bruises faded. So maybe not quite so normal, but I'd take it.

I eased the door open to leave.

"You going to abandon me here? I see how it is."

Logan!

I turned around as quickly as I could manage without pulling the I.V. tube from my hand, and hurried back to his bedside.

"I'm sorry!" I said. "You were sleeping so well. I didn't want to—"

A mischievous grin broke across his face, and even with his unhealthy pallor in the unforgiving hospital light, I couldn't help but think of how handsome he was.

"Logan, you rat!" I said, laughing.

I leaned forward and kissed first his forehead, then his cheeks and nose, covering his face in tiny pecks, until I landed on his lips where I lingered. When I finally pulled away, Logan winced in an attempt to sit up, before collapsing back into his pillow.

"Be careful." I drew in a sharp breath through my teeth. "Does it hurt bad?"

"I feel great," he answered deadpan.

"Oh Logan, I'm so sorry. This is all my fault!" I sat on the edge of his hospital bed and clasped his hand.

"No, Tallulah. I'm sorry. Sorry that I wasn't there sooner. Sorry that I wasn't able to help you."

"But you did help me."

"Hmph. I barged in and got shot, leaving you to fend for yourself."

"No! I mean it! The Chief was beating me pretty badly; he stopped when he heard your footsteps. It let me get away."

Logan nodded slightly, and then yawned. He closed his eyes for a moment, and I began to think he'd fallen back asleep.

I stood to leave again.

"Tallulah?"

He looked up at me through heavy lids.

"Yeah?"

"Next time you want to hang out with me, all you have to do is ask me to get some pizza or something." He smiled and nodded for me to lean closer.

I did.

"Also, I love you," he said and closed his eyes. Before I could respond, he began snoring faintly.

I leaned over him, giving him one last kiss before leaving. "I love you too, Logan," I whispered in his ear. I brushed my hand lightly over his hair. "I really do."

He smiled in his sleep.

When he was better, we would have a lot to talk about. *Did he feel the connection? When I called for him, trying with all of my might to use the Chans, did he know?*

There would be plenty of time for answers after my sister visited him with the baby.

For now, he needed rest.

I did too.

Even though I was worlds better, the slow walk back to my room left me winded, and I was relieved that Daddy and Jack weren't there, waiting. I could sleep. *Maybe I can even get the nurse to give me something to knock me out.*

I leaned heavily on my I.V. pole as I sank onto the bed. I slid under the stiff sheets, and fell back onto the paper-thin hospital pillow. Both felt wonderful. I clicked off the lamp, and closed my eyes.

Three swift taps sounded from the other side of the door, and for a moment, I considered pretending to sleep.

"Dang it," I muttered and clicked the lamp back on.

A uniformed man stuck his head into the room. His orange-red hair, and unlined, ruddy complexion seemed familiar.

"I'm Officer Dirk, Ma'am. I need to get a statement from you and set up a time for you to answer some questions." His voice was flat and emotionless, like the actors who play detectives on television, and I couldn't hold back a tiny smile as I pictured the man practicing his cop lingo in front of his bathroom mirror.

"Ma'am? You ok?" he asked.

I nodded.

"I can come back…" he began, now in a softer, higher tone that had to be his normal voice.

"No. No. I'm fine. A little delirious, I guess."

"I bet."

"Hey. I know you. You said Officer Dirk? You're the cop from the night my sister was attacked."

The police officer looked at his shoes and red crept up his freckled neck and onto his face. *Poor guy.* No wonder he mimicked tough guy detectives.

"I didn't think you remembered me."

"I don't think I could ever forget anything about that night."

Dirk narrowed his eyes at me, serious, and nodded. "Yeah, I guess not. I talked briefly with your sister, but she had to, uh, nurse the baby so I left. I told her I would come back later." He sat down on the bed near my feet. "I figured now would be a good time to speak with you."

I considered this. This police officer seemed like a nice guy, but I couldn't forget that even though Delia, Logan, and me were the victims, the Brooklyn Police Chief was dead in my house when the ambulance arrived.

"Dirk," I said, looking the officer in the eye. I was not going to use magic, but I needed him to take me seriously. "Why you?"

"What do you mean?"

"Well, I assume you know about the, um, scene of the crime. Why weren't there guards at my door, or at least a senior officer waiting here for me when I woke up? How come there's just you, and you waited so long to come and talk to me? What's going on?" Things would end how they would, and there was nothing I could do to change that. Chief Rucker was dead. I needed to know if I was being blamed.

"Do I need a lawyer before I talk to you, Dirk?" I asked.

Dirk paused, and stared at me, searching my face to see...I don't know what he was looking for, but after a minute, he decided he would talk to me. "Look. I'm going to tell you what I know. The only reason that I'm saying this is because I saw your sister that first night. The night she was raped, and I know that's what it was. Rape. She was brutalized, and I have a sister...I just...You don't treat women like that. But you aren't hearing what I'm going to tell you. I am not saying this, you understand?"

I nodded. Maybe Dirk wasn't a rookie after all.

"Your sister never filed a report in Brooklyn, so her rape kit never got sent. It was stored at our station, which frankly, is the only reason that it was never destroyed."

I nodded again. I kept my mouth shut, scared of asking the wrong question and causing Dirk to shut down.

"Since the crime involved Brooklyn's Police Chief, and ya'll only have three other officers, the Sherriff's Department is taking over. The one thing that I got from your sister before leaving was that Chief Rucker was the man who raped her. She's certain, and I believe that the rape kit will be able to validate her claim," his jaw tightened, "Rucker's police cruiser was found parked about a quarter mile down the road from the crime scene. There was a bloody sundress under the driver's seat. We're awaiting testing, but your sister described the garment to a T. So I followed up on your tip. Do you remember? The night of the attack, you told me to look for a red hatchback? Turns out one is registered to a Jason Rucker."

"The Chief's son," I said.

"Then, there's the issue of Rucker's prints being all over the gun that shot your boyfriend. I spoke with the person that's the registered owner of the gun."

"Reverend Armstrong."

"Right. How did you know that?"

"He wears that thing everywhere. And Chief Rucker was happy to tell me all about it when he thought that he was about to kill me." I shuddered.

Officer Dirk nodded, understanding. "Well the owner of the gun said it had gone missing. I asked him if he had any visitors and he said only the Chief. He thought someone else stole it. Said some crazy stuff about you all using magic." Dirk raised his eyebrows.

"Yeah, he's insane," I said.

Thank God Reverend Armstrong gave off the crazy vibe. No one outside of Brooklyn, or his own congregation, would believe him. *I hope.*

"And then there's no evidence that Rucker died of anything other than natural causes. I don't know what went down, but you and your sister are very, very lucky that the stroke, or aneurism, or whatever it was, happened when it did. Sherriff Dirkus said that from the looks of things you all wouldn't have lasted much longer."

"Wait. Sherriff Dirkus?" I asked.

"Um. Yeah. My dad."

I smiled. That's why goofy Dirk was here and not someone with more experience.

"Yeah, it's pretty open and shut. So, no, you don't need a lawyer. Be honest," he said, snapping back on his police persona.

"Chief Rucker said he killed my Mama and Grandma," I said, and instantly, the tears threatened to fall. Some wounds time would never heal, and saying the words brought the pain to the surface as if the deaths happened that morning. I let the tears slide down my cheeks, not wiping them away. *I don't care. I'm not ashamed.*

"We will get the autopsy report, but I don't know that we'll be able to prove it. But Tallulah?" he said, his voice going soft again. He put a finger under my chin and lifted my eyes to his. "He's dead. He can't hurt ya'll anymore. If he did it, and I'm not doubting you that he did, then he paid for it."

The corners of my mouth turned upward in the smallest smile. *The monster is dead.* And I killed him. *I don't feel like a killer. I feel...happy that I did it.* There was no sorrow, or guilt, or regret. He hurt us, and I made sure he could never do it again.

I considered what that meant, knowing that I could never again be the victim. No more silently taking shit from people who thought they were better, and then, in the cover of night, making their lives easier for a payment. *That is not who I am going to be.*

There was a knock on the door and Dirk pulled his hand away from my face as if he'd touched a flame.

A dark-skinned woman, who filled out every inch of her fuchsia scrubs, glided into the room. Her manicure matched her gold eye shadow perfectly.

"Time for vitals and meds!" she sang in a husky, alto voice.

"I'll come back later, then," Dirk said, his cop voice once again up like a shield. "Tomorrow morning." He crossed the room in three steps, and disappeared through the heavy door. I settled back into the thin pillow, watching my nurse as she slipped the blood pressure cup over my arm and let the machine do the rest.

Exhaustion slid over me once again, and I wanted nothing more than to sleep. I realized that for the first time in a long time, sleep could bring peace. That I had nothing to fear. *I'd killed the monster.*

I looked into my nurse's happy, brown eyes, and before I could ask, she said, "How about something to help you drift off?"

It had to be a coincidence. She brought the syringe of medicine into the room with her and sat it down on the metal tray at the foot of my bed. I would know if I had used my Gift. *I would, I think.*

"Yes, please," I said.

She pushed the liquid into my I.V.

I watched as the amber colored serum glide through the plastic tube, on a mission to bring me peace. The delicious cocktail entered my body, sending streams of warmth throughout my system with every heartbeat, melting me into my bed. My limbs tingled and grew heavy in the way that means a deep, dreamless sleep was coming. My eyelids drooped and then closed, but I could feel the nurse's gaze on me, so I forced them open. It was like trying to lift thousand pound weights, but I managed to separate them into thin slits.

My happy nurse shook her head, and said, "Has anyone ever told you that you have the prettiest, greenest eyes? I have never seen eyes like that."

"It's a family thing," I mumbled, and gave in to the medicine, letting the darkness cover me like a familiar blanket.

THE END

Thank you for reading! Find book two in the Blackbird series coming soon.

Please sign up for the City Owl Press newsletter for chances to win special subscriber-only contests and giveaways as well as receiving information on upcoming releases and special excerpts.

www.emshotwell.com

@ mamacrazysocks

All reviews are welcome and appreciated. Please consider leaving one on your favorite social media and book buying sites.

For books in the world of romance and speculative fiction that embody Innovation, Creativity, and Affordability, check out City Owl Press at www.cityowlpress.com.

See the next page for a special bonus, the prequel short story of the Blackbird series,

The Chans

By: Em Shotwell

Available Now from City Owl Press

I had every intention of pulling out of the school parking lot and driving straight home to binge on *Breaking Bad* and frozen pizza. If I was lucky, my plans would also involve a six-pack of Abita Amber and not leaving the couch for the entire afternoon.

Tension knotted in my shoulders and tightened my jaw. I needed to unwind.

The faculty meeting had been a joke. Even more budget cuts. This meant the following school year I'd have to figure out a way to teach a classroom full of bored teenagers how to play guitar using only two half-busted instruments.

Yeah. That should work out well. At least they were good kids. Mostly.

I loved music. I loved teaching. I really loved teaching music…but the bureaucracy and school politics made me consider quitting to go back to college for something else. Anything else.

Cecille would love that, I thought, and then quickly shook away the image of my ex. We'd broken up right after college. She'd had no intention of being a teacher's wife, and it had been a lot easier for me to walk away from the two year relationship than it should have been. Even though I'd really liked Cille—hell, there'd been a time I might have loved her—I'd always known she wasn't the one. My ex had been a placeholder, a dog-eared page in a now-closed chapter of my life. She was never meant to be my ending. But you can't be with a woman for that long and not have her pop into your thoughts from time to time.

Without thinking, I pressed harder on the gas, eager to get started on my afternoon of doing nothing. I had an hour's drive to get from the town where I worked, to Peachton, the town where I now lived. I began to settle into the familiar daze brought on by a long drive, when "Paint It Black," by the Stones, rattled through the speakers of my small Dodge.

I smiled. *Perfect driving music.* I cranked up the volume and rolled down my window. Despite the sharp, ammonia-like odor of an unseen chicken house, the air felt good on my face.

The tempo of the music picked up, making my speedometer inch forward. Outside, expensive historic homes zipped by, before giving way to middle class, ranch-style houses, and the occasional doublewide. As I made my way toward the edge of town, the homes spread even further apart and the Mississippi landscape changed again. One side of the road became open pasture land, and on the other, groves of pine saplings grew in uniform rows, biding their time until they'd be cut clear and a new generation planted.

As I neared the county line, I passed a billboard for a podiatrist group, and my mind again drifted to my ex. I'd heard she'd moved to Austin, married a foot doctor, and was pregnant. *Good for her.*

Me? Well, I'd gone out a few times. Made a few friends. Nothing more. That was fine. More than fine, actually, because I needed to focus on my job. On my kids. On trying to make them care about music. Real music, not that overproduced crap that was played on the top forty station.

Easier said than done. I sighed.

Most of my students moved through my class only concerned with doing well enough to get a music credit, but in my year at The Mississippi High School for the Artistic & Talented I'd taught a couple that had possessed that *spark.* They were the ones that reminded me why I loved my job. I imagined molding one of them into a future Hendrix or Clapton. Only, you know, without the drug problems.

I was about a mile from the highway when I felt the familiar tug. I ignored it at first because of said date with couch and beer. Usually the pull was slight, but the closer I got to the highway, the more intense it became, like a rubber band pulled tight and ready to snap.

My Gram called this feeling *the Chans,* which meant chance or luck in her native Haitian creole. I'd adopted this name for my "sixth sense," but in my gut I knew there was more to it than that. Luck was luck. This, the Chans, was different. Sometimes, it was as if there was an unseen hand holding a piece of chalk and drawing a trail that I was compelled to follow. Other days, it was more like a thick piece of rope knotted at my ankle, gently guiding me along in the right direction.

Today, it was different. Stronger. What I felt was more than a push in the right direction. It was a demand, yelled loud and clear. *GO THE OTHER WAY!* The thought of not following stole my breath, the same way getting bad news can knock the wind from your lungs. I *had* to cooperate, and that was all there was to it.

Crazy? Maybe so. But the thing about the Chans was, it meant good things were bound to happen. And soon.

If I'm being pulled with this much intensity, then the pay-off has to be worth it. This thought was the only thing that kept me from panicking at the sudden fervor I felt to cut a U-turn in the middle of the rural Mississippi road.

So, as annoyed as I was at the idea of putting off my date with Netflix, I gave in and turned my truck around at the next opportunity.

***

"Freaking wonderful," I sighed as I passed the rusted *Welcome To Brooklyn* sign. I'd known the old turn-off road seemed familiar.

A year-and-a-half ago, after I'd moved to Mississippi from New Orleans, I'd stumbled onto this hole-in-the-wall town by accident. Before I'd even made one loop down the main street, sirens had appeared in my rearview mirror. It had pissed the officer off to no end that I wasn't speeding, didn't have any kind of warrant out, and that I knew my rights. After he'd made it clear what he thought of outsiders, and especially "city boys," the red faced policeman had no choice but to let me go.

I'd made a point to never go back.

It wasn't like I was missing anything by avoiding Brooklyn either. It was ugly, as far as small towns go, with none of that *charm* people like to go on and on about. It was a few ancient store-fronts, a fast-food drive-through or two, and a water tower. And the whole dang place felt like it was covered in a film of dust, leaving me with itchy eyes and craving a shower.

I considered turning around and heading back to the main highway, but as soon as the thought entered my mind, I felt antsy. My muscles twitched and my breathing grew shallow.

"The hell?" I groaned aloud. This feeling was new. And I didn't like it one bit.

I looked at the clock on my dash. "Dammit," I muttered. I'd really hoped to finish season three tonight, which meant my ass needed to be planted on my couch within the next hour. And I still had to go on a beer run. Maybe I'd get lucky and my Chans-induced detour wouldn't take too long.

Fat chance.

I coasted through town, minding the speed limit, and followed the Chans to a squat building in a gravel lot. It had one window that had been painted over, and a sign that read "Myrtle's Diner" in red loopy script. My stomach growled at the thought of food, even though I couldn't imagine anything cooked in such a rundown place actually tasting good.

But the diner was where I was being led, there was no mistake. I felt like a paper clip being yanked toward a magnet. And the uneasiness of wondering *why* I was being brought to such an out-of-the way place was nothing compared to the anxiety from the idea of not following the feeling.

I grabbed my iPhone and earbuds from the passenger seat before getting out of the truck. Growing up, I'd learned the hard way that, while following the Chans, it was a good idea to always bring along something to do. The Chans might always work out in my favor, but sometimes there were a few speed-bumps when heading down the unseen path.

A bell tinkled overhead as I pushed open the door of the tiny restaurant.

The inside surprised me. The floor was a black and white checkerboard, and red upholstered barstools surrounded a long Formica counter. Tables and booths were crammed in wherever they fit. The 1950s feel was a big improvement from the rundown exterior, which looked like it hadn't been cared for since the fifties.

Near the corner, a three foot tall Elvis clock watched me from its place on the wall. Its hips swung like a pendulum, counting the seconds as they ticked by.

Huh, I thought, shaking my head. *Everybody loves Elvis…I don't get what the big deal is.*

As far as I was concerned, the "King" was the first in a long line of musicians who were better at creating an image than creating music. And the clock was creepy, the way its eyes seemed to follow me as I walked by, like it knew I didn't like Elvis and was judging me for it.

A short woman with white-blonde hair hopped down from a barstool and greeted me. She wore the ugliest dress I'd ever seen. It had big, weird sleeves, and was cut low in the front, showing off a set of small, pushed-up breasts. The short skirt stood out from her hips and reminded me of a college-girl's Halloween costume, the kind that read "Sexy" in front of whatever it was supposed to be. *Sexy nurse. Sexy policewoman. Sexy random waitress in weird diner in a horrible town.*

"Well hello there," the woman said, snapping her gum. She grinned in a way that made me feel like a mouse cornered by a lion. With a few swaying steps, she closed the gap between us.

What in the hell am I doing here? The thought beat at my brain. Aloud I said, "Hi." I smiled, because I'm not the kind of man who's rude to women, even one who looked like she was ready to eat me alive.

She put her hands on her hips and eyeballed me up and down with raised brows. "My name is Loretta," she drawled, reaching out and squeezing my upper arm. "Now you tell me what it is I can help you with, sugar. Anything at all."

"A menu?" I ignored the blatant come-on. "And a booth would be good."

"Sure thing, sugar. Right this way." Lorretta grabbed a menu from the counter and led me past several empty booths, before tucking me away in the back. As far as I could tell, we were alone in the restaurant.

Should I be scared? I fought back a grin.

I sat down. Lorretta opened the menu in front of me. She leaned in close and pointed with her long, red fingernail to a picture of a chicken finger basket.

"This is good," she purred. "And of course, the burger." Her cheek rested next to mine, as she slid her finger slowly to the bottom of the menu, almost touching my chest, and pointed to the deserts. "Maybe you'd like a milkshake?"

I flinched. The way she panted the word made it sound dirty.

"Uh, I got it. Thanks."

"Well of course you do," Loretta said. She stood up straight and smirked. "Now what can I get you to drink?"

Somehow the top of her uniform had managed to inch down even further.

She didn't seem to mind.

At all.

"A Coke's fine," I murmured, careful to keep my eyes on hers. The last thing I wanted to do was let this crazy woman think I might be interested.

Loretta walked across the restaurant, bouncing her skirt with every step. She stopped to shoot me one last smile before disappearing through a swinging door.

It wasn't that Loretta wasn't attractive. In fact, quite the opposite. With her deep tan and bleached hair, she was the type of girl a lot of guys chased after. And if I hadn't felt like I had walked into some sort of crazy, sexual version of *The Most Dangerous Game*, then I'd probably have at least enjoyed the view. The way things stood I was very glad I'd brought in my earbuds and iPhone. *She has to leave me alone if I look busy...I hope.*

The door was still swinging on its hinges when another lady pushed through. Hard lines dug between her eyebrows and circled her mouth, making her look older than Loretta, maybe fifty-five. I don't know. I never have been good at telling a woman's age. She wore the same horrible costume as Lorretta, reeking of menthols and dollar store perfume.

I stared at the small screen of my iPhone and tried to appear busy. If not for the Chans, I would have left the second I had a clean getaway.

But there had to be a reason for me to be there. *I need a little more time to see what it is.*

When the older woman noticed me, she pasted on a painful-looking smile. "You been helped?" she croaked.

I nodded. "Yes, ma'am."

I scrolled through my playlist to pick a song, and as soon as I settled on *The Dallas String Quartet*, the screen went black.

Crap. I didn't charge it.

Lorretta appeared with my Coke.

Think quick, Logan! In a split decision, I flipped my device over, screen side down, and shoved the ear-buds into my ears. Never afraid to be a goober, I bobbed my head like I was really into the "music."

Lorretta sloshed my drink down on the table.

"What you listening to, sugar?"

I continued my charade, swaying my head, and ignored the woman.

The waitress didn't give up. She again leaned into my personal space and tapped me on the shoulder.

I had no choice but to remove one of my ear buds.

"Sorry, did you say something?" I asked.

"You ready to order?"

"I'll take the burger. Please." I started to put the earbud back into my ear when Lorretta placed her hand on top of mine.

"I love music," she said.

It was obvious I wasn't getting out of the conversation that easily.

"Oh, yeah?" I asked. "What's your favorite?"

"My favorite is whatever you're listening to right now." Loretta playfully tried to pull the earbud from my fingers.

I didn't let go.

"Sorry. I don't share."

"What?" she teased. "I don't have cooties. I promise."

I said nothing.

When she realized I wasn't joking, Loretta's hands flew to her hips. She cocked her head to the side. "Really?" she demanded.

I shrugged.

She turned on her heels and stalked away in a huff.

I took a deep breath and stretched my neck from side to side. *So much for unwinding.* I put my silent earbud back into my ear and waited for my food.

Maybe it hadn't been the Chans at all. Maybe it had been indigestion.

The bell again jingled in the front of the restaurant. I risked turning slightly in my chair. I didn't want to get stuck talking to the other waitress either, so I made sure to appear that I was very into my music.

I only managed the quickest glance—a slender silhouette with long, fair legs, and dark hair pulled away from her face—but it was enough. The woman was good looking, but her beauty wasn't what called out to me. I could have had my eyes closed on a pitch black night, and I'd have known. All of the air left the room, or maybe the air just left me. My heart sped, pounding in my ears, and my mouth turned to sandpaper.

She's the reason I'm here.

I knew as clearly as if the invisible rope had pulled me to this diner was lassoed around the woman, drawing us toward each other.

And as surely as I knew it to be true, I also knew that it couldn't be. *Be careful of wishful thinking,* I warned myself, *because the Chans never involves others.*

Through the years, the Chans had shown me what professors to take, guiding me toward the men and women who did more than lecture a class, but became mentors and friends. Then, it showed me what jobs to apply for. Landing the coveted teaching job at the arts school should have been impossible for a first year teacher, but it had been a breeze despite the stiff competition. The Chans had even helped me when buying my truck, leading me away from what CarFax later revealed as a lemon with a tempting sticker price and a flashy paint job, and taking me instead to the older, reliable truck that hadn't given me a single problem.

However, the Chans had never had an opinion on my love life. *Or current lack thereof.* Yet it pulled me to this woman now, like it had never pulled me to anything before. It wasn't simply a feeling this time, but a force, like the kind that pulls a needle to the North no matter how you turn the compass. It should have freaked me out more than the Elvis clock. But unlike the mechanical man hanging on the wall, it somehow seemed...right. Natural. *Meant to be.*

Is this what love at first sight means? I fiddled with the wire connecting my earbuds. *This had to be how Robert Plant felt when he penned, Thank You. I get it now. Except that Plant's song was written about his wife, and I'm sitting here losing it over a woman I've never met. Chill Logan.*

I couldn't help but smile at the absurdity of the whole idea.

Needing to get a better look at the force who brought me to this godforsaken town, I twisted further in my chair. I caught the swinging of the kitchen door from the corner of my eye, and quickly turned back around. I picked up my phone and pretended to be absorbed in a text, as well as music.

"You texting your girlfriend?" Loretta asked, practically accusing me of a crime.

I held up a finger and didn't answer.

The waitress tapped her foot impatiently, as I continued to "text," before giving up and setting my plate in front of me.

As she bounced away, I could see the relief spilled across my reflection in the phone screen.

It gave me an idea.

Using the screen as a makeshift mirror, I held my phone up slightly, angling it to see the reflection of what was happening behind me. The diner was lit brightly with florescent bulbs, and while it wasn't ideal, my plan worked. *Too bad the phone is dead or I could use the selfie-camera.*

The mystery woman was perched on the edge of her barstool, her shoulders tense, as she talked to the horrible, rank waitress. Her face was round, with wide-set eyes, and her dark eyebrows stood out against her fair skin. Strands of hair had escaped from her ponytail and had fallen into messy tangles near her shoulders. The way her lips were pursed and her eyebrows drawn together, it was easy to tell she was annoyed.

The waitress raised her voice, saying something about a girl named Delia who'd somehow wronged her.

The color drained from my mystery woman's face.

I should say something. No. That's weird. I'd look insane.

The urge to stick up for her almost made me get up and go over there, almost.

Hell, she doesn't even know that I'm here. Besides. It's none of my business.

Thankfully, before I could talk myself into doing something I'd probably regret, the waitress left through the kitchen door. My mystery woman took a deep breath and her shoulders relaxed into place as she sank into the padded barstool.

I was beginning to feel creepy spying on this woman who didn't know I was here while she waited for her order.

Before I could lower my phone, she spotted me. The corners of her mouth tilted upwards, and she stood on the lowest rung of the barstool and leaned forward.

I was sure I was busted and scrambled for a way to explain myself. Embarrassed, I waited for the woman to call me out.

But she never did.

That's when I realized that she couldn't see my phone, and even if she could, she couldn't possibly see her reflection in the screen.

So who is spying on who?

I smiled, and then remembering that I was supposed to be listening to music, I again started swaying my head. I moved more than I ever did when there was actually sound pumping through my earbuds, but I had to be convincing. I didn't want Lorretta the over-sexed hell-cat to straddle me in my booth and frisk me. And now, even more, I didn't want my mystery woman to think I was a creeper who secretly eavesdropped on strangers from dark corners.

But that's exactly what I am doing. Damn. I should probably stop.

I didn't lower my phone.

I continued to watch her reflection, strangely happy because she continued to watch me back. It was bizarre, secretly observing someone who thought she was secretly observing me.

She's pretty. I squinted for a better view of the reflection. *No. She's more than pretty.*

The mystery woman's tied dark hair and natural smile were the opposite of my ex's highlights and cherry pout. My ex had been beautiful, everyone had thought so, especially her.

But this woman, the way she appeared so laid back, the way she didn't seem to be trying to impress anyone, made her sexy in a natural, easy way. Her skin glowed against the bright white of her t-shirt, and contrasted with her sable hair.

And her eyes. Oh man those eyes. They were so green that they stood out, even in the shoddy reflection of my phone. And somehow I knew they weren't contacts. This wasn't the type of woman who'd bother with that sort of thing.

I'm going to talk to her.

I took a deep breath.

What am I going to say? I can't be like, "Hey, I've been watching you watch me." No, that's weird. I'll have to wing it.

I mentally prepared to introduce myself, hoping that I'd find the words and not come across as some kind of a weirdo.

I started to turn when Loretta waltzed back into the room. I watched from the corner of my eye as my mystery woman deflated like a balloon left outside on a cold day. She sat down hard and blushed the color of George Harrison's red Les Paul, while my waitress shot venom at her through black-rimmed eyes.

I sat my iPhone on the table, again screen side down.

A smirk played on Loretta's neon lips, turning her even more predator-like.

Sneering at the woman, *my woman*, Loretta slid snake-like toward me. Each step and movement was calculated to show the sway of her hips, the rise of her cleavage or the curve of her waist. Normally, I'd roll my eyes or simply ignore the advance, but I couldn't help but think of the woman at the counter, watching. I cringed.

The swing in Lorretta's hips grew more pronounced with each step closer.

Good god, is this woman waiting tables or working a brothel?

As if she could read my thoughts, Loretta slid her tongue across her lips, then asked, "You need a refill, hun?" She leaned low and stretched across the table toward my cup, her cleavage threatening to spill out of her dress and onto my poor cheeseburger. *I guess I won't be eating that.*

Had I given her the wrong idea? Or is she like this with everyone? I mentally replayed everything I'd said since coming into Myrtle's. *No. Not unless I've entered the Twilight Zone where "I'll have a burger" had some secret, erotic meaning.*

I pressed my back into the booth, scared any accidental touch would be seen as a flirtation. "Nah, I'm good," I said, even though Loretta already had hold of my cup.

"Fine," she huffed, dropping my drink back onto the table. She stood over me a couple of seconds longer. When I didn't look up, she took the hint and turned to leave. She paused before stalking through the swinging door to give one last withering glance to my mystery woman at the counter. She mouthed something, and then with a wicked smile, stomped away.

Unexplained anger burned through me. I had never even met this woman, so why did I feel the need to jump to my feet and defend her? To follow Loretta through the door and demand that she back off and treat her with a bit more respect?

I'd dealt with the Chans my entire life. I knew that as long as I followed its lead, things would probably end well. Sure, I'd been put in the path of different people before for different reasons, but I'd never felt this...this *longing* to know someone. I'd never felt this need to protect. This desire to make another person happy.

Shit. I sound like a stalker.

An idea popped into my head. *What if the Chans is done? What if it's completed its job? Maybe the invisible rope that pulled me through life really is tied to this girl? What if she's the ending to my story?*

The thought made me happy. Uneasy, but happy.

I raised my phone to take another look. *To check on her,* I told myself.

A grin broke across my face. My girl was once again "spying" on me. She was being more careful than earlier, but she was leaning forward and sneaking looks at the back of my head.

Is it possible? Does she feel it too? I'd grown up believing that I was the only one with my gift, but what if I was wrong? What if here, in this podunk town, there was a woman who was going through life same as me? With the same ability? Thinking *she* was the only one?

No way. Stop it, Logan. You sound dangerously close to someone from a Criminal Minds episode. I sighed and lowered the phone. Enough was enough. The Chans may have *led* me through life, but it sure didn't *control* my life. It would be best for me to finish my meal, pay, and leave.

The older lady walked back into the room with a dish of ice cream, and dropped it in front of my mystery woman with a loud clink. I sat my phone on the table and picked up my burger, almost taking a bite before remembering my food's close encounter with Lorretta's lady lumps. *Ick,* I winced. Behind me, the ladies' voices grew louder. I did my best to ignore them.

"Another man's voice!" the waitress cackled loudly, and without thinking, I again grabbed my phone to take a peek.

My mystery girl's eyes were shining so bright that they seemed to almost glow green. I knew it had to be the reflection, something to do with the fluorescent bulbs and the glass in the screen. *Hell, I teach music, not science, but there is no way a person's eyes could suddenly be that bright.*

I blinked hard and looked again. Her eyes were bright and green, but they weren't glowing. *You're losing it, man. Get it together.*

She stared at the ice cream dish in front of her, and it dawned on me. Her eyes hadn't been glowing, those were unshed tears. *She's trying not to cry.*

The thread that bound us together snapped tight. So tight, I was scared it might break. The thought of losing this connection, no matter how strange, sent me reeling. I had to lift my feet from the floor to keep from standing. If there'd been any way to run to her aide, to stand between her and the horrible woman and not look like a lunatic, then I'd have been at her side in less than a heartbeat.

But we'd never met, and if no one was in danger, then there was no reasonable excuse for jumping into someone's private conversation. Butting into arguments was something I constantly lectured my students about. *Mind your own business.* I repeated the words in every class, every day during the school year.

I sighed. *If I could do it over, I'd turn in my seat and "catch" my mystery woman in the act of staring. I'd smile and say something clever. She'd move from the counter, to sit across from me in the booth, and then I'd dare anyone to make her cry.*

"That's bull and you know it, Myrtle," 'my' girl said, snapping me out of my thoughts. Her voice managed to sound calm and forceful at the same time.

Well, well, maybe I misjudged. Maybe she isn't hurt at all. Maybe those are angry tears in her eyes.

She'd called the woman "Myrtle." *So the older woman is the owner. Figures.*

My already low opinion of the tiny town sank even further. I turned sideways in my seat and pretended to read something on my iPhone, but what I was really doing was watching as a shark-like smile spread across Myrtle's face. The woman walked around the counter and placed a hand on the younger woman's shoulder.

She flinched at the touch, and her eyes again flashed the impossible shade of green. The women's eyes locked, neither wanting to be the first to look away, as uncomfortable seconds ticked by with each swing of Elvis's hips.

Finally, my mystery woman broke the silence.

***

It was impossible. I half expected someone to jump from a hiding place and yell *gotcha!* because the things I'd heard… The whole thing had to be a joke.

Magical Gifts. Our people. Arranged marriage.

A bad joke.

But the smug look on Myrtle's face was serious. And my mystery woman—turns out her name was Tallulah—had bolted from the restaurant, her own face streaked with tears.

I knew that this town was off, but the things I'd heard were…well…there was no way they were true. *And this is coming from a guy who has lived his whole life making important decisions based on the whim of an invisible 'guide.'*

When my mystery woman, I mean Tallulah, had charged out the door upset, I'd leapt to my feet without thinking. By the time I'd dug money from my pocket and thrown it on the table, I made it to the door in time to see her peel out of the driveway, the tires of her old green truck slinging gravel through the lot.

I turned to look at Myrtle, who shrugged, and continued to fish a cigarette from the folds of her uniform before disappearing behind the kitchen door, muttering.

Loretta leaned against the counter, amused. "Can I get you anything else? You see anything you might wanna take to go?" The woman actually had the nerve to wink at me.

"Who was that?" I asked.

"You mean Tallulah?"

I nodded.

"Oh never mind her. She's one of the crazy Caibres. Every small town has its weirdos, sugar. You'd do good to stay away from her and the rest of her family."

"She lives around here then?"

Loretta rolled her eyes. "You gotta be kidding me. Honey, you ain't got a chance of getting in those panties."

I walked over to where Loretta was still propped against the counter and leaned down to look her in the eye. "That's not what I asked," I said, tossing a five in front of her.

"Fine," Loretta huffed, picking the bill up and sliding it into her bra. "Her family owns a produce stand out on the highway, outside of town. Her and her bitchy sister, Delia, work there most every day."

"Thanks," I said.

"Whatever. I'm going on break. If you come to your senses, I'll be out back smoking."

Now what? The impatient pull of earlier was gone. If it hadn't been so intense, so unexplainable, I could almost imagine that I dreamed the whole thing up.

But I knew better.

I'd expected to feel compelled to follow Tallulah when she sped away. Instead, I had the faint feeling of being led to the front of the restaurant, and then...nothing.

What can this mean? If not Tallulah, then what was the reason for me coming here?

I'd been eye-screwed by a walking STD in a short skirt, then I'd spied—creepily I might add—on my impossible dream woman. I'd overheard an argument that could never be real, and ate a few bites of a mediocre burger, before it had been molested by my waitress's free-falling cleavage.

And now...

Maybe it wasn't as intense as I'd thought. Maybe it was all a big misunderstanding.

I shook my head. *No, I didn't imagine it. It was real. That pull was real.*

Gravel crunched in the parking lot, and I looked through the glass top of the door to see the green truck returning. Tallulah maneuvered the vehicle into a spot.

She's back! My stomach tied itself into a giant knot, and it was as if a pair of invisible hands landed on my shoulders, bidding me to stay where I was. I took a deep breath to slow my racing pulse and looked around the restaurant. The terrible women were still outside having a cigarette.

The truck door slammed and Tallulah crossed the parking lot, her lips moving as if she were mumbling to herself.

This was the first time I was able to really look at her and not her reflection. She was tall, at least 5'8, and most of her height came from a pair of slender legs that stretched out a mile from her cut-off shorts. Her skin was flawless, without a freckle or tan line. And she must have ridden with her windows down, because her dark hair had fallen into a tangled mess. Everything about her, from her baggy t-shirt to her dusty sneakers, was unpresuming. I watched as she walked closer. *This woman has no idea how pretty she is. That, or she doesn't care.*

After the whole fiasco from earlier, the last thing I wanted to happen was for her to catch me staring. I stepped back from the door, and again looked around the restaurant, this time for something to do. There wasn't even a free real estate magazine that I could pretend to read.

I was still standing there like an idiot when the door opened, and the bell signaled her entry.

Tallulah walked in, her eyes glued to her sneakers.

She was even more beautiful up close. Her skin was flushed and she hugged her arms close to her body.

I was doing exactly what I didn't want to do, I was staring. I jerked my eyes away. *Be cool, man.*

"Look, Myrtle, I want to say that I'm sorry," Tallulah began, still looking at the floor.

"You shouldn't apologize to her," I interrupted.

Tallulah jerked her gaze upward, and if she was blushing before, now she was on fire. Scarlet colored her cheeks, and her eyes again shone bright. Impossibly bright.

So I hadn't imagined it.

"Uh. Excuse me?" she asked, taking a small step backwards. She glanced around the empty diner, then back to me. "I just…um."

"I know," I said. "But you shouldn't apologize to that woman. She's terrible. And that other lady acted upset because, I don't know, because I didn't want to take her in the back room or something. What is with these people, anyway? I guess you get lunch *and* a show."

Tallulah looked at me, her expression guarded, before the tiniest smile finally crept across her lips, disappearing again almost immediately.

"I'm Logan by the way," I said, thrusting my hand between us. My breathing hitched as I realized that I couldn't wait for our fingers to meet. For her to reach across the space and take my hand, even if it was only for a friendly handshake. I knew that if we touched, she'd feel what I felt.

I also knew, even as I had the thought, how creepy it seemed. *Pull yourself together, man. She's just a woman,* I silently told myself for what felt like the hundredth time since entering the diner.

Tallulah stared at my hand.

I smiled. "This is the part where you tell me your name?" Of course, I already knew her name, but there was no way to say that without making things even more awkward.

Her eyes flashed again.

"Wow," I mumbled, lowering my arm to my side. "You have the most gorgeous eyes."

She stared back at me, and I knew. *She feels it. I haven't lost my mind. She feels it, too.*

I don't know how long we would have stood, staring at each other, but I know that nothing would have made me happier than to drown in those eyes. To let the rest of the world pass us by as we grew roots and lived the rest of our days in one spot, tied to one another by an invisible force.

"You ain't nothing but a hound dog," the Elvis clock sang from the wall, rocking its mechanical pelvis and signaling that it was four o'clock.

Tallulah looked away and the spell was broken.

"I-I got to go," she mumbled as she turned and pushed out the door.

I glared at the ridiculous clock and let out a deep breath. "Damn," I whispered, rubbing my eyes with my palms. "Elvis," I said out loud, "I *really hate* that guy."

Then again, maybe the old icon had a good idea. Maybe I needed to sniff around, find out a bit more about my mystery woman. Looked like I'd be missing my date with the couch after all.

THE END

Acknowledgements

This book is dedicated to the storytellers in my family. I grew up believing the jabberwocky lived behind my Uncle's house, and was convinced (by another Uncle) that the "titty-baby truck" would get me if I threw a fit. My Daddy wrote me poems and my Mama told me stories. The bogeyman was named Sam Pokey and lived nearby. Thank you, my crazy wonderful family, for always feeding my creativity.

I will always be grateful and forever thankful to the people who believed in Blackbird Summer:

Heather McCorkle who plucked Blackbird Summer from the slush pile because she believed in Tallulah and Logan. I owe this entire book to your encouragement, vision, and patience.

Tina Moss for not only putting up with, but happily answering my millions of questions and guiding me through the publishing process. You are not only an editor, but an amazing mentor.

Blythe Johnson, Garrett Shotwell, and Justin Shotwell for reading early versions and getting excited about the story. Cindy Shotwell and Kathy Crosby for always believing that I was, indeed, a writer. Thank you to my friends who let me disappear while working toward a huge goal, and forgiving me when it took over my life.

Thank you to my husband, who I love more than anything. And who believes in me, even when I don't.

About the Author

EM SHOTWELL is an author of Southern-fried-fantasy and magical realism. She lives in South Louisiana with a husband who spoils her and two mini-superheroes who call her mom. Em thinks the most interesting characters are the ones who live on the sidelines, and that small towns often hide the biggest secrets. She is inspired by tall tales and local legends. When she isn't writing about misfits and oddballs, she enjoys spending time outdoors hiking, and debating Doctor Who facts with her obsessed ten year old.

www.emshotwell.com

About the Publisher

CITY OWL PRESS is a cutting edge indie publishing company, bringing the world of romance and speculative fiction to discerning readers.

www.cityowlpress.com